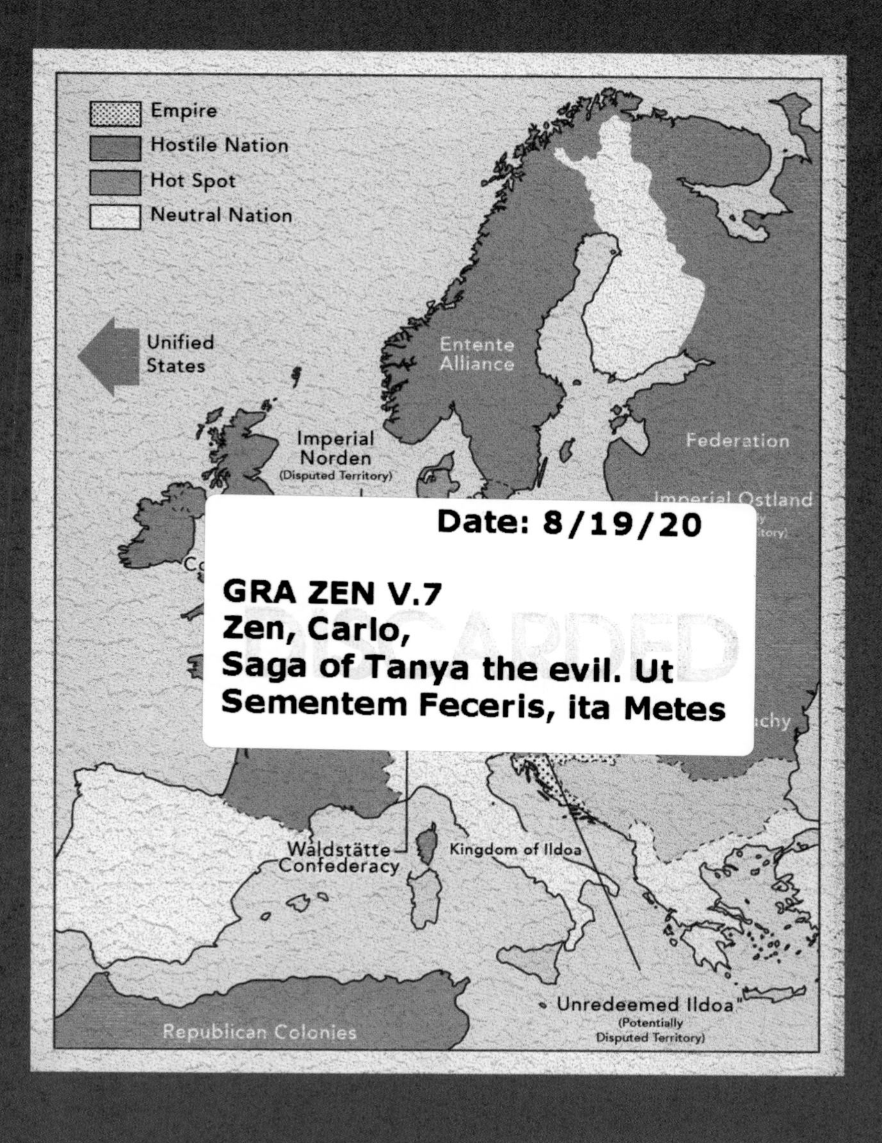

Ut Sementem
Feceris, ita Metes

THE SAGA OF TANYA THE EVIL

"Real coffee?"
"Yes, courtesy of the Lergen Kampfgruppe."
"Hooray for Colonel von Lergen."

Kingdom of Ildoa / venue of the Empire–Ildoa goodwill gathering / a sc

NOT
PERMISSIBLE
IMPERIAL ARMY GENERAL STAFF

Eastern front / date unknown

e from the friendship ceremony of two allies

THE SAGA OF TANYA THE EVIL

Ut Sementem Feceris, ita Metes

[7]

Carlo Zen

Illustration by Shinobu Shinotsuki

New York

The Saga of Tanya the Evil, Vol. 7

Carlo Zen

Translation by Emily Balistrieri
Cover art by Shinobu Shinotsuki

YOJO SENKI Vol. 7 Ut Sementem Feceris, ita Metes

First published in Japan in 2016 by KADOKAWA CORPORATION, Tokyo.
English translation rights arranged with KADOKAWA CORPORATION, Tokyo, through TUTTLE-MORI AGENCY, INC., Tokyo.

Yen On
150 West 30th Street, 19th Floor
New York, NY 10001

Visit us at yenpress.com
facebook.com/yenpress
twitter.com/yenpress
yenpress.tumblr.com
instagram.com/yenpress

First Yen On Edition: June 2020

Yen On is an imprint of Yen Press, LLC.
The Yen On name and logo are trademarks of Yen Press, LLC.

Library of Congress Cataloging-in-Publication Data
Names: Zen, Carlo, author. | Shinotsuki, Shinobu, illustrator. | Balistrieri, Emily, translator. | Steinbach, Kevin, translator.
Title: Saga of Tanya the evil / Carlo Zen ; illustration by Shinobu Shinotsuki ; translation by Emily Balistrieri, Kevin Steinbach
Other titles: Yōjo Senki. English
Description: First Yen On edition. | New York : Yen ON, 2017–
Identifiers: LCCN 2017044721 | ISBN 9780316512442 (v. 1 : pbk.) | ISBN 9780316512466 (v. 2 : pbk.) | ISBN 9780316512480 (v. 3 : pbk.) | ISBN 9780316560627 (v. 4 : pbk.) | ISBN 9780316560696 (v. 5 : pbk.) | ISBN 9780316560719 (v. 6 : pbk.) | ISBN 9780316560740 (v. 7 : pbk.)
Classification: LCC PL878.E6 Y6513 2017 | DDC 895.63/6—dc23
LC record available at https://lccn.loc.gov/2017044721

ISBNs: 978-0-316-56074-0 (paperback)
978-0-316-56075-7 (ebook)

2 4 6 8 10 9 7 5 3 1

LSC-C

Printed in the United States of America

THE SAGA OF TANYA THE EVIL

Ut Sementem Feceris, ita Metes

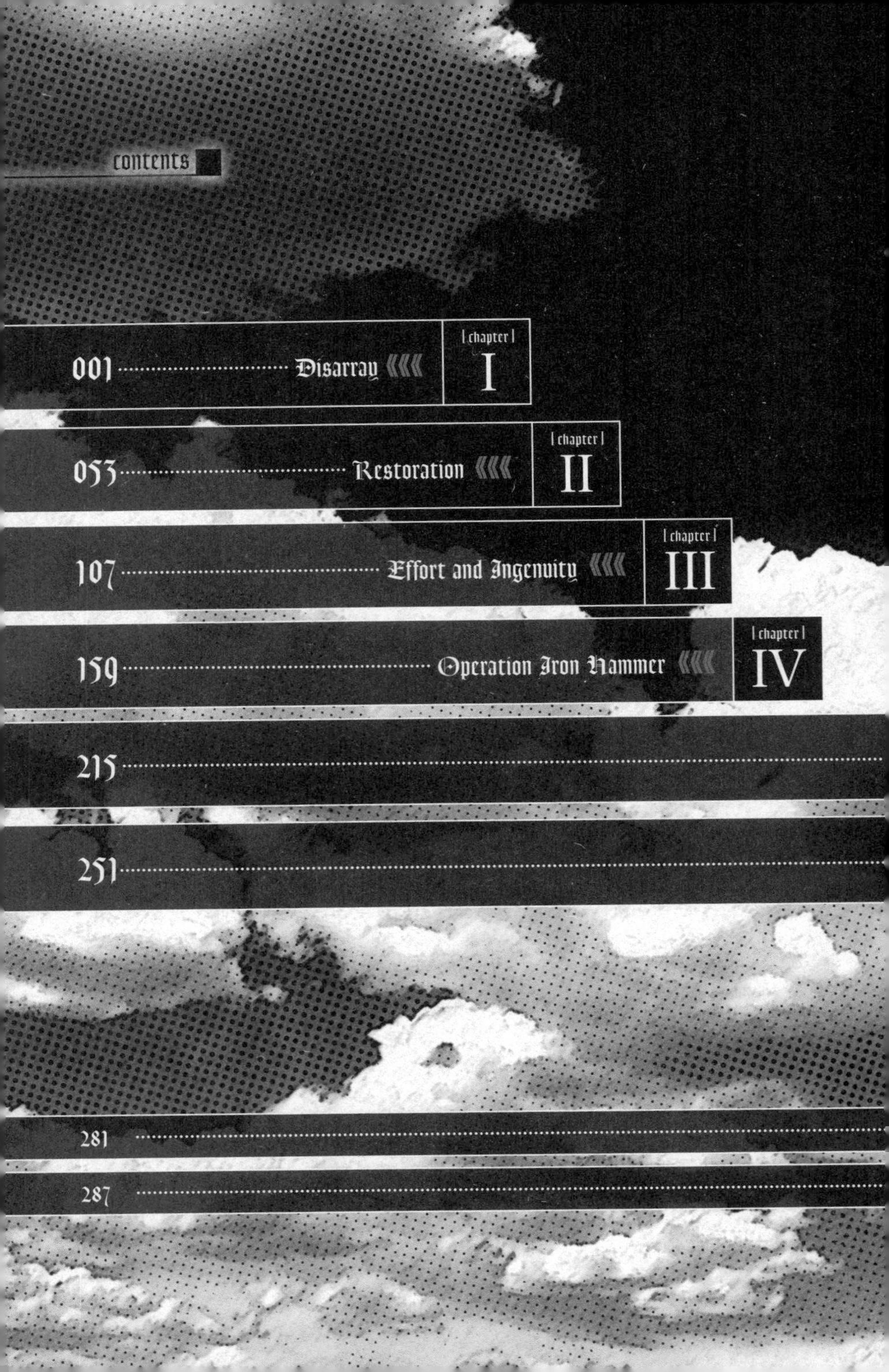

contents

Turning Point
[chapter] V
Excessive Triumph
[chapter] VI
Mapped Outline of History
[appendixes]
Afterword

Prepared by the Commissariat for Internal Affairs

Federation

General Secretary (very respectful person)

Loria (very respectful person)

【Multinational Unit】

Colonel Mikel **(Federation, commander)** — First Lieutenant Tanechka **(political officer)**

Lieutenant Colonel Drake **(Commonwealth, second-in-command)** — First Lieutenant Sue

Kingdom of Ildoa

General Gassman **(army administration)** — Colonel Calandro **(intelligence)**

The Free Republic

Commander de Lugo **(head of the Free Republic)**

Relationship Chart

Empire

【General Staff】

Lieutenant General von Zettour
(Service Corps)
— Lieutenant Colonel Uger
(Service Corps, Railroad)

Lieutenant General von Rudersdorf
(Operations)
— Colonel von Lergen

〔Salamander Kampfgruppe〕

203rd Aerial Mage Battalion

Lieutenant Colonel Tanya von Degurechaff

— Major Weiss

— First Lieutenant Serebryakov

— First Lieutenant Grantz

— (replacement) First Lieutenant Wüstemann

Captain Ahrens **(Armored)**

Captain Meybert **(Artillery)**

First Lieutenant Tospan **(Infantry)**

[chapter]

I

Disarray

Mud, mud, mud.

Regarding the eastern front

APRIL 20, UNIFIED YEAR 1927, UNCERTAIN COORDINATES ON THE EASTERN FRONT

From the perspective of someone looking down on the world below—a bird's-eye view—taking in the scenery from a great height reveals how endlessly monochromatic it is. And more geometric than mediocre avant-garde art to boot.

But a single glance through some binoculars makes it clear that the only thing to be found on the ground is a chaotic, intractable swamp. Shell holes, mud, the carcasses of collapsed warhorses, mud, injured soldiers, and mud as far as the eye can see.

Looking from the sky, even the unwilling are forced to learn what a menace the mud poses.

A listlessness still grips the earth and the coming of spring is far indeed. Lacking any definition, the land truly seems like a mirage. There's no obvious sign of the road that should be directly below, according to the map. No one would be able to read this location accurately.

"Hmph," murmurs the commander Tanya, who shakes her head slightly.

What happened to the mission that was supposed to be nothing more than flying along the road?

"It's a simple order to advance along the main highway," they said! *"You're simply going up to the forward-most line,"* they said.

So why the hell are we out here guesstimating our location using celestial navigation?

Tanya sighs. Her current position can't be clarified any further than "*somewhere* in the vicinity of the front line."

Her group doesn't consist of any old hands who have a knack for pathfinding, nor does it include guides or local troops who can instruct them.

At the same time, they're the stalwarts of the 203rd Aerial Mage

Battalion who pulled off a search and destroy with the air fleet over the notoriously stormy Northern Sea. She can trust them to have a rough idea of their current location wherever they go. There's no reason they should have too much trouble figuring out where things are.

Nevertheless, Tanya is astonished.

The friendly position that should be nearby is nowhere to be seen. The highway that is clearly marked on the map has sunken into the mud, and enemy soldiers are milling around where they don't belong!

It certainly wasn't without reason that she nearly agreed to her subordinate's earlier suggestion of turning around after they first encountered enemies on their path.

Ultimately, after recalling their orders, she rejected the proposal; according to reports from the home country, their comrades were still holding the line out here.

How much easier it would have been to abandon them! In the end, she dismissed that attractive option and their unit continued to advance out of a sense of duty.

And this is what we get. Tanya can't hide her disappointment.

"What the hell is going on here?" She glares at the enemy soldiers infesting the ground below.

This isn't even close to what the intel claimed. The area we're flying over should be the location of the friendly picket line!

And yet! A glance below reveals a revoltingly dense enemy anti-air position.

There was zero mention of this on what was supposed to be the latest map available.

"Fucking hell. Are our troops amateurs?"

The contrast is infuriating.

"The enemy's field engineers seem to be pros. They've done good, competent work."

"...This must have been set up after our line crumbled. The enemy seems very committed to their counterattack."

"You're not wrong, Lieutenant Serebryakov."

All we can do in response is toss our plan in the trash.

I'm loath to even take the time to lament it.

"...The General Staff must not have anticipated this," Tanya adds with a tongue click under her breath before she sighs.

Her annoyance mounts rapidly at the unacceptable situation they've found themselves in. That's only natural when most of the intelligence provided during the pre-mission briefing turns out to be completely useless.

She had no issue with being abruptly transferred to the eastern front.

That's simply following orders.

If the General Staff says "*Jump*," the only proper response is "*How high?*" And being told to reach these coordinates was no problem, either. I've accepted that we're supposed to serve as the General Staff's eyes.

"...I know. I know all that."

But the words that follow are lamentations, complaints, and even curses.

"What is the Eastern Army *doing*?"

Refraining from outright calling them idiots is already a test of self-control.

As a frontline aerial magic officer who has been through officer training at the war college, Tanya is aware of what the General Staff is after. The generals, especially high-ranking ones, want information. The education of high-ranking commanders imparts a gut-wrenching fear of making even the slightest mistake, so they impulsively seek out ever fresher nuggets of intelligence.

It's also wise for the commanders in the rear to be curious about the current situation out in the field. To take an interest in the front and dispatch teams to conduct surveys is model behavior for the military. The only complaint I have is that despite everything, our leaders have failed to get even a basic handle on what is happening out here.

This is what most people would call a "critical error."

"Under the circumstances, I'm not even sure if we can act on our own authority. How are we supposed to know what the government wants to achieve here? It feels a little unfair to not get even one hint. Pretty soon, I won't be able to do much but laugh."

Even if the Eastern Army Group really has collapsed, what happened to enacting plan B, which was supposed to deal with that exact situation?

In merely approaching the designated coordinates, the elite Salamander Kampfgruppe has already been forced to fight three encounter battles with enemy aerial mage units.

If friendly troops are still around...even if they gave their all to prevent anyone from suspecting them of making an unauthorized retreat, it clearly didn't accomplish much.

At that point, Tanya thinks of something that makes everything feel all the more pointless. "*All pain, no gain*" has a horrible effect on the mental health of anyone who is anti-Communist.

"What am I going to do for dinner now?" The futile lament dribbled out quietly.

You can resupply once you reach the objective. That was the happy-go-lucky order we received. To hell with last-minute deployments. Unless a unit that has access to the army supply line welcomes us, we won't be getting a hot meal tonight.

Since everyone knew it would be a long-distance mission, the troops probably snuck a few chocolate bars into their packs, but there's a limit to how long those will last us.

"Fate sure is a nasty bastard. How wonderful. Really impressive stuff here. I wanna hit the General Staff with some quality 37-mil tungsten shells."

But Tanya doesn't even have time to curse the heavens. Directly below is an enemy strongpoint. Only someone with a death wish can afford to get distracted while bad-mouthing people in a spot like this.

Time is never distributed evenly. When you're bored, you have more time than you know what to do with, but in moments like this, every second is precious.

Tanya clicks her tongue regarding another mistake. Since the actual combat mission was to take place after arrival, the whole unit is carrying more gear than usual.

Despite keeping the load to a minimum, a full complement of gear is still a serious burden. Since flying over enemy territory was unexpected, dumping anything they don't need for combat is an option.

But Tanya gives up and resigns herself to accepting the dead weight. Only an amateur would consider throwing away their gear for even a second.

The eastern front is the Empire's most thinly stretched position. Logistics are in rough shape, and supplies are liable to be cut off at any time, which is why the lines are in such confusion—we're one slip away from a real shit landslide.

If we dump our packs now, there's no telling when we'll get resupplied. This is nothing like dropping your stuff on an exercise field back home to move easier in hand-to-hand combat.

"Battalion commander to all units. I don't think any of you is a quick shooter, but just to make sure, there aren't any idiots who dropped their packs, right?"

Ha-ha-ha. The laughter filling the radio channel is a good sign. It's proof that the troops are prepared to respond to whatever comes our way. A workplace overflowing with cheerful laughter has a very low accident rate.

"Enemy mages climbing!"

By the time my adjutant gives the warning, the battalion is fanned out and ready for combat. It's the prompt response you'd expect from a team of vets. Pride fills Tanya when she sees that no one needed orders to take their positions. That said, anyone who pins all their hopes on the morale of the workplace is a failure as a manager.

If we're entering combat fatigued due to our lengthy advance, then the probability of an accident occurring must be taken into account. Working to anticipate mistakes and prevent them is part of what Tanya gets paid to do.

"...We're outnumbered, huh?" she murmurs and immediately reevaluates the power disparity. The 203rd's ability to bring firepower to bear when intercepting is clearly inferior.

The numerical disadvantage is obvious. Even a quick estimate shows we're up against more than three times our numbers.

I don't like it. This reminds me too much of the time we took heavy losses over the Northern Sea.

When I weigh my love for rationality and freedom against the need for emergency evacuation, my thirst for safety wins out.

"I guess we have no choice... What a shit show."

"Colonel?"

"01 to all units. I'm gonna hit 'em with something big. Watch out."

Tanya warns her troops, refrains from clicking her tongue, and readies herself.

What justifies it all is the unalterable truth of what reality demands.

It has to be done, I tell myself as I spool up the orb I rarely use, the Elinium Type 95.

An instant later, Tanya feels disgustingly refreshed. It's as if the fog in her brain has dissipated; a sense of clarity and omnipotence fills every fiber of her being.

"O Lord, declare balance and order good. May peace and the promised kingdom await!"

"Haaah…" Even her sigh seems to overflow with energy, and her fear is both unbearably awful and exhilarating at the same time.

"Stubborn reactionaries! I'll sweep you from the skies!"

Cries are coming over the wireless—actually, maybe it's just the agitated shouts of the enemies who've gotten within earshot? It's terrifying how my consciousness isn't quite steady.

"Scream for me, Commies!" Tanya raises her voice, trying to keep a handle on her sense of self with a yell. "You Commie scum go against the laws of nature! I'm going to teach you a lesson! You need to understand that reality won't be warped by ideology!"

"Blather on all you want! No one's gonna listen to the enemy of our motherland and the party! Get ready to taste the iron hammer of the people, you witch!"

It seems like Tanya's comments were rather provocative. A number of what appear to be enemy officers are polite enough to yell back at her in the language of the Empire. Come on, if they're mages and speak the language to boot, they should just defect from the Federation already.

In general, I'm not a fan of Communists. And nationalists also tend to have some values that I find hard to understand.

Having an attachment to your home is fine, but why value the imaginary entity of the fatherland over your own life?

Tanya stops there.

Objectively speaking, these Communist nationalists—the Federation Army—are the devil, and while they may be a sort of cult, as long as they are the devil, they are the enemy of gods or similar beings.

Gods don't actually exist, but the *stance* of not accepting that sort of being is important.

It's not fair to ignore the points where we can come to a *mutual understanding* just because we have certain issues that we'll never agree on.

I was taught to always look for the good in others. That's what I try my best to do. That's why I'll acknowledge them.

Even Communists can be praised when it comes to bullying and atheism. If I don't assess that fairly, my perspective will be undeniably biased. To put it in extreme terms, I would be extraordinarily lacking in modern intellectual integrity.

Anyone who wishes to be impartial needs to observe intellectual honesty.

With her mind full of such sickeningly pure and bright ideals, Tanya chuckles at the tidbit of irony she's discovered. Perhaps it should be said that she noticed it thanks to her dutiful commitment to intellectualism that she practiced every single day. Having discovered this opportunity to overcome the gap between herself and others in the midst of battle, Tanya even feels her heart warming up.

"Yes! Good! Very good! This deserves a round of cheers!"

It's hard to call it enjoyable, but it is exhilarating.

That's why, with great reverence and while tolerating the psychological contamination of the corrupting Type 95, I find it deeply gratifying to fulfill my duty as efficiently as possible.

Cast numerous overlapping explosion formulas to achieve area suppression.

In theory, that's the optimal solution.

Even for aerial mages, it's nigh impossible to dodge when the entire area around them is blowing up. Talented enemies should never be underestimated. Especially not when they're atheists deserving of some praise. We need to have good manners and make sure to kill them carefully.

"Warning! I'm gonna nail them with explosive saturation fire! Battalion, pull out of this airspace on the double!"

While warning her troops once again, she sets the manifestation area of her spell.

Finalizing her aim, she makes sure to take into account the flight path of the enemy mages still climbing to intercept. It's out of respect for her opponents that she's readying such a dense array of formulas.

Capable enemies are the worst enemies. This is the moment where Tanya should take out as many of them as she can.

Yes, it's time to use the Elinium Type 95 or whatever other cursed object of power the situation calls for. A job is a job. Sometimes duty demands wholesale slaughter. A sad thing for sure, but this is war.

"O, you who guide us. O, you who know serenity."

This violation of my consciousness, my very dignity as a person, encroached upon by something that shouldn't exist…

It's an atrocity that begs the questions *What is morality? What is justice?* Tanya has no choice but to experience the horror of her mouth moving of its own accord as the seconds pass.

How humiliating it is for the words coming out of your mouth to betray your mind. Still, it is a sacrifice willingly offered up in exchange for victory.

"And so we muster our courage, and though the path is thorny, we shall overcome."

The spell is four layers of explosion formulas cast in parallel. That means the mana required and the speed at which the effects will manifest are four times greater than usual. With one casting, Tanya has the ability to lay down suppressive fire equal to an augmented company.

This must be what people mean when they say their brains are fried from overexertion.

"There are the promised laurels—house of glory, a world peaceful and pure."

Despite the fact that it feels like her consciousness is one false move from slipping away…Tanya's attack manages to engulf the ascending enemy mages in a ball of fire and instantly knock several out of the sky.

More than enough for an opening salvo.

Even the Federation Army, notorious for its disregard of casualties, is nothing more than a collection of human beings. They flinch when they get shot, and when their pals get roasted medium well right in front of them, they're bound to shrink away, even if they don't realize it.

"Follow the battalion commander!"

Right as the enemy is wasting their precious momentum by hesitating, Major Weiss makes his move.

"Permission for my unit to close with the enemy?"

"May the Lord protect you…! Do it!"

As soon as Tanya nods in response to his succinct suggestion, her soldiers set off. The company responds with tremendous speed, assuming strike formation. Their impressive maneuvers are pulled off with the practiced ease of professionals, their technique fit for print in textbooks.

Tanya's unit is brimming with Named mages, veterans of the eastern front. Or perhaps they should simply be called "warmongers"? These soldiers have enough combat experience to easily seize the initiative from the enemy, making a mockery of their opponents for faltering on the battlefield.

Weiss's single company, scattering optical decoys as they go, plunges with great ferocity toward what must be close to a regiment of enemy aerial mages.

At first glance, it looks like they're throwing away their advantage in altitude. Really, though, they're simply going with the best option available. The probability of scoring a fatal hit on a mage moving at high speed is miniscule. Not to mention that humans freeze up when confronted with the unexpected. It's a simple matter to trap the Federation mages who thought they were coming to *pursue* us as we *fled*.

When the targets are sitting ducks who have stopped moving, success is all but certain. It's times like this that exemplify how dogs of war are excellent hunting hounds. They can sniff out an enemy's weakness and bite down hard.

A unit's morale is a finicky thing. Suddenly ending up on the receiving end when you're supposed to be attacking is especially bad for it.

Any flagging can make even the most powerful army fragile.

But then again, in an organization as unbalanced as the Federation Army, maybe the number of veterans is low.

"That Godless rabble… Ah shit, is the language region of my brain contaminated again?" Tanya quietly laments the glitch. The battlefield has no intention of affording her even that modest luxury.

"Rusted Silver!"

"Shit! Shit!"

"Today, you die! If nothing else, I'm taking you down!"

Multiple sights are trained on me. There are even some optical sights mixed in with the targeting sights. It shows just how eager the Federation mages are to kill a notorious enemy.

Their decision to pick off the commander first is a sound one. Cut off the head and the body will die. Only an ignorant fool with a bizarre sense of romanticism would curse them as cowards.

After taking a moment to consider the opposing forces, Tanya can't help but bark a dry laugh. The Federation Army has really honed its skills.

"Man, these guys are really a handful. They should just be ground down in the *lageri* by some other Commies instead of bothering us."

Switching to the Type 95 often makes it hard to avoid processor overload. With little other choice, I take full advantage of the device's four cores and promptly open fire.

"May Good News reach every corner of every land."

Who would spontaneously burst into praises for the world and want to fill it with the glory of the Lord? There's a saying that goes, "*You can't fight a war without losing your sanity*," and it's absolutely correct.

So many formulas manifest that it almost seems like I'm taking my frustrations out on the enemy. On the opposite end of my aim are hunks of meat shrieking at the top of their lungs.

That's when a sudden thought crosses Tanya's mind.

"I'll hammer the glory of the Lord directly into them!"

Tanya's adrenaline-addled mind, purified by the creepy holy relic, goes berserk as she follows after Weiss's unit.

"Company, on me! I'm not about to let Weiss beat my score!"

She charges headlong into the engagement.

By the time the wisdom of her actions comes into question, it's safer to follow through without hesitation now that the course has been decided.

The enemy is trying their best to deal with Weiss's company. Their effort is commendable, but what will happen when another company appears at their flank?

"Damn, it's the curse of the witch hag!"

Cries of an enemy caught by surprise and the clashing of mages engaging in hand-to-hand combat—nothing could sound sweeter.

"Hmm?"

At the same time, there's an unmistakable sense that something is off.

"Is it just me or are they absolute shit at close-quarters combat?"

The enemy response is…well, to put it bluntly, they're weak. The Federation mages who had been weathering attacks as a cohesive group up until moments ago have completely abandoned discipline and organization.

Unless their will to fight is completely devastated, units don't usually fall apart so quickly. But these guys came charging even when we were right on top of them. It's hard to imagine them folding like this.

"Compared to when we were fighting at a distance, the difference in skill feels rather stark… No, wait a minute… Could it be?" Tanya grins in satisfaction. "Were these soldiers grown too hastily? I get it now!"

Yes, *relatively speaking*, most aerial mage battles are medium- to long-range shoot-outs. Given that, it's understandable if the focus training becomes lopsided. Especially if time is limited.

Even the Federation can't raise head counts without resorting to drastic measures, leaving them few chances to teach their recruits how to fight as a unit in hand-to-hand combat.

"Ha-ha-ha! This is great! It's an all-you-can-kill buffet!"

Have the courage to be disliked.

A good rule to live by, no? Pretty soon we won't be able to make fun of compulsory moral education anymore.

"Virtues should be taken seriously! Let's cut them down!"

Armchair theorists say that close-quarters combat in a battle between aerial mages is "*absurd.*" On that point, Tanya agrees that it's so high-risk as to be irrational.

But even back in the days when artillery reigned supreme, soldiers still expected to fight hand to hand with shovels more often than not. Whatever the reason for the Federation Army's miscalculation that there would be zero close-quarters engagements, Tanya is happy.

"How is this happening?!"

The Federation mages' shrieks are incomprehensible, but simply looking at their faces makes it clear what they're thinking. Hooray for nonverbal communication, I guess.

With a sneer big enough for her opponents to see, Tanya concisely sums up the cause of their defeat. "We're more devout and more experienced. On what basis did you think you could win?"

Only an amateur would believe it's enough to simply swing wildly and hope that they land a hit. The basic principle of close-quarters combat is simple. Cut the enemy away one at a time and beat them down with an advantage in kinetic energy.

Essentially: You believe in what's certain, prepare for the worst, and then pray you hit… Pray? No, you don't need to pray. I wouldn't consider it healthy to put all your efforts into something as unproductive as praying.

This is no good. Tanya shakes her head again and carves into the enemy soldiers as they buckle in despair.

It's the same as the difference between kendo and *kenjutsu*. Unlike a bamboo practice sword, a magic blade cuts when it makes contact. These mages, barely better than the rawest recruits, can't seem to understand that.

Most humans can't remain calm after sustaining injuries. The timid who try to avoid getting hurt at all instead of focusing on preventing only fatal wounds are nothing more than easy prey.

Cowardice is a good thing. Especially for soldiers. It's far better to be cowardly than recklessly brave. Of course, there's no saving anyone who forgets the caveat of "*as long as you can still move when facing the enemy*."

"It's like sheep to the slaughter. If only every battlefield could be this considerate."

In such a target-rich environment where I can easily raise my score, it's a fine thing to devote myself to work. The time off and bonuses that come with a high number of aerial victories are plenty attractive.

"Ha-ha-ha-ha! What will you cling to, atheists? Your party? Your ideology?"

Even the Type 95's contamination of my mind is a negligible risk when weighed against the prospect of glorious leave. Well, maybe I'm underestimating it a little bit.

Still, in a juicy situation like this where I have a good shot at earning a just reward for my labors, a chance to crush totalitarians, and an opportunity to easily rack up military achievements, it's practically impossible to come up with a sensible argument against not indulging. After all, I can satisfy the capitalist and liberal in me while simultaneously meeting my need for self-preservation all at once.

Accordingly, Tanya continues ripping through the enemy forces with high spirits that border on intoxication.

"God is with us! To think that I would live to see the day I make such fools out of Communists! Come, then! Show me how you squirm!"

This extremely close-quarters combat is basically a dogfight. We keep chasing one another's tails. In this delightful pseudo-pincer, sometimes Tanya gets to pounce on an enemy from the rear, while other times she gets to skewer the idiots distracted by Weiss and his unit; every now and then, she opens up at point-blank range to blow away the guys taking the time to aim at her men.

Just as things start heating up, her wonderful parade gets rained on—by a short phrase uttered by an enemy soldier.

"Oh God..."

Tanya may have mastered only the most basic parts of the Federation language during her officer training, but there's no mistaking those words.

Is it the curse of the Elinium Type 95?

I can hear that prayer awfully clearly.

"Ahhh, shit."

Well, it's ruined.

Those three words say it all.

"A Communist looking to God of all things?!"

Is the Communist Party badge that you wear even on your army uniform nothing but a decoration?! The urge to scream is overwhelming.

It's *treachery.*

This is as good as betraying the values of their revolution. Frowning in open disappointment, Tanya barks, "A bit late for that, isn't it, atheist?"

Is the intensity of the glare that soldier shoots back just for show? Must they cling to something that doesn't even exist?

The letdown is unbearable.

"Gott mit uns!"

I joke right as I'm about to blow the enemy's head off, thinking idly that maybe I should have readied a pickelhaube as a prop for my obscure gag.

"All right, Rusted Silver. I'll admit you're strong...but I swore loyalty to my motherland, too! Even if it's the last thing I do, I'm taking you with me!"

The Federation mage, who approaches while yelling something or other, makes the sign of the cross as Tanya looks on. The moment's been ruined.

I came here expecting Commies, but they're not even proper Commies.

Liars.

Traitors.

"Wake up and smell the logic. Sins must be atoned for!"

As she vents her utter disappointment, Tanya soon realizes that the sounds of combat have stopped.

In the end, war is governed by an impartial equation. Some may call it cruel, but that's mostly a matter of personal opinion.

The strong are the ones who win. Even the Fair Trade Commission, which forbids monopolies, doesn't regulate combat.

Hooray for free markets, Tanya nearly grumbles, only to put a hand to her head instead.

"...Ow. That really hurts..."

I guess I can't overuse the Type 95 while upholding my will and expect zero side effects. Apparently, Being X has never heard of safety standards.

No wonder he has believers who would sincerely follow the saying "*If your eye causes you to sin, pluck it out and throw it away.*"

That's heartbreaking for a learned individualist like me. As a civilized person, I'd very much like to find a civilized solution.

"02 to 01, we've got almost complete control of the airspace."

"01, copy that. Well done."

Oh right. She remembers to add something.

"Your attack was brilliant."

"...They were much weaker in close-quarters combat than expected. I thought it would take a bit more effort than that."

"Indeed. I'm sure the Federation Army has their own struggles. They must be working a lot harder than they expected."

War is also about balance. That said, there's a limit to how long both sides can keep ignoring the screams and betting in the face of such losses. It would be stranger if no one went out of business.

Tanya shakes her head. Though they've defeated the enemy, that was merely the most immediate threat. The problem is what comes next.

"We may be tired, but our losses are within acceptable range. That said, I do wonder if there is any point to defending this airspace."

"I believe that's spot-on, but it doesn't do much for our motivation."

"True. Still, even if it's a pointless thing for you to hear, how can I help it?"

The only time a commander fills their officers' heads with propaganda is when the end draws near. Having nothing but blind faith that there must be a way forward is proof of incompetence.

"A tactical victory is utterly meaningless on its own. At best, we'll get medals. From the perspective of the individual worker, maybe that's not such a bad thing..."

If work isn't incentivized, efficiency plummets. Some people try to use the magic word *rewarding*, but all they'll end up with is not much different from a pointlessly inflated balloon.

The slightest disturbance will cause it to pop, which is useless.

As long as you're a cog in an organization, using others and being used as a cog yourself makes sense. But even if cogs are replaceable, anyone who neglects to perform maintenance is a half-wit who lacks cost awareness.

For Tanya, who boasts extremely good sense, it's obvious that she should supply her subordinates with natural motivation by keeping them informed of the significance and results of their work.

This is the essence of a manager's reason to exist. Human resources must be used with care and wasting resources is unconditionally bad.

"02, our present status is meaningless. We're withdrawing!"

"02, roger. Are you sure?"

"The premise that the General Staff based our deployment on has fallen apart. They have bigger issues than worrying about us acting on our own discretion."

...That's the truth.

"There's nothing else for us to do here."

With a fed-up expression, Tanya strengthens her defensive shell. The moment we reduce our altitude the slightest bit, an obnoxiously dense curtain of anti–air fire will strafe at us from the ground.

If caught by surprise, even an aerial mage isn't safe from getting shot down.

Maintaining current altitude is an option, but the difficulty of performing recon over an enemy position became clear during deployments on the Rhine. While our losses have been minimal, once fatigue accumulates, accidents only get more and more likely. And the point on the map that a few days ago was supposedly the Imperial Army's front line is now this mess.

Better to pull out before we get burned.

"All units, urgent from 01." Tanya swallows her sigh and relays her orders over the radio. "I'm suspending the recon-in-force mission the General Staff assigned to us. We're moving out immediately. Once we're clear of this airspace, I want the commanders of each unit to gather for a midair meeting."

Amid a chorus of *Yes, ma'am*s, the unit circles above the enemy hard point in a perfect display of synchronization meant to provoke the onlookers below before flying away in splendid formation.

Now, then… Tanya waves to her vice commander flying nearby. "Major Weiss, where's the nearest bakery company?"

"Somewhere within a few kilometers, but I don't know for sure."

The emergency midair meeting of imperial magic officers held near the front lines is to discuss bread. In response to her vice commander's expression that seems to ask, *How should we proceed?* Tanya responds with a knowing look on her face.

"At the moment, I don't care where we go. Our highest priority is to locate a hot meal. Let's link up with a logistics unit retreating alongside a load of high-calorie food."

"Then, according to the map, shouldn't we follow the highway?"

"That was my plan as well, but I think that'll be difficult, seeing as it's hard to tell where the highway is exactly."

Plus, there's no guarantee that our troops are even retreating along that route. And it won't be easy to tell what branch they're from, either.

What should we do? Tanya mulls it over for a bit before deciding to call First Lieutenant Grantz, who is flying nearby.

"Lieutenant Grantz, I'm detaching your unit."

If we don't know, we'll just have to find out, obviously.

"Ma'am! What are my orders?"

"Go ahead of us and get in touch with the friendly rear guard. Even if they accidentally start shooting, whatever you do, don't lose your cool and return fire."

"Understood."

The way he smiles wryly as he nods—he knows what he's about. He may not compare to Weiss yet, but Grantz is on his way to becoming quite reliable.

The way he quickly rounds up his subordinates and flies off—prompt and effective, the way a junior officer should be. The ambition and assertiveness he displays are admirable. The precious trust that allows me to send him and his unit off without worrying is something he's earned himself.

"Lieutenant Grantz has certainly become dependable."

"Colonel?"

"Back on the Rhine, he would've been too scared for me to feel comfortable sending him off on his own."

Maybe I have a talent for cultivating subordinates. Considering the rising value of the human capital under my command, I think it's safe to pat myself on the back. The thought brings on a private cringe, but the feeling of pride is undeniable. It isn't a bad thing to confirm an ability to foster growth no matter the circumstances.

The opportunity to bask in triumph lasts for only a moment.

"Speaking of the Rhine… Back then, the situation on the ground was the opposite of what we have now. A retreat this disorderly would have been unthinkable over there. What a time."

Tanya nods in agreement with the comment Weiss utters while flying at her side.

"We have the supplies, but we end up abandoning them… This is why lapses in discipline are such a terror."

On the Rhine front, Grantz (a second lieutenant at the time) wasn't reliable, but the army as a whole could be counted on.

How about now?

"Colonel, Major, look over there."

I turn my binoculars in the direction my adjutant points.

Agh, what a waste!

Those charred wrecks used to be imperial vehicles!

"…I guess those trucks were abandoned along the highway? If the Service Corps back home saw that, they'd faint."

"I can't show Colonel Uger this disgrace."

To the guys in charge of handling the already strained vehicle situation, this would be a sight too cruel. War really is nothing but a colossal waste. Heavy sighs are a tradition now. There's no telling how many I've heaved on the eastern front.

"Hmm?"

"What is it, Lieutenant Serebryakov?"

She seems to have found something, and sure enough, when I look where she's pointing, there's a strange pattern in the mud on the ground.

Any trained soldier would know what it is at a glance: the tracks left by a large unit on the move.

"A division of mechanized infantry? And by the looks of it, it isn't one of ours …"

"What makes you say that? I can't see enough evidence to identify them as an enemy unit."

For better or worse, the puzzled adjutant must be a stranger to routs. After that initial thought, Tanya reconsiders. Come to think of it, the Imperial Army is an entity that wrests victory from the jaws of defeat with the power of logic.

My subordinate's only experience with what happens when an army breaks down and flees in a panic is probably limited to reading about it. After all, humans are creatures who draw on their experience first.

"Visha, more people should take after you and learn to be a student of history instead of their gut."

She responds with an affirmative "Yes, ma'am…" My adjutant is incredibly attentive. There's never a need to repeat anything for her. She shows such promise.

The lesson continues. "Remember this. A routed army will always escape along the path of least resistance. Not even the Imperial Army's mechanized infantry is an exception. But you've seen what it's like down there. Our abandoned vehicles are so covered in mud, it's hard to tell they're ours, but they were mainly dotted along the highway."

What a mess. Tanya sighs. She can't help it if they tried to choose the easy route and all got mowed down.

"So because this unit chose to go through the boggy terrain, it must be the Federation Army?"

"No doubt about it," spits Tanya. "It looks like their priority is continuing the advance. And they seem to be moving pretty quickly."

"Do you think there's a chance they'll catch up with the rest of the army by the time we rejoin?"

"...Well, our mission is clear. Assisting friendly troops as they retreat until we can link back up with the rest of the Kampfgruppe doesn't sound so bad."

"Understood."

"Good." Tanya nods and they continue flying for a time.

Looking at the markings left on the ground and given the lack of a large armored unit or any mechanized infantry in general, the location of the enemy force seems to creep into view.

...That must be the Federation's spearhead.

Seeing evidence that friendly troops were chased down is deeply horrifying. If at all possible, I would prefer for the enemy to not be directly in our path of retreat.

I mentioned to Weiss the possibility of assisting our fellow troops, but...frankly, we don't have the numbers to take on an opponent of this size.

"Colonel?"

Tanya pulls her attention away from the ground back to the sky. Her adjutant next to her is handling the long-range-communications kit.

"Do you have a moment?"

When she nods, she's offered a wireless receiver.

"It's Lieutenant Grantz. He's joined up with a supply unit."

Tanya changes gears and stops her musings to assume command. Then she grabs the receiver and questions Grantz.

"Give me a sitrep."

"Please wait a moment."

She hears Grantz talking with friendly troops in the background. To be frank, that initial reaction doesn't inspire confidence.

"...It looks like no one knows for sure what's happening on the battlefield as a whole. Even the general info we're getting is garbled and confused, so I'm not sure if it'll be much use..."

"Don't worry about it, Lieutenant. You're not to blame."

Grantz's tone is apologetic, but it's obviously not his fault. Knowing who bears what responsibility is one of the bare-minimum requirements of a leader. Taking out your frustration on your subordinates is the worst thing you can do.

"For now, we'll prioritize linking up. Send over the coordinates. Make whatever accommodations are necessary to receive us."

"Understood."

"Good." She hangs up and lightly shakes her head.

I know that I know nothing. You could call it an achievement, but all we've really done is accept our unpleasant state of affairs. Well, misery does love company. Time to share with Weiss.

"Vice Commander, we've made contact with friendly troops, but"—Tanya shrugs and grumbles—"we learned nothing." It's a simple matter to convey how dire the situation is. Weiss clearly understands as he responds with a grim expression.

It's probably not only him. Tanya's face is very likely all twisted up in frustration as well.

"Is the Eastern Army Group a collection of babies?"

"Major Weiss, be fair with your criticism. We've been pretty out of it ourselves ever since Norden. We can't really talk when it comes to performance."

Security is the greatest enemy. Corpses galore. That's just how it is.

"This is war. Everyone gets a turn on the receiving end."

"...It reminds me of the Rhine," Serebryakov chimes in, sounding tired, and Tanya agrees with a nod. Thinking back on it, we did have quite a bit of trouble thanks to a mistake on HQ's part.

The fact that the ones who pay for those mistakes are the people in the field will be an eternal structural issue.

"If experience is anything to go by, we'll have to pick up shovels for trench combat soon."

"Ha-ha. How nostalgic."

Perhaps he's taken Tanya's grievance as a joke. Weiss clowns around, missing her point in a fundamental way.

"Down there should be supplies that were left behind, so scrounge some up."

"Huh?"

"I'm serious, Major. Grab enough for everyone." There's no smile on Tanya's face as she gives the order, not bothering to hide the displeasure in her tone. He must have realized she meant it. He stiffens up and replies in a slightly hoarse voice.

"...Understood. I'll take a company down. Please cover us."

"You got it."

Staying alert while riffling through abandoned gear with backup nearby is not such a hard job. It's just depressing.

It takes hardly any time at all for Weiss's group to collect a good amount before getting ready to move on again. For Tanya, who was on the lookout for enemies, the whole venture goes so smoothly, it feels anticlimactic.

"...That's strange."

The battlefield hasn't been swept clean yet, sure, but it hasn't even been looted? Really? Some theories are beginning to feel more certain.

Not much later, we meet up with the troops Grantz managed to contact. We find them sooner than expected.

Best-case scenario, the imperial lines haven't been pushed back that much...and the worst case is that the retreat is delayed.

After a brief examination of the troops we've just met up with, what stands out the most is how orderly they are. Yes, normally an orderly retreat is ideal.

But...under these circumstances, it's horrible news.

Despite the utter chaos and confusion on the front, this calm, organized unit is retreating far too slowly. In other words, it's proof that the Eastern Army Group's orders are not keeping pace with the developments on the battlefield.

...They can't even smoothly withdraw as a cohesive whole!

Well, this is a problem, A grim expression still on her face, Tanya calls out to the most senior officer nearby. "I'm Lieutenant Colonel Tanya von

Degurechaff of the Salamander Kampfgruppe. What HQ or Command are you attached to?"

"Eastern Army, Twenty-Third Division, Fifty-Fourth Regiment. And you? You're clearly aerial mages…"

The exchange is to the point. Everyone takes a moment to confirm the collection of ribbon bars and rank insignia of those present.

The outcome is rather expected… In terms of medals awarded, this fellow is a notch lower than Tanya, who wears the Silver Wings. But on the battlefield, an officer one notch lower than the Silver Wings recipient is basically a few steps short of a god.

"We're here on emergency deployment orders. I'd like to consult with you about the situation."

"You're welcome to, Colonel."

"Sorry, but who are you?"

"Ah right." The older officer smiles wryly. "I'm Colonel Dirichlet, commander of this regiment."

The manly commander's smile acknowledges that they've both gotten the short end of the stick.

"From the top, I'm Lieutenant Colonel von Degurechaff of the Salamander Kampfgruppe. This is my second-in-command, Major Weiss."

"You've got multiple Named, huh? That's awfully reassuring—if you'll be escorting us, that is."

Tanya finds some hope in the fact that he seems like a pro who has a firm grasp on the situation and understands his duty. It's especially wonderful how his first impressions of her height and appearance don't show on his face.

If you want to do good work, you'll obviously need good coworkers. Knowing you won't be tripped from behind means there's one less direction you have to worry about—which is great. The good thing about the medal system is that you can usually expect people to live up to the ribbon bars decorating their chest.

"I think we can help you out. We're operating independently from the rest of our Kampfgruppe. Until we receive new orders from the General Staff, we can support your rear guard."

"Well, I can't ask you to come under my command, but having your assistance will definitely make things easier for us."

Plus, he understands the chain of command. You don't see this type of commander every day.

"Though we're a Kampfgruppe on paper, at the moment, we're deployed as just an aerial mage battalion. Setting aside issues of command authority, we're quite agile. I'm sure it won't be a problem for us to support you guys for a few days."

"We'd appreciate it."

Then shall we?

He picks up on Tanya's meaningful glance. "I'll take you to our temporary headquarters… There's some pressing business to attend to."

"Thanks. Lieutenant Serebryakov, come with us. Major Weiss, the unit is in your hands. Coordinate with the deputy commander of the 54th Regiment as soon as possible."

After leaving an undefined jumble of tasks to the vice commander, Tanya runs after Dirichlet. His broad shoulders project a sense of reliability.

Yes, we're running.

The jaunt to the regimental headquarters happens at a jog. This is rather impressive. At his age, Dirichlet must be in great shape if he can run down this road in such horrible conditions.

And he appears only even more impressive once we reach our destination.

"We may be some distance away from the front lines, but I'm surprised such a nice house is still standing. Honestly, I assumed you were leading us to a campsite."

Maybe the Council for Self-Government secured it for them? Either way, a building that hasn't been scorched or riddled with bullet holes is noteworthy. It's a proper place to sleep! Tanya smiles, admiring yet again how capable Dirichlet has turned out to be.

"Yes, we were lucky a building was still standing…especially in this weather."

"I must agree about the cold, but what about booby traps?"

"This is the east, Colonel! I wouldn't have moved the HQ in here without having the field engineers examine it first."

A houseful of competent officers—gone in an instant. Even the heartless would be devastated by such a loss. And what a disgraceful error to make. After seeing that blunder happen again and again, it starts becoming reasonable to be paranoid about cleaning out buildings.

"Ha-ha-ha. Do excuse me."

"No, please, it's a legitimate worry if you've heard about whole command posts getting blown to kingdom come."

The cold-blooded conversation we're having in this toasty house really highlights how impermanent our world is.

"Now then, I'll be straight with you. The situation is not ideal."

"While I do want to discuss the wider situation as we go along, perhaps we should begin by exchanging information. Would you like to hear what my unit witnessed on our way here?"

After Dirichlet responds with a "Sure thing," Tanya gives him a brief report. The General Staff may have ordered a general advance, but the friendly positions at the designated coordinates have already fallen. The various traces of an enemy force we saw along the way line up with the fighting retreat Dirichlet's troops have been engaged in.

"On top of that," Dirichlet continues with a pained expression, "it's unconfirmed, but we have reports that some of our troops got nailed with heavy artillery."

"Heavy artillery? You must mean a unit bringing up the rear got hit while lingering near the forward-most line, right?"

"...Apparently not. It was the regiment right next to ours."

That's incredibly strange. Big guns are slow. Deploying artillery in a hurry is practically impossible. We received a thorough education on the Rhine front that artillery is slower by far when compared to infantry.

That's why I figured if a unit got hit by heavy artillery, they had to be on the forward-most line.

"The enemy troops are advancing with considerable speed. We should probably assume they have a unit with a powerful artillery division coming along."

Tanya is about to shake her head and say, *You must be kidding.* But no imperial soldier would joke around at a time like this.

"...I'm jealous. An entire artillery division..."

"I couldn't agree more. But as you know, it'd be asking for the impossible, Colonel von Degurechaff."

Tanya nods readily in response. "Indeed."

Human lives are expensive, but shells are cheap. The Federation is already blessed with human resources, and now they're calling up artillery divisions?

It would be difficult to call this a fair playing field. Ultimately, the existence of the invisible hand of God that Adam Smith[1] was talking about means the world is unfair by design.

"Lieutenant Serebryakov, review our encounters with enemy troops on the way here. I want to know where that artillery division is. If need be, send out a unit to perform recon-in-force."

"Yes, ma'am. Right away."

Serebryakov is already drafting the order even before her mouth stops moving. She's an excellent adjutant. Someone who will do *what* they're told *as* they're told! Truly a blessing, especially considering the times.

"Now then, what's our defense plan? From what I've seen, we can't even establish an integrated defense on a division level."

"That's correct. We can maintain only intermittent contact with division HQ at best."

So? Tanya raises the question of their grim future with her eyes alone, drawing a wince from Dirichlet.

"I suppose you can say we just barely received the brief for a fighting retreat, but it's unclear if the other units are managing to pull out or not."

A jumbled retreat? Argh… Everything is coming to a head. Tanya shudders and gazes at the ceiling.

"And where is division HQ?"

"Here."

Dirichlet rolls out a map on the table with a dry rustle, and after he points out the location…hope flares ever so slightly. Not as bad as I feared.

"This is close to our railroad… Looks like we have a chance to regroup."

"I'm sure we could. The problem is time."

[1] **Adam Smith** The extremely moral author of *The Theory of Moral Sentiments*. He probably never dreamed the phrase *invisible hand* that he used once in *The Wealth of Nations* would get the words *of God* tagged on… He's also known as the father of modern economics.

Ahhh, time. We meet again. Time, time, time. That is the one thing the free market cannot remedy, I must admit. Finding a way to reliably secure a supply of time would revolutionize global economics.

"Failing to regroup means we'll be obliterated."

"Exactly. I hate to point out the obvious, but that also means these next few days will decide the battle."

Tanya nods to say that the colonel's comment is spot-on.

If they can just reorganize their lines, the division could rise from the ashes. All they need is more time. Whoever came up with "*Time is money*" knew what they were talking about.

"By the way, while I still want to discuss the regrouping in detail...can you tell me exactly what happened on the front lines?"

"What do you mean, Colonel?"

"It seems like your forces were ripped apart before you even got started..."

Dirichlet's shoulders slump as if that hit a nerve. After a few moments of silence pass as he carefully chooses his words, Dirichlet takes out a standard-issue cigarette ration. "We had just repelled a probing attack the enemy conducted along the whole front the other day. Since we had managed to drive them off, the mindset that we'd 'pushed them back' must have set in not only in my regiment but throughout the entire division. That hubris came back to bite us. There were faults in our defensive positions." With a sigh, he begins smoking.

"Faults?"

Seeming somewhat tired, he rephrases. "Well, it had less to do with the actual line of defense and more to do with our mentality. I think everyone was overly focused on a spring counteroffensive."

"A counteroffensive?"

"That's right," he spits in response to Tanya's question. "Division's orders were to prepare for an advance. No one was paid a second thought to defending the ground we were holding."

The positions at the front hadn't been fortified or dug in. The patrol lines must've fallen all too quickly. It's all coming together now. The Imperial Army was already committed to mounting an attack. From the get-go, the plan was to advance farther. In that case, it's not that surprising no one ordered the troops on the front to diligently construct defensive positions.

This is especially true on the eastern front, where the average soldier's main struggle is against the cold and the mud, not incoming fire. Apparently, these troops forgot that supply-route maintenance, equipment repairs, and more rely on the existence of trench works.

"...The enemy caught us unprepared."

"That's right, Colonel. I guess the damn Communists have a good grasp of human weakness."

Dirichlet's comment is logical.

At the very least, it's an unquestionable truth in Tanya's experience. Her demeanor seems to say, *Well, they're Communists.* "They've certainly broken a lot of people. They must have a solid understanding of how to go about that, finding weak points and revealing just how vulnerable people can be. Boy, sure is a rough bunch for anyone with good sense."

"Ha-ha-ha. If even an officer like you is willing to say that, then tell me, where do I find sanity?"

"We're at war. Such a thing is a rare luxury."

The common sense of war, the nonsense of peace.

There's no reason to think it especially strange that the supply of rationality fluctuates so erratically. This is simply the nature of the market. Even so, Tanya firmly believes in the righteousness of market principles. Too many simpletons like Being X obsess over the moral dualism of good and evil as is. That's more than enough reason to not give up on the market.

"Couldn't have said it better myself. Getting back on topic, we currently lack intel. To remedy this, we'd like your unit to conduct a recon mission for us, Colonel..."

"Scouting the area and recovering the remnants of our defeated friends while we're at it, right?"

"Will you do it?"

"We got enough practice on the Rhine. Leave it to us."

Frankly, it's rarer to receive a mission we haven't done before. When Tanya pounds her chest to display her willingness to undertake it, Dirichlet cracks a bitter smile.

"...It would be tactless to ask at what age you served on the Rhine, huh? All right, Colonel Degurechaff, we're counting on you."

Tanya nods. Their trust is not misplaced.

From there, all the preparations are made without a hitch. After a short briefing about the rough location of the position, Tanya departs from the provisional HQ ready to begin the reconnaissance mission.

"Okay, we need to grab Weiss and Grantz."

"...Everyone's here already."

"Fantastic."

Are aerial magic officers just the sort of people who naturally know how to be in the right place at the right time? Tanya's subordinates are already waiting by the time she zooms out of there.

These guys have great timing. War dogs are all about how you use them. Moments like these, they come in handy.

"Major Weiss, you're on patrol duty. Split the battalion in three and get a handle on our situation. Reports say the enemy has an artillery division operating nearby. Locating it is our highest priority."

That force might be hunting me. Revolting. If nothing else, we have to confirm whether they exist or not. Otherwise, I'll never sleep.

Ah, damn, that's right. Something needs to be done about Tanya's empty stomach before bedtime. Our terrible foe, hunger, has dulled many a mind throughout history.

"Before we leave, I'd love to snatch some provisions from the field bakery company."

"Understood. But you don't need to worry about provisions."

"What?"

"Colonel Dirichlet was kind enough to have a supply company from his regiment deliver us calorie-dense meals. Since they're on active duty in a war zone, they understand that sort of request."

What consummate professionals. Tanya nods in satisfaction. When the one in charge has a good head on his shoulders, everything runs smoothly. It's something to be thankful for. One less thing to worry about.

"Lucky us. All right, then let's send out scouting parties starting with the people who've already eaten. It's urgent that we get a full picture of our operational area. First, we'll check out the riskiest direction..."

Tanya prepares to further detail the need to check their surroundings, but then her mouth closes. A harsh sound pierces her ears. After the unmistakable *whoosh* of a flying object is followed by a low rumble, Tanya instantly screams.

"Incoming!"

It's the sound of shells streaming down.

A familiar roar.

Ahhh, those bastards got us.

"Shit!"

The enemy stole the initiative!

"Enemy attack! Climb..."

Lieutenant Grantz is about to take off when she shouts him down reprovingly.

"No, find shelter! They've got us pinned! Take cover in the trenches!"

After diving into the nearest crude trench, Tanya spits, "Damn it, I can't believe we're too late!"

The guns are practically serenading us to announce our disadvantage. Anyone who's ever experienced the difference between warning shots and a true bombardment in a trench, their ears will remember even if they prefer not to. Once you learn it, you never forget.

Hiding in a hole on the receiving end of heavy-artillery fire is far from pleasant. Against the familiar backdrop of the riotous battlefield, Tanya screams in spite of herself.

"It's too soon! This is happening way too soon!"

A full-scale bombardment this quickly? At this point, I'm uneasy about everything.

We managed to get to cover, but these are the most basic of trenches. If my survival comes down to whether they can withstand a direct hit from a large shell, I'd say it's extremely unlikely. And even if we want to fortify them now, we don't really have the materials or the tools.

So what do we do?

Surely not *pray*?

That'd be ridiculous.

Most people would call this utter humiliation.

"Damn! I guess this is what you'd call the worst," Tanya utters, acknowledging the indignation.

This is a war on freedom.

My choices are to either submit to that scum the irritating Commies call God or forge my own destiny, obliterating Being X and those Commies alongside him.

Fine, let's do it.

The answer is simple.

As a civilized person who loves freedom and modernity, my duty is clear.

"Officers! Rally your troops!" The impacts, explosions, and the resulting thundering force Tanya to raise her voice. Shouting at a volume that might injure her vocal cords, she cuts through the noise to what's to be done. "Get ready to counterattack! Battalion, prepare to strike on the double!"

"What?"

"It's a preparatory bombardment— Hello!! Get going before the enemy infantry shows up! Pop 'em in the nose the moment they get here!"

That's how it always was on the Rhine front.

After the shells come the humans.

There's no reason it should be different in the east.

"Major Weiss, rally the battalion! Do we have a line to Colonel Dirichlet? If it's dead, then send a liaison."

"Look over there!"

When Tanya turns her head dubiously to look where the finger is pointing, she notices that's the direction of the house serving as provisional headquarters, the building they just left moments ago. Except it isn't there anymore.

...Ahhh shit, those fuckers. Now we have to talk about headquarters in past tense!

"...I get it now."

It's clear why the enemy decided to go all out with their initial salvo, why they could fire for effect immediately—the Federation Army artillery had their target zeroed in from the very beginning.

Figuring out the scheme took only a little deduction. That lone house hadn't simply survived. The structure had been left intact on purpose to serve as a target.

"Regimental headquarters has been wiped out!"

"I can see that. And the colonel?"

"...I don't think he made it."

Weiss's reply is simple and clear.

My wishful thinking came back to bite me. Tanya fills with regret. For once, it seemed like there'd finally be a capable colleague to hold down the fort. Who could have predicted that he and the rest of HQ would be blown to smithereens?

I didn't see it coming. Ahhh, what a wonderful confession of ineptitude. I should be shot for not even considering that possibility even though we're at war. What negligence! Carelessness! Failure!

This is the kind of incompetence that makes me sick.

"Fine, we'll act on our own discretion. Assume Colonel Dirichlet fell in battle and that the chain of command is unclear. We will consider this spot to be headquarters temporarily."

"Shouldn't we find the second-in-command in the Fifty-Fourth Regiment?"

"It's a waste of time."

My adjutant's suggestion is fine in most cases but mistaken under the current circumstances.

A handoff of command with no proper meeting would throw everything into disarray. There's no way we can afford the luxury of devoting pointless labor to something impossible now, when every second counts.

"B-but—"

"Lieutenant Serebryakov."

"Yes?"

"Have you forgotten? Time is finite. Extravagance is the enemy."

Right as Tanya is about to continue the lecture, she shuts her mouth when it becomes apparent that the artillery fire has halted. On the Rhine front, the end of the bombardment was a signal of what always came next...

"Enemy attack!"

Shrieks erupt in all directions and the familiar sound of gunshots begins chattering. The textbook progression of events makes me want to curse our enemies. But something in the air seems off; I have a bad feeling that insists on being heard. When I listen to figure out what's causing it, the answer is simple. There isn't enough sound.

"...I don't hear enough LMGs!"

Given the gunshots booming from every direction and the few explosions mixed in, each position must have begun to mount a counterattack according to the defense plan. Did they lose all heavy equipment during the retreat? Our outbound fire sounds miserably weak.

"There isn't even a silver lining to find. What the hell is going on?!"

What should sound like a unified orchestra of imperial firepower is instead warped and jerky, like a broken phonograph. Individual units are putting up valiant resistance, but coordination is clearly lacking. This is the moment when regimental or divisional fire support should be raining down, and its absence is conspicuous.

The cause is simple to explain. The enemy lopped off the head of our local chain of command with their opening attack. Their damn artillery division or whatever did a real fine job!

In short, this is the worst-case scenario.

Considering how we no longer have the means to mount an organized defense, we're in serious danger of seeing the entire regiment collapse. "We really screwed this one up." Tanya curses at the heavens.

Even if she wants to take over, she hardly knows anything about the Fifty-Fourth Regiment's defense plan, since she was operating under the assumption that Colonel Dirichlet would be handling it. Most importantly, a new chain of command hasn't been established yet.

I had assumed we would have time to discuss things in detail after we finished a search of our surroundings! That was so mindless of me! Even I wouldn't deny that the blunder deserves a firing squad.

No. Tanya shakes her head. The priority now is assuming command, not self-criticism. In order to get through the crisis, she raises her voice as high as she can manage.

"Listen up! Officers of the Fifty-Fourth Regiment, gather round! Yes—you guys!"

She revives the dazed and confused troops by invoking command and rank. It's a primitive but battle-tested method. Never make fun of the simple, classic approach, especially in emergencies.

"Colonel Dirichlet and the others are dead. I'll be taking command temporarily!"

Convincing the dazed officers of the Fifty-Fourth Regiment that I'm the boss is an easy task. Standing there blankly, the officers would be best described as…cogs that do as they're told.

These guys exist to follow orders, so if we give them the appropriate lubrication, there's still hope.

"C-Colonel?!"

"Hurry up and bring me your second-in-command! Get a move on!"

After lighting a fire under the rumps of the Fifty-Fourth Regiment's officer corps, Tanya starts scattering sharp words of encouragement.

"Go to your positions and prepare to intercept! The enemy is coming—you know what to do!"

These are orders born of defined pledges.

"Move! Move! Get ready! Officers, do your duty!"

They're magical words that light a path for lost troops who don't know where to start. As long as they understand the purpose of intercepting the enemy, the training that's been drilled into their heads will overpower their confusion to some degree.

"Ready up!"

"Hurry! To your posts! Pick up the pace!"

This instinctive reaction of those blank-faced troops must be the result of daily training.

When they first jolt into motion, the speed is sluggish, but the shift to a defensive posture isn't lethally slow.

Even at a temporary foothold during a withdrawal, an army will always need at least a bare minimum of preparation.

"…Probably time to get moving ourselves. Very well. Major Weiss, I believe the possibilities are opening up."

With this, things should be okay for the moment. Tanya is finally getting a sense that things are in motion.

Honestly, it's a shame that there's no chance of getting anything close to the near-instantaneous response of the Salamander Kampfgruppe, but this is a moment to make do.

Once you're in the game, you have to give it your all for a chance at victory.

"Tsk! Have we still not found the second-in-command?" Tanya immediately spots the young officer she grabbed just a few moments ago wandering around aimlessly and screams at him. "Hey, you! Where's the Fifty-Fourth Regiment's second-in-command?! I'm pretty sure I ordered you to bring him here!"

"...Who's in command?!"

"It's *your* unit! You don't know?!"

"Ma'am, I, uh... I was only just assigned here—attached to the HQ section. I literally arrived the other day..."

Still dumbfounded, Tanya realizes her mistake.

As the rest of the troops yell and run in every direction, Tanya and the other outsiders—the mages of the 203rd Aerial Mage Battalion—have nothing to do. *In that case...* She regrets not sending Weiss and the others out to search sooner, but it's too late.

"Take cover back where the provisional headquarters used to be! When a high-ranking officer shows up, explain what— No, wait. Just give them this message: 'The 203rd Aerial Mage Battalion has temporarily assumed command. Contact them immediately.'"

What in the world is happening...? Tanya peers up at the heavens. The last time she looked up, there was a fine ceiling overhead. Now there's nothing but irritating cloud cover.

Shouting curses is about all she can do at the moment.

"How did these complete amateurs become officers?! The hell is going on?!"

Suppressing the urge to click her tongue, Tanya shakes her head.

It would have been nice to at least have discussed a plan with the Fifty-Fourth Regiment...but it seems like there's not enough time. Given the situation, something needs to be done now. Reflection and regret are luxuries only the living get to enjoy.

The ability to worry is quite a fitting way to prove to ourselves that we're still alive.

"...We can't coordinate with these guys. We shouldn't even try. Instead of teamwork, we'll just pile up a heap of individual victories until it becomes something resembling team play. I guess that's the plan, then."

Necessity justifies it.

"Let's take advantage of an aerial mage battalion's mobility."

What a nostalgic operation theory. I remember how, back at the war college, I suggested it to General von Zettour during a coincidental meeting.

A unit specializing in mobility that excels at single strikes and can respond quickly with small numbers—an aerial mage battalion really is the optimal reserve force for tasks that require flexibility.

They're the optimal manhunt specialists. Now, turning back to more immediate concerns, it's time to get Tanya's thoughts in order.

The situation is extremely unfavorable.

Chain of command has collapsed.

The transfer of command is ineffective.

And to top it off, enemy numbers are grim.

But that's no reason to neglect the things we have to do. On the contrary, we should apply ourselves even more steadily and carefully than usual.

"Battalion, attention!"

The order elicits a perfect reaction.

The members of the 203rd Aerial Mage Battalion turn to me in a synchronized motion as if an electric current zapped them from their heads to their heels.

It's something that was drilled into them countless times in training.

The way Major Weiss, First Lieutenant Grantz, and First Lieutenant Serebryakov are standing tall at the head of the formation speaks to how perfectly disciplined the troops are.

They're pros. I feel nothing but satisfaction seeing them work. Which is why I'm confident I can expect them to perform admirably in the future as well.

"In brief, our mission is to support our allies! Don't expect the other units to do anything but defend their positions!"

"That isn't too much work for them?"

The formal beauty of Weiss spouting a joke at the appropriate moment to lighten the mood, the exquisite timing of his interjection… Nothing can replace the peace of mind and confidence of knowing that your vice commander can read the mood.

"Assume that you're splitting roles. While they hold ground, flank our numbskull enemies and scatter them."

Tanya's smile is like a silent *You know what to do.*

It's the same job as always.

"Battalion, this is business as usual. Mop them up the way you always do, turn in reports like normal, and then return to base like any other day."

It's exceedingly easy for aerial mages to cross distances. They're the ideal reserve force: exceptionally rapid to deploy with the mobility the Imperial Army has been craving.

The Imperial Army's forte is running around within established positions to conduct interior lines defense. It's a tradition that is drilled into every cadet at the academy, and then, as a finishing touch, they carve those concepts into the officer corps' very flesh and bones at war college.

In other words, the current conditions are all anticipated scenarios. Protecting a base by using interior lines tactics to fend off encroaching enemies is no exception.

"Enemy soldiers!"

"We have enemy contact! Get in there!"

Even the hand-to-hand combat within the position is performed with no hesitation.

This is the 203rd Aerial Mage Battalion, after all. We have plenty of members who have been around since the Rhine. Their proficiency with shovels is beyond excellent. Once you get used to using them, shovels are extraordinarily handy tools. A stab to the privates and then a whack to the head is a surefire way to incapacitate the enemy.

"Elimination complete, yeah?!"

"Colonel, over there!"

When I glance over, I see a group fleeing from the direction of the gunfire. To put it plainly, it's the sad troops who can be described as the remnants of the defeated army.

The way they're retreating in a panic instead of facing the enemy… suggests there's a hole in our lines now.

"What the hell? Patch it up!"

I learned this well at the academy. With defense by interior lines, the defensive lines frequently require repair. You can find as many examples as you can look for of a collapse in one corner leading to a total rout.

I learned at war college: Ignore a breach in the lines for too long and you'll be forced to switch to mobile defense, but even mobile defense requires a certain amount of space to be successful. In a trench battle, you can abandon the first line—assuming you have the depth to weather a sustained attack.

But in the end, defense in depth is another theoretical ideal, one you can't rely on in a static defense where there isn't much space to spare. Which is why the instructors kept emphasizing how critical it was to maintain a solid defensive line.

"Shit, what are the guys on the west side doing?!"

Is there some vulnerability on that flank? Soldiers fleeing from the direction of the western defensive position is about the worst sight I can think of.

Tanya needs to go and find out what's happening there. Right as she's about to rush over, a sound rings in her ears, alerting her to just how serious the situation is.

An echoing call of that most vexing "*Urá!*"

Agh, damn it all to hell. It's obvious what's going on. That's a cry you get used to hearing when you're on the eastern front!

The better you hear it, the more pressure the enemy's advance puts on our troops. Their morale is peaking while ours is falling apart.

It's clear we're about to be overwhelmed by enemy forces. One glance is enough to tell the cause. I can see it even if I don't want to.

The ones running are all pale-faced youngsters and men who look pretty old to be on active duty. An ad hoc unit of newbies and reserves. When it dawns on her, there's no way to disguise her sigh.

These guys are vulnerable.

They're too fragile.

They're far below the standards of the powerful Imperial Army Tanya knows. Having been continually fighting on the front line, that's her honest opinion.

"...They're raw recruits."

Tanya nods at Weiss in silence.

"Shall we withdraw to the second line?"

Nein. She shakes her head.

A retreat would be difficult. If we could move in an organized way, a withdrawal would at least be a tactical option. It would be more logical than a futile attempt to maintain the crumbling line, which can hardly be called optimal.

But with the headquarters destroyed, an orderly retreat is impossible.

It's nothing but an empty theoretical option that can't be realized. No, if we're unlucky, it could be even worse than armchair theories. What would happen if the disarray spread rapidly so that even the points currently holding out ended up peeling off?

A classic loss of leadership followed by a classic rout. A feigned retreat followed by a counterattack would be impossible to pull off without a solid foundation.

Troops who believe they're already defeated are useless in a counterattack.

I never thought I would have to prioritize the sure thing over the rational. War really forces some horrible choices on people.

Tanya makes up her mind.

"Prepare for an assault battle. Major, you'll command the 203rd."

"Huh?"

Weiss is a veteran, too. If his eyes are asking me *Are you serious?* that means he understands what I'm trying to do. He's found the rational in the irrational.

"I agree wholeheartedly that it's unwise, but we have to do it."

"...Understood."

"I'll command the infantry. Lieutenant Serebryakov, you and your company follow me. The rest of you, go with Weiss. Watch the timing for the counterassault."

With a curt "Let's break it out," Tanya swiftly hands out instructions and sets off in a deliberately casual jaunt toward the friendly troops who have transformed into shells of a defeated force.

"Dig your heels in!" You couldn't call it a terribly loud shout, but she musters all the volume she can. Sadly, despite the fact that an aerial magic officer with her rank clearly visible is screaming at them, none of them returns to their positions.

Not only that, but they stare at her blankly. Apparently, their understanding of the world has broken down.

Fine. Tanya frowns a bit.

Why are officers called officers? Because they do what needs to be done when it needs to be done.

Hasn't it been said that soldiers should fear their own officers more than the enemy?

"Consider this fleeing before the enemy."

"Huh?!"

Her adjutant's vacant reaction is the expected response.

Though Serebryakov has worked her way up the ranks, she was originally a draftee. And given her temperament, Tanya can understand why she would hesitate.

Nevertheless... Tanya gives the order with confidence.

"Prepare to fire!"

"Preparing to fire, ma'am!"

Training and discipline are nothing more than the optimization of conditioned reflexes.

Her troops respond immediately.

It's only twelve people, but they are aerial mages—seeing them lining up to attack is jaw-dropping. And the pressure of a company of aerial mages is especially potent in a war zone.

Anyone who still has the presence of mind to be frightened on a battlefield can obviously comprehend threats.

Instincts can be extremely handy when controlled. Saying humans are like beasts is perhaps too strong a comparison, but humans do have instincts. If we brand them with intelligence, the appropriate regulation and management of people under extreme situations can be achieved.

Urging the troops on has no effect. What a handful. Tanya switches to more provocative language. "What if the people back home found out? It would probably render them speechless. You should be ashamed of yourselves, you utter buffoons!"

When she scans the terrified faces, all of them are recoiling. Troops who can no longer feel shame are a handful. This is pointless. There's little reason to keep trying.

If giving up isn't an option, then is the only thing left to do to take things up a notch? Probably. Tanya steels her resolve and opens her mouth for the third time.

"Attention." Her voice is small, and no one listens.

At this point, that's not surprising. By the time soldiers are routing, they're nothing but a mob of individuals consumed by terror.

But people being scared isn't useful.

And these troops have to be put to use if the Empire wants to win the war. This is total war, i.e., a conflict where the entire population plays an active role in the war effort. The situation has gotten so out of hand that I almost want to laugh.

Tanya repeats again, with composure, "Attention."

Hmph. She sniffs, reaching for the gun at her hip.

Paying no mind to the fact that her action rattles even the weak-kneed soldiers, she aims horizontally and waits until the last second to lift the pistol into the air to shoot.

"Attention!" She raises her voice and checks the response, but the outcome is only a commotion… "Arrrgh." Her patience runs out. "Lieutenant Colonel Tanya von Degurechaff is calling you to attention! Shut up and listen!"

After emptying an entire magazine, she raises her voice again. "What are you doing? What about your posts? Who's your commander?"

"C-Captain Ryan's dead! W-we're done for!"

Did the tension break? One of the kids screams that their unit has been wiped out, his face an unnatural pallor. This is a good opportunity. In response to the numbskull panicking over the insurmountable odds, Tanya sighs.

There's no denying that it's going to be a tough fight.

But so what?

It's not as if running away is going to help anyhow.

People who flee despite the lack of an escape route are lemmings. If you're just planning on falling into some water and drowning, then fighting to the bitter end seems more promising.

"Wiped out? Soldiers, are those legs just for decoration?" Tanya laughs at them. "Aren't you still alive?" Her expression changes in an instant. "Or what? You there, right in front of me. Are you saying you guys aren't imperial soldiers? Are you Federation soldiers who have kindly come to inform us that our western position has fallen?"

When she glances at her subordinates, Serebryakov and the others seem to catch her drift—they place their fingers on the triggers of their weapons.

The one issuing a warning and the ones being warned are all soldiers. Everyone understands what's going on.

If she doesn't need to explain every little thing, that'll make this go quicker. Fantastic. Tanya continues, feeling quite satisfied.

"This is simple. There are imperial soldiers, and there's a position that needs to be held. It's obvious what needs to happen."

This can't be called a threat. It's just proof that there really are idiots in the world who can't regain composure without having a gun pointed at them.

True idiots are constantly falling short of the lowest expectations of sensible people like Tanya. There's nothing to guarantee there won't be a deranged fool mistaking us for enemies and firing.

"Are you enemies? Or are you Imperial Army, like us?"

"What do you want from us, ma'am? There was nothing we could do!"

"If you have complaints, you can tell them to a counselor, if you like—after you survive. Right now, you have a decision to make. Will you take back the position with us? Or will you resist us as an enemy? Give a clear answer. I can't wait all day."

"...Are you serious? Why are you doing this?"

"That's obvious. We need to save our position right this instant."

It's good to see some startled faces remaining. It will stay secret that Tanya is incredibly relieved when she surveys the ragged remnants and spots some survivors with faces that are just barely passable for soldiers.

If we can find more instructors, it'll make things easier. Leaders take on a lot of responsibility.

When someone is staggering toward you, you should call out to them. What a human thing to do, right?

"Lieutenant, you can still fight, yes? Great, round up your men."

"I—I..."

Rank insignia, age, ribbon bars. Even if you can't actually tell a person's worth from a badge, it is one criterion that can be used to make decisions.

"Didn't you rise through the ranks? Unless you're a fool who's just been letting the years go by with your thumb up your ass, do what you need to do. If you can't, I'll lay you to eternal rest right here!" When Tanya smiles encouragingly to say, *C'mon, you can do it,* the effect is immediate.

"Ha-ha-ha! Ha-ha! You're a monster, huh, Colonel?"

"The fatherland's enemies approach. Are you saying I should flash them a loving smile?"

How rude! She puffs her cheeks out to pout.

"Yeah, you're right, Colonel."

"Damn straight, Lieutenant."

"Understood… All right, fellas, let's do this."

His muttered words are low, heavy, and mixed with a sigh. There's no mistaking that will. If a soldier still has enough energy to sigh, he passes muster.

With a satisfied nod, Tanya offers a hand.

"Good, good. What's your name, Lieutenant?"

"Second Lieutenant Barchet at your service, Colonel."

"All right, Lieutenant Barchet. Let's hop to it, shall we?"

Time to go to work. Tanya smiles faintly.

Now we have the people. Even if we detach some mages to support the defense after we take back the western position, it won't need to be that many. If we do it right and get them organized, we might be able to cover most of the flank with them.

It's always wonderful to have a reason to feel hopeful.

And you can't look down on the powerful desire to work. Being able to expect a bright future is fabulous. All right, then. Tanya smiles. "Follow me! Let's go!" She waves her pistol to encourage them and then runs off.

I'm not a big believer in mind over matter, but then again, mindless corporate slaves can only produce empty victories.

We'll just have to devote ourselves to our work as members of a proper human society.

"C'mon! We're counterattacking!"

"If you're going to die, at least die falling forward!"

"You imbeciles need to be taught how to fight like infantry from aerial mages? Get your asses in gear! Run!"

Hmph. Tanya slumps her shoulders and even makes a joke to her adjutant when she comes jogging over.

"Man, we should never act like a blocking unit. Things got a little dicey."

"...It was rather intense."

What? That was nothing. Tanya shrugs. Sure, it's a pain in the neck, but it's the easiest way to "persuade" someone without risking a call from Legal.

It was a piece of cake, no sweat.

You could even call it a civilized conversation.

Rallying troops together, reorganizing them, and reminding the mob of their duties is so human—Tanya rather likes that part.

Luckily, there are no other disputes at this urgent juncture.

Relieved that they might be okay after all, Tanya takes direct command of the provisional unit that will reinforce the defensive line.

As that group is hurrying back to the front, a monster appears out of nowhere, rearing its ugly head.

Hulking frame. Painted red star. Though they've never seen it before, there's no soldier on the eastern front who could mistake that familiar silhouette. More than a few people are cursing.

"Tank! Is that a new model?"

Several aerial mages abruptly cast explosion formulas as they're conditioned to, which function both as a smoke screen and an attack. Sadly, it doesn't seem to have any effect besides putting up some concealment.

"It's sturdy! Shit, it's a new model for sure! Aim for the treads! If we can stop it, we can slug it to death!" Barchet yells an appropriate order. "Bring up the anti-aircraft guns! We can use them to pierce the armor!"

I take that back. He seems to be fighting this war with nothing but an infantry mindset.

"Sheesh, Lieutenant. I can't have you forgetting us. Mages, follow me! We'll pry their lids off and heat them up like canned rations!"

"Yes, ma'am!"

The reason aerial mages reign in urban areas is their ability to conduct combat in three dimensions. We're more flexible than helicopters and smaller and nimbler than the humanoid weapon platforms you see in science fiction.

Well, blasting through the canopy of a tank is easy enough. That doesn't change even in an encounter battle in a village.

"Major Weiss! Leave some intact so it can be used as cover."

"You can leave it all to me!"

"The enemy is running scared! This is where we start our counterattack! Charge!"

Let's clean them up! Leading from the front, Tanya's time serving as a sort of blocking unit ends almost the moment it begins.

The counterattack drives off pretty much all the enemies, and once Tanya can sit back and admire their handiwork, she sighs as if to say, *Finally.*

Even if the enemy strikes with artillery support, as long as they don't have aerial mages, too, they won't get anywhere.

On that point, perhaps the Reich should give an award to the Federation "comrades" who sent all their mages to the *lageri*. It sure makes our battles easier.

"Hmph, I guess that's that?"

"Magnificent work, Colonel."

"Lieutenant Barchet? It's all thanks to your support."

Without the different branches cooperating, there is no chance of victory. An army that does the obvious as a matter of course is best. You can say that an organization's performance depends on how well it can stick to basic principles.

"So can we leave this up to you now?"

"Of course. When this is over, I hope you'll let me treat you to a drink."

"As you can see, I'm not allowed to imbibe. Make it a cup of your finest coffee."

If Tanya drinks at her age, neither military nor civil laws will protect her. The Empire is rather unforgiving when it comes to minors drinking or smoking.

"Oh, how thoughtless of me. Would some milk or meat from the east be all right?"

"Let's make it a can of pineapple. Now then, if you'll excuse me."

Ha-ha-ha. Time to leave the rest to Barchet and swiftly switch gears to the next task.

"02, what's our status?"

"No losses, three light wounds. Nothing that will knock us out of the fight."

"Very good. Then we'll move around the outside of our troops' defensive line. Let's treat ourselves to the fun of kicking the Federation Army in the flank," Tanya barks. To her, it's an easy job. No, strictly speaking, it's probably better to say that it's more easygoing, since the outcome is clear.

As long as there are no mages mixed in with the Federation troops, the imperial aerial mages can run wild. That artillery division is the only enemy worth fearing in the vicinity, but given that there haven't been any incoming shells since the initial bombardment, they're probably either out of ammo or building a position and thus left out of the equation.

So far, nothing's happened to disprove that theory.

"...Sheesh, I guess that's it for now?"

The enemy attack has been repelled. The infiltrating enemy unit has been eliminated. Tanya nods in satisfaction at these results, which on the whole can be termed a successful instance of ideal interior lines defense.

"Colonel, I found the second-in-command of the Fifty-Fourth Regiment."

"Lieutenant Colonel Kreisler, at your service. Thanks for the helping hand."

"Likewise. I'm Lieutenant Colonel Degurechaff."

Filling each other in, as if they had agreed to ahead of time, the discussion about everything that had been neglected during the panic is incredibly smooth. As expected, sending Weiss in to negotiate really helps move things along.

Things would have gone more smoothly if I hadn't sent a useless greenhorn officer with the message.

Is that why? She finds herself, in the natural course of things, praising the capable one with a good recommendation.

"Your Second Lieutenant Barchet did a fine job. We met him partway through this ordeal, and I must say that officers who are promoted from the enlisted like him are a precious resource. I realize you're short on people, but I'd even like to have him if I can."

"Oh, you knew him? He was from my battalion."

"Oh my. Well..." Tanya apologizes and bows her head. She can't help but notice the past-tense nature of his reply.

"I'm sure he would have been happy to know someone with the Silver Wings Assault Badge thought highly of him."

"...You mean?"

"At the height of the counterattack, he got hit with a Federation grenade. He was groaning until just a short while ago, but the surgeon told me..."

There's no need to add *We couldn't save him*. If anyone on the eastern front shakes their head with such mourning, the meaning is clear.

"I had a comrade. He sleeps; I walk. Oh Lord, please have mercy on his soul."

"Couldn't have said it better. Well, my unit is withdrawing. If we go now, I think we can make it to the next marshaling point. What are you going to do?"

He must be inviting us to go with him. Give and take. It's a mindset I appreciate. But Tanya shakes her head.

No aerial mage unit should travel the same road as an infantry unit.

"My troops are nimble aerial mages. We're used to being the rear guard. We'll stick around here for a few hours after you've left and then head to the marshaling point at our own pace."

"I really appreciate it...but are you sure?"

"Of course."

Tanya responds with a broad smile.

In contrast to slow-moving infantry, aerial mage units are made for mobility. To put it another way, their ability to shoot and scoot is their chief feature. If there's no need to hold a position, they can simply fly away. That's a strategy that works well on the eastern front, where the usual order of the day is defense in depth—though the static defensive battle the unit just fought in is not a great example.

Anyway, outside of times when operating as a Kampfgruppe, there's not much appeal in sharing the fate of another unit.

"Oh, we'll just throw a wild party with the jettisoned supplies of the Fifty-Fourth Regiment—if you don't mind forgetting some choice rations."

"...So your Silver Wings aren't just for show, huh?"

"Oh, they definitely are. All right, Colonel Kreisler, I hope we both have good luck."

"Yes, stay safe out there."

The good-bye ends with salutes and well wishes. Tanya and the 203rd Aerial Mage Battalion members watch as the others leave the crumbling building.

"Are you sure you don't want to withdraw with those friendly troops?"

Tanya nods at her vice commander with absolute certainty. "Major, we and the infantry move at different speeds, as I'm sure you know."

"Yes, ma'am."

Honestly, considering how we can consistently outrun the Federation aerial mages, if all we want to do on the eastern front is escape, it's extremely easy. Not to mention that the huge group of foot soldiers making up the Fifty-Fourth Regiment serves as a great decoy. Our retreat should go quite smoothly.

"We have the leeway to take it slowly. I see no problem with staying here until we have cover of night. Sleep in shifts now, while you can."

"The beds were all blown away..."

"I'm sure you'll be able to find enough for half an aerial mage battalion. The troops who aren't getting some shut-eye should have some tea and high-calorie chocolate."

"That's quite the leisurely shift."

You're not wrong. Tanya agrees with her vice commander's grumble but doesn't forget to tack on a warning. "If there's no enemy attack, that is."

"Certainly. Then, if you'll excuse me, I'll go first."

"Yes, switch up in two hours. I'll wake you, so get some shut-eye."

"Understood." Weiss salutes, and as she watches him go, Tanya realizes the first lieutenants are standing next to her.

"Lieutenant Serebryakov, you too. Get to bed. Lieutenant Grantz, you're with me. Go look for some coffee beans or something."

"Coffee beans, ma'am?"

"Sort through the remains of the Fifty-Fourth's regimental HQ. I'm sure you'll find at least one bean. If that doesn't work out, grab some of the troops' tags and we'll trade them in for luxury goods when we return to the rear."

"Got it. I'll task a few people."

As the mages set off with their shovels, Tanya makes good on her words and chomps into some chocolate.

In any case, we've earned a breather. All that's left is to make our way back to the rallying point and join up with the rest of the Salamander Kampfgruppe.

To be frank, when coordination is doubtful, cooperating with another unit is an absolutely terrifying prospect.

It was hard to not let it show on Tanya's face. Synchronizing on the fly is hard to pull off even for pros. To cooperate with amateurs who are fuzzy on even the basics is sheer horror.

A ragtag crew is basically a walking nightmare.

If someone makes a mistake and ruins themselves, that's their own fault. Sadly, the fundamental principle of war is collective responsibility. And your life is what's at stake.

I'm not about to entrust that to someone I can't believe in.

How would that be any different from getting treated by some quack doctor who doesn't have a license to practice medicine.

Even in cases of disease or injury, I'm extremely reluctant to leave my fate in the hands of a doctor. But it must be done. As long as they guarantee professional standards, they deserve my respect.

Quacks and other fakes, however, should be shot. There's no waste more toxic than an incompetent fool who thinks they're an expert. That goes the same for soldiers at war. If you're receiving payment and putting your life on the line to fight, there are no compromises allowed. Troops who can't be put to good use are nothing but dead weight, not even usable as meat shields.

If you're not a pro, don't even speak to me. Don't bother me. If at all possible, make yourself useful and cause some damage to the enemy. While it's incredibly self-centered, Tanya is confident that these sentiments are utterly human and normal. That's what a human is to Tanya von Degurechaff.

Being taught that humans are political animals who construct society to serve their own interests is one of my earliest memories from Japan, my onetime schoolhouse.

Back then, I probably didn't fully comprehend it.

"Sheesh, you can't sniff at lifelong learning, can you?"

There's no limit to the amount that can be invested in human capital. It's a virtue to learn whenever the opportunity presents itself. Ultimately, there's no such thing as a professional who stops learning.

"I guess that's a pro's job, huh?"

In that respect, the members of the 203rd Aerial Mage Battalion and the Salamander Kampfgruppe are model, certifiable experts.

They enjoy combat just a bit too much, but, considering the current situation, Tanya can only rate them highly. Personality, education, and taste are all secondary factors when it comes to evaluations. The main criterion is whether or not they can properly fulfill their duties.

In other words, people who can't do their jobs well are garbage. In private life, I'll be respectful. But working with them is impossible. If it's a choice between war maniacs who can fight a war or good-natured people who can't do anything useful, I want the former beside me when I'm on the front line...

Then Tanya is suddenly struck by something.

"...Why am I assuming that I'll be fighting in a war?"

If you say it's because she's currently at war, then there's nothing else to it.

But for a peaceful peace-loving liberal democrat like Tanya, the state of war should be *an exception*. Not a natural state of being.

War shouldn't be used as a justification for anything.

"Fucking hell."

This war needs to end.

Tanya swallows the words instead of saying them and turns on her heel, a glum look on her face.

[chapter] II Restoration

"The Lergen Kampfgruppe?
I've only ever heard the name."

Interview with a retired imperial soldier

»»» UNIFIED YEAR 1976 EDITION OF DR. BAXTER'S *RECORD OF THE EASTERN FRONT* «««

Every historian knows that the Lergen Kampfgruppe was a ghost on the eastern front.

The oral histories all seem to indicate that the unit did, in fact, exist. It's rare for someone who served on the eastern front at the time to not know the name.

Imperial, Federation, and even Commonwealth soldiers continue to speak of the distinguished Lergen Kampfgruppe—of its stunning achievements, the brilliant feats and undying wartime exploits.

At risk of being uncouth, they were glorious given the context of their existence. They and only they managed easy victories no matter where they fought. Call them heroes—or to be poetic: legends.

Most would expect this legendary Kampfgruppe to be universally praised. But that's not what happened. Everyone knows them, and yet nobody knows them.

The Lergen Kampfgruppe's true nature is shrouded in mystery. To this day, even the few survivors who say they were members aren't sure what the truth is. One reason for that is surely the extreme rate of attrition on the eastern front.

Of the Lergen Kampfgruppe's order of battle, almost none of the units made it to the end of the war. On paper, the Kampfgruppe was wiped out apart from a mere handful of survivors.

That wasn't unusual on the eastern front.

Undeniably terrible, but it wasn't exceptional. The war, the eastern front—it was just that kind of animal. That's how bitter the fighting was.

One returnee spat, "Hearing about it isn't enough to understand." He snapped at me with a broken look in his eyes. "It was an extreme environment where corpses of friend and foe alike got tangled in the mud only for the armored units to churn them all up with their treads. Then the aerial mages burned what was left, and to top it off, airplanes constantly fought over the sky. I'll never forget the smell that hung in the air."

Still, the depth of the Lergen Kampfgruppe's mystery can be summed up with the word *abnormal.*

It's not as if there are no records. Its commander, Colonel (at the time) von Lergen, was a respectable staff officer whose existence is confirmed.

He was a verified officer of the General Staff.

Knowing that he served under the two ravens Zettour and Rudersdorf for a long time in the field of operations, the hard fight he put up on the front lines should come as no surprise.

But the records of his era are notorious among scholars of history for critical lapses so numerous as to be strange.

Colonel von Lergen's post-war rank seems to suggest a deep connection between the Lergen Kampfgruppe and him, but the connection itself is incredibly unclear.

APRIL 22, UNIFIED YEAR 1927, EASTERN FRONT, A CERTAIN IMPERIAL ARMY MARSHALING POINT

Unexpected is probably the best way to describe it…

The 203rd Aerial Mage Battalion's retreat went rather smoothly. The anticipated Federation pursuit was surprisingly sluggish, and the battalion completed its withdrawal to the designated line of retreat without a hitch last night.

While taking a simple rest and even getting maintenance done on our orbs, we still have the wherewithal to grimace at some ersatz coffee and spread plenty of margarine on rye bread that was allowed to rise properly. If I say it that way, is the leisurely pace we're taking here conveyed properly?

Additionally, once order is reestablished, the organization's power can be wielded much more successfully. On this point, the ones who benefit the most are the Salamander Kampfgruppe and the 203rd Aerial Mage Battalion at its core. This is obvious, given how the unit was formed.

Created to serve as the hands and feet of the General Staff, a strike force with special emphasis on rapid response and mobility will receive the highest priority. We're even capable of sending personnel to a depot to receive supplies if need be, though that would be nonstandard operating procedure.

The combination of a convenient air route and a rail network means aid can arrive much swifter than Tanya could have wished for.

"Captain Ahrens, reporting! We're here to link up with the main force!"

The armored officer with a cheeky expression on his face is the definition of dashing. With his well-fitting uniform topped with his crumpled crusher cap, he cuts the classic figure of a tank man. Compared to Tanya, who is covered in mud and fed up, he must have had a more pleasant trip.

But the fact that he has come at all makes everything forgivable.

"We've been waiting for you, Captain!"

As they exchange salutes, Tanya and the rest of the aerial magic officers breathe sighs of relief. They're all so excited for reinforcements that everyone, aside from First Lieutenant Grantz, who was already on duty, jumped up and raced over. Even straitlaced Weiss is slapping Ahrens on the shoulder with a big grin on his face.

"Finally, reinforcements." Cracking a smile, Tanya expresses her genuine feelings. "It's incredibly reassuring, isn't it, Major Weiss?"

"Yes, it certainly is. Things just felt unbalanced with only the aerial mage battalion."

Letting the armored troops take care of anti-tank combat, as is their job, lessens the burden on us dramatically. It was a great king who once said that artillery turns an ugly brawl into a war. Tanks are surely similar.

"And the others? How long do you think it'll take for them to meet us?"

"The guns and infantry are supposed to be coming behind us, but… I'm afraid I don't know the details."

"Ah, but just knowing they're on their way makes me feel better."

"Oh, I have one other related report. We ran into Lieutenant Colonel Uger from the General Staff, whom we met during our reassignment, and he gave us a message for you."

Oh? Tanya's face shifts in curiosity. What kind of message would Colonel Uger go out of his way to leave with Captain Ahrens?

"And the contents?"

"They're dispatching a wave of reinforcements to the Kampfgruppe."

"As long as he's not just saying that."

Regardless of what she says, feeling slightly guilty, she knows that Uger is a specialist of integrity. She doesn't want to expect too much, but she figures it's all right to hope.

"Anyhow, what's our status?"

"What you see is what you get, Captain Ahrens."

"You mean…?"

"That's right." Tanya nods. "It's bad. Everything's in terrible disarray. I'll let Major Weiss fill you in on the rest. Get the details from him."

Both officers acknowledge their orders. Tanya has complete faith in the two of them. Their personalities and tastes may be hawkish, but she has no qualms about their abilities.

"What are you going to do, Colonel?"

"Oversee the fortification of our position here with Lieutenant Serebryakov. It's a pain that these guys in the east know nothing but trench warfare, and we have to think about what to do when the chain of command falls apart."

As Captain Ahrens watched Lieutenant Colonel von Degurechaff leave with her adjutant, he commented with a wry smile. "She's worried about the chain of command falling apart?"

Of course, he couldn't deny the possibility, but… While it did make sense that the Imperial Army, which employed decapitation tactics, would be wary of falling prey to those exact tactics…

"The colonel worries so much."

"According to the colonel, though, we'd probably be categorized as idiots who let our guard down too much, right, Captain Ahrens?"

"What do you mean?"

His blank stare was met with Major Weiss's dead-serious expression.

"During a fighting retreat we participated in before you arrived, we ended up defending a strongpoint. There, we saw the senior officer of a friendly unit get blown up along with his whole HQ."

"…That's awful. It's like they're playing games with us."

To get turned into a punching bag… It couldn't have been a very fun time. Weiss nodded at Ahrens's quiet comment.

"We're not in a position to pick and choose. The colonel's policy of doing our best no matter the circumstances is a roundabout way to avoiding trouble as much as possible."

"Yeah. Let's do what we can."

"That's the spirit."

As they nodded, they both sighed.

"Even grumbling is a pretty rough time in this unit. It'd be different if we at least had a few cigarettes."

"Oof, Captain Ahrens, you have no idea how much I envy you."

"Why's that?" But he realized almost immediately. "Oh, you're not allowed to smoke."

"Yeah." Weiss nodded. "Under the colonel, smoking's prohibited. Our lungs won't last otherwise. In the past, orb performance was the greatest limiting factor. No one used to fly so high."

Major Weiss was an aerial mage. A job where if he burned out his lungs, it would come back to bite him. It wasn't as if smoking got you any points before the war, but nowadays, unless an aerial mage was a truly serious believer in nicotine, cigarettes were a luxury they went without.

"The progress of technology *is* remarkable. The armored units have seen similar developments. Our main guns used to be peashooters!" Ahrens laughed, and Weiss seemed to agree wholeheartedly.

"I recently saw something similar. I heard today that unless rookies can aim for the tank treads, there's no hope of even delaying the enemy."

"But surely you and the colonel are different. You're probably sick of destroying Federation tanks by now!"

"No, just fed up with how tough their armor is. Even for the vets of the 203rd Aerial Mage Battalion, punching through the defense of their main battle tanks is a feat."

It didn't used to be so hard to destroy tanks. Ahrens had heard it was a given that even if it took a bit of time, just about any aerial mage could defeat enemy armored vehicles.

"There are only a few types left that we can pop as easily as opening a can."

"Really?"

"Yeah," Weiss replied, his face grim. "Aerial mages can perform some anti-tank combat, but our hands are pretty full with our main tasks… Anyhow, we've been chatting for a while now. Let's get you up to speed."

"Yep, thanks."

APRIL 24, UNIFIED YEAR 1927, EASTERN FRONT, KAMPFGRUPPE'S TEMPORARY POST

Ordering everyone to stay alert, pointing out lapses in care, and taking every possible precaution to keep operations safe. It's only natural to do that as a commander, but making sure it filters down into the whole organization is difficult.

The task is hardest in the relief that comes once the dust settles and warm food is served. This is the moment the tension drains from everyone's shoulders. It's hard for soldiers not to feel like they've finally reached safety in the rear.

It cannot be overstated that in these moments, not a speck of battlefield tension remained in most of the Imperial Army units.

The troops were convinced that they'd succeeded in their retreat. Mistakes that stem from truth are the most insidious. This small victory relaxed the Imperial Army too much.

The alarm announcing the approach of a large Federation force only began to ring after the enemies were already quite close. Still, if the enemy is coming, everyone already knows what to do.

The troops dozing with their knapsacks as pillows are slapped awake, and it takes only an instant for them to leap to their stations.

"Enemy attack! Enemy attack!"

"All units to your posts!"

The duty officer races around yelling, and the troops whose light sleep has been cut short curse without restraint as they leap to their places in preestablished harmony.

"Obstructing our sleep? Fuck! Someday I'll sue them for being a public nuisance!"

Tanya is no exception. She heads for Kampfgruppe HQ, barking loud protests the whole way. The moment she reaches her command post, she knows what she needs to do.

"Status report!"

"It's a division at least, ma'am. Enemy attack."

"Shit, we're not even finished constructing our position yet! Don't people from the Federation know the etiquette for visiting someone?!"

The imperial fortifications are still incomplete. It sounds better if you say *They're currently making every effort to finish it*, but the truth is that they may or may not have managed to dig some spider holes—that's the level of progress we're talking about.

And that's not all because when it rains, it pours. We're suffering a rampant shortage of light machine guns on the eastern front. Neither the freezing winter nor the muddy spring has been kind to the standard-issue LMGs crafted for us in the home country.

The density of fire from the frontline units here is terribly low compared to what imperial forces were putting out on the western lines.

Under the circumstances, we can't expect the strongpoint to pin or stop the enemy completely, even if there are trenches. It's only natural that the commander of the defense would want to make up for the lacking firepower of the infantry by working the armored troops and aerial mages extra hard.

"Colonel, it's the command post."

"Patch me through."

The only saving grace is that the chain of command is still functioning. Tanya can see clear benefits from unified command at the division level as a member of the organization.

"Aid the defense? Understood. The Salamander Kampfgruppe would like to provide support with armored troops and fly strike missions with aerial mages. Do we have your approval?"

This is the negotiation stage of the briefing that needs to happen before everyone can get to work.

"This is CP. The left wing of defense line two is in the most critical condition. Can you shore them up?"

"We can, but it'll mean having the aerial mages stick around there."

"I realize it's a lot to ask, but please provide as much support as you can. I'd also like to request that you pull a company of aerial mages to use as reserves once the situation stabilizes."

It's not that she doesn't see what the CP is trying to do, but no commander is thrilled to get a proposal like that. Everyone wants to have reserves nearby.

"Salamander 01 to CP. I'm fine heading over there as backup, but it's unclear whether we'll have the extra troops, so I can't guarantee you any reserves."

"...Well, just if you can, then."

"I can't offer you something from nothing."

"...Understood."

Luckily, the other side gives in, and the issue is neatly resolved. We don't even have much to spare, so I appreciate being able to conserve even a little.

It's the same reason there's a big difference between pushing the system to its limits and keeping some slight redundancy to ensure its overall health.

Now, then. Tanya puts down the receiver and, upon turning around, begins assembling sortie orders.

If there's any conversation more obnoxious than the one I just had, it'll be this next one. Tanya shifts her gaze to her tankman.

"It's probably only the 203rd Aerial Mage Battalion that will attempt to attack, so, Captain Ahrens, your armor will be supporting the defense."

"Colonel?! We can head out there, too!"

It's the answer she expected. To be fair, anyone who doesn't have that attitude probably isn't cut out to be an armored officer.

"I need the tanks on defense."

"But, ma'am!"

"Denied! Fire at the enemy and draw them in! If we don't leave a strike force inside the strongpoint, we won't be able to keep them in check!"

Ahrens makes his argument only for Tanya to flatly refuse it. A subordinate's assertiveness mustn't be praised unless the timing is right.

He learned how to fight tank battles on the eastern front; she needs him to understand and accept.

"...Yes, ma'am."

"Good." Tanya nods and then turns her gaze on her old hands. These guys can do any mission. They're reliable enough that she can leave this job up to them.

Time for war—she's about to grin when she notices Ahrens looking like he wants to mention something. Well, a superior officer's job is to listen to what their subordinates have to say.

"Captain, if you have something, go ahead and say it."

"Are you planning to sortie at full strength from the start? We don't currently have a complete picture of the enemy force's strength. I think scouting should maybe be priority..."

"Yes, that's right. The enemy unit's size is unclear, Captain Ahrens." As she adjusts her hat on her head with a *boff*, she nods with a wry smile. "If we don't know, we just have to go find out."

"So you're taking the entire battalion out for recon-in-force?"

"It's more of a search-and-destroy mission, but yes. Because," she continues bitterly, "we expect at minimum for there to be an artillery division."

"You mean divisional artillery?"

The way Ahrens's face twists up into a *You've-got-to-be-kidding* look as he repeats what she said is not entirely unreasonable. The threat that a division of artillery poses is in another dimension compared to divisional artillery.

"Unfortunately, it's not a misunderstanding." Tanya continues, "I can see you wishing you misheard, but what we're facing isn't comparable to divisional artillery. Be ready for a whole division's worth."

Boof—she gives him a punch in the stomach.

Later, Tanya will remember this moment bitterly and be glad that she said to prepare for the worst.

Not long after the mage unit sorties and begins their search, they pick up a large amount of communications. The signals should give a strong indication of where the enemy artillery unit is located, but they're encoded. Even so, specific repetitions are enough to get an indirect confirmation.

With a quick "Let's go!" Tanya leads her battalion in a beeline for the determined location...only to be confronted with the unfortunate reality that her predictions were correct.

Apparently, no expectations are more likely to be dead-on than the ones you wish were off. Setting aside whether it's statistically significant, Tanya is forced to see that her worst fears are quite reliable.

"Sheesh, I'm jealous. What beefy artillery support!"

What she's looking at in the distance as she comments quietly is the Federation position—and what a magnificently arranged artillery position it is. She can't help but hate how even the corps artillery battery is lined up in such an orderly way. A bombardment from that alone could be enough to annihilate our forces.

"Prepare for anti-artillery combat. This is officially an assault mission now."

A single order brings three formations to instantly appear, ready to strike. Their flight path will allow them to hit the enemy's position with an air-to-ground attack. Once they're in place, all that's left is the easy job of nailing the flammable shells on the ground with a few explosion formulas.

If we don't hit them hard enough… Tanya ventures to shout in a condescending tone. "Troops, we're gonna show them the kind of flying attack aerial mages are capable of! Now let's go!"

"03 to 01, there's an enemy mage unit!"

Tanya responds to her adjutant's warning with a grin—because of course there are enemy mages. It has always been natural that aerial mages provide air support for artillery. Whenever you see artillery, the first thing you do is go hunting for mages.

"Engage them! Take 'em apart!"

"I'm detecting a company of enemy troops, and it's headed this way!"

"Ha, is that all?"

It happens as she's murmuring what a small number that is to support a division of artillery—the far-off battery suddenly begins to fire.

This is the exact moment that I notice the elevation on the guns is weirdly high…

"The enemy artillery is aiming at us!"

At the shrieked warning, Tanya looks back to the artillery instinctively and notices the cannons are aiming awfully high.

Well, isn't that just luxurious as hell!

They've got anti-aircraft cannons mixed into their artillery position!

"I doubt they'll..." *...hit us.* She's about to grin wryly when she realizes: *If we're up against curtain fire from anti-aircraft guns... they've probably already finished firing solutions for this airspace!*

"Break! Increase altitude!"

The reason she gives the sudden warning is that she trusts her gut. You should always pay attention whenever you have a bad feeling about something.

Immediately after she has the unit veer off their strike path, the shells that burst below eerily scatter shrapnel where the mages just were moments ago.

"Timed fuses? Tsk, they're certainly prepared."

And on top of that, at the moment we break our formation to evade, the enemy mage company swoops in on us!

"Enemy mages charging!"

"Three rounds of explosion formulas! All companies open fire!"

Even if we outnumber them and surely aren't at a disadvantage in terms of training, it's not great that they've caught us off-balance. And considering how well the enemy troops seem to be cooperating, I'm hard-pressed to say I feel great about our current situation.

Tanya, a good person, has trouble understanding why the badder the guys, the more friends they have. Evil always comes in gangs.

"CP to Salamander 01—it's urgent!"

"This is Salamander 01—currently engaged. Shit, these guys don't let up!"

She casts an explosion formula on the heads of the charging enemy mages and dodges an optical sniping formula.

"CP, what's your urgent request?!"

"We've spotted another enemy battery! It's a rocket-launcher unit! They're setting up in the opposite direction of your current heading, and if they open fire, our position will be completely suppressed! Take it out as soon as you can!"

Charging into one artillery division is bad enough, but now there's another one? Even if your philosophy is that more is better, the Federation's idea of "more" is astonishing.

"Don't be ridiculous! We're in the middle of taking out one position right now!"

"If we're under a blanket of rocket fire, the armored units won't be able to do a thing. Colonel, please."

"CP, this is Salamander 01…send the details."

Swallowing the expletives is a challenge. But Tanya asks for the details out of her sense of duty. It has to get done…

"Major Weiss! You heard them! We're splitting the unit in two."

"They're asking an awful lot, huh? We'll do all we can!"

"I'll leave a company with you! Stay here and keep bullying these guys! I don't expect anything more than harassment! Feel free to go nuts, but don't overextend yourselves!"

"Understood!"

"The rest of you, follow me. We're going hunting for self-propelled rocket launchers. Prepare for a search-and-destroy mission. It's a damn busy day, but make sure you get your jobs done!"

APRIL 26, UNIFIED YEAR 1927, EASTERN FRONT, FOLLOWING THE START OF THE FEDERATION'S SECOND OFFENSIVE

Enemies, enemies, enemies. Wave after wave of them as far as the eye can see. It's a surge of pressure no less terrible than anything seen on the Rhine front.

A massive waste of matériel.

The profitless enterprise of war.

An idiotic battle of human-capital attrition.

When you fight so hard to repel them, refusing to be crushed, only for their energy to never flag or waver, even the hardiest soldier has no choice but to recoil from their fierce attacks.

And if you succeed in repelling them, the feeling that remains is far from joyful. It hardly feels like a victory; you just get the dimmest sense that you were able to defend.

Later, while wandering the battlefield snatching up the gear the enemy left behind or cleaning up and working on rebuilding the line, it's very noticeable even if you wish it wasn't...how all sorts of the enemy's plentiful gear has to be deemed "origin unknown."

"This is strange. It can't be that...," Tanya grumbles as she gazes at the abandoned Federation Army tanks that dot the landscape just as the report from the defending troops described.

The presence of Commonwealth tanks doesn't bug her so much. As a hostile country, it's not so out of the ordinary for their equipment to be on the eastern front. But what about the tanks from the catalogs of "neutral countries" sitting out there?

"Huh? Who even knows where these tanks are from!"

The ominous word *lend-lease*[2] crosses my mind.

I knew it. I anticipated this. But the shock of actually seeing it is impossible to describe.

It's not fair, I want to say.

I hope you rot, I want to curse.

No, wait. Tanya notices a strange feeling mixed in with her distress. *Curse*? You mean a libertarian like me thought to rely on a supernatural power?

Of all the—! She can't help but shudder.

Are my thoughts being contaminated by God, the devil, or some similar notion?

That's erasure of me as a modern individual.

When I think about how I might have taken a step closer toward the negation of my dignity, free will, and determination—a denial of everything that matters to me—all I feel is fear.

It's so horrible that simply suppressing the urge to vomit is a struggle.

Wishing is just too superstitious. If I'm going to end up on the side of the cackling Being X, it'd be better to blow my brains out.

Still, even while Tanya draws a clear line between praying and wishing, she can't help but hope.

Our reinforcements had better arrive tomorrow, as scheduled.

[2] **lend-lease** Literally a leasing service for lending! Could be weapons and ammo, battleships, tanks, or fighter planes! Don't confuse this with weapons sales—it's merely a service to lend out extra materials. Or at least that was the logic that was used to explain away furnishing countries at war with weapons.

APRIL 27, UNIFIED YEAR 1927, IN A VILLAGE NEAR THE FRONT LINES OF THE EAST

A rare visitor. That is Tanya's first impression of the colonel wearing the brilliant insignia of the General Staff.

That said, she's happy to see him.

Colonel von Lergen has come to the quagmire of the eastern front bearing coffee beans and reinforcements. Only someone out of their mind who hates coffee and wants to monopolize the war would be unwelcoming.

In other words, someone the exact opposite of extremely sensible Tanya. She doesn't imagine she could understand them.

So Tanya welcomes the incoming troops with a huge smile. Naturally, she doesn't forget to return—with textbook style—the salutes of the officers leading the column.

"I feel like it's been ages, Captain Meybert, Lieutenant Tospan, Lieutenant Wüstemann." Tanya grins as if to say, *Nice work making it back*, and then extends her respects to the colonel. "I owe you thanks for guiding them."

"What? No, it's fine. I have business here anyhow."

"On the forward-most line of the eastern front?"

"That's right."

It's not rare for a member of the General Staff to come observe things in the field, but Tanya stiffens up—*Wait a minute*—and Lergen lowers his voice.

"I need to talk to you. Is there somewhere we won't be disturbed?"

"Sure, one moment."

She doesn't even have to wonder what's up. It must be important. Seems like anti-espionage operations are high priority as well. Though she wanted to brief the troops herself, she can leave that to her subordinates.

With that settled, Tanya raises her voice. "Officers, gather up! Major Weiss, Captain Ahrens, fill in the returnees on the frontline situation! Lieutenant Grantz, you're on duty while they're doing that!"

"""Understood!"""

The snappy, disciplined response is encouraging.

"Lieutenant Serebryakov, follow me."

"Yes, ma'am!"

I've participated in exercises where we practiced tactical operations without troops on military maps while General Staff oversaw us, but come to think of it, this is my first time getting a lecture from such a high-ranking staff officer as Colonel von Lergen.

I have to stay on my toes, thinks Tanya as she tenses up again.

"All right, let's take a walk. This way, Colonel. Allow me to show you the front line."

With her adjutant guarding their rear, Tanya leads the way, heading for the aftermath of the battlefield that had only just calmed down after the recent fierce battle.

She's confident she can protect one colonel, but…she's still anxious that there could be snipers or remnants of the defeated troops lurking about—it's bad for Tanya's heart.

That said, they've mopped up already. Since a certain degree of safety is guaranteed, she gives him a rough explanation, describing the lay of the land while beginning to expand on how they're preparing for the next defensive battle.

This kind of report is rather normal, but since they're on the forward-most line, there is wreckage of destroyed weapons and such all around.

Perfect. She points out one of their most challenging foes. "…This is a defeated Federation main battle tank."

"Hrm?" Lergen's eyes pop. He must be fairly perceptive.

Happy for the opportunity, he approaches, shaking his head as he examines the armor itself. "…I've seen it on paper before, but in real life, the armor is surprisingly thick."

"It can defeat most attacks. According to my armored officer, even our tank guns can't penetrate unless it's at awfully close range."

"Makes sense." Lergen grimly nods. "At this rate, most of the active main battle tanks will need to be downgraded to reserves. The pressure to upgrade is increasing."

Tanya and Visha maintain a respectful silence while Lergen openly heaves a sigh.

"They may be our enemies, but…I envy them. They still have this much energy to spare? To think they can develop and commit new tanks like this…"

Clong-clong—Lergen raps on the armor with a knuckle. His comments reveal his perspective on the situation as someone coming from the rear. That said, it's probably the viewpoint of any staff officer confronted with the need to update primary equipment of whole armies.

"Have you fought one of these things yourself?"

"I've battled similar tanks several times," Tanya responds, inviting Lergen's follow-up.

"So what's your honest evaluation of them, having faced them before? Your personal opinion is fine."

"The skilled members of the 203rd Aerial Mage Battalion can just barely break through the top armor. Current anti-tank doctrine won't cut it anymore. We should assume that the ability of a normal aerial mage unit to combat tanks has been severely limited."

"No doubt about that. So they can even repel 57 mm shells, then?" He winces, mentioning in passing that he read that tidbit in a report. Lergen is an observer with integrity. He has no shortage of imagination and is capable of revising mistaken preconceptions. Truly a model staff officer.

Which is why Tanya feels safe offering a bit of her personal opinion. "I'm not even sure 88 mm could do it. It's an evolution of dinosaurs, but everything on the eastern front does change abnormally fast."

"So just reading the briefs isn't enough. You really can't get a sense for things unless you come out and see it for yourself. They say the devil is in the details, but the field has a quality all its own."

"What the General Staff needs is experience on the front. With all due respect, this is a trap that those of superior caliber are especially liable to fall into. Smart people tend to understand things intellectually first and foremost."

"A sensible thing to say." Lergen nods. "You're absolutely correct. Assuming you understand without proof is terrible. Knowing and experiencing are two very different things. Well said, Colonel."

"I'm honored to have you say so, sir."

"And this is exactly why I have a favor to ask of you."

When he flicks his eyes toward her adjutant, Tanya knows what to do.

After waving off her adjutant with a "Leave us, please," she takes a cautious glance around, but nothing is out of the ordinary.

And since they're talking in low voices behind the wreckage of a tank, eavesdropping probably isn't an issue.

"So may I ask what the secret is?"

"Feel free to consider this a personal request. Just don't tell anyone."

"Yes, sir."

Tanya straightens up, and Lergen, openly hesitant, broaches the matter.

"I'd like to ask you to look after a guest, Colonel."

"A guest?"

"Yes, that's right… A military observer."

Hrm? Tanya cocks her head. *Should a provisional unit like the Kampfgruppe be taking observers?*

But that question is obliterated the moment she hears what Lergen says next.

"It's a colonel from Ildoa."

"A military observer? A colonel?!"

But, but!

Unlike Colonel von Lergen, Lieutenant Colonel Tanya von Degurechaff is an officer in the field, so she says what she needs to say without reservation.

"Colonel von Lergen, *we're a Kampfgruppe.*"

"I know that, of course. And?"

"You don't get it. To be frank, I'd ask that you consider Eastern Army Headquarters or at least Divisional HQ instead."

"It's too difficult?"

In response, Tanya nods deeply and shoots back, "With all due respect, do you mean to say it's easy?"

The Kampfgruppe, by its nature, is a temporary unit. It doesn't have a permanent headquarters, and it was never supposed to. The silver lining is that the core of the unit, the 203rd Aerial Mage Battalion, has so many officers that she can use them as staff.

In other words, everything runs smoothly thanks to all the effort put in on the ground—essentially unpaid overtime. It's obvious that if they suddenly have to look after an important visitor, they'll be overworked.

"We don't have extra personnel in the Kampfgruppe. And since it's unclear when or if we'll ever get replenished, taking proper care of an observer is..."

"It must be out of the question."

It's less *difficult* and more *impossible.*

Tanya tries to state her case clearly, but she's unable to finish when she hears Lergen say that.

So if you get it, then... She glares at him before she can stop herself and is caught entirely off guard by his response.

"Even so, I have to ask this of you."

"Ask?! Forgive me, but you, a colonel, are *asking* me, a lieutenant colonel?!" The reply is out of Tanya's mouth before she knows it. She's never seen Lergen bow his head before.

He's a General Staff officer, a hotshot from central, not to mention an elite on track to become a general. Of all the things he could do, he's bowing?

Tanya shakes her head, confused. "Please excuse me, but are you telling me this isn't an order from the General Staff?"

"Not officially."

Once he says that, she's even more bothered. She has no idea what the colonel is trying to get at.

"This is a strange thing to ask, but...could you please speak candidly? What in the world is going on?"

"...That's a natural question to have. Well, where do I start...? But you're right—I should be frank. Colonel von Degurechaff...starting today, I've been appointed the commander of a mobile task force above the Salamander Kampfgruppe."

Tanya doesn't even try to hide how ridiculous she thinks the news is and snaps, "I haven't heard a thing about that. Personnel is making that kind of move *now*?"

"Yes. The paperwork is all done. Written orders have been issued."

That's the efficiency of someone who's spent time in the General Staff. This is the kind of familiarity with the organization's regulations that earns a military bureaucrat so much honor.

But that flawless adherence to procedure gives her pause as well.

"...That's awfully efficient."

If they were really so thorough, Tanya should have heard something. Communication is fundamental to an organization. A talented military bureaucrat should know how to avoid causing malfunctions in the lower ranks by keeping everyone appraised of their plans and thoughts.

The fact that Tanya didn't get word of it at all means either that failed to happen or purposely wasn't done...

In other words, there must be some reason behind it. In which case, it's simple. Tanya has a general idea of what's going on.

"It'd be great if you could share the truth with me and not just your official cover..."

"You always get straight to the point, don't you?" Lergen winces.

Tanya feels bad for him, but this is important, so she closes in a step and asks, "Could you tell me what this has to do with the Ildoan officer? Wait a minute. Sending an officer here as a personal request is..."

That would normally be beyond the realm of his authority. There should be no way that a personal request from Colonel von Lergen results in Tanya welcoming a military observer into her Kampfgruppe.

What if the Lergen Kampfgruppe was set to take the observer...? He would never be able to hide his tracks with this farce of saying the guy's just an observer... What if he's not hiding it, and we're all partners in crime? Then it would make sense...

What could be the reason? Why is that necessary?

As that line of thought nears the critical point—*Ohhh*—a hypothesis springs into being.

"I'll ask you straight. Is this about diplomatic negotiations? *Are you, a General Staff officer, planning to perform them?*"

"...This war can't go on any longer. Can't we agree that it has to end at some point?"

That's essentially saying yes!

"I heard about your argument regarding the necessity of an immediate end to the war from Lieutenant Colonel Uger. I'd like it if you could think of this as a related parting-gift-plus-covert operation."

"...So accepting the observer plays a role in the negotiations?"

"We're expecting a handsome reward. It wouldn't hurt to spend a little quality time with our Ildoan friends, would it?"

"What does General von Zettour think about all this?"

"Probably, '*Show them what's going on.*'"

Ahhh. Tanya's shoulders slump. It's true that the higher-ups in the General Staff are open-minded. He might actually say that. And considering Lergen's position, it's clear that he must already have authorization.

"They say a picture is worth a thousand words, but..."

"Show the peace-addled Ildoans the military might of the Silver Wings."

"May I say something?" Tanya cuts in.

He's calling it battlefield observation, but this person would actually be a guest. It would be best to show them a neat and tidy Imperial Army. In fact, if that's one of the main goals and they don't take it seriously, I'm somewhat worried about the upbraiding that might come from the homeland.

"I'm sure you're aware that they call me Rusted Silver..."

"It's not as if you're advancing by wildly spilling the blood of your allies. Don't worry about it." He laughs, and Tanya smiles wryly, thinking how bold he's gotten.

"With all due respect, Colonel. Human lives are precious irrespective of friend or foe."

"You surprise me, Colonel. Let me be frank. I had no idea you were a humanist. When did you convert?"

"That's a malicious misunderstanding. I'm nothing other than a decent individual who was born full of affection for mankind."

"In that case, the least you can do is exercise some neighborly love and demonstrate what someone with the Silver Wings is capable of. The Imperial Army has got to show our ally just what sort of army we are."

This should go over well is Lergen's tone, and the way he nods makes her feel as though she doesn't need to worry. Or actually, maybe she does?

"Is this gunboat diplomacy?"

Lergen grins in response to her question. "It's a gesture of friendship toward a pal who's in a bit of a precarious spot."

So the idea is to give them a stern warning.

Lergen may not be aware of it himself, but between the chilling smile about his lips and his frigid eyes, he's the spitting image of the ideal General Staff officer. As usual, he's a prime example of how even a good individual can be a member of an evil organization.

"Ooh, how terrifying. I can't help but shake in my boots."

"We're looking out for our ally, Colonel."

In what way is this looking out for someone? Even if Tanya asks, he'll tell her it's a state secret. The risk of touching something sensitive is too great. She just nods vaguely and casually shifts the conversation toward impending practical matters.

"So? How long am I supposed to have this guy?"

"Basically, the General Staff wants to make it look like everyone involved in the negotiations is present on the eastern front. We can get a lot of things moving on the pretext of entertaining him."

"So it'll be a while, then?"

"There will be a slew of phantom commanders, bureaucrats, and staffers joining the Lergen Kampfgruppe, and they're going to raise some hell."

At first glance, the response doesn't seem to have anything to do with what she asked, but the meaning is clear. This temporary measure could easily become permanent. At the very least, this will probably continue until some sort of decisive moment comes. Even considering the General Staff's personnel policy, which is so strict about regular shuffles and meetings, the scale of this could be measured in not months but years.

The worst part, laments Tanya as she runs the pros and cons through her head, *is that...*

...I don't have the right to refuse.

The soldier Tanya von Degurechaff has been through General Staff training. In other words, her assignments are all decided on the General Staff's discretion. She's basically an employee who has signed a general office-worker contract.

She can't choose her boss, her subordinates, or her assignments.

And the orders don't come from a company but from an army. If she refuses, she won't get off with simply being *fired*—it's entirely possible that a firing *squad* would make an appearance. And she's a civil servant, so she has no right to go on strike. Goodness, these are bad working conditions. Though she was already aware, reality is rough.

"...If you don't mind, I'd like to go over some of the practical issues with the operation."

"You should face virtually no practical issues. Almost immediately after I arrive, I'll get sick and be sent back to the rear."

"So I'm the second-in-command?"

"You'll continue to command your Kampfgruppe. And the Salamander Kampfgruppe will probably be permitted to keep its name, since you're below the Lergen Kampfgruppe in the order of battle."

"I see. So in the end, I'm the deputy commander of the nonexistent Lergen Kampfgruppe, and all I have to do is command the Salamander Kampfgruppe."

"Exactly. But...," he trails off and gets a look on his face that says he's sincerely sorry for what's about to come next.

"What is it, Colonel?"

"There's one thing you'll just have to put up with for me."

"Put up with?"

"Yes." Lergen speaks with a mournful expression. "Publicly, your achievements will be reported under my name. So basically..." He bows his head, openly mortified. "I'll be stealing your successes, if in name only. Of course," he rushes to continue, "the General Staff is fully informed on this matter. I'm sure you'll be given every consideration possible during performance evaluations. The catch is that it's likely you won't get the decorations and hammock number you deserve... I beg your understanding." He bows low, and when he apologizes, it seems like he means it. "I'm sorry, but please agree to this."

This is what it means to sigh—*Haaaah...*

Tanya isn't disappointed. As she calms her leaping heart, the feeling she can't suppress is relief.

With this, Tanya now has someone she can nominally shove off all her accountability onto, and on top of that, the guys making decisions in Personnel will owe her one. Why would I turn down such a great opportunity? Anyone not morbidly obsessed with being in the spotlight would be thrilled.

For Tanya, a rational modern individual endowed with incredible self-restraint, the answer is obvious.

She takes a breath and comes up with some nonsense.

"I...am a soldier sworn to serve my country."

Her position is clarified by something that's plainly obvious.

When specifying the scope of a job, nearly all explanations can be omitted by simply bandying the word *responsibility*.

By definition, soldiers must obey orders. Unlike misguided self-proclaimed soldiers, Tanya is the officer of a regular army, so it's natural what she would do.

"I can't say it doesn't bother me in some ways, but I understand."

Tanya doesn't forget to make her appeals, either. If she doesn't want to be a convenient pawn, she'll have to point out her devotion and contributions, albiet nonchalantly.

Not properly emphasizing what a hefty sacrifice this will be and how much she brings to the table will affect her later promotions. Also can't forget to inject some human emotion.

"That said, it would be great if the peculiarities of my situation could be taken into consideration in the future."

She makes her demands simply. When it comes to compensation, be neither too bold nor too modest.

"Honestly, I'm so relieved."

"Huh?"

"I though you would shoot me."

"How funny you are."

"All right." Lergen must have caught his breath. After shaking his head a couple of times, he speaks. "Your supplies will come with a little extra while the observer is there, for appearances. Not that we can make you a Potemkin[3] unit, but…"

Any offer must benefit both sides—at least on the surface.

This isn't the kind way to put it, but making a deal is a double coincidence of wants based on good sense. You can sell even hundred-yen water for five hundred yen. But someone who tries to sell it for ten thousand has clearly forgotten the word *trust*, which is required for a business deal.

Investment is not speculation.

Lergen said that this will be taken into consideration during her

[3] **Potemkin** Well, it definitely looked good. *Window dressing* is an awful way to put it. He just did what he could for his own benefit.

This is a classic example of glossing over the truth with unrealistic results. But you know, if you can't trick the inspectors, you never get promoted. What choice did he have?

evaluations, so at this point, it's simple to ask. To put it plainly, all Tanya hopes for are some modest material demands being met.

"Then please see that I get coffee beans and chocolate, and some socks at the very least. Enough for the Kampfgruppe would be great."

"S-socks?"

The colonel looking blankly at her is wearing a clean uniform, so he probably doesn't understand right away—that on the muddy eastern front, a single missing sock is enough to give an officer headaches.

"There's a limit to what the standard uniform designed for use inside the Empire can handle."

"Still, I'm surprised to be petitioned for socks."

"I don't know how it was before the war, but now, serving outside the country is the norm. It would be great if that could be factored into the plan."

"Got it." Lergen nods, but he still seems perplexed. "We have asked for opinions from the front lines, though." He sighs; it must have hit him that the surveys didn't work. I'm sure it had something to do with whatever the overriding agenda was at the time.

"Well..." Tanya is compelled to point this out with a wince. "It's probably hard to bring up socks when asked about the war situation."

"I'm sure it is. But never in a million years did I think the day would come that a recipient of the Silver Wings Assault Badge would requisition socks. War is just full of the unexpected."

"Indeed." Tanya nods in wholehearted agreement.

She thought she knew what she was getting into when she joined up to build her career, thought she knew that war was a conglomeration of absurdities. Yet she never imagined she would have to use her connections to secure a supply of socks.

Who *could* predict such a thing? That the gears of that incredibly elaborate precision war machine known as the Imperial Army would have such a struggle to supply its soldiers with socks?

"Okay, I'll leave all that up to you, thanks."

"All right. Then let's hold a little show of turning over command later."

"Sure thing. Shall we do it with the battalion present?"

Ceremony, ceremony, ceremony. That said, we're *zoon politikon*. Political animals simply have to accept that these things are mandatory.

"No, that won't be necessary. The Lergen Kampfgruppe only exists on paper. I want to keep the number of people who know what's going on as low as possible."

"So we'll just be preparing documentation? Then should my adjutant, vice commander, and I control the information?"

"It probably doesn't have to be that strict. Although it'd be nice if it could stay among the officers."

Hmm. After thinking for a moment, Tanya voices her request. If there's paperwork involved, it'll be tricky to limit to officers only.

"Could you allow for the soldiers attached to the command post as well?"

"That's fine. Well then, I appreciate you taking the observer."

"Yes, sir." Upon accepting the job, she immediately raises her voice. "Lieutenant Serebryakov! Lieutenant Serebryakov!"

"Yes, Colonel!"

I call my adjutant back in and get straight to the point. If you have to ask someone an annoying favor, it's best to ask someone you can trust.

"Colonel von Lergen has instructions for us. Prepare to receive a guest on the double!"

"Yes, ma'am! A guest? Prisoner camps aren't under our jurisdiction…"

"No," Tanya snaps before she can stop herself. "Not a prisoner. This is a guest who needs to be served coffee and warm bread."

"Huh?"

"A guest! You know, a guest!"

"Y-yes, ma'am."

Her confused-looking adjutant is probably imagining nothing but prisoners. For a second, she doesn't seem to get it, and a rare expression for her—only comparable to a frozen computer screen—appears on her face.

"I'm talking about a real guest! There *are* people in this world who don't shoot at us, you know!"

"Yes, ma'am…" Her adjutant still doesn't seem to understand at all, so Tanya realizes she has no choice but to break it down for her.

"A military observer from an allied nation, Lieutenant. If we don't have good manners, it could cause an international incident. Make sure there's no trouble."

"Ohhh." She starts to nod in understanding but then stops and looks at Tanya with questioning eyes.

"What? What is it?"

"Ummm, Colonel. What exactly should I do?"

"Huh?" *About what?* Tanya starts to ask, but then Serebryakov shyly explains.

"I mean, it's our first time..."

"Mm, oh, I see."

She doesn't have to ask what she means.

It's at this moment that Tanya realizes why their communication is failing. A Kampfgruppe is an organization specializing in combat...

"Manners are a whole other pain. And what about an orderly? Who's going to keep him company...? Considering he should probably have some protection, too, it'll be a good idea to have some magic officers or non-coms..."

These guys aren't much good at anything but brawling.

Is this the harmful result of being overly specialized in all-military activities? It's certainly a problem right now, and the fact that Tanya can't give in to her despair and hurl the mission back up at her superiors is frustrating.

"I'm pretty sure there's a manual... Eh, I'll have Major Weiss read it over. I want to review etiquette while we're at it."

APRIL 28, UNIFIED YEAR 1927, EASTERN FRONT, AT THE SALAMANDER KAMPFGRUPPE'S CAMP

She must have fallen asleep looking through the materials on how to do the unfamiliar job of accompanying a guest. When Tanya's eyes open in her provisional bed, she understands why a few seconds later.

"Warning! All units to battle stations!"

An echoing call, the thudding footsteps of troops rushing around.

Aaaah, damn it.

"Seriously? Again? Shit, these guys are busy..."

Why not sabotage your own side once in a while? Are they forsaking workers' rights to get cheap labor? What are you guys even Commies for?!

Regardless, Tanya is an officer and a commander. No one is going to accept excuses just because she has a sleepy face.

She puts her cap on as she races to Kampfgruppe HQ, but awkwardly, she arrives last.

"Colonel!"

"It would seem I'm late. Sorry about that." She bobs her head. "What's the situation?"

Her straightforward question gets a straightforward answer. An organization in which everyone understands their role is the embodiment of efficiency.

"The aerial mage battalion members have assembled. They can leave at any time. The armor and infantry troops are at their posts. And the artillery is also in position."

"Nice work, Lieutenant. I appreciate it—oh, and this, too!" Tanya cheers with a smile. She didn't expect some nice coffee the moment she woke up!

How wonderful it is to have subordinates who give you what you want before you even ask! Despite being specialized in combat support, the wonderful First Lieutenant Serebryakov faithfully performs all her duties.

Sipping her coffee, Tanya pauses. The enemy may be attacking, but preparations have been made. There's no need to panic.

That means I can have a moment of peace alongside my coffee. Teatimes and coffee breaks truly symbolize readiness.

"Colonel, it's Command at the base."

"Well, they're quick. Okay, let me talk to them."

She takes the receiver, and the exchange hardly differs from those of a few days prior. If pressed to name a difference, perhaps it's that Tanya's superiors are getting a little bolder with their plans now that her unit has received reinforcements.

Today's mission is more aggressive than the last. Although I suppose it's more that we don't have to stick around defending a static position.

"Attention, all units! Our mission as the Salamander Kampfgruppe is to support the main army."

"Does that mean we'll be defending like last time?" Captain Ahrens asks in disappointment.

He must really hate being on defense. Tanya doesn't possess the burning desire to leap into battle, but she can understand the feeling of wanting to act assertively to break through a problem on your own terms. Obviously, relinquishing the initiative is never a pleasant experience.

"That's a good question, but no, we won't be." She continues, "Hmm. Remember this, Captain Ahrens."

I can't say I like it, but the fruits of one's experience should be displayed: On the battlefield, *rough and ready* trumps *polished but slow.*

"If the outnumbered side stops moving, they'll be swallowed up. Our only choice is to take the initiative. Our superiors at Command want to attack."

"Then you must mean…?"

"Yes." She responds to Ahrens's eager look with a nod. "You'll be going out, too. We're deploying at full strength."

"That's what I always hope for!"

Very good. Tanya nods as she proceeds to briefly outline the operation. "The main forces will intercept. While they're doing that, we'll go around and tear into the enemy's flank."

Ultimately, it's business as usual.

We'll break through this issue with an appropriate concentration of forces achieved through careful application of the Imperial Army's specialty, mobility. It's a formidable way to move using the orthodox tactic of hammer and anvil.

The grinning aerial magic officers must realize by now: Whether it's the Rhine, Norden, the eastern front, or the southern continent, the task is the same.

"You can call it a classic, textbook maneuver battle, but it's also something we're very familiar with."

Tanya expresses how little problem she thinks they will have completing this mission. She has full faith in them and their abilities.

"I'm counting on you, Captain Ahrens," she says, giving him a little slap on the rear. "We'll open up a hole, then you and the infantry will cooperate to keep up the momentum. If anyone can do this, the Salamander Kampfgruppe can."

A proven track record, trust, and ability. Anyone in a management position thirsts for the precious gem known as reliable firepower. Especially so in war. Those without experience are incapable of imagining how rare a sure thing is amid the fog of war.

"All right, Captain Ahrens, Lieutenant Tospan, I expect you to cooperate as best you can with troops of the main army."

""Yes, ma'am!""

"I'm putting Captain Ahrens in charge, as he's the senior officer, but given the nature of the operation, you'll probably be fielding requests from the other infantry units. Pay no mind to the rate of supply usage and just do as much as you can."

Regardless of how I feel taking advantage of other people's resources, I hate having mine ground into the dirt. But losing the right to be picky is just one of the tough parts of war.

"Captain Meybert! I'll give you Lieutenant Wüstemann's company of replenishments as artillery observers. Have them do whatever you need them to do!"

"Thanks, but are you sure?" He glances toward the eager young officer.

Tanya thinks for a moment—*Hmm*—and then asks the man in question, "Lieutenant Wüstemann, how's the replenishment company doing?"

"We can go! I think we can handle the bare minimum of action."

Good intentions. But that answer doesn't meet Tanya's standards. What she needs is quality. Unless it's a unit that can really move, they won't be able to keep up.

"All right, you stay here and support Captain Meybert."

"But, Colonel, we can—"

"No, Lieutenant. I appreciate your passion. But we won't be able to coordinate. For now, stay out of the way."

He looks somewhat disappointed, but he'll make a good warrior someday. Not that Tanya can understand or sympathize.

Anyhow. She refocuses and turns to her babies.

"The battalion's ready to sortie at full force," says Weiss.

"As always. All right, let's move."

Major Weiss and the other members of the 203rd Aerial Mage Battalion acknowledge with a nod. How reliable! These are Tanya's accomplished, reliable babies. Accomplishments and reliability really are important. And it's also reassuring that she can trust her buddy, her adjutant, when they take off together.

She's also her partner in a little playacting.

"Another maneuver battle, huh, Colonel?"

"Yeah." Tanya nods back at Serebryakov. An aerial mage battalion is worth its salt only if it can move; troops who don't understand their job cause more harm than the enemy. The other way around yields a great advantage. "We've got the numbers of a normal battalion, but I expect the fight of an augmented one."

"You can count on us!"

The two of them speak nonchalantly but under the assumption that everyone nearby can hear them. Her adjutant responds in an exaggerated way, her voice loud and clear.

Is this a special kind of talent, the way Serebryakov casually melts the battalion's tension away with her willingness to deliver? What a valuable individual she's grown into.

"...I do wish we could get our numbers back up."

People who can read the atmosphere are so precious. She knows how to lower her voice when discretion is called for.

"We'll have to train up the fresh troops."

"...If there are any worthy ones, that is."

"That might be asking a lot. We can't expect much out of replenishments lately..."

Tactically speaking, recruits are a burden. Battle-ready rookies are as rare as any other fantastical creature.

But Tanya finds something funny in her adjutant's words, and grins. "Lieutenant Serebryakov, you've really been through the wringer, huh?"

"Huh? Um...?"

"You and I were once replenishments, you know! Keep those helmet straps tight. I don't want to have to request a new adjutant!"

I was partnered with her on the Rhine front when she was still a corporal. We were paired simply because there wasn't enough fighting power and we both happened to be replenishments.

Tanya nods in response to her adjutant's apologetically bobbing head and takes a quick look at the battalion ready to sortie.

Gear, check; personnel, check; atmosphere, check. All that's left is to do the work we know so well.

I can't say it'll be easy. But we'll be fine if we do a solid job.

We'll head out, set our course for enemy territory, and fly due east. Knowing how and when to move whole corps and divisions is practically the Imperial Army's specialty.

The values aerial mage battalions are lauded for: mobility, firepower, and shock value.

Tanya cracks a grin at the front row of imperial soldiers loosely in attack formation as if to say, *That's about enough bluster out of you.*

Problems are there to be solved.

"Okay, troops, let's do this. It'll mostly be a ruse, but...let's make it look like an encircle-and-annihilate operation. The enemy will see a battalion swinging around to assault them from behind. Let them taste the fear of being surrounded."

Since the Imperial Army is outnumbered, if all it does is diligent base defense, the troops will be ground down under that numerical disparity. Our only choice is to take the initiative to upset the enemy and give them a good reason to retreat.

More specifically, we'll have aerial mages popping up all over the place to harass and confuse them. It's a poor man's tactic, but it's not uncommon for it to give even a Goliath problems in a guerrilla battle.

Accepting your own weaknesses and focusing on needling those of your enemy is an admirable tactic—even if you're compelled to use it by an unfortunate strategic environment.

"This goes without saying, but our actual objective is the defense of the front line. We want to threaten the enemy's communications lines in a way that leads to their withdrawal. Do not under any circumstances disrupt the lines out of bloodlust, thinking you'll annihilate the enemy's field army."

"So this is a classic feint, then?"

"Exactly, Major Weiss." Tanya briefly affirms and then shrugs with good grace. "This is no normal power disparity, after all," she murmurs before continuing soberly. "We can't *actually* encircle and annihilate them. There's a limit to how outnumbered we can be. Before we even get a chance to surround them, we'd be blasted apart."

In order to perform an encirclement, you need a good number of troops. Consequently, war is all about numbers. Pulling off the sort of splendid victory that happened at Rossbach[4]—against an enemy double your numbers—is actually quite difficult.

[4] **Rossbach** A battle that broke out during the Seven Years' War.
Frederick the Great led the outnumbered Prussian Army with some weirdo operational finagling and managed to win. The loss ratio was about 1:20. Frederick the Great was a weirdo, but he was strong.

"It's rather sad for a battalion that once sent three divisions scattering like Boy Scouts."

Weiss's lament is correct. It's bad news for us that the enemy is getting stronger.

"Heh. That's big talk for an officer who once turned tail and ran from some guns firing at the sky."

"Touché. Sadly, my issue lately is getting in trouble for not running away."

That's how it went in Dacia. Unfortunately, unlike the Dacian Army, the Federation is in possession of a respectable instrument of violence.

And to go a step further, the Federation Army is becoming more professional.

I have noticed them transforming from an organization overemphasizing their ideology to a military apparatus that prioritizes results, which is troubling. I suppose we can't hope for the miraculous loss ratio like that practically legendary battle at Hoyerswerda.[5]

"In other words, it is what it is."

"…Still, this should be an encounter battle. I doubt the enemy would have a ton of anti-air guns ready."

"That's a good point, Lieutenant Grantz. Shall we test it by seeing if you get shot in the gut again?"

The vice commander childishly jabs with a dicey remark directed at the junior officer. He must be teasing, but Tanya steps in.

"That's enough, Major Weiss. Don't pick on your subordinates."

"I only learned from my superior, ma'am."

"Then let us agree to regret my moral lapses. All right, Officers, time for work."

[5] **Hoyerswerda** The Prussian Army (led by Frederick the Great's younger brother) and the Austrian Army fought with about equal numbers. After the battle, the Prussian Army estimated their losses at no more than a hundred. Meanwhile, 600 Austrian troops died and 1,800 were taken prisoner.

ABOUT TWO HOURS AFTER SORTIEING, ON THE EDGE OF THE IMPERIAL ARMY, SALAMANDER KAMPFGRUPPE

After beginning their advance and mopping up some enemy units, Tanya has just finished a scuffle. Since the mission is simply to probe the enemy flank, no major clash with their main forces is expected.

There could be comparably few encounters.

"We've advanced to the designated point. According to Captain Meybert, his troops can still provide artillery support."

"Got it." Tanya nods in response to her adjutant's report. "Report to CP. And let's wait for Captain Ahrens. Keep a sharp watch on our surroundings. Preferably in a skirmishing line..."

"HQ! HQ! Requesting immediate backup!" "The right flank is collapsing!" "No supporting artillery yet?!" "Where are the air support mages?"

"Huh? There's some kind of confusion with our troops. Check it out."

"That's strange. I don't see anything... One moment." She must realize it when faint flashes go off in the distance. "Colonel, over there."

"Aaah, shit. So the right flank is getting pummeled?"

Even if the unit set to circle around to the enemy's rear is in place, if the foundation—the main troops—is being suppressed, the operation can't proceed. We did our part, so what the hell?

Performing any more labor under the circumstances isn't worth it. Still, grabbing some popcorn wouldn't be very professional. It's clear that doing nothing would result in dismissal, reshuffling, or demotion.

An officer is an officer precisely because they make decisions based on the big picture. An officer is a manager who thinks for themselves. Responsibility grows in proportion to authority. Being responsible is my duty.

Unlike jobs that are only nominally seen as managerial, an actual managerial job requires independent thinking. Otherwise, how can you ever expect to play a critical role in the future? If you only do as you're told, the best you can hope for is a bit part.

But then... Tanya winces.

There are too many people who can't even do what they're told, so it's true that always following orders is mistaken as the highest virtue in the lower ranks.

Still, the only job available to someone who abandons thought is something that anyone can do. Adding value requires creativity. The right to that discretion isn't given to just anyone, though. Having the privilege is proof that people expect results from you.

In that case…

If I can accomplish things here, I should.

The little bit of extra work involved to seize one of the enemy's new equipment or gather intel is within the scope of my salary. If I can expect a bonus on top of that, then it's actually a pretty fair deal.

Hmph. Tanya recalculates in her head and makes up her mind.

"I'm leaving this to Captain Ahrens. Tell him to continue supporting the main force's flank."

Her adjutant, Lieutenant Serebryakov, looks at her in a way that asks, *Are you leaving?*

Tanya nods with solemn determination and says, "The main force's right flank is taking a pounding from the enemy's new weapons. The balance between the hammer and the anvil is unstable. Busybodies may be detestable, but I can't just stand on the sideline and watch our troops suffer."

"You're right, ma'am."

"Good. Put me through to Command and round up the unit."

Her adjutant acknowledges the instructions, and Tanya feels confident leaving things up to her. Now then, it's time to use the long-range communications kit to earn a favor for later.

"HQ, this is Salamander 01. Priority response, please."

"Salamander 01, has the enemy received reinforcements on your part of the line, too?"

Even if I'm making the suggestion to someone under duress, things should go more smoothly if I lighten up the atmosphere a bit first. When the response comes back tense, Tanya opts for a more affable answer.

"Negative. We've advanced to the designated line. We're currently capable of dispatching an aerial mage battalion to support your right wing. The majority are Named who survived through the Rhine, from the commander on down. Just say the word."

"HQ, roger. You're not having any issues holding the line?"

"If the rest of our troops are racing over, then certainly not. Besides, holding this line means nothing if the right wing of the army collapses."

"...One moment, please."

HQ doesn't hesitate on this point. Considering the time it took to ask the question, the commander pretty much got on the line immediately.

"Colonel, you can go over there?"

"Yes, General, if need be."

"Need does be."

This matter-of-fact way of speaking isn't bad. The more appropriate and quick an officer's decisions, the more reliable they are on a fluid battlefield.

"So?"

"There are lots of rookies on the right side. We thought we gave them a zone that would be easier to handle, but the enemy's got a new model out there. If you have the troops to spare and can afford to send them out, please do."

"Understood."

"Thanks."

With that one word, HQ hangs up. Impatient much? In other words, that's good. Being late is a problem, but being early is never bad.

And it agrees with Tanya's temperament.

When she flicks her eyes over, the response comes at once.

"The aerial mages are all present, ma'am!"

"Thanks, Lieutenant Serebryakov. More than anything, I appreciate your efficiency. Although I suppose we owe it just as much to the fact that they weren't broken out into a skirmish line yet."

"No doubt about that, ma'am. Is this business as usual?"

Tanya's adjutant knows the drill, and Tanya nods at her.

"Kampfgruppe, a message from your commander. The aerial mage battalion is going to support the right wing of the main troops and intercept the enemy's latest weapon. Other units should continue holding their forward positions until further orders."

Leaving the rest with an "I'm counting on you," Tanya gathers her babies and heads out.

Once they take off, the battalion is neither overexcited nor excessively relaxed. They're a fighting force tensed like a well-trained muscle.

How incredibly sad that we can't take pride in this as the Imperial Army standard.

"…Seems like things are still in chaos?" Tanya murmurs to herself in the sky. She's used to friendly signals being tangled when on a rescue mission, but the static is still quite bad.

The closer she gets, the worse she feels.

"Group leader to all Kampfgruppe hands. The enemy has new orbs. I regret to inform you that they walk the walk."

"The defensive shell's too thick! Explosion formulas aren't penetrating!" "Concentrate your fire! Focus opticals on a single point!" "It's no good! The shield's too hard!"

Lieutenant Colonel Tanya von Degurechaff races across the sky as those signals shriek in her ear. With her blond hair trailing behind her, she grasps her computation orb with her fair, slender fingers.

She must look like a Valkyrie. Or perhaps she flies with enough grace to be termed an angel.

That said, on the inside, she's a perfect self-preservationist. But it's not as if that prevents her from doing her job. She boasts a proper understanding of their circumstances.

She'll do what she can and draw as much attention to it as possible. That's the clear and simple truth. But it's not as if someone like that doesn't have feelings about the situation.

A sort of complaint slips out.

"…So these new models are giving us trouble?"

"New models? I'm disturbed by the Federation Army's lack of reason. They could have just used gear they're used to like us."

Grantz acknowledges. Tanya had only intended to talk to herself, but he responded in good faith. Well, communicating with subordinates is also a superior officer's job.

"There's no doubt about it, Lieutenant. This is going to be a pain."

"But I'd say that's precisely why we're the ones heading out."

Grantz was probably being serious when he said that, but Tanya can't quite suppress a smile. "Well, look at you! Quite the officer now. Ah, I remember the days on the Rhine when you were but a trembling little lamb."

"They say to strike while the iron's hot and the shells have warmed me up, so…"

He's even learned to wag his tongue. Tanya's impressed. Before, he would have clammed up, the young thing. He's really come a long way.

"So you think you can take the heat? Did you hear that, Major Weiss?"

"Nah, it's too soon. His turn of phrase was witty, I'll give him that, but it was also a bit too on the nose."

"You're not wrong. Okay, let's take the chatter down a notch. I realize I'm the one who started it, but it's probably not very nice to be bantering away up here while our fellow troops are in a grueling fight."

""Understood.""

"Of course, it's good to have some breathing room before a battle."

"Hmph," she snorts. Then she tunes in to the communications of nearby imperial troops beginning to ping back and forth.

"Group leader to all units! Report in—report in with your status!"

"Don't leave your position! Stay in formation!" "Wait, who's commanding the Third Company?! Wasn't it 01?!" "Requesting urgent backup!" "Use the correct protocols! What airspace are you requesting support for?"

"We need artillery support! Is there no artillery support?! Sector B-23! Hurry and suppress them!" "Observer mages, send the coordinates—now!"

Things really do seem to be chaotic. Tanya wants to sigh.

"The communications we're picking up from our fellow troops are a mess."

Serebryakov nods at Tanya's murmur with a solemn expression. "On the other hand, the Federation Army seems to be in good order. Though we're only catching fragmentary glimpses, I'm getting the impression our side is overwhelmed."

"The Reich's troops, overwhelmed by the enemy? Hmph." Tanya scoffs.

An army that surpasses its quantitative inferiority with qualitative superiority and organizational might is frightened of the enemy?

That's no way to fight a war.

I have no intention of blindly believing mind over matter, but the issue of morale should not be neglected.

First off, even the magic word *worthwhile* can produce workers who won't hesitate to endure terrible conditions.

You mustn't underestimate the power of words.

"01 to 02, seems like we're going to get more of a welcome than we thought."

"02, roger. Just as you say, 01."

"Colonel, Captain Meybert is saying they don't have enough forces to defend the position."

"...He has a point, but wait."

Tanya meditates for a moment. *Should I split even just Lieutenant Grantz off and send him back?* Both of the captains she left behind are competent and trustworthy to an extent.

Meybert is an artilleryman. Whereas Ahrens is a tankman. They balance each other nicely. In particular, Ahrens is a capable armored unit commander who will surely undertake a mobile defensive battle.

Of course, even a unit of tanks can't rage on its own indefinitely. And with only replenishment mages to both defend the position and perform artillery observations, which need to be accurate, I worry. Plus, getting artillery support and having Meybert take his turn is great and all, but as long as shells are a finite resource, we can never be free from having to conserve them.

But it's not as if things are falling apart *right now*.

"*Non.* He'll have to make do with what he has. This won't take long."

There won't be any dividing of the forces on her watch.

Rather than wavering, Tanya settles on rushing the enemy with her troops concentrated to put a swift end to things.

"Let's hurry, then, ma'am."

"Let's. We can't keep those guys waiting."

With that, Tanya faces front and grits her teeth. One look at her appearance and her blue eyes filled with courage speaks fathoms of her fearless bravery; her white teeth grinding together seem to be channeling the pain of her fellow soldiers.

But internally, she's sorely regretting her decision.

In a nutshell, Tanya is feeling wary after hearing the news that the enemy's new models perform better than expected. She had only moments ago been scheming, since the new orbs are out and about, to clash a bit and seize one if possible as part of other intel-gathering activities.

Most of the time, new models are experimental. Even so, seizing one from the Federation would be quite an achievement. Those were her superficial calculations. It's not a happy thing to see these models getting results on the battlefield already.

I figured the enemy wouldn't have time to get used to them…but was that a mistake?

There's no way of knowing without making contact.

"Group Leader, come in. This is Salamander 01. Come in."

For the time being, the signal is good. And requesting only data doesn't cost anything. Tanya braces herself to hear that they're too busy, but when she gets on the line anyway, they ping her right back.

"Salamander 01, this is Group Leader!"

"Group Leader, this is Salamander 01. A mage battalion from the Salamander Kampfgruppe is currently headed your way. Send us what you've got on the enemy's new model."

Just the fact that she's been successful establishing contact with the right wing makes Tanya's cheeks relax into a smile. It's confirmation of organized resistance. Not collapsing is a good sign.

"Unfortunately, I can't do that."

"…You can't? I beg your pardon, but what do you mean?"

"The front is currently in disarray, and we're unable to send any detailed reports."

"Whoa, hold up." Tanya furrows her brow, and the controller responds in an entreating voice.

"I've heard of your unit before. If possible, I'd like you to report back with the details of the right wing's situation when you arrive."

"My unit isn't outfitted for scouting or observation. We're charging in to conduct an assault."

"Group Leader, roger. That's why it's an 'if possible' request."

"Salamander 01, roger. I understand and respect your request. We'll give it our utmost, but just know that there's a limit to what we can do."

"Of course. Over and out."

Hmm. Tanya occupies herself in thought for a moment. It was a short conversation, but there was something strange about it. Frontline units are often in chaotic situations, but this seems to be something beyond merely getting attacked. She gets the feeling they're crumbling in a panic over their inability to deal with a new type of enemy.

Even if we *are* careful, are we plunging headfirst into danger?

"Major Weiss, what do you make of the communications we've been listening in on?"

"Our fellow troops are in bad shape. From what's coming over the wireless, it sounds like they're total amateurs. They're wailing and crying on an open channel."

"Are those rookies we're hearing, though?"

"It seems like the magic officers up through company level are bewildered."

"Whew"—she whistles in spite of herself; it's all she can do; things are such a mess.

I can't say the warmongers under me are representative of the Imperial Army's standards for company commanders. Still, though, still. Being an Imperial Army company commander requires, as it should, certain abilities. As with ancient Roman centurions and boatswains on ships of the line, if middle management is rotten, the organization has no future.

What we need is...people in the position to support the men on the ground, like the capable First Lieutenant Schwarkopf she once served under. *So the guys at that level are out of their minds?*

"Saving the right wing might be a bigger challenge than anticipated."

My subordinates are war maniacs, while I'm into self-preservation... Her internal regret is intense.

"This is no good, Major. It's embarrassing to show up late."

"Let's do our best. Grantz and Visha are young enough."

Heh. Tanya decides to respond to her vice commander's joke. "Whoa there, don't forget I've got some formidable youth myself."

"Ummm." The tiny noise is her adjutant. There's no mistaking that voice. When she looks over immediately, the expression on her adjutant's face is *Oh shit.*

"Lieutenant Serebryakov? What is it?"

"If you'll excuse me, ummm... Colonel, that is..."

"What is it, Lieutenant? Are you trying to leave me out?"

She's stunned to get a nod in return. "You have a certain class to consider at your rank..."

"...I see. Well, I suppose that's true."

Tanya thought it was weird, but with that response, she can't really argue. Status and dignity are powers that come with rank.

If someone described her as far more mature than her age, how could anyone say that's wrong? If her internal maturity is coming through, and people count that as a virtue, who am I to disagree?

"CP to combat controller team. The Salamander Kampfgruppe is on its way. Should arrive within 600."

Anyhow, now that we've come this far, I'll get caught up in the trouble if we don't put a stop to it. I'll just consider myself lucky that the wall of meat shields hasn't been wiped out yet, so we can still support from behind it.

"All units, get ready for combat. We're going in!"

Under the guidance of the combat control team, we begin our charge, but something's strange.

If you asked me, I couldn't tell you what, exactly. Yet, suddenly it's obvious. We're receiving wireless signals far too clearly!

...Why the heck aren't the enemy mages jamming us?

In Dacia, we knew they simple didn't have the ability.

In Norden, we knew the Entente Alliance wasn't actually expecting a full-on fight.

But this is the eastern front. A bizarre zone where the Imperial Army and the Federation Army pit their national powers against each other by endlessly squandering their production capacity on a massive, meaningless war of attrition.

It's too weird for aerial mages not to be jamming at all. And if the enemy aerial mages are putting up a fierce fight with new orbs, it's even weirder.

Twisting up her doll-like face, Tanya raises her guard a notch.

When the only scenarios she can imagine are bad, her brow furrows.

"Ch-Charlie Leader to Salamander. Currently data linking."

Just the brief that reaches her ears paints an unambiguous picture of how serious the situation is.

The front line is so full of holes, it's absurd to call it a line. Has the stronghold that was supposed to be here already been overrun? The lines are so broken, she's seized by the urge to whine.

"...What a clusterfuck. I'm honestly shocked. How have things gotten this bad without the front collapsing?"

Although looking from our side, it's basically already crumbled.

"It's a miracle they're still holding out. I guess the veterans have their training to thank."

Is it purely the skill of the lower-ranking officers that's keeping things together?

There must be a handful of capable guys mixed in who are just barely staving off a decisive collapse. That's the best way to hold ground.

But the data she picks up as they charge into the fighting zone are truly astonishing.

The enemy mage company busted through the imperial mage battalion stationed here, splitting them apart so that each infantry unit was isolated. In other words, this was an unmitigated trampling—and that's *of* imperial mages *by* Federation mages.

"I can't believe this... Shouldn't it be the reverse?"

If you want to accuse me of arrogance, go ahead. This is still difficult to accept.

The Imperial Army is being overwhelmed in terms of quality by the Federation Army? Ridiculous.

"Could they make this much of a turnaround? Or is it the rumored security mage unit? Either way, this is no joke."

"But, Colonel, this is strange."

"Wait, Major. What's strange?" Tanya asks, focusing on the enemy unit.

"The enemy company's movements are... How can I explain it? They go in such straight lines."

"...I see what you mean."

It's so obvious, I'm kicking myself for not noticing it until he brought it up. They aren't looking terribly majestic out there.

"And even if they're up against elites, our troops are working too hard. It's not bad; just not sustainable."

They must have a special reason to be resisting to this extent.

"And plenty of our positions are still standing. This really is strange."

Let's just be frank. All this is unexpected.

Outstanding aerial mages are air-to-ground-attack professionals. If the enemy is using their new orb model, the broken troops should be a pile of corpses.

We can't simply laugh off their survival as the aftermath of a tough fight.

"...Could they be bait?"

Attacking to draw out aerial mages is a classic trap. If there's even a slight chance that's true, Tanya needs a decent excuse to turn around right now.

"Can you contact any friendly troops and make sure it's not a trap?"

"How could I ask them something so inconsiderate? Please don't be ridiculous."

"You guys get so considerate at the weirdest times."

Tanya's subordinates screw up their faces into *Huh?*s while she makes the call herself.

"This is Salamander 01. I have a question. Is the enemy not shooting at you guys? Or are they shooting but missing for some reason?"

Thankfully, her message gets through without any issue.

...That's still weird. Tensing her little mouth, she begins calculating an escape. She considers what route to take as she waits for a response.

"You've got to be kidding! They're firing like crazy and if we get hit, it'll be a disaster!"

"Got it. So they're stubborn and coming out with a ton of firepower, but getting hit isn't very likely."

"...And their defensive shells are stupidly strong."

"By that you mean?"

"We can't get through them without a direct hit from an 88 mm."

"...Yeesh." Suddenly, she just wants to cradle her head in her hands, but given the eyes of her troops, she opts to cross her arms instead. "So this is a different animal we're up against."

The answer is that our enemies have obtained ridiculous firepower and heavy armor. The idea must be to make up for accuracy issues with intensity. Considering how hard the defensive shells and protective films are, they must be specialized.

...These were developed with not addition but subtraction.

The designer is definitely optimizing for wartime mass production.

Compared to Chief Engineer Schugel, the Federation guys are actually pretty rational. Who'd've thunk?

Luckily, the enemy mages are moving pretty slowly, so we should be able to take care of them. We just have to put some thought into our tactics. In other words, a bit of tightrope walking is necessary.

This time, there's a wall, so it should be easier... Or at least that's what Tanya thinks before she remembers this is a rescue mission and clicks her tongue in frustration. Time to start over.

We can't abandon our troops on the ground.

Ahhh, damn it. I can already see the enemy.

What should we do? Our only choice is to give them a whack, obviously.

"The fundamental tactic of counter-mage combat is the hit-and-run. Let's give it a shot, troops."

Though there's some distance between us, several enemy mages are already in range. I slam some mana into the Type 97 Assault Computation Orb and don't spare any of the solidified mana I'd prepared ahead of time, either.

This explosion formula is like a long-range artillery barrage, but luckily, our troops have fallen back a bit, so there's no danger of accidentally hitting them. Of course, I've already accepted that sometimes you'll accidentally hit people, but...that's not something that needs to happen at the moment.

I manifest the formula with my orb.

Flying at high speed, I focus up and aim as best I can and cast. That combination of logic and magic manipulates the fabric of reality, and as a result, a powerful explosion goes off in the middle of the enemy group so quickly that there isn't any time to evade.

It's a precise, unforeseen blow to these numbskulls bunched up for a strafing run on helpless ground troops. I poured as much mana as possible in during that short time before I fired. And I'm sure it was a bull's-eye.

Even Tanya expects success with a certain degree of confidence.

"Of all the—! They're fine?! My target is fine?!"

The shock is too great. She's so astounded that she hangs motionless in midair.

The scene before her makes her eyes nearly pop out of her head. And it's not just her.

"...Ngh. That's a surprise. I've never seen anyone take one of your hits and not only stay in the air but not even have their flight disturbed."

Her adjutant's comments are the truth.

That explosion was on a scale that a normal mage would have gone down just from being in the blast zone. In the Rhine, in Norden, and even on the southern continent, Tanya and her aerial mage unit have proven they are capable of such destruction.

But that ended in this moment.

The Federation mages withstood the attack.

"Honestly, it's hard to believe, but...ready the next volley!"

I switch to a guided type of formula, up my impact, and fire along with the rest of the unit.

"The guided formulas connected just now!"

"Target is still unharmed!"

Whoa now, hold on. This is a resilience that makes you want to burst out laughing. The 203rd Aerial Mage Battalion, full of Named and with one of the most fearsome rosters of the Imperial Army, can't even pierce a single enemy defensive shell?

"The enemy's coming up fast! Ngh?! We're being targeted!"

"For fuck's sake!" *Shit!* Even as she curses, Tanya keeps her hands busy to do her job. "How solid can you possibly be?!"

This can't be happening. Tanya avoids that comment and reconsiders her choice of formula. She decides her only option is to try something with penetration boosted to the max.

"Do it with a focused-type optical! Punch through!"

In parallel to her gripes, she loads some lead shot, casts, and fires.

"It's a direct hit!"

Arrrgh! Teeth grindingly enough, the enemy appears unfazed after sustaining another hit—even though it was an optical sniping formula with boosted penetrating power.

No. She adjusts her evaluation, noting that there was some impact.

Their protective films are gone. And apparently, it's not impossible to affect their defensive shells. From the increasingly unstable way they're flying, it appears they've been injured.

Is that...blood? At least it's proof that the shells can be pierced. That's a good sign.

"Take note that if you focus your formula, you have a better chance of penetrating."

Finding something that might work is a happy joy. Tanya quickly reconsiders her attack method. The enemy is sturdy. And they have firepower. A good option is to snipe them from a distance. A great option is to rain fire down on them from above.

"Use those legs! These guys aren't as mobile as we are! Let's pummel them!"

Given the circumstances, we'll have to think of what to do with the troops on the ground afterward. For now, our top priority has to be intercepting these mages. After all, I've taken on the risk to push out here. I'm not about to go back empty-handed.

So the plan is to toy with the enemy using our high speeds.

And things go more smoothly than expected.

"Charge! Charge! Show 'em how you move!"

"Give Weiss backup! Don't stop firing explosion formulas—we'll use them as a smoke screen!"

She has the battalion lead the way and Tanya herself stays back with the rear guard to fire at range from above. Though they aren't as effective, explosion formulas limit enemy visibility, so they're the best option.

Of course, in the heat of battle, explosion formulas always come with the risk of hitting friendlies. Only units as highly coordinated and skilled as the 203rd Aerial Mage Battalion could ever hope to pull this off.

None of us are idiots who would shoot our own. We don't stumble into the line of fire, but neither do we slack on support.

I can't overstate how much I appreciate veterans. Especially in this melee, we're lucky to have sharpshooters.

With focused opticals, it's possible to penetrate those thick defensive shells the enemy's suddenly sporting. Not that they'll be downed in a single hit, but there's no doubt it's effective.

If we can slow them down like that, finishing them off will be no problem. All that's left is for the troops up close to cut them down with their magic blades or for the rest of us to pump them full of holes from afar.

"Zone clear!"

"Nice work, Major!"

In any case, I suppose it should be said…

The Federation mage battalion attacking the right wing of our main army puts up a tough fight in vain and gets swept away by the 203rd Aerial Mage Battalion.

Soon after, their organized resistance collapses.

"Way to go, troops!"

With a satisfied nod, Tanya quickly takes stock of the damage to her unit.

Her own company escaped with burns. Neither of the other two companies had major losses, either. She anticipated there might be some, but happily, that was a miscalculation.

Also, this is incidental, but the unit on the receiving end of the enemy strike was really hounded but apparently managed to keep casualties to a minimum. For future reference, it will probably be good to look into the ratio of losses.

But right now, it's time to chase bonus achievements.

They may be wonderfully powerful, but even these Federation soldiers who came at us prepared to die are human. Regardless of how it is when blocking units are involved, if your unit gets decimated, it's impossible not to be conscious of your mortality.

That's how humans work.

"They're faltering! Announcement from Salamander 01 to all units! Shift to pursuit! Obliterate the enemy's will to fight!" What a delight it is to shout the order to advance. "Let's go!"

The bunched-up guys are doomed at this point.

Ha-ha-ha—look at them go! Tanya laughs. Watching disciplined violence get transformed into *formerly* disciplined violence is lovely.

There, Tanya finally regains her more intelligent side. *I guess I got a bit too high on the abnormal circumstances of combat,* she reflects in frustration.

Her original objective was to seize one of the enemy's new orbs. If she shot them down, there's no reason she has to let that distinction go to someone else.

"We're going to search the enemy crash site. The purpose is to recover a set of gear. I want to recover a body, but if we can take prisoners, that's even better."

She decides to prioritize acquiring one of the new enemy computation orbs.

If we can recover a corpse, we can learn about how their soldiers are outfitted and what their nutrition is like, so add on another order to the list.

"We don't have much time. Get it done."

Luckily, she's able to borrow some NCOs from the local unit as it flails around trying to get organized, so there are plenty of people.

Of course, what she gives them is an order, but she doesn't forget to add a "please" to be nice. If your staff hates you, your abilities as a manager are limited. It's natural to avoid harsh wording unless it's absolutely necessary when dealing with people.

The fact that there are too many newbies who don't understand that is vexing. And then there's the despair when they learn that they've signed on as general-purpose workers.

Well, I learn from history. Tanya smiles wryly.

That is, I follow precedents.

If you do what ends up formulized as the result of trial and error, things will usually go well.

"Also, find out how many casualties our fellow troops took."

"Ma'am?"

"I want to know how the losses stack up. It's always painful to make sacrifices, but I think it's important to know what they are."

I'm acting like a politician, but I guess that's handy know-how.

Pretending to care about these sort of losses is a mandatory skill for those with ambitions to climb the ladder. Having an empathetic attitude is an important social technique. You especially can't neglect it internally at an organization if you're hoping to bend people's ears.

Regardless of the truth, appearances are critical. This is the equivalent of saying *Sorry for your loss*, but politics have already proven that even that much is effective. There exists an incomprehensible concept called the "sympathy vote." Some people choose someone simply because they don't hate them—and this phenomenon is widespread enough that those votes can decide an election. That's what humans are like.

That's why whether or not you actually feel the pain of the world, it doesn't hurt to pretend you do when you have time.

"Understood."

My fighters fly off with dreamy salutes.

Surely they don't doubt my intentions.

Having them express sincere sympathy will be more credible than Tanya grinning as she offers condolences.

Phew. At that point, she sighs and voices her impressions.

"They were tough. That armor! I can't get behind that sort of hardness."

Not even the Republican Army Named on the Rhine front were that durable. Of course, they were that much more mobile and had that much more firepower, so if anyone's asking which one is the better deal, I'd have to say that using the Federation's new model makes you a bit of a sitting duck, but...being able to produce a defensive shell more durable than a Named is enough to be a threat to most on its own.

"A level of toughness that lets you ignore differences in altitude is disconcerting."

Nodding at her adjutant's comment, Tanya painfully spits, "That took some doing even for us! A normal infantry unit would be out of luck. They'd be broken before their guns could penetrate the defensive shells."

She's forced to admit that this really is a problematic new model. Since they're so sturdy, it takes time to shoot them down.

Considering the Federation's materialistic attitude, this could be a huge problem—we can't ignore it. The casualties that would result from a run-in between Federation mages and our ground troops would be simply unacceptable.

Well, things would be different if the main ground forces were centered around a crack team of experienced NCOs.

"This is horrible. Our newbies are running around in a panic, and the Federation forces are just casually chasing after them."

This is a pointless war of attrition devoid of even a hint of discipline. The realization that the nature of the conflict is beginning to shift toward amateurs merely butchering one another is anxiety-inducing.

The Empire has stumbled right into the muck of the eastern front and gotten sucked into the depths. This battle almost seems like commentary on that plight. What if the global situation worsens while we're struggling here?

The Imperial Army is being ground down on the eastern front. No wonder Ildoa so much as squirming in the south is enough to set off shivers in the unflappable General Staff.

With time, the deterioration of the Empire's strategic environment will accelerate. That's the honest truth. Which is why...Tanya had no choice but to accept Colonel von Lergen's proposal.

We have to take this Ildoan guest and bind him to our side. *What a headache*, thinks Tanya as she imagines just briefly what's to come.

TO THE UNIFIED YEAR 1927 SPRING CONFERENCE ON COMBAT RESEARCH, REPORT ON THE NEW ENEMY ORB SEIZED ON THE EASTERN FRONT

My first impression is that it's crude.

There's no need to wait for the detailed technical analysis—the samples we've seized speak volumes. The new orb of Federation make that has appeared on the eastern front is constructed nowhere near as precisely as is the imperial standard. In the test officer's view, "It's like they have no concept of subtlety."

According to the test battalion, "They've misunderstood mobility so badly, I want to scream at them to double-check the definition of an aerial mage. On top of being unforgivably sluggish and having a poor turn radius, it underperforms when compared to previous generations at similar altitudes. Due to this critical lack of precision crafting, users are more likely to hit friendlies than the enemy."

Thus, everyone has come to the same unwavering conclusion.

That is, "This model is not suitable for our army's operations."

It boasts impressive firepower, but frankly, aside from its toughness, it's difficult to say it surpasses our models. The previously stated opinion on the Federation's new orb is unlikely to change.

That said, members of the Imperial Army reluctantly admit this orb possesses several distinct advantages.

One is that, since they're not crafted with precision, they don't demand as much skill from their users. The new orb is eminently suitable for mass-producing and issuing to mass-trained soldiers.

The second point is the high rate of survival. They may be sluggish, but the defense provided is high; an average infantry unit would have a hard time shooting down someone with one of these.

In conclusion? The General Staff is fretting. These properties make it clear that the new orb will be a natural enemy of the Imperial Army. Everyone scoffs, saying it's a sign that an army that specializes in human-wave tactics is about to send in a huge amount of aerial mages.

An enemy with numerical superiority is going to challenge our top-quality army with so-so quality, and a lot of it.

This is going to be a major problem.

Report on the Type T3476 Computation Orb from Technology

[chapter]

III

Effort and Ingenuity

"Why doesn't anyone find this strange?!"

Ildoan Army military observer (Colonel Calandro)
during his inspection of the eastern front

»»» MAY 1, UNIFIED YEAR 1927, ILDOA, GENERAL GASSMAN'S OFFICE «««

When he walked into General Gassman's office, the general himself stood to merrily welcome (or at least he wore a mask to that effect) the "mere" colonel.

"Colonel von Lergen, welcome to Ildoa. You must be exhausted after such a long trip. Please make yourself comfortable."

The man's amiable demeanor brimmed with affable warmth. Someone who didn't know better might have shed tears in response to this mask. It's hard not to be touched by such kindness coming from a general.

That said, the expression plastered on Colonel von Lergen's face was also a mask. His words of gratitude, implying he was terribly moved, were practically a type of formal beauty.

"I thank our beloved ally for their hospitality."

"Well, we've been neighbors for so long. We should help each other out when we're in trouble." He offered a fine cigar made in the south. "Care for one?" Even in the Reich's capital, these had become scarce.

The ostentatious recommendation of a smoke made it impossible to not grasp the general's implication. Though Lergen smiled and thanked him, he had mixed feelings. "...When we're in trouble, yes, you're quite right."

"Ha-ha-ha. No need to be so stiff. I'd appreciate it if you didn't pay so much attention to our rank discrepancy. After all, our countries are friends. I'd like to be as direct as we can."

"Very well." Lergen took advantage of that sentiment as he began to speak. "I'll get straight to the point. Regarding your mediation of a compromise..."

"Let's hear it."

Nodding and smoking, the men continued their conversation.

"Allow me to be frank. The Imperial Army seems to be having a hard time in the east. We'd like to help you in some way."

"...The Southern Continent Expeditionary Army Corps is so grateful for your generous assistance with supplies."

"Oh right. There's that, isn't there?"

"I hear from the men in the field that there tend to be delays."

"Not everything can go perfectly. I hope you'll understand. Even if we have a duty to our ally, Ildoa has its own issues as well."

"I realize that."

"So you can take that into consideration for me?"

"Yes." Lergen nodded at the general.

It was a bit difficult to tell what he was thinking. His gaze somewhat dubiously urged the general on. Well, it surely went both ways. Lergen yearned to know how Gassman and Ildoa felt about everything, too.

"To be honest, the Southern Continent Expeditionary Army Corps is considering pulling out. If necessary for negotiations, that is."

"Oh? That's promising news." Gassman nodded with interest but then proceeded to cut to the chase with the same smile on his face. "But, Colonel von Lergen, you seem to be misunderstanding something."

"Misunderstanding? I don't know about that." When Lergen feigned ignorance, Gassman rained criticism on him, still smiling.

"Who should the Empire really be talking to first? You're currently fighting major battles—what about recovering peace there? That seems to be the most pressing matter to me."

"You're requesting negotiations while at the same time suggesting we should first negotiate with the party that's attacking us? You'll have to excuse me, but I don't quite understand how the Kingdom of Ildoa does things."

"Well, the Federation's violent handling of the situation has its logic. But," he continued, looking tired, "I'm sure you know everything has a cause."

Even if they were aware of them, the Empire couldn't accept the current situation. That was why Lergen the messenger had to play his part according to the script.

"General, please forgive this question, but what kind of logic do you mean?"

A small sigh. Gassman shook his head and spoke. "The provisional discussion plan your country proposed. Even for a starting place, honestly, it's too greedy. Speaking objectively as a mediator, it brings your willingness to negotiate into question. Listen," he continued, sounding somewhat exhausted, "the Federation wants an unconditional cease-fire with zero reparations or cessations."

That's expecting an awful lot. Lergen snorted. As the one in charge of negotiations, conveying that they would never swallow such outrageous terms was as good as his duty.

Which was why he, a colonel, had to take such an attitude toward a general. Under normal circumstances, he wouldn't get off with merely breaking out in a cold sweat, but it must have been permitted here due to the mutual tacit understanding that this was simply how it would go... *Well, that's quite, uh, something.*

"And in response, the Empire proposes a cease-fire that demands reparations, makes requests involving territory, and even assumes 'local referendums have been held in occupied areas.'"

"Seeing as the Empire is the victim here, those seem like modest requests to me."

"I understand your position, suffering as you have such terrible losses. But your requests strike me as much more avaricious than simple compensation would warrant."

No matter what anyone said, surely the necessity of security was ample justification. Lergen's strict orders from the home country were to secure a safe space. The General Staff was close to pleading for a safe zone even if territorial gains were kept to a minimum.

With the state's security hanging in the balance, Lergen had no choice but to ignore his rank and butt heads on the matter.

"With all due respect, General, please just laugh about it."

"Oh? So you have some self-awareness?"

"Please remember that I'm forced to say what 'we demand.' This isn't my personal opinion but strict orders from the home country."

Phew. The bitter look on the general's face as he sighed was a good indication of how rough this was going to be.

"So not open negotiation but a working-level meeting. I'd sure like to reach an understanding...but isn't that inflexible attitude of the Empire's the reason the Federation is attacking?"

"What an utterly two-faced thing to say. Leave the bait-and-switch offers of negotiation that end in attacks to the ancient barbarians."

"Fine. I understand well what the Empire is saying. As its ally, we'll—yes, we'll take proper measures."

"Thank you ever so much for your consideration. Please do as you see fit."

Both Gassman with his "Leave it to me" and Lergen bowing a *Thank you* understood the exchange, and the wordplay was recognized as negotiation to find a common ground.

To Lergen, representing the Empire—the party under fire—it was undeniable that the pushback he currently faced was weakening his position.

On his way back to the imperial embassy after respectfully leaving General Gassman's office, he abruptly looked to the sky and wished for the troops to be victorious.

Please win.

How much better he would have felt if he could have stayed on the eastern front and led the Lergen Kampfgruppe himself! It was unbearable to only be able to hope.

"...Hmph. A Kampfgruppe commander who remains only in name is a pitiful wretch indeed."

All he could do was believe—in the troops in the field and the friends he had left there.

MAY 1, UNIFIED YEAR 1927, IMPERIAL CAPITAL BERUN

In the War Room, where the air was thick with the purple smoke of cigars and cigarettes, and fortresses of stubs were being constructed in the ashtrays, Lieutenant General von Rudersdorf, sitting at the head of the table, spoke to request a report.

"What's the general status on the eastern front?"

His voice wasn't loud by any means, but it carried. The reply came from a part of the mechanism, the precision war machine, known as a staff officer.

"We've halted the enemy's general offensive! The front lines are hanging together by a thread." The expression on the Operations officer's face was pleased. His somewhat-less-exhausted and impatient look said more than words could about what was going on in the area he was charged with. "The organized retreat is a success! Order is being restored in all units!"

"Nice work," says Rudersdorf with a glance at his friend sitting next to him. The man's expression was rather stern. Lieutenant General von Zettour sounded tired.

"How's the mobilization and supply stockpiling coming?"

"Not great. Since the forward depot has been demolished, the planned reorganization has to be put off for a little while."

As a result of pulling the front line quite a ways back, the forward depot that had been built under the assumption there would be an advance was utterly demolished. Over the course of the winter and into spring, most of the supplies they had diligently stockpiled were burned. Perhaps the fact that they had destroyed most things before the enemies could get their hands on them was the one silver lining?

...But if that was the silver lining, it was clear how bad things were.

"The air fleet is solidly operational. We withstood the enemy's attempt to cripple the air force and just barely managed to secure air superiority in all sectors."

"Good." Zettour nodded, though he had a few questions. "Assume the enemy air units could have reinforcements and keep working to maintain control of the skies. We've been handling requests for planes and personnel as they come up, correct?"

"Yes, General. About that. The two reconnaissance units you urgently deployed are up and running. We're now capable of performing tactical reconnaissance all along the eastern front."

"So we made it just in time."

It was mostly the Operations men who sighed in relief. Their manager, Rudersdorf, especially, looked delighted, his face cracking into a smile.

"The recon net we carefully built was paralyzed so easily, we couldn't be sure about the enemy's intentions. You really saved us, Zettour."

"Hearing you say that makes it worth the struggle of scraping them together."

"So? I realize you haven't analyzed the materials yet, but...how do you interpret the enemy's offensive?"

"It's extremely awful but just shy of lethal."

Ultimately, the Empire's forces had been hit at a bad time.

That was the undeniable truth.

"...The eastern front and the southern front are both a bit worrisome."

"Oh right." Zettour seemed to remember something and asked his old friend a question. "How's the diplomacy going? What does the negotiation team have to say?"

"According to our man on the ground, they've still only held some preliminary discussions. He reported that both sides said what they had to say and that the issues are more serious than simply finding common ground."

So Lergen's saying it won't be so easy to get their support. He never thought it was something that could be accomplished overnight, but the fact that the Emp was facing an enemy offensive while the negotiations were still under way was another example of bad timing.

"What do you make of the Federation Army increasing military activity under these circumstances?"

"...I'm sure they're priming us and figuring it makes a good bargaining chip. They seem to want to make us realize how weak we are," Zettour murmured bitterly. If the Imperial Army concentrated on the eastern front too much, Ildoa could start to stir on the southern border.

Looking at the big picture, it was a classic feint.

"You mean if we get too involved in the east, Ildoa will be jumping for our throats?"

"No one can rule that out one hundred percent. We have no choice but to be frightened of these nightmare scenarios. Can you say any different, General von Rudersdorf?"

"...But it makes me wonder if that's what they're actually after."

Rudersdorf was still going around in the same loops of doubt and worry. They had been through this debate several times before. It might be a feint. Or it could be the main attack disguised as a feint. Or possibly both of those things.

The Federation had a talent for this sort of negotiation and pressure. Maybe this was a ploy to get secret negotiations to go to their advantage. Or it was possible that the diplomacy was a ruse and they were planning a huge offensive.

Vexingly, each hypothesis had its logic and was probable enough.

"I understand that. We're facing a military dilemma." Smoking his cigar, Zettour confessed his true feelings in a sober voice. "If we hit them back, we'll get drawn in further. But if we continue retreating, we'll lose our foothold. On top of that," he continued with gravity, "I must admit we don't know the enemy's intentions or capability due to lack of intel, so we're ill-equipped to deal with them. We thought several times that we had wiped out the Federation field army… However, the truth is a shock. The size of the enemy's reserve forces is nothing short of dizzying."

Staff officers, especially, understand that sinking feeling of having failed to evaluate a situation correctly. And being unable to get an accurate grasp on the enemy's strength is a veritable nightmare.

The Federation Army doesn't have the ability to start a major battle, not right now. That analysis of the situation turned out to be gravely mistaken. "Of course," he took care to add, "the enemy must also be trying too hard. Without a serious balancing act and creative accounting, it would be impossible to mobilize so many troops. But one thing we can say is that if they have so many forces, they're more flexible about taking losses than we are. It makes you aggravatingly envious, doesn't it?"

"How can you talk about it as if it doesn't concern you?"

"Oh, it does. On the contrary, I consider it urgently every day."

"I'm not sure you can talk, as someone so good at scraping people together."

Zettour grumbled a response to Rudersdorf with a shrug. "I'd like you to remember that '*Service Corps*' isn't just another way to say '*alchemists*.' I can try all I like, but I won't be able to provide the infinite resources we need from a finite stock."

"Hmph." Rudersdorf snorted and, with his cigar between his teeth, asked in a strained voice, "So you mean logistical limitations will hold us back?"

"Regretfully, that is correct."

"So what, then? Are you saying we should retreat?"

Even with Rudersdorf glaring at him, Zettour had to give the same answer. "I can't deny it. The only way to fix the eastern front at this point is to assume a long haul and reorganize the lines while putting up a delaying defense. I won't say we have to fall back dramatically, but if we can to whatever point is doable, the logistical burden will lighten proportionally."

"And then?"

"If we buy time, at least we'll make it through this crisis. If we can stabilize the lines, we can probably have enough time to come up with a solution."

There is no other way. It was a cliché way of putting it, but to Zettour, it was also his sincere understanding of their situation.

"You've gotten awfully rusty, haven't you?"

"Huh?"

That's why he froze at his friend's remark.

Rusty?

...Do you have some other brilliant idea?

"War is solved not with hesitation but with a strong will. Blooming late is an armchair theory. We need to get our way and put the enemy in a hard spot through decisive action, even if it's quick and dirty."

"You want to punch some more glass? Let's not. I'm not a fan of putting an extra burden on wartime production."

"This again?" Rudersdorf sighed and turned to his friend with a stern look. "You're being stingy during a war, Zettour?"

"Please amend that to say that I'm aware that the amount in my wallet is limited. All you have to do is ask—*I'm* the one who has to conjure things up. There are physical constraints to what we can mobilize. We don't have a genie's lamp here, you know!"

"If it's bankruptcy or defeat, I think bankruptcy is the better option." Rudersdorf snorted.

His unsentimental view was the correct one for an Operations man. If you went out into the country, probably everyone felt that bankruptcy was fine.

But Zettour cocked his head. "I wonder. We've already—yes, *already*—

run through the country's assets. Even if the war ends, what will have become of us?"

"Yes, I'm sure that's an issue. But we'll cross that bridge when we come to it! Even if it's something to worry about, now is not the time. We'll worry about it once we're able to end the war."

"What?"

"Are you saying we should concern ourselves with finances while fighting?" He laughed at the absurdity. "That's not our job, Zettour. Our duty is to win. We can't use the budget as an excuse for defeat."

It was a valid, coolheaded understanding of their situation.

As a soldier, he couldn't deny it. But for Zettour, it was equally difficult to agree.

"To that end, I've got a bit of a gamble to make."

"A gamble?"

"Now, while the enemy is on the move, is a once-in-a-million chance."

"...You mean a large-scale invasion of Federation territory?"

"That's right," said Rudersdorf, and Zettour understood immediately. This was one of Rudersdorf's typical plans to solve things with his fists.

If it goes well, great. But what if it fails?

"Hold on—are you insane?"

"The enemy has left its nest. Well, our lines are in a sad state, true...but if we rebuild them, it's a great opportunity to encircle and annihilate."

With a fierce grin that seemed to proclaim that their chance had arrived, Rudersdorf looked every bit the valiant general a model Operations man should be, that mass of fighting spirit.

"If we can do a good job, we should be able to push the lines up. It'll be a sort of pursuit battle. If it goes better than Open Sesame did..."

Don't be ridiculous, Zettour said with his dissenting eyes.

Enveloping the Republican Army on the Rhine front with their revolving door took an awful lot of preparation. The idea that if they worked extra hard, logistics and intel would be solid sounded like something out of an old folktale.

"We're not on the Rhine anymore!"

"It has to be done."

"It's too great a risk. You're saying we should put everything we've got on the table right now? Just load all our eggs into one basket, why don't you?"

"Beggars can't be choosers."

Well, that's probably an accurate way to express it; I see, so the Imperial Army is slipping into poverty. Even so, Zettour had to argue back.

"The best way to avoid a gradual decline is to plunge straight to the bottom?"

"Being risk averse is healthy. But consider this, my friend. You can't call standing by and watching things get worse 'good risk analysis.' What we need is action. Action that is as drastic as possible."

"You can talk about it all you like, but an operation like that is impossible."

"Why?"

"I'll give you the short answer!" Zettour spat. "The supply network won't be able to hold out!"

"Force it."

"Tell that to an alchemist or a wizard!"

Zettour was pointing out with a grimace that it wasn't his job. As the person scraping the bottom of the barrel to make ends meet and just barely keeping the eastern front from falling apart, he had an objection or two.

Frankly, the Empire was nearing the limits of its national strength. They had surpassed the acceptable number of losses in the east ages ago, and the personnel shortage in the Imperial Army was growing increasingly severe.

They had drafted the young, plus recruiting the elderly and women to work as reserves, and they even had the prisoners of war laboring. It still wouldn't be enough.

"...I just don't think we should move. That would use up the last of our dwindling energy."

"No, Zettour, it's the opposite. We need to act while we still *have* the energy. Above all, the Federation Army has started a maneuver battle!"

"But why does that mean we have to respond in kind?!"

"The enemy has left its base. You could say we've lured them out of their cave... You're the one who sowed the seeds, Zettour. You've got to reap what you sow. And it's harvest time!"

"Wait, what are you saying I did?" Zettour asked, puzzled, and Rudersdorf replied in exasperation.

"You're the one who sowed the dream of self-determination among the people in the east. They're trying to make an anti-Federation flower bloom in the occupied territories, so now's the time to take out the main forces!"

Zettour could only mumble "Mmmph" in response, so Rudersdorf continued with growing intensity.

"The Federation can't hold out! Just as the imperial family of Russy crumbled, so too will the Federation's Communist Party scatter like rats!"

"Show me the evidence that supports this. Are you sure it's not just wishful thinking?"

"History testifies."

"I'm gonna pass on lending my ear to that jerk. As far as I know, history's the worst kind of liar."

"Ha-ha-ha," laughed Rudersdorf as he shrugged at Zettour's remark. "That's a good point. But if fate or what have you is really so fickle, perhaps it can be grasped with an iron fist."

"That sounds like something you'd do."

"That goes for the both of us. Anyhow, first we need to tighten up the lines. If possible, we'll counterattack. Make the arrangements."

MAY 1, UNIFIED YEAR 1927, EASTERN FRONT, SALAMANDER KAMPFGRUPPE HEADQUARTERS

To someone who just arrived from the south, even spring on the eastern front must feel cold. Regardless of how well he may have wanted to present himself, the colonel appears somewhat warmly dressed. I suppose the fact that he came prepared with cold-weather gear means his research of the battlefield is laudable.

Either way, the social animal Tanya takes care not to forget social norms: a warm smile, a polite demeanor, and a sharp, soldierly salute.

The colonel, who returns her salute as he approaches, must have the same stance. He's plastered a fishy smile on his face.

"It's certainly good to meet you. I must admit, I'm not sure whether to call you Fräulein or Colonel..."

"I've heard it all, sir. My hands and feet run red with the blood of my enemies. Frau or Colonel, as you prefer."

"Well, that cuts to the chase. Oh." The man's expression stiffens. "Let's finish up introductions. I'm Colonel Virginio Calandro. I've been dispatched from the Royal Ildoan Army as a military observer."

"I'm Lieutenant Colonel Tanya von Degurechaff. Nominally, I'm the deputy commander of the Lergen Kampfgruppe, directly under the General Staff, but I'd appreciate it if you remember that in reality, I'm the commander of the Salamander Kampfgruppe."

The first step in labeling people is experience and rank. Tanya feels a personal fondness for Colonel Calandro from that initial amiable moment where both of those criteria came into play.

To be blunt, it's good business, I think? Anyone showing up here can't be too inept.

"I've heard of you and your alias White Silver from Colonel von Lergen. He told me you were a living recipient of the Silver Wings Assault Badge, a Named, and a true soldier—so I must say I'm a bit surprised by your appearance."

"I profit by being small. Less surface area that can be hit."

"Oh, that'll make things rough for me. Maybe I'll walk through the battlefield in a half crouch."

"I hope you won't find this question rude, but what kind of combat experience do you have?"

"I trained with the Alpine Regiment, but this is the first time I'm participating in such a large operation, Colonel. It must be quite different from one or two little covert ops."

He's an officer flexible enough to banter but handy enough to be thrown onto the forward-most line in a pinch. *Phew*, Tanya thinks as she feels the burden on her shoulders lightening.

It's much easier to handle a capable officer than an inept one. Of course, given that her each and every move is being watched now, there's no time to relax, but still.

"Oh, don't be modest. You're a specialist in delicate situations. If I may be so presumptuous, I think they made a fine choice in sending you."

"And thanks to that, I've been flung all the way onto the eastern front."

"Ah yes." Tanya finds herself sympathizing with a bitter grin. As someone who was sent to the front lines because she does such a good job, she can relate to that gripe. "Here you are on the forward-most line. On behalf of the Empire, I humbly welcome you."

"Thanks. I'll mainly just be watching and listening. If you could show me things as they are, that would be perfect."

"Understood. As a host, I hardly meet the minimum requirements, but I'll do what I can, even if it's not much."

"I appreciate it."

MAY 2, UNIFIED YEAR 1927, EASTERN FRONT, IMPERIAL ARMY CAMP

"Colonel von Degurechaff, we've made contact with the enemy."

At First Lieutenant Serebryakov's announcement, Tanya jerks out of her pleasant doze. Just like Pavlov's dog.

The sound of the word *enemy* is enough to banish her light sleep.

She swallows her sigh and acknowledges with a shout, "I'll be there right away!"

Parting with her bed and beloved sleep, Tanya resolutely sprints for headquarters and is already holding back sighs by the time she's looking over the brief.

"Enemy contact, huh? So it's sooner than the General Staff anticipated."

It's rough to suppress her rage and condemnation.

The enemy has advanced too quickly. Not faster than expected but faster than we could have ever imagined. I don't want to think that the General Staff's understanding of the situation disagrees so much with ours on the ground that they're optimistically assuming we'll find the kind of environment they hope for.

Does this mean the enemy is more capable than the General Staff estimated? More powerful?

Either way, it's not a favorable development for Tanya. Regardless of how things are done in sports, this is war. Overwhelming a weaker enemy is far more practical and profitable than competing against a stronger one.

"...I guess all we can do is cry over our helplessness. We can't even choose the opponents we want."

Tanya adjusts the priority of things in her mind. Reflecting and assuming are both luxuries now. If she doesn't first eliminate the threat facing her, the future of free thought is in danger.

"Major Weiss, let's have the details."

"A few moments ago, Captain Ahrens encountered a group of enemy tanks. We took no losses. Five enemy tanks were destroyed; however, since infantry showed up as reinforcements, he's decided to withdraw."

"So the report came in late? That's unusual for Captain Ahrens. Was the radio out of order?"

"There seems to have been a light rain."

Rain isn't kind to radio waves. That said, I don't really want to believe that a mere drizzle could cause that much of an issue... Are we just having critically bad luck?

What's worse is that we can't rule out the possibility of mechanical failure. The precision of the "precision" machinery we're using to the fullest on the eastern front can't be counted on. It's hardly surprising, given that by the time we're employing our equipment to the fullest on the eastern front, we're already using them in a way that was unexpected, since they were made for operating in our homeland.

It really is irritating. A *tsk* slips out.

"Colonel Calandro's arrived, ma'am!"

What switches her mind's gears is the shout from the person outside on guard duty.

When it rains, it pours... Tanya leaps to her feet as etiquette demands and snaps off a textbook salute.

"Sir!"

"Thanks, Colonel."

It's been ages since an officer superior to her has entered the command post during combat. It doesn't make things easy. But whining that this is exactly why Tanya told Colonel von Lergen she was against this won't help now.

"Sorry, I didn't mean to interrupt."

"The General Staff has given us orders for how to handle this."

He seems to understand that she means not to worry about it. With a bob of his head, he thanks her and apologizes again.

"Can you tell me what's going on?"

"I just got here, too. Let's have the duty officer, Major Weiss, explain things."

She tells Weiss to fill them in, and he nods his understanding before beginning to speak. "The advance armored unit made contact. They ran into enemy tanks backed by infantry, so our tanks have begun their retreat. We're about to have First Lieutenant Tospan's infantry unit go out to meet them."

"Where did they make contact?"

"It's this area on the grid. Specifically, I think around here."

Weiss pointed to a location on the map—"Please take a look"—in response to Calandro's question.

Tanya has climbed up on a chair to look at the map with them and the topography makes her want to click her tongue in frustration.

When she glances at Calandro, she sees that he seems to have a good understanding of the situation.

"...It's awfully near that residential area, isn't it, Colonel?"

"Yes, that's a pain."

Unfortunately, the map's accuracy seems only up to par for civilian purposes and had probably been appropriated for military use, but it still got the job done of providing a basic picture.

That spot is indeed a residential area. No, technically, it's probably more of a town or village... But in any case, the amount of cover there would make it very different from a field battle.

"It may be presumptuous of me, but may I ask a question? How does the Imperial Army generally handle situations like this?"

What a pointed inquiry. Tanya grins wanly at Calandro. For better or worse, armies love manuals. Operating in residential areas is a stiff military and legal challenge, so as a military observer, trying to learn from the seasoned Imperial Army is the correct attitude for the Ildoan colonel to take.

If there's any issue with it, I suppose it's that she has to tell him that no such handy thing exists in this world.

"As you know, residential areas are headache inducing. Embarrassingly... though the home country must be actively deciding standard operating procedures...they haven't been yet established."

"Is that true?"

"Yes," affirms Tanya. "I keep thinking how much easier things would be if they were." Tanya is lamenting this fact from the bottom of her heart. If there was a by-the-book way of doing things, she could simply follow that and avoid a lot of responsibility.

"All the officers must feel the same. If you had a standard policy, then you could avoid hairy issues by simply applying the rules set out by the higher-ups."

Although when he says that to her so bluntly like that, she has to wince.

"The way you explain it is a bit extreme, but in general, you're right. The practical issue now is that when a residential area is in our way, we're forced to proceed at a snail's pace."

Due to the balancing act with the land-war convention, the Empire hasn't seriously considered research on urban war; that's only to be expected. Since the Federation isn't party to any of the international treaties, they should have thought about it, given the possibility of an attack, but...since the Imperial Army is specialized in interior lines strategy, you could say a weakness has been exposed.

"So even veterans with plenty of experience aren't sure what to do...?"

"I beg your pardon, Colonel, but it's the opposite."

"The opposite, you say?"

Contrary to Calandro's puzzled look, her subordinates are nodding. They understand quite well what Tanya means.

There's some difficulty in claiming it as a civilized opinion, but there are hardly any places less suited to war than a residential area. There are just too many obstacles to have any real fondness for it.

"Anyone who has had a bitter experience in a residential area feels the same."

She glances around the room and there happen to even be people with experience being injured in a similar battle. Even the veteran lineup of the 203rd Aerial Mage Battalion's officers is a good sample of the loathing.

"Am I wrong, Major Weiss?"

"This conversation is liable to make my old wound act up. I do wish you'd spare me," her subordinate, who had been shot in the fight against the Republic, said with a wry grin.

Even a veteran like him is no exception to the rule that it's virtually impossible to keep a lookout in all directions in a residential area.

Flying also requires keeping a 360-degree watch, but the only obstacles in the sky are clouds. Honestly, it's far harder to search for enemies in places where people live. And in an urban environment, well, you can call it a concrete jungle. It would be so much easier if we could just go around it.

Faced with Tanya's and the others' sighs, Calandro seems to get the idea and winces. "Ha-ha-ha. Experience points, hmm?"

"Something like that."

"Well, let me ask you more on that later. For right now, I'll stay out of your way while you take command."

"Thank you." She extends her gratitude for his consideration and then speaks in a purposely normal tone. "So, Major Weiss?"

"Yes, I know. Are we heading out?"

His reply is immediate. This is what an outstanding vice commander should be like. "That's right." Tanya smiles in satisfaction.

She's glad she can save time by omitting the explanation. Still, although it's contradictory to say so, explaining things is her duty. It makes sense, since a superior must see that everyone is aware of their intentions to the extent possible.

Work among professionals who aren't overly reliant on one another entails a sturdy foundation of concise, accurate communication and confirmations.

"Considering the less-than-stellar wireless performance we're getting, let's move HQ up. We can meet with Captain Ahrens and get a handle on the situation."

"Understood!"

He responds immediately to the order. It's so reassuring to feel like you're able to trust someone enough to let them handle things. I suppose you can say having to do checks is extra work.

Ehhh, maybe it's rude to call it extra work, Tanya reflects in her head as she speaks to the military observer beside her. "It's as you've heard, Colonel. What would you like to do?"

"Hold on—are you trying to tell me to lie low because it's dangerous?"

"I wouldn't say that, but neither can I make light of the risks. Of course, I don't want headquarters to be attacked, either…but this close to the front lines, literal encounter battles are to be expected."

Stray fire or harassment from a hidden sniper…

Near the front lines, even if it's a noncombat area or not technically considered part of the front, safety is never assured. Claiming an area is 100 percent safe is a scam. And Tanya is no scammer. She's a civilized individual of integrity armed with modern reason and an awareness of norms.

"We've minimized said risks. But…" Tanya drives her point home. In addition to compliance, their public image has to be considered. Naturally, the most definitely important factor is the law.

All that said, neither can she discount how carefully everything has been checked and rechecked to make sure there are no ethical issues.

Whether for self-protection inside the organization or signaling in society, preventing problems related to the initial handling of these things is paramount.

"We cannot guarantee that the Federation will immediately recognize you as a military observer from the Royal Ildoan Army and hold back in their attacks."

"…I understand your concern, but I'm not sure I approve of being treated like an overprotected child. I'd appreciate it if you'd let me watch."

"Understood," Tanya says with a reluctant nod. "Respectfully, we have nothing to hide from our ally. If you insist, then please observe to your heart's content."

"I realize I'm asking a lot, Colonel. Sorry."

She'd like to say, *Then maybe watch yourself.* Given the strict orders she has from Colonel von Lergen and the General Staff, she's so worried something might happen to him that the comment threatens to pop out of her throat.

But contrary to what's inside, Tanya's mouth forms a polite reply.

"No, it's not so much at all."

Perhaps it's because she's such a sociable animal of politics? Lieutenant Colonel Tanya von Degurechaff is fully capable of employing respectful flattery with an ingratiating smile.

"This is an honor of a role entrusted to me by the General Staff. I've been told to grant your every wish, so don't hesitate. I'm at your service."

"Then about that..."

"Mentioning the risks is just a part of my duty, so I hope you understand."

"I respect your obligations, Colonel. With that in mind, I'd like to do this of my own accord."

Calandro declares his volition before all the staff at HQ.

If he's coming along despite Tanya's serious reluctance and warnings, then all that's left to do is arrange an escort. Now, no matter what happens, her duties have been perfectly fulfilled.

Even if he gets shot and killed, she'll be able to make some excuse to the General Staff. Hopefully that doesn't happen, but it's important to anticipate the possibility.

If I must... Tanya maintains an outwardly courteous attitude and says to her adjutant in a slightly put-out way, "Be Colonel Calandro's guide."

"Yes, ma'am!"

Regardless of how Serebryakov is at entertaining, she makes a great shield as an escort. Tanya is happy to be able to trust her to protect him in the case that anything should go wrong.

And by assigning her to guide him, she can get him out of HQ for a moment—perfect.

"Oh, Colonel, one thing."

"Yes, what is it?"

"If you don't mind, after we move, I'd like to watch your meeting about how to handle the situation."

For a moment, Tanya thinks in silence. Honestly, she wants to refuse. Whose idea of a good time includes holding a sales meeting in front of an executive from a client company?

But Tanya's position prevents her from saying *nein* outright to the military observer. Whoever said *Wretched is the lot of the government official* is worth taking seriously.

"...If that's what you wish, then of course. But—" Though she chooses her words carefully, she has to add, "I'm terribly sorry, but may I ask for your express consideration during the action?"

"What specifically? Of course I want to cooperate as much as I can."

"Thank you." Tanya bows and, with full realization that she's being offensive, makes her request in detail. "During the operation, I want to make commanding my highest priority...so can we temporarily disregard your superior position—the fact that there's a full colonel present?"

Basically, this is an impudent request for permission to make Calandro an ornament. But she simply has to get him to agree to it. Educating a superior while simultaneously fighting a war is more than Tanya can handle.

War is a problem you must always tackle with every last bit of your strength. Cutting corners could lead to problems that not only lower society's estimation of you but directly affect your assets and very life.

"Of course. Consider me a bystander."

"Thank you." Suppressing her relief, Tanya bows deeply. *It's really so helpful that he understands. Of course, I still probably won't be able to ignore him completely. This'll be hard.* Even if she thinks that, though, she can't say it aloud.

It'll be a struggle to perform as usual under the gaze of an important visitor. But it is what it is. When it comes to doing it, it must simply be done.

Thus, burdened with these slight worries, Tanya and the principal commanders of the Kampfgruppe begin moving to the front line. They may be experiencing a bit of poor weather, but there's probably no one else on the road besides the Kampfgruppe's vanguard. They're blessed with relatively good ground conditions.

More than anything, she appreciates that the horses, vehicles, and people can travel without much issue. Tanya and the others meet up with Captain Ahrens's armored troops without a hitch.

It's going about as well as anyone would expect, I suppose... Troops rush about receiving supplies or delivering them, getting plastered in mud as they do so.

On the forward-most line, they have no choice but to prioritize function over form. Provisional HQ is constructed promptly, but it does only consist of a single tent.

Still, Tanya and the others are used to that by now. To Calandro, who looks around, fascinated, there must be something novel about it, but it'll feel normal soon enough.

The place grandly called a "meeting room" is a basic, rough collection of folding chairs; a wireless kit; and maps. That said, even with the minimal equipment, their work can still be done.

"Gentlemen, it's as you've heard. Let's get a handle on the situation." In this space appropriate for an operation briefing, if only superficially, Tanya kicks off the discussion. "Captain Ahrens, what's your status?"

"After encountering the enemy armored unit, you mean? It was a mess."

"Like usual, then?"

"Yes, ma'am." The expert nodded with a wince. It's doubtful you'd be able to give a quick explanation of the situation if you lack the skill to grasp it.

"Before long, enemy infantry started showing up. Since the enemy was entering a residential area, we decided that to avoid a battle in the streets, we should retreat temporarily."

"Mm." Tanya comprehends the situation and finds it irritating.

If there are enemy troops in a residential area, then this will involve the chore of pseudo-urban warfare where we conduct a sweep block by block.

The Kampfgruppe has the ability to do that, if nothing else. Sending in the golden duo of the mage battalion and infantry would make it possible to clear those areas. The issue is that that would take too long.

Since we aren't in a position to creep up around the enemy base and attack, we have to pay close attention to time.

It happens while she's thinking about what to do.

"...The Federation troops entered a residential area?" Calandro asks a question.

"Um, Colonel Calandro?" *He may be a bystander, but apparently he's inquisitive, too*, Tanya thinks as she suppresses the urge to pull a sour face and replies politely. "Can I help you with something?"

"If they enter a residential area, that makes it a fight in the streets. Does that mean the Federation soldiers are fine with that?"

Replying to his question would slow down the functioning of HQ.

Really, she'd like to scream, *You're in the way* and kick him out, but violence won't be tolerated in this instance.

This is exactly why I told Colonel von Lergen that accepting a full bird colonel as an observer would be difficult for a Kampfgruppe with a lieutenant colonel as its superior officer. But frustratingly, headache inducingly, even sighing would be a breach of etiquette in this situation.

I guess I have no choice. Tanya resigns herself and throws it at a subordinate. "Captain Ahrens, answer the colonel's question."

She shoots him a look that says, *You know what I mean*, and he's well trained; he seems to have grasped her intentions.

Straightening up, a model officer, he begins explaining the situation in an expository tone.

"Yes, ma'am. A large-scale unit of enemy infantry has holed up in a residential area. As you pointed out, sir, they may be intending to resist from inside the buildings."

"In a residential area? How did you confirm that?"

"After the armored troops clashed, it was mainly the infantry who checked out the situation. The mages who flew in as support have also been observing."

"...I see. So the Imperial Army is using aerial mages for search missions."

Apologies to Calandro, who's murmuring something or other, but Tanya can't have this level of Q&A interrupting the flow of her meeting; we can't fight a war like this.

"Colonel, may I continue?"

"Yes, sorry. Please do."

"Thank you," she responds politely, but internally she's hurling protests by the dozens. *An officer ranking above me! And from a country that—even superficially—is supposed to be our ally! How am I supposed to work like this?*

I'm going to have to bill the General Staff for tons of entertainment costs.

"Troops, it's as Captain Ahrens said. If the Federation soldiers are holed up in a residential area, orthodox methods will take too long."

"Then please leave it up to the artillery."

"Exactly. Now's your time to shine."

"There's the issue of how much ammunition to conserve… Shall we go all out?"

Tanya nods at Captain Meybert that she's fine with that. She's really just delighted that her artillery maniac has learned to worry about how many shells are left.

"If it's an encounter battle, wouldn't this be a good time to use our mobile artillery?"

The reason we've been supplied with something so expensive as self-propelled guns is that the Imperial Army's General Staff values mobility in the extreme. Our ammo concerns are unavoidable and frightening, but the obvious benefit is that problem areas can be leveled with artillery shells.

"We can use mages as forward observers. Guide the guns and eliminate the points of enemy resistance. Get support from Lieutenants Tospan and Grantz and their mage-infantry composite unit for suppression as necessary…"

"Hmm? Please wait a moment."

"Yes, Colonel Calandro? What is it?"

The flow of things is once again interrupted. The mental cost of politely swallowing the comment *Again?* is no joke.

I definitely need to draw up that plus the opportunity cost and invoice the General Staff for the full amount. All of it! I'm not leaving out a single *bitasen*. If I don't invoice for everything within my right to invoice for, including supplemental compensation for my subordinates who have to do everything with me, I'll be a disgrace.

"You're calling in artillery fire? On a residential area?"

"Yes, that's right."

"Seriously?"

"Huh? Errr, what about, sir?"

Her blank expression is genuine. *If the enemy is in an obnoxious spot and we have artillery, why should my seriousness about attacking with artillery come into question?*

No. She shelves that question. Calandro is not from the Imperial Army. Perspectives often vary between insiders and outsiders. The reason must be a difference in organizational culture.

"To suddenly order an artillery barrage on a residential area in an encounter battle is…worrisome."

"With all due respect, this decision takes into account what we've learned in battle. It seems like both sides were in the processes of advancing, and that's why we ended up in an encounter battle, so this will be particularly effective, as they haven't fortified their position yet."

"I'd like to ask one thing just for reference… Are you actually being serious, Colonel?"

"Yes." She nods.

Is combat doctrine that different in the Royal Ildoan Army? Still having no idea what the questionable part of this is, she doesn't really enjoy getting a taste of that vague middle-management-position misery that involves explaining your intentions to a superior in front of your subordinates.

"We're carrying this out with firm resolve. If you'll forgive me for speaking according to my experience, these sorts of encounter battles are not uncommon on the eastern front, and I determine this to be an appropriate measure."

If there's anything to be worried about, it's time. Using even a second of it on this discussion is already a huge waste. The stress of wondering if the enemy is building up a position as they speak can't be good for my mental health.

"Surely it must be against the law of war, though."

"…What? Excuse me, but are you having some kind of wild misunderstanding?"

"Misunderstanding? What exactly do you think the law of war is?"

"International norms that must absolutely be adhered to."

"Forgive the abrupt question, but…have you ever learned them?"

This isn't a conversation she wants to have in front of her subordinates, but she replies because she has no choice. "You're asking if I've studied the law of war? It's only natural, but I consider myself to have thorough knowledge of the standard legal curriculum."

"Really? Because it sure doesn't seem like you understand…"

When Calandro gives Tanya a doubtful look, she glares right back. "I've completed the standard law courses at both the imperial academy and the General Staff program at the war college. While at school, I also did research on interpretations in practice."

Ahhhgh... It's too bad for Colonel Calandro, but to Tanya, laws are the most important system of norms.

Things that aren't written down might not exist. But only monkeys make light of laws that have been put in writing.

"...I'll be frank, Colonel von Degurechaff. Isn't attacking an area presumably inhabited by civilians a clear violation?"

"Ohhh, I see."

"Colonel?"

That's what you're on about?!

"You're referring to the rule prohibiting combat in residential areas? Generally speaking, I think it's correct of you to question whether it conflicts with the rules of engagement." Tanya nods as if to say she couldn't agree more. But it's actually quite simple to unravel this misunderstanding. "On the eastern front, however... Don't worry, Colonel Calandro. All manner of issues pertaining to these laws has been dealt with."

"Dealt with? What are you talking about?"

Though she's amused that the day would come that she's having a debate about legal interpretation in a temporary field HQ like this, she doesn't forget that the clock is ticking. Unfortunately, given that they're fighting a war, this sort of extravagant time usage should probably be curtailed.

Thus, Tanya gives a concise conclusion.

"The law of war doesn't apply to this scenario."

"It's not applicable? Don't be ridiculous; exceptions don't—"

"They don't exist, true." Tanya nods with that matter-of-fact observation. Because you get burned if legal interpretation isn't done correctly, she's given this close consideration. Laws are not for breaking; they're for dodging. Fighting a law head-on means an emergency evacuation in the very end.

"Strictly speaking, the Federation is not party to several of the international treaties and is therefore not afforded their protection."

It's a boss's duty to show their subordinates that there are no legal issues with their actions. Neither civil nor military law supports the ordering of illegal actions.

If something is gray, you can still call it white, even if it's a stretch. But black is always black. Being "in the black" is permissible, but when we're talking about the laws of modern society, being a black sheep is no good. As a civilized individual, it's something I want to avoid.

"...You're sure about that?"

"Yes, and cities on both sides have already become battlegrounds."

"W-wait a moment, Colonel von Degurechaff. On both sides?"

"Our side's cities have taken a pounding during Federation offensives. I'm hard-pressed to call it civilized, but it's reality." Tanya continues, implying that she hopes to gain his understanding, "Either way, Legal has already given their stamp of approval to shelling cities, and as a combat unit, we merely follow Central's legal interpretations. Will that do?"

"...That's quite edifying, Colonel von Degurechaff."

"Yes, I thought we would find a legal way to avoid problems. But I never thought all manner of barbarism would be justified with the simple words *The treaties don't apply*. It's quite a shock." She smiles wryly and continues, "Either way, there aren't very many armies as law-abiding as ours, and that goes for both international laws and military regulations. And I'm also proud to say my subordinates are doing a great job."

"...You call that law-abiding?"

"Even if only nominally, the Kampfgruppe comes directly under the General Staff. It probably also helps that its core unit is an aerial mage battalion. Since aerial mage battalions operate over a large area, officers are given a thorough legal education."

You can't be fighting a war without a legal defense. That's obvious, is what she's showing him.

Her simple, clear answer must have made an impression. Taking advantage of the fact that Calandro has gone silent, Tanya returns to the stalled conversation with her officers.

"Okay, troops, sorry for the delay, but let's get back to the matter at hand. We're going to wipe out enemy resistance. But this time, it's enough to repel them in a general way. Captain Meybert." She turns to him as she addresses him by name. "I want to do this based on your proposal. You'll have aerial mages as support, but a field of rubble will be an obstacle for the rest of the troops. I hope you have a plan in mind."

"Yes, Colonel. My combat plan is...as you see here..."

He's marked several important buildings for bombardment.

They're all high-rise buildings that'll give us trouble if the enemy has holed up in them… Well, in this remote residential area, those are clearly church towers, but… The idea seems to be to get ahead by obliterating all of them.

It's easier than destroying concrete pillboxes—and probably more effective.

"The classic strategy? Fine, I approve." Nodding, she points quickly at the map to show her officers, confirming the combat plan. "Doesn't need to be flashy. Just crush the enemy's gun positions and suppress them."

Artillery plows, and the infantry advances. Even in a residential area, that principle doesn't change. That's what unlimited war means.

"The plan is for Captain Meybert's artillery to strike a blow to the enemy's firepower, but we should probably consider how the rubble will block our advance. So," Tanya adds cautiously, "I need the observer mages to guide the guns accurately so as little debris is created as possible."

"Then in terms of training level, I'd like to have Lieutenant Grantz's unit observe as opposed to Lieutenant Wüstemann's…"

"Your opinion makes sense, Major, but Lieutenant Tospan's unit pairs the best with Lieutenant Grantz's. Lieutenant Tospan, can you pair with Lieutenant Wüstemann?"

She glances over to see Tospan's unconcerned face. But even this easy-going fellow has learned some things in the Kampfgruppe.

"If that's your order, we'll do our best, but at such short notice…"

The fact that he's able to recognize the task as difficult is commendable. The Tospan who can say no is much more useful than the Tospan who says yes to the impossible. He's made fine progress toward becoming a well-fitting cog in the system if he can recognize what he can't do and reports that to his superior.

If you don't acknowledge these small improvements, personnel will have stunted growth. To Tanya, who is considering writing a few books about personnel development, it's a critical realization.

Thinking about harmony surely makes me a peace-minded individual. Biting back a wry grin on that point, Tanya reconsiders how to handle this.

"Then there's only one thing to do, huh? Major Weiss, can we put your company on direct observation?"

"No problem."

"Good. Then your unit's on observation. Lieutenant Wüstemann's will be reserve firepower. Lieutenant Grantz's will be working with the infantry. Captain Ahrens, sorry, but the armored unit will also be support for the charge."

""""Understood!""""

"All right, then." She makes a quiet excuse. "My unit will stand by here as reserves. If need be, I'm sure we'll go in, but we have a guest, after all. Don't you dare let them break through."

I have to protect Colonel Calandro, so I can't go to the front line.

What a beautifully empty assertion! It would cause too many side effects—or, rather, problems—to use it for every little thing, but as an excuse to not go to the front line, I should appreciate it as more than adequate.

...That said, what if something *did* happen to Calandro? Tanya's future career prospects would be dark indeed.

"I trust you all, but...just in case, I'm counting on you, Lieutenant Serebryakov!"

"Understood. I can handle it."

Good. Tanya nods, still calculating things out in her head. The problem with Calandro really is his rank more than his temperament.

Getting ready to attack and into position in a war takes up a surprising amount of time and effort. Being in the right place and accomplishing the task as planned is proof of excellence in itself.

Perhaps you could say it's the kind of craftsmanlike job that can be pulled off only when commanders on all levels understand their role and the noncommissioned officers are displaying their leadership skills.

"All units are in position."

"Quicker than planned? Well done," Tanya replies to her adjutant after a satisfying glance at her watch.

"Lieutenant Tospan is requesting the use of a smoke screen before they charge."

"Tell him to remember the basics of trench warfare... Errr, oh. I guess he doesn't know them. Tell him to use it *as* they charge. Why go out of our way to alert the enemy to our presence ahead of time?"

Clutching the receiver, her adjutant, who acknowledges with an "Understood," is the type who comprehends good communication. Tanya feels confident leaving things to her.

So then my critical task is... Tanya picks up the lined phone next to her. "Captain Meybert, are you ready to go?"

"Leave it to me. We'll have those belfries ringing in no time."

"...Ha-ha-ha, good. I love it when church bells ring."

"Oh?"

Her subordinate sounds skeptical on the other end of the line, but Tanya confirms, "Of course. For whom the bell tolls, right? I'm not against it. I plan to watch through my binoculars."

"We'll do our best to make it worth your while. Please wait for the appointed hour."

"Will do." She replaces the receiver and confirms the slightly awkward time until Meybert's scheduled to move. Everyone reached their positions sooner than expected, so there's no need to hurry.

Glad to see her troops displaying that arrive-five-minutes-early spirit, Tanya nods and considers calling her adjutant to prepare her some coffee.

Times like this, it's fine to take on that relaxed observer air... And maybe that negligence is what gets her in trouble.

"Colonel von Degurechaff, may I have a word?"

When the actual observer enters the provisional HQ and speaks to her, Tanya fights the urge to respond with her true feelings—*Again?*—and greets him properly.

"Sure, Colonel. What can I do for you? Apologies, but we're about to move, so if you can make it quick, it'd be much appreciated."

"Of course. Let's make it quick."

"Great."

When he tells her to "take a look at that," she turns in the direction he points. In the residential district they're about to invade, she sees...oh, a church?

"...It appears a church is being targeted for bombardment?"

"Ah, I understand your concern. But"—Tanya smiles—"don't worry. There's nothing wrong."

"Huh?"

"Under Federation law, that's property of the state. Sadly, the Federation doesn't have the concept of church property."

"Wait... What are you talking about, Colonel?"

Calandro, staring at her blankly, must be a man of common sense. On this point, Tanya can understand his confusion quite well. A normal, civilized person can't sanely praise the rejection of personal property.

The rise of Federation Communism is downright terrifying, is it not?

"Interpreting the law of war is Legal's job. The notice we were given was that, since it's virtually impossible to distinguish between private and state property in the Federation civil code, attacking facilities doesn't violate the—"

"Wait!"

She looks up when he interrupts her. "Hmm? Was I mistaken about something?"

"Colonel von Degurechaff, you must be aware, but purposefully attacking religious personnel is in blatant violation of the law of war, I'm fairly certain."

"Yes, that's absolutely correct. Is that what you were worried about?" Tanya nods as if to say that she has finally understood his concern.

Calandro brims with law-abiding spirit; alerting her to possible illegality out of a sense of duty as a good citizen is absolutely the right move. *But...* Tanya is also a professional with a respect for the law.

"It's right to fear that people connected to the church might be present. But when I checked, I didn't see any special emblems."

Staring back at the colonel's blank face, she says, "I'm not kidding" and holds out a pair of binoculars. She surveyed around the church towers and everything she could see from their base but didn't spot any emblems that would prohibit them from attacking.

"I've had several officers take a look to confirm. Since you're here, I'd appreciate if you checked as well. Do you mind?"

"...If I find something, does that mean the bombardment will be called off?"

"Of course. I would never order my subordinates to fire knowingly on a place of worship. With your confirmation, we'll be even more sure, which is great."

She's not fibbing or anything—she would genuinely appreciate his cooperation in checking the situation. With only imperial-soldier eyes on the situation, it does end up being a bit biased. Even if this person isn't neutral enough to be considered a third party, the observations of a soldier who isn't from the Empire will be terrific evidence on a report.

Well, I don't actually like places of worship…so I admit that I don't *not* want to shell it, but still.

Actually, Tanya wants to shell it quite badly.

Even so, if it's protected under the law of war, then as vexing as it may be, she'll hold the guns back. Waging war out of personal feelings turns it into a conflict of beasts.

Even war has a minimal number of laws, and Tanya is a stranger to the self-destructive impulses of those who would actively break the rules.

Rules are not for breaking. They are for forcing your opponent to break. Laws are not for antagonizing. They are a tool to have as your ally for knocking your opponent into next week with the power of legal principles.

"S-so you're actually going to fire on the church? It's right in the middle of the town!"

"Yes, it could be an advantageous firing position, so we should crush it ahead of time."

"…So you're going to be fighting in the streets?"

"Yes, I believe we've discussed how it isn't a legal issue in the Federation, but did you have an issue with that?"

"Errr, no, but…no, but…"

If your opponent doesn't know the rules, won't keep them, or for whatever reason doesn't use them, there's no reason to be *considerate*.

"Just to confirm, you're sure there are no religious personnel over there?"

"Mm." Tanya winces at him.

"Are you suggesting there might be?" It's a leading question, a technique used often by lawyers and public prosecutors in court.

If she says no, he'll ask for proof.

If she says there might be, he'll accuse her of going against the spirit of the law.

The action doesn't fit the spirit, the idea, of the law. So he approaches her with a classic trap, but Tanya is confident she won't fall for his subtle scheming.

Since the question is typical, the answer is also in the textbook. If you know it, you can avoid the trap. It's an excellent, accurate example of how knowledge can save your ass.

Knowledge is a weapon. If you're going into a fight, you should carefully arm yourself.

"I have no idea what you're talking about. You're saying there are emblems there even though there aren't?"

Yes, Operation Never in a Million Years Did I Think That. It's the defense most recommended by seasoned lawyers from the lawsuit superpower.

The trick is to neither confirm nor deny while not refusing to testify, either.

"Are you saying there aren't?"

Maintaining a blank expression and tone, Tanya replies simply. "Please consider that they haven't displayed any emblems. I can't fully rule out the most extreme possibilities, but if there aren't any displayed, then we need to wonder what their motive is for not displaying them."

"In other words?"

"Even if there are religious personnel present…I think it's very likely Federation soldiers are garrisoned there. Either way, my troops are more important to me, so I'm of the opinion that we should eliminate the position. Oh." She politely adds one more thing. "And regarding your visual confirmation…did you see any emblems?"

"…No, but…"

"Thank you for your assistance. Ah, it's almost time to go. I guess I got caught up in that discussion… But all right, I'll take the liberty of returning to my military duties now."

Watching Lieutenant Colonel von Degurechaff go, Colonel Calandro wandered outside the command post in a daze.

What he saw through the binoculars clenched in his hands was a Federation residential area somewhere between a village and a town. As he was trained to do, he had scanned the area, and when he saw all the imperial units in position, he still had the feeling this was unacceptable.

"...What's going on?"

This wasn't the Middle Ages. Invading the streets. Encirclements. Civilians would probably get caught in the crossfire... But the even more basic question was: *Is this what armies are for?*

"What are the Imperial and Federation armies thinking?"

He seemed to recall reading in some report that attacking cities was becoming accepted as normal. But seeing it before his eyes...it was beyond his understanding.

"This is absolute madness."

He didn't notice the imperial officers hesitating at all.

Not just Degurechaff. Everyone was waiting for the agreed time with their barrels pointed at a residential area.

"Are these scenarios really just going to repeat forever? Does morality fall silent before raison d'état? How many corpses need to be piled up for this to end?"

When leading an attack, commanders are compelled to be unusually tense. Everyone hopes to defeat the enemy without any losses, but obviously, wishes don't always come true.

And it's only natural for Tanya to worry, since even though it's listed officially as the Lergen Kampfgruppe, if the Salamander Kampfgruppe crumbles, it's she who will be held accountable.

Is it really my job to create a combat plan with the heartfelt hope that it doesn't contain any flaws, get saddled with the baggage that is Colonel Calandro, and then earnestly cross my fingers that Being X doesn't show up to get in the way?

I'm truly hard-pressed to call this waiting period "pleasant." Even if it seems like the one in charge is simply kicking back, the truth is that my job is to battle the stress weighing on my digestive tract.

Please, Tanya thinks as she opens her mouth to speak. "Damage report!"

"Very few casualties, ma'am!"

How grateful she is to hear that from her adjutant, who has tabulated all the losses from each unit!

"Nice work!"

There is nothing that reduces stress so much as being told that you were worried for nothing. She heaves a relieved sigh with a giant smile on her face.

"We're currently mopping up the end of the enemies and rebuilding the lines."

"There's no need to get every last one. Unfortunately, if we did a thorough search and pursuit, our units would be broken up. Let the runners run."

"Are you sure?"

What choice do we have? Tanya nods. Once a location is tentatively captured, a commander is wont to prioritize securing it. In order to secure a location to which they can advance and loose the next arrow from, she needs to make sure the troops will be able to move.

"Our mission isn't search and destroy. There's no reason units should scatter just because we have time on our hands."

Her mouth is forming the word *therefore* when she notices with a smile that an officer she has been expecting to show up has appeared at their provisional HQ.

"Reporting back in, Colonel."

"Oh, nice work, Major. You did an excellent job guiding Captain Meybert's artillery. Lieutenant Tospan's men must not have had much rubble to trip over."

"Great," her vice commander answers; he's so reliable. She glances around to double-check, and seeing Colonel Calandro isn't there to overhear them, she waves for Weiss to come closer. "By the way, about the church…"

"You don't need to worry about that. I confirmed at my discretion during the mop-up operation. It really seems to have been empty."

Tanya doesn't actually think Major Weiss would give a false report over something like this, but…was it really empty?

"Oh? I thought I saw some movement."

"Open graves and the aftermath of stolen burial goods."

"What?"

"Maybe they were raided by the Communists before we arrived? It seemed as though they were sending anything of value to the rear."

"Makes sense." Tanya nods.

The Federation troops are really not slacking on their hatred of the Imperial

Army lately. That is, they don't want to leave so much as a speck of anything valuable behind for the Imperial Army to find. The malice is tangible.

This is what it means to lack kindness, charity, and goodness of spirit.

"Sheesh, the Communists are always one step ahead of us."

"Huh?"

"Did we not research them enough? Their propaganda apparently says that we're on the brink of defeat. And," she continues with a smile, "apparently, they're always one step ahead of us. So those Federation guys tell the truth once in a while."

"Ha-ha-ha. Good one."

Wincing, she says, "No, I'm serious." She's not actually averse to acknowledging how sensible they're being about this.

They've struck at the truth with their propaganda. Even capitalists aren't perfect.

But... At the same time, Tanya grins. Unlike the Commies, who are incapable of admitting their mistakes, capitalists take failures as a given. This is the proper application of human engineering. She's had her fill of guys like Being X who deem themselves perfect and unerring. The capitalist strengths are adaptability, improvement, and evolution.

And in terms of *should*s, the Commies are definitely a step or two ahead of capitalists, including me, when it comes to having an ideal of how things should be. It wouldn't be fair to not commend them for having the courage to step up to the cliff's edge.

"That said, it's vexing that I have to admit how efficient their looting was. All right, let's give Colonel Calandro a tour of the demolished abandoned church and put his law-abiding heart at ease."

"Oh right, we still have that pain in the ass to deal with."

"Major Weiss, watch what you say. You could cause an international incident."

"Do excuse me... I'm just reminded once again of the gap between the front line and the rear."

"Me too, Major." *Seriously, though.* Tanya is compelled to say with a sigh, "I can't believe he thought we were going to shell a church..."

"For real. Even I apply the international laws and standards."

Exactly, thinks Tanya. At some point, before she knew it, Calandro started viewing his hosts as savages, and she doesn't like it one bit.

"I know plenty about laws, so I don't want to be called a barbarian. It's honestly so unfair."

MAY 3, UNIFIED YEAR 1927, EASTERN FRONT, NEAR THE FRONT LINE, KAMPFGRUPPE GARRISON

It probably sounds cool if you say *a victory nap in a seized building.* But actually, even just having a corner of an old building to make into a bed is such a huge upgrade in comfort.

After a good night's sleep and a breakfast fit for a human, just as Tanya is thinking with a wry grin that it seems like it will be a civilized day, she gets a message from headquarters.

The higher-ups just do what they want. Tanya is allowed a single sigh. Then all she can do is solemnly obey.

She's simply telling the officers of the Kampfgruppe gathered for a meeting that they'll be retreating.

The officers of the aerial mage battalion accept it relatively quickly—they must be used to the home country's absurdities. *Surprisingly*, it should probably be said… Captains Meybert and Ahrens and First Lieutenant Wüstemann don't even seem terribly dissatisfied, which is quite something.

So the one who reacts as expected, in a way, is First Lieutenant Tospan?

"Orders to retreat? If you'll excuse me, we did just suppress a residential area, but the fortification of our defensive position is going smoothly. I don't see the need to—"

"In other words? Ah, errr, I didn't mean to interrupt. This is a good opportunity. Please finish what you were saying, Lieutenant Tospan."

"We can defend. I don't see why we have to abandon this position. Isn't the worst case that the enemy will retake it and we'll end up giving them time to strengthen their foothold in the area?"

"That's a good question, Lieutenant Tospan." Tanya nods and, sparing no effort to educate a newbie, inquires about his current perception of the situation. "Is that how you see things?"

"Yes, Colonel. The conditions on the front lines aren't so bad. Aren't we strengthening our foothold despite the encounter battle with the Federation Army?"

My word! He makes more sense than she expected. She's pleasantly surprised to get to witness his growth. And when you count that his infantry unit performed during the suppression, she has to admit that he's capable of getting the minimum done.

Which is why she puts all the necessary energy into mentoring him.

"That probably is how it looks from the ground."

"So you mean...?" The puzzled look on Tospan's face means there's some work to do with regards to application. He's not the kind of guy who you can give him one and he'll get to ten on his own.

Sadly, he's also one of Tanya's officers.

That said, it's a matter of course as a soldier to do the best with what you have on hand. And Tospan is making an effort in his own way. I have no complaints about assisting him as a superior officer. I do feel that I'm a little hyped-up about education, even for me, but as a good citizen, that's only natural.

On the other hand, Tanya can't help but point out with a wince, "You can't just live in the two classic dimensions. Modern warfare is three-dimensional!"

"Huh?"

When Tospan still doesn't follow, Tanya appoints an aerial mage to explain. "Major Weiss, how do the lines look from the sky?"

"They're too tangled."

Meybert and Ahrens both nod that they understand; they may not be magic officers, but they have been trained. Tospan's blank look must mean he requires more education.

That said, even if he can't get to ten from one, it's too soon to fault him.

For a lower-ranking officer, this is the current standard. The Peter Principle[6] was well stated; it'd be selfish of me to expect more without promoting him.

[6] **The Peter Principle** A paradox where if ability is the criterion for promotion in a meritocracy, the end result is extreme incompetence.

For example, say there's a capable company employee. He's capable, so once he is promoted to section chief, if he has abilities beyond that position, he'll probably be promoted to head of the department. But if he hits his ability ceiling, he'll stay an ordinary, useless section chief forever. That's the principle governing all organizations! Doesn't that mean they're actually full of people who can't do their jobs?!...is the horrific discovery that was made.

"From your point of view, we've got the pressure on them."

"Yes, ma'am. As long as, like my unit, the others are advancing, I don't see why…"

"That's probably not mistaken, but it's also only a flat view. If you look from above, you can say the forward-most line is in chaos. Listen, Lieutenant." She continues her explanation. "The way things are now, it'll be extremely difficult to operate smoothly. For example." She gives a concrete reference. "Suppose I request artillery support for your unit. Now, say that the enemy position is right in front of your nose… You don't want to accidentally get blown away, do you? Or, rather, I doubt the artillery would even agree to such a reckless order." She glances over to see the artilleryman frowning.

"…It's not a distance we could be responsible for. As long as there wasn't an order to blow Lieutenant Tospan up along with the enemy…"

It happens just as Captain Meybert says those words.

As if it was the sign, the sound of shell impacts echoes. If you're used to getting shot at, you recognize it even if you don't want to. It's close, and it *is* us being shot at.

"A bombardment?!" someone yells, and all the officers at HQ simultaneously develop the same fear.

"An enemy attack?! Of all the—! The search…"

What is going on? Tanya nearly says when the artillery officer, Meybert, shouts, "They're behind us! It's coming from behind us!"

But when he says the bombardment is coming from the rear, Tanya shakes her head. "It can't be!"

The rear has been infiltrated, and we didn't realize it until we were getting fired on?! *Are we really such a bunch of numbskulls as that?* Tanya can't accept what Meybert is saying.

But on this point, Meybert is a professional artilleryman.

"I'm pretty sure these are our guns! We're coming under accidental friendly fire!"

Wha—?! After a moment of speechlessness, Tanya realizes he's probably right.

We *did* get hit with our artillery's irritating calculation errors on the Rhine front…

But there's another impact. And it's even closer this time!

"They…they have observers! The real barrage is coming!"

Thanks to Meybert's warning, Tanya understands the situation much better and she clicks her tongue. *This isn't a calculation error! It's even worse! We've been mistaken for the enemy!*

The base piece fires a round and makes adjustments. I have experience guiding them. And I've been shot at like this before. I just never thought our own guys would be shooting at me!

"All units, take shelter! Shelter now! And keep an eye on the sky."

Tanya knows from experience: If you can stop the observer mage, you can at least delay the firing.

"Shit, I guess I have no choice!"

She manifests an electronic countermeasure with the Elinium Type 95's overpowering output. All the communications in the airspace are temporarily overwhelmed, and Tanya calls to the observer mage who must be out there, her murderous intentions plain to see.

"In the name of God, I say unto you! This is the Salamander Kampfgruppe! To the idiots firing on your own troops in grid-square C-39, cut it out! I possess neither the mercy nor the patience of the Lord!"

"Salamander Kampfgruppe? Um, what's your call sign…?"

"Dumbass! You've got a lot of nerve after firing on us," Tanya rages. She truly cannot stand this. "Make them stop right now! Listen." She kneads her urge to kill into her words and launches her fury at the flying freeloader. "Salamander 01 to observer mage! Where are you flying, you absolute waste of air?"

With not so much as a peep in reply, I suppose I can't even expect to solve this with words. As my anger at those insufferable amateurs continues to build, I resign myself to the fact that Tanya may have to shoot down someone on her own side.

Anyone who shoots at me, regardless of nationality or organization, is an enemy. The logic that *my enemy is every idiot who fires on me* is violent but not wrong.

"The identification signal is ready!"

"Send the flare up, then—hurry!"

Her adjutant's rapid efforts are truly the work of a pro. *Teach those amateurs what's what!* She gives the order. If they don't acknowledge the stream of smoke pouring from the signal flare, then she'll just have to retaliate.

"There! Did you see it?!"

"Uh, I see it, but..."

"I'm not saying it again! Cease your observed fire! If you don't, I don't care what your IFF says—I'm treating you as enemies and counterattacking!"

"Wh-why is your unit over there?"

"You think we're the enemy in disguise? Fine. Just try firing for effect on the Salamander Kampfgruppe. The aerial mage battalion will bring its full force to bear in an anti-artillery assault!"

I'm confident we could overrun a division of artillery. The Imperial Army's batteries are relatively weak, so I can obliterate them in one shot... What a depressing thing to be so confident about!

"Do I need to teach you guys that my score on the Rhine isn't just a number?!" Tanya's tone, filled with fury and loathing from the pit of her stomach, is meant to show them she is serious. She doesn't want to attack troops on her own side. But the plank of Carneades exists in the field of law, too.

I have the right to defend my plank so I don't drown.

Crushing the artillery in order to at least protect Mr. Ildoa from these fools trying to weaken my shield, the Salamander Kampfgruppe, is equivalent to emergency evacuation.

Their reaction is slow, so Tanya screams in irritation. "Battalion, be ready to sortie in response! If they fire, treat them as the enemy!"

"Understood, Colonel!"

There is only one criterion by which friend and foe can be distinguished on the front lines: whether they shoot at you or not. That's it. You can't change that core truth by quibbling about IFF, identification signals, what badges people are wearing, or anything else.

"If you fire on us, we'll take care of you the way we deal with Federation artillery units! Give me whoever's in charge over there! Apologize! If you can't do that, then we're fighting to the death!" Tanya doesn't even try to hide her annoyance. Just then, she notices her encoded wireless receiver screaming.

"H-HQ to Salamander CP, come in—it's urgent! Come in—it's urgent!"

"Salamander 01 to HQ, please explain."

I guess it's fine, since it's not on an open channel.

"It was a misidentification. The observer mage didn't get enough training..."

But hearing the word *misidentification*, Tanya explodes. "I want your excuses officially—on paper—at a later date! How are we supposed to keep morale up when we're under observed fire from our own artillery?!"

"It was the observer mage's mistake. Because the fighting is so chaotic..."

"Don't they even know standard procedure?! What do we even have identification signals and communications ciphers for?!"

"Very sorry. I'll have him write a formal apology..."

Oh, the bureaucratic reply.

"Great! Send one copy to the General Staff and one here! You'll be officially censured afterward!" Tanya slams down the receiver and takes one deep breath before exploding again. "These fucking amateurs! What do they think war is?! The lives of imperial soldiers are on the line! Take this seriously! No confirmation—are you kidding me?!"

This is people's lives. There's no recovering or taking them back.

Under no circumstances will I tolerate a casually mistaken bombardment. *This is a major incident that put people's lives in danger—what are they thinking?* Tanya is shocked at this disaster brought about by a lack of professionalism.

"Shit! Why can't our observer mages tell our own troops from the enemy?! What are they even observing?!"

I can understand being fired on by the enemy.

We can just fire back. That's only fair.

Being fired on by your own artillery is not fair.

I can even accept an accident due to gun trouble or whatnot during a rolling barrage. Just because a shelling is scheduled doesn't mean the trajectories can be calculated with 100 percent accuracy.

"Give me a casualty report!"

"No serious losses. Just a few shells fell on our defensive position; there won't be any notable casualties."

Major Weiss responds promptly and Tanya has to ask back, "What? You're sure?"

"Yes, Colonel."

Her vice commander wouldn't give her an unconfirmed report. Knowing that, she understands that he's being serious.

"...I'm...really glad to hear that."

"Haaah...," she sighs in relief. Suffering casualties over something like this would be despairingly absurd. The fact that they were fired on makes her furious, but the news that they haven't incurred losses is a hopeful-enough reality to cool her raging head.

"Just to confirm, no damage to tanks or guns?"

"No, ma'am. If necessary, we're ready to fire against the artillery."

"Ha-ha-ha, right now I'm thrilled that it doesn't seem to be necessary."

The command post is relaxing before her eyes, a warmth returning to the atmosphere. No damage is truly the blessing in this curse.

Sheesh, thinks Tanya, but her troubles don't end there.

"Excuse me, Colonel."

"Colonel Calandro? I was worried there would be an international incident if you were killed in friendly fire. Very glad to see you're safe."

Calandro pops in, looking fit as a fiddle.

"Yes, thankfully I'm fine. Your artillery units are surprisingly sloppy."

"And thanks to that, we survived. I never imagined the day would come that I'd be delighted at their sloppiness. Of course, maybe it's because they're sloppy that we were fired on in the first place."

"“Ha-ha-ha.”"

The stupid ones get mocked for being stupid. It's a natural principle.

"Still, I admire your unit. Fearing actual firing for effect, you were taking shelter, but the efficiency with which it was carried out... Your defense against artillery fire is impressive. It seems you've trained your men quite well."

"You're going to make me blush. It's just that I've been in many an artillery battle on the Rhine front..."

"Maybe it's impossible for me to comprehend, since I haven't experienced that terror myself. It brings the importance of experience into sharp relief."

"Yes, my adjutant, vice commander, and I have a wealth of that." She brags slightly that they're elites who have been through hard times.

"Now then, I'm sure you know why I've come... Do you mind explaining what happened?"

"Certainly." When Calandro expresses interest, Tanya laments to him. "To put it plainly, as you've gathered, we've been fired on by our own artillery. The cause was the observer mage mistaking us for Federation troops."

"Mistaking? Wow, '*fog of war*' is right, huh?"

"Truly. But luckily, we managed across the board to avoid getting hit." Tanya comments that it was the blessing in this curse, but Calandro eyes her with suspicion.

"That's what I'm wondering about, Colonel. I'm surprised you were able to stop them before they fired for effect. How in the world did you do it?"

"Huh? I called them up, gave them the cipher, and told them to cease fire."

"Which is a feat of coordination indeed... So how did you pull it off? Regardless of the theory, the practical details elude me. For future reference, it would be great if you could tell me."

"We're risking our lives, you know; it's just the case that all our safety mechanisms functioned."

"So you can't explain the finer points? As a military observer, I'm desperate for that sort of info."

"I see," she says, but beneath her polite smile, Tanya sneers. *It's not happening.*

No matter how hard he digs, she can't tell him she got them to stop by threatening them!

Just try leaving that on record! Something listed in the official record becomes something that officially happened. If it got into the record that I was fired at by mistake and threatened them, it would be a stain on my CV!

This is different from logic in a moment of rage. Once you have the breathing room to think about long-term preservation of the self, you need to keep up appearances.

Perfect résumé, perfect career, perfect future. This three-item set must be defended with one's life.

"First the friend-or-foe identification signal and then an appropriate conversational exchange. And the grace of God. Yes, I think that's about it."

Calandro leaves the room with an "I see" and a "Thank you," either because he realizes I'm busy or because he wants to observe the situation some more.

Whichever it is, I'm grateful he's gone.

"I can't believe I have to deal with this ineptitude… The instructors who sent these idiots to the front can rot. Observer accuracy is the root of the Imperial Army's firepower!"

If we're getting lax with that, the future is bleak.

"…As losses reach their limit, the quality of the replenishments is bound to drop."

"I know, Major Weiss."

It'd be stranger to replace veterans with part-timers and expect things to function without issue as normal… Would the General Staff really cling to such stupid wishful thinking?

Hmm… Tanya sinks into thought for a moment.

The more she regains her composure, the stranger it all seems. It's common knowledge that the army is running short on fighting power. She can't deny that committing newbies to the front is a *theoretically* sound last-ditch measure.

But that's not what happened. The essential point is that the Imperial Army still has some sturdy personnel left. *Running low* and *running out* are two different things.

"…Unless the home country has mental issues, something weird is going on."

It was just such a shit show. It's difficult to imagine that coming out of nowhere. I'm not citing insurance statistics, but usually an accident is preceded by a flood of previous smaller stresses.

The incident this time seemed much larger than a simple mistake. So then has the quality of the troops shifted so radically? In the span of a few days?

"In the past few days, we had the advance order from yesterday and the sudden retreat order today."

Talk about getting jerked around. Normally this would be an indication of how much chaos the Imperial Army is facing.

Normally, that is…

"…Not experiencing confusion in the field would be more of a surprise, but actually right now, things are fairly orderly?"

She thought maybe the idea was to purposely tangle the lines, but in any case, this is too quick of a reversal. It's easy to say, *The lines are tangled, so retreat for now*, but much harder to pull off.

If it was so simple to retreat with the enemy right there, they would never need a rear guard.

"…But the higher-ups mean for us to do it."

And, she adds in her head. *We can't say that there's zero confusion. But for a unit riddled with rookies, those guys have been operating in a relatively organized fashion up until now!*

This is blatantly suspect. It couldn't have happened unless someone somewhere was manipulating things.

"In which case, the question is the aims of the actor."

A modest advance, a clash, and a tidying up of the lines. If we were going by the textbook, the order would probably be to build up a defensive position, but…what are all these newbies doing on the front lines? What are they planning to do by freeing up the veterans?

"Recon-in-force? But if they want to push all the lines up…"

Usually it would just be a Kampfgruppe like us sent in. It's not something you need the whole army for, and it isn't the Imperial Army's custom to perform reconnaissance in force with a whole corps.

"Colonel? Is something wrong?"

Tanya suddenly realizes she's been in her own world for quite a while. It wasn't until her adjutant prodded her with a stare that she noticed.

"Oh, no, I was just thinking. An officer's bad habit."

Anyhow. She shakes her head. Leaving her questions on a note in the back of her mind and recalling her role, she knows what she needs to do is simple.

She re-confronts the situation before her.

She has to present her subordinates with a plan to remediate and give them their next orders.

"Troops, I'm glad we didn't end up having to charge on the numbskulls in that other unit. If something had happened to Colonel Calandro, it would have been an international incident, so I'm glad we escaped that, too."

""""Ha-ha-ha!"""" The officers who burst out laughing, including Tospan, must all be beefing up their nerves here on the eastern front. Tanya finds adaptability to be a powerful force.

Wow, she's compelled to marvel.

All that's left is to alternate an appropriate level of tension with appropriate rest. That's the task of Tanya and the other personnel-managing members of the General Staff. Human resources function perfectly when managed appropriately.

"Let's seize apology and consolatory gifts from headquarters. The requisition I leave up to she who is supposedly the most merciless among us, Lieutenant Serebryakov!"

"Wha—? I—I object, Colonel!" But Serebryakov's sputtering protest is the minority opinion in the Kampfgruppe. All the officers must have been fleeced by her multiple times.

"That's our commander, always keeping a sharp eye on her subordinates."

"Yes, I hope that my eye for people, at least, is accurate, Captain Ahrens. But she's robbed more than just the magic officers?"

"I certainly have no desire to play cards with her." There's something sad in Ahrens's eyes as he murmurs that. It must mean she's beaten him more than once.

She glances around and sees that all the officers seem to agree.

"Captain Meybert, Lieutenant Tospan, judging from the looks on your faces, you agree with Captain Ahrens? Did you hear that, Major Weiss?"

"Sure did. What an embarrassment. She's utterly ruthless."

The duet of sighs plays out perfectly.

As a light topic of conversation, it's not bad. Maybe it's a bit obnoxious, but it's important to share a sense of humor if you're going to be working together. Tanya had been worried that she couldn't connect to her subordinates in that way, so she feels like she has stumbled upon some handy material.

"...I'm not going to tell you to have mercy on the enemy, but you might want to rethink being so heartless toward your friends and fellows."

"Colonel?! Major?!"

""""Ha-ha-ha!"""" The laughter reviving inside Kampfgruppe HQ is a sign that precious normalcy is returning. Harmony is invaluable.

"All right, troops. That's that for the settlement. Make sure you tell Lieutenant Serebryakov what you'd like later." Tanya tenses up her expression to head back to the point. "We need to retreat to the designated line in order to tidy up the front. Major Weiss, you're on rear guard. Captain Ahrens, you're in charging of securing our route." When she glances at them, she sees the faces of veterans who know what they're doing. "So the aerial mage battalion, with their mobility, will protect the rear, and the armored forces, with their breakthrough capacity, will lead the way out. Let's set ourselves up for a solid withdrawal!" She makes her intentions clear. "Lieutenant Tospan, operate under Captain Meybert. Assist the artillery in their retreat. Lieutenant Serebryakov, you'll go with them and escort Colonel Calandro."

"Understood!"

The fact that she can leave that to her adjutant means she has a great adjutant. *You can't find support like that just anywhere.* She thanks Serebryakov and doles out tasks to her other equally trustworthy officers.

"Okay, Major Weiss, Lieutenant Grantz. We'll leave last as usual. Boy, it's a drag that managers don't get paid for overtime."

"Same as always, then. But I'm one of the lower ranking of the lowest ranks, so I'd like to apply for overtime pay."

"Oh?" she blurts as Grantz's uncharacteristic banter catches her by surprise. *Right, Weiss is mid-ranking, but Grantz is still lower.* "The privileges of being a lieutenant. Sheesh, I can't argue with that. I'll make sure we get you a form to apply for the overtime allowance. If we can get Legal and General Affairs to sign off, you'll get your extra pay."

"...Your kindness brings tears to my eyes."

"Ha-ha-ha. Well, just think of it as being an aerial mage on call to scramble includes your flight, rapid response, and overtime allowances."

"That's just what I'd expect a manager from the homeland to say."

By the point he raises his hands in surrender, Grantz must have accurately comprehended the power differential between them. *Very good*, Tanya thinks, shooting a wry grin at Weiss.

"Well, I am a general staffer who came through the war college, remember. I know a thing or two about military administration."

"So, then?"

"If I could, I'd get one of those refined desk-polishing jobs."

Weiss's face says he finds that unexpected as he murmurs, "So you wanted to work in the rear, Colonel?"

"That's right, Major. Perhaps I'm a different animal than you. It's not as if I was hoping to be serving on the front lines."

"This is what it means to be truly surprised."

"Why do you say that?"

"It just doesn't sound like the sort of thing an officer who has stood on pretty much every front would say."

"That's for sure." She groans at Weiss's comment. Even she finds her perfect attendance–like score odd. Maybe she needs to pay more attention to her work-life balance.

"How much better would it have been—how much better!—if that wasn't true." She smiles bitterly and nods. "That said, you can't wish the world into being a certain way. Ever since I got mixed up in combat in Norden, I seem to have a connection to war."

Or more like ever since I was hurled into this world by Being X? Malicious beings really cause nothing but trouble for good civilized people.

"Ha-ha. Maybe that's what you call fate."

"Fate? You have no idea how much of a relief it would be if I could shout, '*Nein!*'" She sighs heavily. "We're at war even as we have this ridiculous conversation. For someone with common sense like me, it's truly painful."

"If I may, ma'am, I agree."

"Oh, you understand, do you? That's great, Lieutenant Grantz."

Major Weiss, who pipes up with a "It really is," has spent as much time with Grantz as Tanya has. He probably has a thing or two on his mind. "I'm impressed with how far you've come. How about a simple quiz, then?"

"A quiz? What should we have him do?" Tanya asks, her interest piqued.

"Hmm, what about having him explain the war situation?"

"Good. Okay, let's get to it. Lieutenant Grantz, I'll ask you just like back in the academy. Explain this order to retreat and the background to it."

"Yes, ma'am." Grantz stiffens before speaking. "...It's a sort of weird way to reorganize the defense lines."

"How so?"

"It's a question of timing, Colonel. Isn't it strange to reorganize the lines while there's still combat continuing in various places...instead of after the fighting is over?"

"You felt the same way, hmm?"

"Yes... You thought the same thing, ma'am?"

"...I have the feeling that maybe, just maybe...the home country is planning a major counteroffensive? The way they're moving forces around feels a bit peculiar. It feels somehow deliberate. Oh, but that said..." She smiles bitterly. "This is just one officer's guesswork. I think that's enough chatter for now. Time to retreat; let's do it. We'll withdraw to the rear and thank headquarters for those shells."

""""Understood!""""

[chapter]

IV

Operation Iron Hammer

The General Staff is an organization
that sees things through.
If they need a sorcerer, then let's
show them some sorcery.

From the notes of the Imperial Army General Staff

MAY 5, UNIFIED YEAR 1927, THE KINGDOM OF ILDOA, GENERAL GASSMAN'S OFFICE

A messenger, for better or worse, is tasked with accurately conveying the sender's intentions. To put it another way, being a messenger requires the resourcefulness to deliver the words as stated, unaltered. When an officer performs a messenger mission, it's something different.

Colonel von Lergen was in the awkward position of realizing that he hadn't fully understood that until just now.

No matter what he thought, he was in the position of making the facial expressions the home country intended, speaking in the voice the home country demanded, and saying the words the home country wished him to say.

The job could hardly be summed up as merely talking. General Gassman had his usual cheery, affable smile plastered on his face, but Lergen got straight to the point.

"Regarding the matter you proposed earlier, there's been a reply from the home country."

"And what was it, Colonel von Lergen?"

Facing the general, who had straightened up, Lergen took a deep breath. Let's admit it. To say what he was about to say, as a colonel to a general, took no small measure of resolve. So he braced himself and spoke with extreme seriousness. "I shall now relay the message from the home country. All right?"

He paused to take a breath.

"Eat shit. That is all."

Doing the work to achieve a cease-fire and peace—that is, to end the war—required a show-no-weakness, take-no-prisoners attitude, bizarrely enough.

"Oh? That's the reply from your home country?"

"To put it plainly, it was nothing more or less than that."

If he'd had a mirror, he probably would have seen a conceited imperial soldier in it. Lergen knew his face didn't appear threatening. That's why he forced its stiff muscles into an expression approaching overconfidence.

...Considering how long he had spent practicing in front of a mirror at the embassy, he wanted to believe he was pulling it off. If he wasn't, he was nothing but a clown.

"In response to the Federation Army's nonsense about repelling us with force, the home country has invoked Operation Iron Hammer. Based on an existing policy, they're currently refusing Communist ideas with guns and powder, as if it was their most cherished dream to do so."

"That's quite a militaristic way to put it."

Gassman, shrugging, must have realized how far backward Lergen was bending over. Up against a soldier-politician with a long career in military administration, Lergen came off as having secondhand experience no matter how he tried to play it. It was only natural that a green, mid-ranking officer would be scoffed at by a cunning general.

"I hope you'll excuse me. But, sir, the Federation's pronouncements are equally high-handed. I'd appreciate it if you could overlook it."

Lergen had already accepted that his role was that of the clown.

"Do you know the first thing about negotiation?"

"Of course I do."

He had known ahead of time that he would be snorted at and glared at.

From the moment they met, it had been implied that the Empire and Kingdom of Ildoa would clash, with the former seeking a settlement in its favor and the latter saying, *Quit being so demanding.*

"I was concerned you had forgotten. I do hope there is still a role for Ildoa to play. Very well. For now, can we review the Empire's terms?"

"Yes, of course." Lergen nodded respectfully, but contrary to that attitude, he had been dispatched with strict orders to not budge. As long as that was the case, it would probably look like superficial politeness to the general.

...And it would only be a matter of time until it was obvious that he was acting that way on purpose.

"Let's set aside the demands for reparations and a disarmed region for a moment. Would you be willing to alter your demands for the cession of key strategic points and the citizen votes in occupied territories?"

"The home country notified me that, if necessary, we can accept that occupied territories would become neutral, although that's assuming that the treaty guarantees they're established as self-governing regions."

"Colonel von Lergen, to be blunt...we want you to rethink the voting and the fixing of the divisions."

"We can't do that."

Gassman didn't even try to hide the bitter look on his face when Lergen refused so flatly. Perhaps that was only natural, as the Ildoan side surely had an idea of what they were up against even during the preliminary negotiation stage.

But Lergen truly couldn't yield in this instance.

"No wiggle room at all? Really? If you could cede us some ground on this point...Ildoa could arrange things with the Federation almost immediately."

"General, I'm overwhelmed that you would speak so courteously with a mere colonel, but even so, I must decline. I hope you're able to forgive me."

"I would hope that you could understand the good intentions of your ally."

"We simply shan't be taking advantage of them."

"...Let's speak heart-to-heart as soldiers. Where's the middle ground? How can we settle this? I want to know the limits of your demands. Could you tell me?"

"Frankly, we want reparations. We're also hungry for territory. But let's get to the essential: The Empire wants peace of mind."

"Peace of mind?"

"We want the guarantee of safety—that we won't be attacked again."

Strategic sneak attacks and being surrounded were the reality of the Empire's geopolitical circumstances. But both of those things had become traumatic for them.

There were times the Empire felt anxiety and even fear. The Imperial Army General Staff wanted to be liberated from that terror no matter what it took.

...Peace had to mean the end of fear.

"Conversely, if all the other terms are met, the General Staff will accept with or without reparations and with or without territorial cessions."

"...The complete security of the Empire's strategic environment?"

It was clear to Lergen that Gassman was about to say, *There's no way.* And yes, it was easier said than done. And it wasn't only the dilemma of guaranteeing complete security but the fact that just because one person was able to sleep peacefully under ideal terms didn't mean their neighbor could as well.

The secure strategic environment the Empire so wished for was, on the other hand, too advantageous. Let's face it: It was a hurdle too high for the other countries. Even the General Staff would admit that.

...But public opinion in the Empire thought differently. The public felt that security was the minimum. Anything less, and the imperial public wouldn't accept.

"Hence why I'm presenting this request."

"It's too much. Are you saying you think it's realistic?"

"The Empire has already dealt with the west, handled the north, and cleaned up the south. The only threat remaining is in the east. Under the circumstances, it seems like a minimal ask. Why do you think it's too much?"

The reason he continued to emphasize that this was a line that couldn't be crossed was simple. If the terms were like any cease-fire that finished after ten years or so, they were afraid they might end up in another idiotic war.

What the Empire needed was a *final and eternal framework for peace.* That was why Lergen had to stubbornly, uncompromisingly maintain the position that they would not yield.

"Colonel von Lergen, get a grip and be reasonable. As your ally, Ildoa feels compelled to warn you."

"You needn't worry."

"Oh? Even though your army is under pressure from the Federation's?"

"...With all due respect, the Imperial Army is fighting on enemy territory, not our own. I believe you can comprehend, then, who is ahead?"

Though he knew he was just playing with words, he had to employ some bravado and say they weren't losing. He had heard once that diplomacy sometimes required an honest liar, but now it hit him what a realistic complaint it was.

"Have you ever heard of logistics, Colonel? I'm sure even the Empire can't advance forever. Considering the rate of attrition in the east, I suggest out of the kindness of my heart that you prioritize an early settlement."

"From one perspective, you may be right...but we know we're one step away from victory."

"That's great if true. Colonel, I'll tell you this... Where that last step will take you may not be the world you hope for."

Lergen knew he was being told that hope had remained at the bottom of Pandora's box. But who peeked in and checked anyhow? You don't know if the cat is alive or dead until you look, right?

"Maybe not. But," Lergen continued with a wan smile, "we've sown our seeds—the seeds to solve the problems on the eastern front."

"...You mean you've planned for the issues that will come up after your counterattack succeeds?"

"Naturally, we're prepared."

After seeing Colonel von Lergen off, General Gassman remained alone in his room smoking a cigar; he sighed in spite of himself.

"...I'd like to think it's just a brave front."

As far as he knew, the Imperial Army's current situation was far from ideal. Even if they weren't completely battered, it was probably appropriate to describe them as "awfully exhausted." Unable to overcome the toll of winter, they had only just managed to regroup after sinking into the mud, no?

And that was when the Federation had knocked them sideways.

It was a total surprise attack. And the Imperial Army's response was far too late. It was an uncharacteristic blunder that ended in even their supply depot getting hit.

What said the most was the movement of the front line. Between imperial units pulling far back by the kilometer and reports of a rout, their position wasn't such that they could be putting up a brave front. Perhaps it was properly termed a *quagmire*? It had to be frustrating. Yet the Imperial Army showed no signs of compromising.

"It's fine for the negotiations to take a while, but…at this rate, will it ever come together? Unless one of them achieves a major victory and the other suffers a terrible defeat, we may not get anywhere."

As the mediator, the longer the negotiations dragged on, the larger he could claim his role was. But honestly, if it was going to take too long, the whole mediation maneuver seemed less appealing.

"…I suppose I just have to wait for Colonel Calandro's report."

MAY 5, UNIFIED YEAR 1927, IMPERIAL CAPITAL BERUN, GENERAL STAFF WAR ROOM

The Imperial Army needed a breakthrough on the eastern front, a plan to pull the disordered units away from the front lines that were being backed up on them, to regain discipline, and to avoid a total collapse.

Of course, in the field, what needed to be done was getting done. Noncommissioned officers roared pep talks, lower-ranking officers endeavored to get things under control, and the higher-ranking commanders ran around working hard to reorganize everyone. Thus, order was reinstated.

To put it plainly, the issue was what their next move would be, given their strategic environment.

They were in the process of gathering enough fighting power for a counteroffensive: airborne rangers, air forces, armored units for mobility, and what little shells and horses they could find. But working like alchemists, the Service Corps had managed to scrape together the minimum—the bare minimum—of supplies necessary for the attack.

Still, no one could deny that it was all done very quickly. And more than anything, no one was sure that the prep for this emergency plan was really enough.

Normally, there would have been a careful risk assessment. But at present, all they had was an operation plan based on forced guesses made under strict time constraints.

You definitely couldn't call it a thorough job. And more than anything, their track record of failing to grasp the enemy situation made them extra hesitant.

The trauma was deep-rooted. The General Staff's failure to predict the enemy offensive cast a heavy shadow over their ability to judge the situation.

Their plan for a counteroffensive to deal some serious damage to the enemy field army as soon as the spring ground solidified missed its mark.

It was such a blunder that everyone had to admit that they had done a horrible job analyzing the enemy situation. If they faced off again without a plan, they would surely be swept away.

In order to recover, desperate for a move that would break through their strategic difficulties, the General Staff mustered all their wisdom, collected what few possibilities remained, and put together a sole hope.

The name of the plan was Operation Iron Hammer.

The idea was overly ambitious maneuver warfare focused on hitting the brunt of the enemy forces with one powerful strike.

Even the primary architect of the plan, Lieutenant General von Rudersdorf, had to admit that Operation Iron Hammer was an all-or-nothing gamble.

"Hey, Zettour, what do you think?"

"It's too high-risk for a final plan. That's about it. Operation Iron Hammer has a rationale I can't deny, so I agree with you there. But it just doesn't feel right."

"It's the best we have right now."

The main idea of Operation Iron Hammer was to use a river in the enemy's rear area as a huge wall for defense. In order to do that, the plan was to have troops drop at a crossing. While the airborne unit cut the enemy off from their rear area, the "iron hammer" made up primarily of armored forces would ram into the enemy military district to divide and envelop them. It was perfect in theory.

You could say getting them to tidy up the lines to make up for their numerical inferiority and managing to identify the enemy military district through the combined effort of east and central Intelligence despite the unplanned nature of it all was a historic achievement.

But, but, but…

"The fact that we have to just hope that this one attack will solve all our problems is…exceedingly pathetic."

"Hope? Stop making it sound like we're praying, Zettour. The already

oppressive atmosphere in the General Staff will get even gloomier. Besides, it isn't our job to look to the Lord—though we could ask a chaplain to..."

Lieutenant General von Zettour nodded solemnly that Rudersdorf was right about that, but he couldn't help but express his internal doubt. "We're staff officers. Our job isn't to pray for miracles but to perform them. I don't have any objections to that. But do you think we really can?"

"We need a miracle, so it's our duty." Rudersdorf spoke matter-of-factly, declaring that there was nothing to be confused about. "It must be done, so we'll make it happen."

If you get it, then quit whining was the look Rudersdorf shot at him, and Zettour shook his head and murmured, "That's how it's always been. We do what we must."

Operation Iron Hammer hinged entirely on whether the drop was successful or not. In order to send in the ranger paratroopers, a battle for air supremacy would be unavoidable. The imperial military was only just barely able to cover the necessary costs—fuel, planes, personnel, and so on.

"Rudersdorf, I'll be straight with you. At present, our air force is like a rubber band stretched to its limits. Please remember that." Zettour warned him out of the sense of duty that went with his position. Saying they didn't have any more room to extend further was the same as saying he could see them about to snap.

...Ultimately, and sadly, they couldn't count on the air force to be capable of a second strike. At this point, they had already mobilized every last transport plane and personnel they could muster. It wasn't even likely they would be able to get adequate supplies to the rangers being dropped at the Federation river crossing.

And he couldn't shake his worry about how long the lightly outfitted rangers would actually be able to hold the bridge. It would be a battle against time. If it took too long, the damage would be irreversible.

"We've done what we can, so all that's left is to believe in our troops out there fighting."

"Hahhh," Zettour sighed. He respected his friend and was terribly envious of his unflappable courage.

"You're always like this."

"Like what?"

"I envy your decisiveness and how certain you are. I'm incapable of that much confidence. All this walking on thin ice has worn me out."

"Hmph," Rudersdorf snorted. He thought highly of himself, yes, but that's what a staff officer had to do. And as long as a staff officer was defined thusly, a high-ranking officer who had been through the staff curriculum would necessarily end up arrogant.

He took pride in his power, in his devotion to his duties, and in his abilities as a specialist.

"No risk, no reward."

"I agree with you, Rudersdorf, albeit with a reservation."

"What reservation?"

Zettour nodded, shrugged, and hit him with exactly what he wanted to say. "It has to be a risk taken after eliminating what risks can be eliminated."

"You just don't know when to give in, do you?"

"General von Rudersdorf, I'll take the liberty of saying…that no, I don't." Zettour's heavy sigh mixed with the anxious tapping of his trembling left fingers on the table. Irritated, he shook his hand out and took a cigar from the case. The words that slipped out before he put it in his mouth were his true feelings. "No sane person would approve of this gamble. If this were before the war, the one who came up with it would be sent to a sanatorium!"

"Are you saying it's madness?"

Obviously. Zettour nodded firmly.

A long-range airborne operation and no solid prospects for supplying the rangers who dropped? If this failed, they would have lost their invaluable reserve ranger paratroopers—that fact alone was headache inducing. And they'd have to abandon the eastern defensive lines to counter.

If they lost this bet, imperial units could collapse across the board… Though it was true that if they won, it would be a great achievement. They could also expect it to have a positive impact on the secret negotiations going on in Ildoa as they spoke. If things went well, it might even lead to a cease-fire and peace.

Sadly, all these hopes came with the caveat of victory. This was a military operation in name, but in essence it could be described only as a gamble. It was incredibly risky—perhaps even too risky.

"What else could you call it? The basis of the logic may be just barely sound, but in practice, it's a parade of impossible hurdles... How many examples are there outside textbooks of a maneuver battle punching through an enemy military district? It's nutty," Zettour grumbled, and just as he was setting his cigar in the ashtray, he caught a glimpse of his reflection in the window.

As usual, he was looking a bit pale... His exhaustion was written all over his face. Whether it was the curse of overwork or caused by stress, he wasn't sure, but his hair wasn't doing too well, either.

The same went for his friend next to him feigning pep and motivation.

"There's no guarantee that we can break through." *Am I wrong?* he asked with his eyes, and Rudersdorf frowned slightly.

His old friend was a man like a great boulder, but unexpectedly, he was showing his true feelings—Zettour knew that.

"General von Rudersdorf, frankly...I can't be sure of this plan."

"It's fine to be cautious. But you can't waver when it comes to execution. There are plenty of examples in military history of hesitation ending in failure. Aren't you supposed to be a specialist in that field?"

"I am, but setting theory aside...I'm also human, you know?"

"Oh?" Rudersdorf moved his eyebrows to indicate his interest, and Zettour, wincing, carefully proceeded to say what was on his mind.

"The worst-case scenario is enough to stop this old man's little heart. Sorry, but I can't take this calmly."

"I've been wondering since before," Rudersdorf said, frowning. "Aren't you being awfully timid? What in the world is wrong?"

"I don't know."

"What?"

Even questioned with that confused look...Zettour himself couldn't pin down the cause of his hesitation. Since he understood how unscientific and illogical it was, he was having trouble explaining it, but could it have been intuition?

It was absurd, but maybe it was his experience giving him a warning. So, realizing he was being vague, he expressed his worry. "We can't estimate the risks. Honestly, that's the whole thing. We don't have a clear idea of the possibilities."

He wasn't even sure if it was because they didn't do enough preliminary analysis or their fighting power wasn't amply prepared. He had done both of those things to the best of his ability. He had done all he could.

Yet he didn't have the usual certainty he did before an operation. Something was missing.

He could think, *Well, if…*

He could wish, *Or maybe…*

But as for whether he could sit and wait for victory leisurely puffing a cigar…he couldn't fool himself. Something was bothering him.

"That's not like you. I was sure you'd come to the discussion with everything figured out."

"…There's too much of the unexpected in war."

There were too many things he didn't know. Ever since the fighting had started, there were so many events he didn't understand and couldn't have anticipated.

Strangest of all was how, looking back, everything seemed inevitable—to the point that now he wondered how he couldn't have seen it all coming. It made him want to scream.

Was it because so many of his plans had failed that he was losing confidence in his judgment?

"Yes, you've been talking that way for a while now. You realize you're not fit to be called a superior officer if you're lacking willpower, right?"

"That's not my intention. I just don't want to confuse recklessness with bravery."

"We solve this by acting."

Faced with such fortitude, Zettour felt something was off. He had thought that given the situation in the east, his old friend would have been fainthearted as well, but on the contrary, the Operations man remained unchanged at his root. The way he continued to emphasize action as their only option was very Rudersdorf.

So did I really make a rare mistake in reading his intention?

"…Make use of our mobility. Launch an attack directly on the border of the enemy's military district. An airborne operation, a battle for air supremacy. We've even made all sorts of preparations for preliminary espionage. But the risks are still too great. Honestly, I don't want to keep doing this."

"That's only logical, but we do have some history of producing reliable operation plans, you know. I wish you in the Service Corps would trust your colleagues a bit more."

Zettour laughed, as if that was the funniest joke he'd heard all day. There was no less common word in the General Staff than *reliable. And in the first place, can you really call someone who recommends this high-risk operation as the only option* reliable*?*

The fundamental goal of staff education was to take someone who was contrary and turn them into someone who was useful and contrary. *Has the Imperial Army General Staff, who plans to take the initiative and do what people hate, who takes the initiative and attempts to carry out flexible, fly-by-the-seat-of-their-pants missions, ever once selected a "reliable" operation?*

"You mean the guys who are always betting on the outcome?"

"We have no choice but to roll the die. Am I wrong?"

"...As irritating as it is, no."

MAY 5, UNIFIED YEAR 1927, EASTERN FRONT, SALAMANDER KAMPFGRUPPE COMMAND

In military history, things tend to be discussed as if they happened according to plan. It's written that the mission was a go, but there's nothing recorded about the chaos leading up to the action.

The Imperial Army's Operation Iron Hammer has begun.

From the very first moment on, the commanders in the east, grumbling as they go, perform their duty as a precision war machine.

"There's a message! A message from HQ! Officers, gather up!"

The Salamander Kampfgruppe, deployed on the eastern front as the Lergen Kampfgruppe in name, is no exception. Having adjusted their position with some delicate combat during their retreat, they are on standby for further orders from the home country, so the officers gather swiftly.

"I wondered what was up, and it seems it's a major operation. Iron Hammer? So we're going in and pulling out again… Busy, busy."

Major Weiss shrugs, reluctant, but he's one of the ones who has the mental capacity to handle it. Acclimated officers know the importance of responding quickly to changes in the situation.

Old hands are invaluable because even if the game changes, they identify common rules and optimize by applying their existing knowledge.

"It's ridiculous. They think the troops can attack when they're this disorganized?"

First Lieutenant Tospan, on the other hand, is the type to make a mountain out of a molehill. For better or worse, officers who learn through experience evaluate things based on how difficult they seem.

This is a good opportunity, thinks Tanya as she surveys the command post, glimpsing the idiosyncrasies of her subordinates.

The smiling First Lieutenant Serebryakov probably shouldn't be counted. For better or worse, she's used to the impossible problems the General Staff throws at them, so she's not a good point of reference.

First Lieutenant Grantz—an honest guy—has begun silently shoving chocolate bars into his pack. Sometimes I wonder if he can really command, but he does what is possible in the field at his level, so he deserves credit for that.

Captain Meybert is apparently caught up in the numbers related to his duties with the artillery. Just as I'm thinking what an interesting response that is, I notice First Lieutenant Wüstemann sounding upset as he questions his superior, Weiss.

"Major, regarding this Operation Iron Hammer, there's no preliminary plan?"

"Maybe the bigwigs in the General Staff have one, but are you trying to say we should?"

"…Right, well, that is, what should I do?"

"You don't need to think so hard, Lieutenant. Just follow orders. You'll be told to go, you'll be told to come back, and before you know it in all the confusion, the battle'll be over," Weiss spits in an exasperated tone, and the look that crosses his face must be a symptom of that frontline syndrome officers jaded from the field get?

No. Tanya shakes her head.

"All right, Officers, shall we get started?"

"""""Yes, ma'am."""""

Properly trained officers are able to switch gears extremely fast. Up until just a moment ago, they were trading gripes, but now they all have their specialist faces on.

"Colonel, what's going on? Forgive me for asking, but I don't see the Ildoan colonel..."

The question Weiss poses on behalf of her subordinates is utterly valid. The Kingdom of Ildoa's military observer has been around the command post for a while, so his absence sticks out whether she wants it to or not.

"I had Colonel Calandro give us some space. Because, you know..."

A high-ranking outsider is a massive obstacle when trying to get candid opinions from her subordinates. The moment the home country sounded us out about it, she asked him to leave them, assuming he wouldn't agree.

But luckily, he understood. A guy with a head on his shoulders like that is a treasure in any situation. I'm sure he'll go far in Ildoa.

I'm serving on the forward-most line; our esteemed guest is serving on the forward-most line's bench. It'd be a lie if I said I wasn't a little envious...*but I'm too off topic*, thinks Tanya as she changes her focus.

"Okay, let's make this quick. We've been ordered to undertake Operation Iron Hammer, a major counteroffensive."

"There was no sign this was coming, huh? I wish they would take into account the disarray of the frontline troops. It's frustrating that the home country tends to plan operations with brainpower only."

"It's probably about maintaining secrecy, Captain Meybert. The General Staff is often concerned with that." She defends the higher-ups a bit but knows that Meybert is probably right.

The orders were for a front-wide advance. Given the fighting power they have mobilized, it'll probably be a corps-scale maneuver battle. It's easy to propose finding the limits of the Federation's offensive and knocking them back while they've got the pressure on all along the front, but it's another dimension of difficulty to pull it off.

"Telegram. Here you go, Colonel."

"Thanks."

Looking over the paper the signaler hands her, Tanya is stunned by the astonishing reality of what it says.

"Huh? How incredibly..."

"Colonel? What's wrong?"

"Oh, just surprised at the home country's judgment, Major. They're so, uh, fearless. The plan for the operation itself is relatively simple, but it's quite a gamble."

"A gamble?"

"Yeah." Tanya nods at Weiss. "Operation Iron Hammer is what I'd call a 'vertical envelopment.' I guess you could say it's nearly the quintessential maneuver battle."

The one who flinched first in response to the words *maneuver battle* was the armored-forces man. For better or worse, a decisive armored officer doesn't hesitate to ask questions.

"...Have we secured the air superiority minimally necessary to fight a maneuver battle?"

Tanya nods to acknowledge Captain Ahrens's good point.

The ground units can't get very far if we don't have control of the sky. Fighting a maneuver battle without that control is a pipe dream. Nobody wants to travel under fire from Jabos.

"Don't worry. Our air force has taken care of it... We were shot at by enemy artillery and even some numbskulls on our own side, but we haven't had any harassment from enemy planes, right?"

"...So it wasn't just a coincidence? I assumed it was God's protection..."

"Believe not in God but your fellow soldiers, Captain Ahrens. Apparently, our dear air force has been doing good work for us."

How wonderfully efficient, even Tanya marvels... The planes that had been scraped together did take control of the airspace.

"But how?"

"The damn Federation air force was too spread out trying to cover their advancing infantry. We took advantage of that situation."

The air forces nominally mobilized to assist in the withdrawal and tidying up of the lines had waged a battle for the sky and gained, if temporarily, air superiority. For the first time in a while, the eastern sky was the Empire's playing field.

That last achievement was reported only moments ago.

"I found out about it just now, but...ranger paratroopers are going in ahead of us. Airborne units will drop in the vicinity of a large river in the enemy's rear area. Apparently, the objective is to block off a crossing point... and the aerial mages will cover them."

"An airborne operation? To a crossing in the enemy's rear?"

"That's right." She nods at Weiss, who seems taken aback.

Honestly, aside from the fact that they're committing too many troops, it's a classic operation. If we fail, the airborne units holding the crossing will be wiped out... It's a huge risk.

Surely even the General Staff, which so values decisive measures... wouldn't permit such a gamble if there was no hope of success.

"It's an altered version of the trick we used in Arene. Dropping only aerial mages wouldn't be enough, but if we're paired with the ranger paratroopers, they probably figure we'll have the numbers and firepower to suppress the enemy."

The method of taking the initiative and hitting the enemy with what you yourself would hate—it must be a cliché by now, when speaking of how to compete.

It can't be a bad idea for the Imperial Army to put up an enthusiastic fight against the harassment masters of the Federation's Communist Party.

"Our job is to lead the charge—as the central penetrating group."

"So, then?"

Her officers are a bit too eager to fight, but affirming the anticipation of your subordinates is part of the job of a good boss.

"Establishing a communication line with the troops who drop into the enemy rear area is a critical task. Our orders are to charge all the way to the river. It goes without saying that if we're late, the ranger paratroopers could be annihilated. It's a major responsibility."

When she puts it into words, the burden is clear.

Above all, the enemy rear area is...*far away.*

Frankly, it'll be tough to join up with the rangers during the period they're able to continue fighting without being resupplied unless we crank out some serious speed. Even the Salamander Kampfgruppe, which has been mostly mechanized by this point, doesn't stand a very good chance of operating on schedule when clashing with the physical obstacle of enemy troops.

"Who's all being assigned to the district?"

"We'll be in the same district as the Second Armored Division, the Fifteenth Division, and the Third Composite Mechanized Infantry Division. In effect, it'll be those three self-propelled divisions plus the Mobile Kampfgruppe as the vanguard group."

Considering the Imperial Army is committing mechanized troops—which is rare—you can say that at least in form, they're sending their very best, but…there's no way these units will be able to coordinate effectively when their chains of command have barely interacted before.

If they're counting on the flashy work of impressive individuals to naturally produce something that resembles teamwork, the risk of something going wrong is higher.

"May I ask a question that strikes to the heart of the matter?"

"Sure, Major Weiss."

"They may not have trenches, but I'm concerned that we won't be able to navigate the densely packed Federation troops. I have trouble believing three divisions will be enough to break through…"

"You're right. Troops, even the General Staff wouldn't simply tell us to punch through with no plan."

The dry chuckles of "Ha-ha-ha" she hears are a good sign.

At least being able to trade jokes and snark means they're in a much better place in terms of strategic views and logic than a bunch who are trapped in the depths of their thoughts after their minds start wandering from the stress.

"Take a look at the map, everybody."

Given the info we received from above, plus the map, we can get an approximate idea of their intentions. That's an ability an officer is required to have, and a natural one for a staff officer to possess.

"So we're…supposed to attack where the enemy positions overlap?"

"That's right. The Intelligence fellows in the General Staff must want us to head through this gap."

With all the shocked faces in a row, Tanya can guess what her subordinates have imagined. Tanya's vets—Weiss, Serebryakov, and Grantz—are quick to compose themselves… Perhaps they have good crisis-management skills, so they know how to escape a risky situation.

"Did you have something, Captain Ahrens? You can be honest."

"...It's quite something *if they've managed to grasp* where the enemy has control?"

The army's administration is vertical. Even a commander who does everything in their power to defend their own district would have a hard time maintaining smooth control over their troops if their district and authority overlapped with their neighbor's.

But only an amateur could declare that ranks and clear assignments exist to prevent that sort of issue. No army on this earth can immediately tell which district an enemy attack is occurring in.

Even GPSs make mistakes, so how are we supposed to tell with just the maps and communications circumstances of this era?

So the optimal answer, in ideal theory, is to strike right between two districts. The only issue is the simple truth Ahrens has put forth with a frown: *If they've managed...*

"If you'll excuse my asking, how *reliable* is this information?"

"The Intelligence guy from the General Staff guarantees it..."

Ahrens shakes his head as if to say, *You've got to be kidding*—he's actually a pretty good actor.

"Can we trust that analysis? General Staff intelligence has been hit-or-miss, especially when it comes to the situation on the eastern front."

"That's a good point. Not that I'm not worried about it at all, but...as a staff officer, I'll say that the General Staff has its strengths and weaknesses like anyone."

In the education curriculum, there end up being areas covered in depth and others that only get summarized as far as the textbook goes. It has to be that way when you're cultivating not general-purpose geniuses but specialists with specific functions.

Which is why Tanya says, "Actually, in terms of intelligence analysis, the General Staff is pretty good at military and *only* military affairs analysis. Once politics get mixed in, in the strategic analysis realm, they could use some work."

"So you're saying you've managed to nail down where the enemy districts are?"

"Major Weiss, why are you asking *me* that?"

"Oh right, do excuse me."

Tanya grimaces at her bowing subordinate. It's not that she can't understand wanting to ask. Tanya herself would like to carefully question the General Staff about how confident they are.

She'd like to grill them, actually: *Are you* sure *this time?* But she can't ask that. How could she possibly ask that?

So she just makes it seem like she's joking.

"Well, I'm sure the Intelligence officers know what'll happen if we fail. I know Lieutenant General von Zettour, and he's the type who doesn't hesitate to learn from the enemy."

"Learn from the… You mean?"

"Yeah." She nods at Weiss. "Even the General Staff only has so much patience. They'll probably start implementing Federation-style punishments for these guys if they keep screwing up."

"That would make the Intelligence officers take things pretty seriously."

"Ha-ha-ha, right?"

Once the atmosphere relaxes slightly, Tanya quickly introduces the main topic of their discussion. Assuming the intel they have is correct, if they want to act, it's a battle against time. They can't go off on too many tangents.

"You remember how we got that order to retreat the other day, right…? That was when they figured it out. It may be a little rough, but they're definitely the newest data available. That's better than being given a detailed map from a month ago." Tanya confirms that everyone is nodding in agreement before continuing. "Now that we know what the situation is, we need to consider tactics. We're a Kampfgruppe made up of tanks, infantry, mages, and artillery, and thanks to the coordination we've built up over successive battles, we can deliver a solid blow."

In any endeavor, the first step toward success is an objective understanding of the situation. That old aphorism about knowing your enemy and yourself is the simple truth. In that sense, the Salamander Kampfgruppe can be optimistic about its small yet coordinated composite of firepower, but on the other hand, it's about the smallest possible strategic unit.

If it's going to charge into a proper enemy army, a hard fight will be inevitable. So Tanya sneers.

"...Unfortunately, we're only a single Kampfgruppe. So we'll use a cheap trick."

"A cheap trick?"

"Yes, Captain Ahrens. I'm counting on you. Get us to the river no matter what."

"Huh?"

》》》 MAY 7, UNIFIED YEAR 1927, EASTERN FRONT, FORWARD-MOST LINE 《《《

The concentrated guns took the enemy completely by surprise in the counterattack.

For thirty-some hours after the order to advance was given, the Imperial Army clashed with the Federation's at various points along the line. Meanwhile, the aerial mage battalion the Imperial Army was so proud of sortied along with the air fleet. Lucky for the imperial ground troops, the balance of power in the sky was tipped heavily toward the Empire.

Encouraged by the favorable conditions, multiple imperial ground units chose to attempt a fast break. In order to meet up with the ranger paratroopers as quickly as possible, they made a beeline east for the river.

The Lergen Kampfgruppe—that is, the Salamander Kampfgruppe—was tasked with securing a route for the rest of the vanguard, which consisted of the Second Armored Division, the Fifteenth Division, and the Third Composite Mechanized Infantry Division.

They were formed up with Captain Ahrens's armored unit and the aerial mage battalion out front and Captain Meybert leading the second echelon of guns, infantry, and replenishment mages. Having the first echelon cause an impact, the second expand it, and the following divisions sustain it was a simple tactic, but that was why it was sure to work.

The orthodox way is extremely profitable as long as you can pull it off.

On that point, there is no great difference between the organization and doctrine of the Salamander Kampfgruppe and the ground forces. But compared to the other units, which found themselves in battle after fierce battle, the Salamander Kampfgruppe had a strikingly easy time of it.

There was a single secret to their comfortable advance.

Tanya's trick was to have the aerial mages employ tank desant,[7] thereby suppressing their mana signals and gathering enemy attention on the other aerial mage units.

The Federation Army had its hands full trying to deal with the overpowering mages; it may have actually been a good thing that the Federation was so well protected against mage attacks from the sky.

From the imperial communications Tanya was picking up, it was clear that the Federation troops were ambushing aerial mage units the moment they were detected, and even if they weren't able to do that, they could use the mana signals as a way to locate the imperial forces on the battlefield.

So if you want to hide a tree, use a forest.

If you want to hide aerial mages, use an aerial mage battle.

The Federation troops were on careful guard against the aerial mages in the sky, and thus, the Salamander Kampfgruppe and their powerful aerial mages were able to break through to the meeting point—or, rather, they succeeded in slipping past.

As a result, they achieved a speedy advance that broke previous eastern-front records. They enjoyed an almost anticlimactic breakthrough.

An aerial mage unit probably won't take too much damage in a tank desant. That was what she expected when she had the mages ride in on the tanks, and Tanya is impressed—*Not bad*—by how much it helped in enemy detection.

While the visibility from inside the tank is limited, desant personnel, entirely exposed, have a broad view of the field. Being able to keep a careful 360-degree watch is brilliant. And on top of that, it mechanizes them so they don't have to move on their own.

Wars should be won with the least effort possible. In that sense, using tanks as a ride isn't a bad option—if you can shut your eyes to the breakdowns that accompany self-propelling...but in this instance, Tanya considers them within the permissible range.

[7] **tank desant** The utterly natural result of people riding tanks. It's a special tactic where putting soldiers on tanks allows them to keep up better with the mechanized rate of advance. It also allows the tanks and infantry to support each other more closely, which is perfect.

And you put them on the outside, not inside. It's a harsh job, getting rained on by enemy attacks targeting the tanks. Whether this is true or not is unclear, but some say the average survival of tank-desant troops is two weeks.

She's daydreaming about reporting up the chain to suggest transporting mages by tank when one of the mages raises an alarm after spotting movement.

"An infantryman! At one o'clock! There's an ambush!"

The surprised mages react swiftly. Upon discovery of the target, they load a magic bullet with a formula pre-manifested and aim for one o'clock.

Just as a couple of tanks are about to begin searching fire as harassment—

"Wait! Don't shoot! That's one of ours! It's one of the ranger paratroopers!"

First Lieutenant Grantz's shout from the forward group of tanks makes everyone lower their weapons.

"Lieutenant, there's no mistake?"

"The paratrooper helmet! It's one of ours!"

"All right." Tanya promptly gives an order, standing tall on her tank. "All units, wave your caps! Caps!"

When approaching an almost surely nervous field unit, there's a good chance you'll be shot at unless you make it clear you're not an enemy.

And troops standing on tanks waving their caps all at once speak volumes to the lack of hostility on our part.

"Don't shoot! We're friends! We're Imperial Army!"

"Wh—? Huh? A friendly unit?"

Yes, the crowd of waving caps and helmets seems to say, and the rangers who looked to be attempting to turn an anti-tank gun on us immediately relax.

That was almost a bad scene. Tanya sighs, relieved. If she had blown away the rangers they were sent in to save, it would have ended in court-martialed disgrace.

"...Tank desants are not half-bad."

I guess there's a reason the former Soviets and even Americans used this tactic, Tanya reevaluates. She didn't think meat shields should be used so explicitly, but she revises her mistake.

She has success right before her eyes.

"Nice work, you guys."

Grantz, running out front, shares an enthusiastic embrace with the airborne officer leading the group. Watching them punch each other in the shoulders is such a moving scene.

"Sorry we're late!"

"Glad you made it!"

Tanya's unit and the paratrooper rangers mingle, praising one another's efforts. From the way the rangers' expressions, hollow with exhaustion, break into smiles, she can see, whether she wants to or not, how desperately they must have fought these nearly three days isolated in enemy territory. Their struggles couldn't have been just any ordinary struggles.

Thinking she'd like to be of any help she can, Tanya speaks. "I'm the commanding officer of the Kampfgruppe, Lieutenant Colonel von Degurechaff. Is there anything you need?!"

"We've been out of ammo for a while. Aside from the mages, we basically have nothing... If you have bullets, it would be great if you could share them with us."

"I'll arrange that right away. I hate to make demands in exchange, but we'll borrow a bit of your water."

"Water?" He points at the major river running under the bridge as if to say, *It's right there.*

But Tanya is a modern individual who values the concept of property. "Hey now, you guys fought hard to take that, didn't you? How much? Let's make it a fair trade of ammo for water."

"Ha-ha-ha! It's true that we captured the river. I must be tired."

"That won't do. Not getting enough sleep?"

"I'd like to get some serious Z's in a proper bed for the first time in a while. After that, I'll take a commemorative photo."

These troops have given up their break periods to fight through battle after fierce battle. It's their right to request proper rotation days, and it's a commander's duty to make sure they rest.

"Rest well," Tanya replies casually before murmuring, "it's such a huge operation. A commemorative photo isn't a bad idea... Maybe we should take one, too."

"It's not bad at all. I'll handle camera procurement!"

"Lieutenant Serebryakov? Good. I'll be looking forward to it."

"Yes, you can count on me!"

So reliable, thinks Tanya with a wry smile as she turns, filled with emotion, to look at the water. With a river like this, the enemy won't be able to retreat like they might want to. That's how bridges become fateful choke points.

"...I guess all that's left is to carry this thing out."

MAY 8, UNIFIED YEAR 1927, THE GENERAL STATE OF THE EASTERN FRONT

By the time Federation Army Command realized what was happening, the Kampfgruppe vanguard was already deep behind their lines.

If even one hole opened, the Imperial Army would come flooding in to force their way into the wound with firepower and infantry. Preventing a breach would require striking the flank of the attacking unit, but due to their loss of air superiority, the Federation Army couldn't even move troops freely.

We shall be victorious.

The moment the Imperial Army commanders were confident of that, their thirst for victory grew even more. Meanwhile, having even a small breach in their lines was a huge drain on Federation morale. The units that were otherwise holding strong on the front lines were forced to retreat due to the threat facing the rear communication lines.

Looking at this from a position of levelheaded objectivity, with the Federation Army's numerical superiority, the balance should have still tipped in their favor. But without air superiority, control of the battlefield returned to the imperial side.

At that moment, the Federation's plan for a major offensive on the eastern front completely stalled out. Far from eliminating the imperial paratrooper rangers who had dropped in their rear, if the Federation troops didn't retreat promptly, they would be under heavy siege.

THE SAME DAY, IMPERIAL CAPITAL BERUN, IMPERIAL ARMY GENERAL STAFF OFFICE

Between the state of wireless communications and reports from the field, even the General Staff far in the rear could tell that the operation was going well.

Even if they couldn't get a complete understanding of the situation until more details arrived, it was clear from the communications that had come in that they were successfully eliminating resistance and advancing.

Still, reports of success from the ground were categorically different from the supposition of an advantage analogized from corroborations.

With staffers walking restlessly by the communications equipment every few minutes and even high-ranking officers puffing endlessly on hand-rolled tobacco instead of their precious cigars, the General Staff Office was practically overflowing with smoke and tension.

Just as everyone's suspense had built to the perfect storm of impatience and conflict, the message they had been waiting for came through like a blessed rain.

"The breakthrough is a success! They broke through! It's a message from the airborne unit's command! They have contact with the Sixth Paratrooper Ranger Regiment and the Lergen Kampfgruppe!"

"...The Lergen Kampfgruppe?"

"Sorry, that's what we're secretly calling the Salamander Kampfgruppe." When some of the staff officers looked confused to hear their colleague's name, a member of Operations explained in a low voice.

"And they managed to do the hardest part, splitting them down the middle?"

"It's confirmed."

"...They really pulled it off, huh?"

After doing all they could and being even arrogantly confident in their plan, they had been forced deep down to seek divine protection in this tightrope act. *So we made it across?* The worry left the faces of a few of the officers. The annihilation of the airborne unit they had feared had been escaped for sure, and if things went well, they might even get excellent results.

Everyone was hoping they could look forward to the next report.

"How about the flanks?"

"We'll know when we get a follow-up... Excuse me." The communications technician clung to the telegraph and took notes for a little while. When he looked up, beaming, he raised his voice. "They're in wireless contact with both flanks!"

A sweet outcome—or hope... The gloom pervading the room was swept away, and the staffers, who had started to feel trapped, were abruptly energized. It was the instant that, for the first time in so long, they were able to regain confidence and certainty.

Their smiles seemed even childlike as all their thoughts turned to the achievements that were being made.

An Operations man summarized the situation and raced to the back of the room to give the good news to Lieutenant Generals von Rudersdorf and von Zettour, who were keeping an eye on overall progress. "The left side needs a little more time to eliminate resistance, but the enemy lines are seriously shaken, so forming a pocket is only a matter of time!"

"We caught them?"

"Yes, General von Rudersdorf! We were able to catch them!"

"I see." The general smiled in satisfaction. "...So we got 'em..."

There was a hint of relief in his nearly soliloquy-esque remark, loud enough for only Zettour sitting next to him to hear. He must have been doing his best not to let his subordinates see his concern. It was deeply unbearable for him to be capable of nothing but hoping for success. Perhaps you could call it a specific type of isolation that high-ranking staff officers experience during in-progress operations.

The moment they were liberated from their worries, both Rudersdorf and Zettour stood up so fast, they practically knocked their chairs over and cheered, ""Hooray!""

All the staffers spontaneously smiled, and soon unsparing admiration was being directed toward the plan's architect, Rudersdorf.

"Congratulations!"

"What?" Rudersdorf demurred with a shake of his head. "No, this is thanks to the airborne unit and the mages accompanying them who persevered for us. It wouldn't have been possible without them holding out for three days and nights in enemy territory." He continued, seeming deeply moved, "I'm just overwhelmed. The least we can do is thank them. Start the decorations applications ASAP."

"Yes, sir."

If he left things up to the staffers who sprinted off with a "Leave it to me," he was sure they would get them done.

The buoyant mood had everyone shouting toasts with the sweet nectar of victory.

But in any gathering, there is always someone sober.

"...So all we have to do now is finish it off." Zettour snorted. He was happy, but he wasn't ecstatic. There was no way he could forget how on the Rhine, they had stumbled in the final stages despite winning a major victory.

"...So we'll encircle and annihilate them using the river. Paratroopers, topography, and the division of enemy military districts... With those conditions, I'd like to say that creating the pocket will clinch it, but..."

"General von Zettour, I get what you're trying to say. We won a neck-or-nothing battle. So we should make sure to wrench definitive results out of it."

"You got me. If you put it so cautiously, I can't complain. If this operation is a success, you'll have my eternal admiration." *Rudersdorf, you win* is what he essentially said with a smile. "That said, an achievement is an achievement. It deserves a genuine celebration. I'll treat you to wine from the Service Corps's secret stash."

"Ohhh? If it's wine I'm depriving you of, I'm sure it'll be delicious."

Zettour rose to the challenge with a shrug. "You can count on it." As the one in charge of mobilizing matériel, he strove to be impartial, but for a victory of this level, he felt an offer of wine was permissible.

"Colonel Uger, sorry to make more work for you, but send over a dozen or so bottles later."

"Understood."

Lieutenant Colonel Uger, who took on the task with a reassuring attitude, was not only a rear-area specialist, he was also a bit of a wine connoisseur. Surely he would select the right bottles.

He could be entrusted the task of choosing bottles for a gift of wine, where one combination could change the meaning entirely! A thoughtful fellow like that who was also an outstanding soldier was a precious asset to the Service Corps.

It came down to trust. When considering an individual who had racked up achievements to be trustworthy, it was only natural to think of that person as a rare commodity.

"...Proper reasoning..." Zettour cracked a wry smile. *That's me, all right.* Was it a bad habit to always be thinking about the correct procedure and structure? When it came to a single gift, it was difficult to deny.

Either way... He shook his head.

It was possible to minimize the error in their calculations. Inferences, predictions, and then action—that was Zettour's duty. In that case, knowing what to consider in this war situation was fairly simple.

First, the Imperial Army was currently dividing and encircling the Federation forces. After splitting them into thirds, it was strengthening the encirclement and then finishing the process with annihilation.

Even a gamble could become a new page in history if you pulled it off.

Future students at the officer academy would end up with more material to study. *But what a pleasant feeling that is.*

That said, nothing means anything until it's firmly in hand, Zettour reflected and shook his head. *We probably can't let our guard down yet.* It would be especially problematic if the enemy decided to try to force their way through the encirclement and find a way out.

"...But if enemy command is operational, then yeah..." By the time he murmured that, he had come up with a new plan. Their victory was already fairly certain, but...it would be an even surer thing if they made one more move.

"All right, let's crush them."

The Imperial Army had been making frequent use of decapitation tactics in this war. A direct attack on enemy headquarters would render their chain of command definitively helpless at a decisive moment.

Sending an aerial mage battalion in on a direct operation against enemy headquarters had been effective on the Rhine, in Dacia, on the southern continent, and even on the eastern front.

Basically, it was an optimal solution.

It may have been a high-risk operation that required air superiority, a minimum of support, and well-trained aerial magic officers and veterans, but when the conditions lined up, its impact was unrivaled.

"Colonel Uger, allow me to ask one more thing of you."

"Yes, sir, anything you need."

"Contact the Salamander—errr, the Lergen Kampfgruppe. Have them check if it's possible to attack enemy HQ directly."

"Are you sure? I don't know if we should go over regional command's head..." Uger pointed out the need for consideration with a frown. But the polite, proper process of getting permission from the regional army headquarters would be overly cautious. The balance between decisive and prudent action is always difficult for an officer. He and Rudersdorf both seemed liable to gaze blankly off into the distance, but Zettour smiled wanly.

"Colonel Uger. You're an excellent officer, but you don't know much about how field officers feel, do you?"

"Huh?"

"On the front lines, what is useful is just. I'm sure that as long as Colonel von Degurechaff is after her prey like a hunting dog, the eastern army group won't have a problem."

Uger blinked as understanding began to come over him. This sort of flexibility was rare in a staffer. *I'll make a note on his performance evaluation later.*

"I'll sound out Operations. Let's get to work."

MAY 8, UNIFIED YEAR 1927, EASTERN FRONT, SALAMANDER KAMPFGRUPPE COMMAND POST

"General von Zettour really runs his people into the ground... I can't believe he's asking us to strike enemy HQ directly."

"Isn't that always what happens? Well...and officially, this is a message for the Lergen Kampfgruppe."

"Yep, it was." *That was the show put on for outsiders.* Tanya smiles at her adjutant. Though form is a pain in the ass, it must be upheld as necessary procedure.

"I'd really like to answer *No can do* in Colonel von Lergen's name. Should I just think of him as below me and have him wear the mud?"

Tanya is half-serious.

That said, she doesn't have time or energy for disguises, and disguises are against the rules. If she's trying to follow the rules in good faith, then she isn't permitted such neglect of her duties.

I guess I have no choice... She shakes her head and then opens her mouth with resignation. "...I guess I'm tired enough to talk about things that are impossible. War follows such an erratic schedule—it's no good."

"I agree, ma'am. But what should we do?"

"The enemy is as fit as ever. We succeeded in surrounding them, but that doesn't mean their stockpiles have run out. I'd like to take my time, but the General Staff prefers a quick surgical procedure."

An encircled enemy is a cornered rat. Tanya, who would like to win with the least effort possible, has no enthusiasm for a plan that involves charging into the desperate Federation forces and getting bit. And there probably aren't any more supplies coming.

"It makes me miss the additional acceleration apparatus."

"Right. If we had those, this would be a lot easier." But as soon as she replies, she's so shocked, it's as if she'd been struck by a bolt from the blue.

Thinking calmly, she decides it's clear that something is off. *Can I really be missing one of that engineer Schugel's inventions?*

Sheesh, war is really doing a number on me.

Even if you report in that you can't accept the risk of losses and express your reluctance, any army has a clear hierarchy—no one is permitted to refuse a valid order.

Our target is a group of positions that appears to be Federation Army HQ. It's within a short plane ride from the river crossing we took, and the 203rd Aerial Mage Battalion has been given strict orders from the top: They expect an attack.

If told to go, I go.

With no time to even lament how pitiful she is, not being allowed to say no, Tanya is stuck taking her battalion on an operation to strike enemy command.

As expected, perhaps it should be said... Despite the fact that the Federation Army's defenses were supposedly thrown up in a few days, their main position is just as well defended as any on the Rhine.

"The resistance is tough! Shit, is this a bear in the hole castle?"

The enemy's fire density, scale, and, above all, desperation are enough to make even the elite 203rd Aerial Mage Battalion wary.

"Enemy mages are on their way up!"

"Direct support for HQ?! They could have just left it wide open for us!"

Tongue-click-inducingly enough, they've got reserves waiting for us. They're making the right use of troops according to the theory. It's so correct, it makes me sick. If this was a sporting event, I'd probably praise their wisdom and wish them a good game, but in wartime, rivals are to be killed or avoided.

Thinking to take advantage of the altitude difference to smash them with an attack, Tanya manifests a formula. When she casts it at the mages coming up to intercept them, she immediately realizes it didn't work.

"These are the new models!"

She doesn't even need Major Weiss's shrieked warning. Only Federation mages with defensive shells via the new model would be able to keep flying no problem after taking explosion formulas from Tanya and her troops.

"So we can't pierce their defensive shells from a distance?! Fuck!"

Using an optical sniping formula with the penetration jacked all the way up will give her a chance. *But it's not like we can leisurely fight it out in the sky over enemy territory.* Then, just as she's getting irritated about her plans being ruined, something happens.

A first lieutenant rushes ahead, leading his company in a charge.

"Company, follow me! Close-quarters combat should be effective against these guys!"

Grantz, all vim and vigor, makes a bold decision. Tanya wonders if she should stop him but decides that she should honor her subordinates' self-starting attitudes whenever possible.

"Major Weiss, back him up!"

"Are you sure?! We'll stick out!"

She understands her vice commander's implication—that making an overt move here is dangerous—but they've already proven in battle that the new models are weaker at close quarters. Tanya begins to think that rather than clinging to the comfort of fighting at a distance, which would needlessly consume both time and energy, charging in is the right idea.

"That fool Grantz is right this time! Support him in the sky!"

Having Weiss handle an escape route and support is precaution enough. With someone at her back, she can advance and mop up.

"Lieutenant, our company's going after Grantz! Charge that echelon!" Tanya waves her arm—signaling "Let's go!"—and is leading the way when she gasps in shock. Suddenly, Federation anti-air positions begin to open up.

Being shot at by the enemy is fine. I mean, that's war. But this is...

Tanya's eyes nearly pop out of her head.

They're going to send a hail of flak up into an area where their own mages are flying?!

"They're not even going to try to distinguish between friend and foe?! These assholes," she spits and immediately begins giving new instructions. As long as it's zone fire, which isn't likely to score any critical hits, all they can do is up their defenses.

"Don't rely on optical deception! Put that energy into your defensive shell! Then pull back for now!"

They abort their strike and turn around. If they had fallen into disarray and gotten separated, her subordinates would have ended up flaming dragonflies. No, even just being too slow would have been bad. If the Imperial Army's computation orbs didn't excel at the mobility and climbing necessary to ascend to greater altitudes, things surely would have turned out poorly.

"They're really putting up a fight... Shit, I never thought we'd fail during a charge."

It's a different era from when we hardly broke a sweat scattering the Principality of Dacia's ranks of infantry. A desperation that says *We won't let you come anywhere near us* has condensed into thick defensive fusillade coming from the anti-air-guns and MG positions.

Of course, it's possible to hit them with formulas from a long-long distance...but it's undeniable that accuracy and power would be awfully low compared to a closer range. And if we merely pump more mana in to make up for that discrepancy, our fatigue will jump to multiple times' normal. War just isn't simple.

"What a hassle that enemy mages have blocked our charge."

Hard defensive shells, fire that doesn't connect. And when you take the fight into close quarters, they respond with the tactics of dodging like crazy and devoting themselves to defense. So basically, they fill the tank role. I never dreamed I'd be in a war fighting to the death against tanks.

As Tanya is about to fret about what to do, she recalls how important it is to be practical. Getting rid of the tanks will be difficult. In that case, *we'll just leave them alone.*

"I'd like to torture them to death, but their backup is in the way. Ignore the enemy mages for now."

"What?"

In response to her adjutant's stunned murmur, Tanya grins ferociously. "Let's break through the mages. We'll attack the enemy surface position directly."

"We could end up being vertically pincered! Please reconsider."

"Don't worry," Tanya says boldly in reply to her adjutant's quivering expression. "You know how well those mages can aim. Any numbskull gets hit, it's their own fault. And if they shoot, their misses will rain down below and make less work for us! All right." Tanya raises her voice. "01 to all units. 01 to all units. Ignore the Federation mage unit! I say again, ignore the Federation mage unit! Stick to checking fire as we pass by and concentrate on getting through!"

There's no reason to smash into a fortress like diligent idiots. The tanks are tough but have limited firing capabilities, so we'll just go around them.

But since there's no art to a mere detour, we'll try for the delightful feat of getting the cross-fire lines to overlap so the enemy winds up taking themselves out.

"Let's go, troops! Follow me!"

We get into three strike formations. The way everyone charges at once with a shout of "Let's get 'em!" probably seems as reckless as a bunch of stampeding boars.

The enemy mages bunch together to try to intercept, and that's the moment their luck runs out. We manifest enough explosion formulas to count as harassment and then launch them to act as a smoke screen. By the time the enemy mages realize, it's too late.

The flight is so smooth, the word *gliding* seems natural. The 203rd Aerial Mage Battalion's charge is successful. They slip between the

Federation mages and the ground positions and are lucky enough to continue their descent.

"God is with us! Troops, let's teach these atheists a thing or two about reality!"

The only disappointing factor is that she is compelled, out of consideration for her safety and results, to boot up the Elinium Type 95. Even if its influence isn't immediate, there's nothing to guarantee there won't be any at all, which is irritating.

"I sympathize with our enemy, that they aren't able to cling to God, even in times like these. No, perhaps they've been spurned and only deny God's existence out of brokenheartedness."

"...Whoa, whoa, Major. I'm not a fan of that sort of chatter."

"Huh?"

"It's my personal view, but I'm giving you a warning. Take war seriously."

"Do excuse me."

Tanya nods that it's fine, and the unit continues along its strike path. In response, the panicked enemy decides to carry out their prescribed defense plan.

...But that is the worst-possible reaction to an unexpected action.

The Federation surface positions stick to their zone fire. As a result... Tanya sneers with overt glee.

"Ha-ha-ha! This is wonderful! Federation troops are killing one another with stray shots!"

The attacks from the ground run into the altitude the Federation mage unit is flying at, whereas the dive-bombing 203rd Aerial Mage Battalion doesn't get so much as grazed.

Exposed to the dense anti-air fire, the Federation mages can't shift from defense to attack even if they want to. Taking advantage of that opening, it's a simple task to hurl explosion formulas at the anti-air cannon positions.

"Manifest formulas! Hit 'em!"

The explosions cast from so close burst. When you don't even need to seal them in a magic bullet for delivery, the casting speed, area covered, and power are on a whole other level. Mage-covering fire, which can be triggered with perfect timing that even grenades can't match, is the pinnacle of violence in an extreme situation.

"Enemy positions have gone quiet!"

Nodding at her adjutant's report, Tanya raises her voice. "We're going to have guests after us! Let's withdraw a bit!"

"...Tag?"

Tanya smiles at Serebryakov, impressed with her intuition. "Why not? Let's play with them."

The Federation mages with the new computation-orb model have only tough defense. Without interference from any other units, it'll be no problem to slaughter them. If they leave their base to give chase, they'll be done for.

Of course, luring the enemy out is a classic move. So naturally the question comes up whether it's really so clever to stage a fake withdrawal. Commanders from every era and nation have mustered every bit of their cunning in order to make the enemy pursue, but...I suppose we just got lucky?

She's not sure how to take it, but basically they didn't have to do anything. Glancing back to see the enemy giving chase with reckless enthusiasm, it's almost disappointing that her worries were for nothing.

Or did they conveniently misunderstand Tanya and her unit turning around as "fleeing" from them? A party's tank has no business making follow-up attacks, but apparently, the Federation mages don't have enough experience to know what happens when you carelessly follow an enemy.

The moment the 203rd Aerial Mage Battalion takes the only roughly aimed fire, they pretend to scatter but immediately round about for an assault.

The Federation soldiers thought they were chasing fleeing enemies, so when the situation suddenly changes, precious seconds go by in their hesitation and confusion, and the elites of the Reich close in and attack.

On this point, I have to admit that the Federation soldiers were brave to stand their ground.

They have fought more daringly than Tanya can comprehend. Sadly, strength doesn't come in proportion to will. With the exception of their durable defensive shells, she's hard-pressed to say they'll have much trouble taking care of them.

After a few minutes of mixing it up in the sky, the only ones left in the airspace are the tenacious members of the 203rd Aerial Mage Battalion.

"We've eliminated all the enemy aerial mages, right? Major Weiss, report in on our losses!"

"A few were caught up in an explosion formula. All companies are still combat able, but we have eight injured. The most badly injured is a numbskull who got shot in the ass. As long as he's not sitting in a chair, he'll be fine."

"So even if only lightly, a quarter of our members got hit?"

She decides to swallow her next thought: *It sure doesn't feel like we're fighting the Federation Army...* They've taken a lot more wear and tear than she imagined they would from assaulting this position. And on top of that, the Federation mages were full of such fight, it made her eyes pop.

...I knew it already, but the Federation Army is growing stronger. Though under siege, the Federation's organized resistance shows no sign of collapsing.

Normally by now, their discipline would be failing with a catastrophic rate of acceleration, so...I'll admit that their stubbornness has increased.

"We may have achieved limited air superiority, but we don't have much time. Just in case enemy reinforcements are on the way, let's do our strike and blow this joint."

"Yes, ma'am! As the documents indicated, the location of a building thought to be enemy HQ has..." He's about to say *been established*, but Tanya stops her vice commander and shakes her head.

"No, there's a very good chance that's deception."

"What?"

"The enemy's probably waiting for us. I can't see that as anything but a trap."

She truly doesn't want to charge into a danger zone. Her whole heart is against it.

Tanya has no interest in approaching a heavily guarded Federation Army headquarters. The Federation has made remarkable progress in anti-mage combat since the time the battalion attacked Moskva directly. Approaching carelessly could leave them with unimaginable burns.

And in the first place, this is an additional task on top of joining up with the paratrooper rangers at the river crossing. There's no reason we should be worked this hard simply because it's possible.

We could end up Swiss cheese.

"Colonel?"

"Federation resistance is tougher than we knew. The headquarters is sure to know what they're doing."

"...Yes, you're right."

"So we can't just be a bull who obediently charges at a red cloth." Tanya works to convince her second-in-command that rushing straight for the Communists' red flag would be risky. "Think about it, Major. Deception is a classic tactic. Expecting the enemy HQ to be incredibly inept is thinking too wishfully."

"So you're saying...they're deceiving us about the location?"

"That's right." Tanya nods firmly. "Is that huge HQ-looking thing really HQ?" she asks rhetorically, as if to say, *Surely not.*

She's hoping it's not, but she's unsure of the truth. Still, it just has to be reasonable and probable enough to persuade Weiss.

If the commander in an assault fails, there's no problem at all as long as they make a plausible excuse.

"...Just as idiots and something-or-other are crazy about heights, Communists like standing out. But lately they have more soldiers."

"Understood. So then we'll have to start from the search?"

Tanya replies with an expression that says, *Regretfully so.* "Make a careful examination of the area. Stay in assault formation and circle around in an effort to search and destroy."

"Got it."

Off goes her second-in-command with a renewed determination. She feels bad for what she's done to him, but since the purpose of the deceit was to keep the losses and fatigue her friends experience to a minimum, her conscience deems it good.

Work should be done with integrity, but it also has to be accomplished within a fair pay grade. Selling your labor for unreasonably low prices only warps the entire labor market to be unfair. The logic is simple. Even ace-level pro baseball players get pressured by their juniors...to push for higher salaries during yearly negotiations.

Since we've already done our original job, and this is just an additional order, Tanya has no reason to try so hard to attack the enemy HQ. Of course, in the interest of self-preservation, she's done the minimum work necessary.

Even if we haven't completely trampled them, since we conducted the assault, we've already carried out the home country's order to *"attack enemy HQ directly."* Even in the case of the Moskva raid, the true purpose was to achieve strategic results by demonstrating that it was possible to arrive in Moskva and attack.

Decapitation tactics achieve something regardless of whether they succeed or fail.

Locating the enemy, collecting geographical data. She can also say that they held the enemy back. As Tanya is thinking that those things together will make a report, she's hit with unexpected news.

"We found them!"

Grantz's jubilant shout echoes almost surreally as it enters her ears. *How can he be happy on a battlefield?*

After a moment of genuine fretting, Tanya refocuses with a start. "What?" She gapes. "You found them?!"

This subordinate of hers isn't clever enough to joke around at a time like this. So did they really discover a hidden base?

"Colonel, is there something special about your nose?!"

"Are you trying to get me to say there's a reason they call me a war dog?"

"C-Colonel?!"

I'm not saying the lie turned out to be true, but I guess you just never know what is going to happen in life.

"Lieutenant Grantz, if you have time to chitchat, be serious about the war—we're at war. You can't do a proper job if you're screwing around."

Anyone as serious as Tanya can't fathom such a thing as joking around during a war.

THE SAME DAY, IN THE AFTERNOON, IMPERIAL CAPITAL BERUN, IMPERIAL ARMY GENERAL STAFF OFFICE

The Imperial Army's Salamander Kampfgruppe carried out a raid on a Federation Army group headquarters. The first report of it was forwarded via the Eastern Army Group to the General Staff, where everyone was waiting with bated breath for results.

At the first word that the raid was underway, anxious staffers began to gather; the room grew so densely populated that even though it wasn't terribly small, it began to feel cramped.

Is it here yet? How about now? They waited for the next report, guests who were not particularly welcome since, whether consciously or not, they leaned heavily on the shoulders of the technician clinging to the communications set.

Communications personnel and staff alike wanted to be liberated from this anxiety as soon as possible—it was unbearable. Even if the former wanted to be free from the imposing presences of the staff and the latter, the suspense, waiting as if every second was an hour, was something they undeniably shared.

Nothing yet? Not even now?

Everyone's entire being was shouting with an incoherent voice. And it was in that atmosphere that whenever a telegram arrived from the front lines, the poor duty officer had to shake his head that it wasn't related and somewhat stiffly, perhaps because he was nervous, get the message delivered to the proper department by officer-messenger mail.

For a time, everyone was made antsy by practical messages from the occupation troops up north or the Southern Continent Expeditionary Army Corps or a scheduled check-in to do with the western aerial battles.

The staffers had run out of patience, and the utterly exhausted duty officer was getting sick of their stares, but then he received a message that made his expression change.

Forgetting even the suppressive fire of looks from the sharp officers focused on his face, he ran his bloodshot eyes over the text and then looked up.

"It's from the Kampfgruppe."

"What does it say?"

Even if the asker didn't mean to press him, he ended up reading it aloud. "From: the Lergen Kampfgruppe. To: the eastern front and the General Staff. We've attacked them directly. I say again, we've attacked them directly."

A direct attack! They went in on a raid and made a direct attack! The message was short but incredibly clear.

"They carried out an air raid on a number of enemy command personnel, including communications personnel and other facilities. The eastern army is currently assessing the results… Wow, though, they did it."

The room erupted in a cheer—"Whoooo!"—and Lieutenant General von Zettour, who was observing from a distance in a corner of the room, nodded at Colonel Uger in a not-dissatisfied way.

"That's why I call her a hunting dog."

"Yes, it's well said, sir. She really did a great job."

MAY 11, UNIFIED YEAR 1927, EASTERN FRONT, JOINT DEFENSIVE POSITION OF THE RIVER AIRBORNE UNIT AND THE KAMPFGRUPPE

"Theater warning! The Federation troops under siege have begun to move! They're attempting to punch through the encirclement!" the technicians on duty at imperial communications apparatuses all down the eastern front tense their expressions and shout all at once.

It's bad news that comes as the Imperial Army is about to begin celebrating the victory they assumed was theirs.

"Now?! They're still capable of organized maneuvers?!"

"I thought they lost all ability to resist in an organized way! What's going on?!"

Of all the… Everyone suspects for a moment that it's a mistake, but having been warned that the Federation is coming, leaving is no longer an option.

All along the eastern front, officers are slapped awake out of nowhere. Those who were off duty and thought they could sleep easy for the first time in a while are no exception.

Not to speak of commanders, who have to rush to their posts and take reports from the officers on duty. Thus, like all the other officers along the eastern front, Tanya zooms to her command post, and when she hears what's going on from the concerned-looking Major Weiss, she's so shocked that she yelps, "What?! They've almost broken through?!"

"Yes, ma'am... Part of the left flank, where the airborne unit is, is being breached as we speak."

She glances at the map that has the latest information written on it... and the enemy troops who should be completely encircled are flooding into the left flank.

It's less the pressure is on and more like it's about to burst.

"It's so sudden... What an unbelievable scene."

The fact that she doesn't shriek, *Of all the ridiculous—!* must be due to the minimum necessary self-control engaging. Tanya considers herself fairly acclimated to her job as an officer, but there's still a limit to what she can take.

Troops under heavy siege breaking through and escaping? Regardless of theory, in practice, it's almost unheard of. Just look at military history from any place or time.

At Cannae, being surrounded by half their number was enough for elite heavy infantry to be totally wiped out.

Not that there aren't examples like Dyrrhachium,[8] but in that case, the power ratio was one to three. It's hard to fight a siege battle when you're the one side of that equation.

Extreme examples such as Chipyong-ni aren't nonexistent, but I wonder if the defense of a regiment with air supremacy can really be applied on the scale of a whole army.

At Austerlitz and at Tannenberg, there was no question that the side that capitalized on its mobility to surround the enemy was likely to win. Surrounding and beating on the enemy is simple but a sure thing. So someone with Tanya's common sense would never doubt their success.

But now the siege was being broken?

"Sensibly thinking, it's impossible. How is the enemy able to maneuver in an organized way? And more importantly, what are our troops

[8] **Dyrrhachium** A balding, womanizing king heavily laden with debts managed to encircle a great and just senator's army that was much larger. Then the king lost. Of course he did. The king with debts was Julius Caesar, and it was one of his few defeats.

doing? Shouldn't they be building defensive lines with the rest of our guys by now?"

Unlike when the airborne unit suppressed the crossing on its own, both flanks should have received multiple reinforcing units by now, including armor.

Are they late? Or having trouble? Or are they just idiots who let the enemy get through? *No.* Tanya kicks the thoughts getting her nowhere out of the back of her mind and allots the majority of her brainpower to figuring out what remedial measures will patch up the situation.

"Shit! Hurry and round everybody up!"

"They were at separate posts in order to both manage the position and support the defense… I'll have them rush back."

"Yes, do that. Ohhh, no, wait."

She adds that Major Weiss should stay and calls upon the young officer who is easiest to order around.

"Lieutenant Grantz! I'll leave spurring them on to you. Get everyone together no matter what it takes!"

"Yes, ma'am! Right away!"

Feeling good about him racing off, Tanya rapid-fires orders to prepare for the enemy attack. "Lieutenant Serebryakov, go make sure the airborne unit is prepared to blow up the bridge! If they need support, you can give them Lieutenant Tospan's infantry!"

"On it!"

"Major Weiss, I'm sure you're tired, but I want you and your unit to stand by. If the enemy can pull off an organized escape, it's entirely possible they could come attack us here."

Just then, a subordinate interrupts to call her: "Colonel!" It's Captain Meybert, who seems to be rethinking the bombardment zone as he peers at the map. "Excuse me, but…it's about the bridge. This mission could be completed by artillery. If need be, do consider destroying it via artillery barrage."

"What? You can target it?" Tanya shoots back, somewhat skeptical. After all, shells are surprisingly inaccurate. The guns Meybert has at his disposal are highly advanced, including the fact that they are self-propelled, but even then, they connect with the intended target only every few shots. Unlike precision-guided munitions, the accuracy of indirect shelling is only in the realm deemed "good enough" when suppressing an entire area.

"If it's just that bridge, we can take it out with direct fire. At the very least, we can create a temporary obstruction."

"You can hit it?"

"If you order us to."

There doesn't seem to be any excessive bravado in Meybert's attitude as he volunteers for the job. Tanya's cheeks ease into a smile at his professional way of putting it. He's a guy who's hyper focused on his specialty, so if he says he can do it, he probably can. "All right." Tanya nods and tentatively accepts the offer. "Just make the preparations for now, Captain Meybert."

"Who decides whether we destroy it? Can I?"

"Hold your horses, Captain."

It's worrying that she has to wonder whether he just wants to shoot, or gets an ego stroke from being entrusted with difficult work, or something similar.

"I'll make one thing clear. You can't forget that destroying it isn't actually optimal." She doesn't neglect pressing her point. "If you rush just because you want to cause some destruction, we'll have problems…"

"Of course, I know that."

"Very well. The likelihood of us being attacked here isn't very high, but just in case, I authorize you to destroy the bridge on your discretion if it comes under attack. But make sure you talk to the airborne troops first. Do *not* blow them up."

The artillery officer nods his understanding and occupies himself with some calculations. Passion in one's work should be encouraged, not reproached.

"Now then." Tanya waves over her vice commander. "Major Weiss, at any rate, we… Hmm?"

"I'm back."

The look on her adjutant's face as she jogs over and salutes is fairly tense. Weiss must realize, too. They exchange glances and swallow their sighs, and Tanya questions her as she salutes. "Thanks, Lieutenant Serebryakov. Have the bridges the other units control been blown up?"

"…Apparently, they weren't allowed to…and now it's too late."

"What…? Not allowed to?" Before she can ask why, her adjutant is already replying.

"The paratrooper rangers were told to hold the bridge without damaging it. Other units apparently received similar orders, so…" It was evident what she was trying to say. The bridges under our control were all supposed to be kept undamaged and passable, so the Federation Army's escape route was still hanging over the river.

What in the…? Tanya closes her eyes in spite of herself.

If the bridges are still up, that means there are places where it's possible to cross. If the enemy breaks through a single point, there's an undeniable risk of their escape.

"So they weren't able to destroy them. This is a problem, Colonel." Weiss nods as he comments, and Tanya snaps in reply.

"The General Staff is greedy."

"Greedy?"

"Yeah," she responds to the vice commander's confused question. The urge to occupy an undamaged bridge is one every staff officer has had in map maneuvers. If you can do that, you have a way to advance swiftly. And you can secure a supply route. In other words, a bridge is something that makes it possible to go somewhere that would otherwise be inaccessible.

…So then, considering that we're in the middle of working out a diplomatic compromise, perhaps the General Staff is using the bridges as a threat against the Federation Army— *If you don't accept our terms in this negotiation, we'll invade.*

Securing a bridge that serves as a route to attack is convincing proof. There isn't much else that would pressure the enemy so elegantly in terms of making it clear that invading is possible, so I get how they feel.

But though we may have the enemy encircled, we're spread far and thin. If we can't hold them, blowing up the bridges should be an option!

"I don't know if this is just posturing or if they're serious…but apparently, the higher-ups want to demonstrate that we can invade. Of course, the ones who have to do all the work are us in the field."

"Demonstrate? Sorry, but to whom?" Serebryakov asks, and when Tanya sees her blank look, she realizes her mistake: The negotiations going on in Ildoa are top secret.

"Oh, it's nothing. Never mind. Forget about it, both of you."

"Yes, ma'am."

Her adjutant and vice commander politely acknowledge their understanding, so Tanya politely nods.

It's terrific that they mind their manners even on the battlefield. Tanya is proud of her subordinates, but she suppresses a sigh as she laments her misfortune as the one stuck dealing with things her superiors find inconvenient.

She has to make sure the disappointed-looking artilleryman next to her gets it. "Captain Meybert, you heard her. I take back that permission I just gave you."

"…I'd like to act on my own authority…"

"Captain, the home country wants us to secure an attack route. Are you telling me you can do that even if you destroy the bridge? Is that kind of action possible on your authority?" She shoots him a glance that says, *I can't allow it. You understand, I'm sure*, and then switches gears. "Captain Ahrens, defend the bridge. An armored unit defending a bridge—mm, yep, just like in the movies. It's no fun if the villain gets beaten too easily!"

"Leave the defense of the position to us. We'll coordinate with Lieutenant Tospan's infantry and the airborne guys to protect the bridge."

"Good. It feels great to have someone I can trust with things. Okay then, as for the rest of you: We got the short end of the stick. We have to hurry and support the other troops."

So it is that Tanya takes off—*Let's go!*—leading only the 203rd Aerial Mage Battalion, which makes rapid response such a breeze.

Putting the swift deployment aerial mage forces are known for on display and heading straight to the rescue is a job they've been used to ever since the Rhine. You could say it's a skill they've mastered.

But the few differences from the Rhine worry Tanya to no end.

Especially troubling is the status of the air fleet. For a time, after a successful battle of annihilation, it had taken control of the eastern skies, but now it was gone. Judging from friendly radio and other communications, the fleet's operating rate had plummeted.

Have the planes been worn down that much? Or was the preliminary plan not enough? In any case, the expansion of the air forces is so slow, it can't even be compared to how things were during the Rhine.

Surely the eastern army's aerial mages are out, but…it doesn't seem like we can expect much from them. Unlike Tanya and her troops, who had it easy at the beginning of the offensive with their tank desant, those who tangled with the Federation forces head-on are utterly exhausted and suffered terrible losses. With obstacles to proper leadership mounting, their ability to respond in a rapid way is essentially about to give out.

"Our job is to prevent the enemy from withdrawing, but…we're basically already too late."

"So…we won't make it in time?"

The two mid-ranking officers with dark looks on their faces discuss the situation. Tanya answers Major Weiss bitterly.

"Air interdiction is impossible without more friendlies. It's only a matter of time before they seize the bridge."

The Imperial Army is spread far and thin. Encirclements are inevitably that way. If the enemy concentrates on one point to wage a fierce breakthrough in an organized fashion, it's nigh impossible to stop them completely.

And if the various factors to keep it from happening aren't functioning…then there's trouble.

"I agree… Shall we be the vanguard to retake it?"

Asked if they should take it back if it gets taken, Tanya shakes her head. "I thought about it, but there's not much point. I'm confident we can destroy it, but if it's about occupying it, that's the infantry's forte. So a flying aerial mage unit isn't the right force to apply. Furthermore," she adds, "the Federation Army, having come this close to collapse—I don't want to think they could really arrange organized reinforcements at this point—they're desperate, too. Trying to retake a stolen bridge would occupy them for too long and could even end in failure."

True. The officers nodded—they have a good grasp of battlefield psychology. When it comes to securing an escape route, both commanders and their soldiers do everything in their power.

This is often misunderstood, but the existence of an escape route is only one of the factors that affect how well soldiers are able to hold out.

Certainly if their retreat is threatened, that's frightening, but having their retreat cut off can birth soldiers who no longer fear death, which is a threat of its own.

"In that case…what is being asked of us is to reduce the number of enemies who are able to escape."

"You mean a pursuit battle, in the end, is fought best by slamming the enemy's weak point?"

"Right." Tanya nods at Weiss. That's her hunting dog. The habit of sniffing out and biting into weaknesses is commendable. Tormenting the weak can be praiseworthy, but only when the weak in question are your wartime enemies.

"Enemies trying to flee have such fragile spirits, you know? Let's beat them up."

"If *you're* the creep following them home, Colonel, I feel bad for them."

"That's funny—I was about to sympathize with them for being tailed by you guys."

I guess we have that in common. The officers share a mild joke—what a cozy battlefield. The team has great vibes and an excellent drive going on. *The Federation Army must be so cold and distant; I'm sure we're in a much better situation organizationally.* Tanya is proud of her personnel-wrangling ability. It's nice to have confidence in your management skills.

"We'll crush what remains of enemy headquarters. That'll prevent an organized escape." Having changed the mission objective at her own discretion, she continues, "Let's go!" Regardless of whether she understands the enemy, she's confident that she understands herself.

An aerial mage battalion—and an elite one at that—can consider all sorts of different tactical options. Even so, it's still just one battalion. Even elites who can deploy swiftly, have outstanding firepower, and are always polishing their cunning combat skills can't free themselves from the limitation of numbers.

So Tanya chooses to ditch the interdiction mission that requires ability in numbers in favor of a harassment attack with the objectives of decreasing and disturbing.

To discuss this change of plan beginning with the results it achieves, the 203rd Aerial Mage Battalion once again carries out perfect decapitation tactics.

"...Given the large amount of signals coming from over there, that must be the place. Let's get 'em, troops!"

Having gotten a ballpark idea of where the headquarters is from the formations and wireless activity, they pick out units that seem capable of operating in an organized fashion and attack once more. She leads her unit—they rampage as if to show off what aerial mages are really good for—and the one-sided throttling of the Federation troops who have lost control of the sky is the easiest job since Dacia.

Even the Federation Army, which had given us so much trouble, became a bunch of sitting ducks once deprived of air superiority. It was so frustratingly easy that Tanya is sure the air fleet would have been able to stop them if they hadn't been running late.

As it stands, the 203rd Aerial Mage Battalion, which is able to respond quickly in an organized way, wreaks incredible havoc as a single operational unit. It was such a big job that when they return to the Kampfgruppe's provisional forward base, Tanya feels the fatigue weigh on her shoulders the moment they are met by Captain Meybert of the group left behind.

"Any issues while you were here?"

"No... Captain Ahrens said he wanted some action, too."

"Ha-ha-ha, I just had so much time on my hands."

Outrageous. Meybert's report makes Tanya justifiably indignant. Ahrens hasn't the slightly idea how blessed he is. Any civilized individual vastly prefers boring guard duty to a firefight on the forward-most line.

"You mean staying behind as defense was boring? Wish you would have traded with me, then!"

"Ha-ha-ha-ha!"

Ahrens cracks up and Tanya glares at him. *Ugh, you piss me off.* Maybe the aerial mage battalion is being exploited.

Thanks to which, it has to work so hard during this escape interdiction mission.

She can assume that their successes will be properly valued, but...she doesn't like noticing that the higher-ups have this scheme of working capable units to the bone. The General Staff's judgment is logical, but for those on the ground, it's a hard-boiled logic.

Tanya would like to expect that they'll be rewarded proper medals and leave.

Ahhh—it's there that she switches gears. After all, it'll be hard to get a leisurely paid break if she doesn't finish off the work in front of her.

They've pulled off a major operation, achieved a lot, and they just need to make good use of the victory. I can't imagine Lieutenant General von Zettour and the General Staff will make the same mistake they did on the Rhine front that time.

"Okay, no matter where they were breaking through, we've given them a solid beating… We can probably consider the Federation Army incapable of organized resistance now."

So.

With that bit of wishful thinking mixed in, Tanya makes the mistake of dreaming of a bright future.

"Maybe the encirclement will hold, but…"

"Yeah, you're right. Some might get away. Unfortunately, you'd be hard-pressed to call the cleanup effort perfect. Still, we set the tone. If we just wait for the good news…"

"Telegram!"

"Oh?" Tanya's eyebrows move, and it's only until that moment that she expects a positive report.

Once she realizes the sobered signaler is wearing a pained expression, it's easy to tell that the news isn't what she had hoped for.

"The left flank's bridge has been seized!"

It's the predictable bad news. The way multiple sighs are heaved at once is almost comical, as if they had planned it in advance.

"I guess that's according to expectations. It's too bad, but we can't hold it all down."

"Indeed," rejoins her vice commander; he and Tanya had resigned themselves to the fact that at least one position would fall.

That's why they've been able to maintain composure this whole time—and why in the next moment, they're shocked speechless.

"…The first, second, and fifth crossings have been captured! The enemy is escaping in an organized fashion!"

"Wha—?" she gasps. To Tanya and the others, this is the rudest possible surprise. If the head is crushed, the arms and legs are supposed to fall to pieces!

"The airborne unit on the left flank is under attack from an enemy tank division...and has been breached! Multiple enemy units including armored troops are currently breaking away!"

"How?! We definitely..." *...crushed their headquarters.* She's about to say those meaningless words when she realizes. "...Did they plan on that happening?"

Did they assume headquarters would be lost and use its functions as bait from the start? The Federation Army commanders prioritized the escape?

She wants to say it can't be true. It was clear from the interviews with POWs and the survey of enemy formations that the Federation Army was a command-by-direction army!

If the encirclement wasn't broken in reality, she would laugh this off as a delusion. But now, that's impossible.

"So they were the rear guard from the very beginning?! Fuck! That's some serious preparedness!"

The Federation Army is a unwaveringly strict pyramid. For...better or worse, it prides itself on its iron discipline, so its head should have been its weak point. Even Tanya believed without a doubt that if the head was crushed, the lower body would be paralyzed.

"So the lower units were able to coordinate and make adjustments without the oversight of headquarters? Shit, that makes them a thinking army!"

"A th-thinking army?"

"The same as us—the same as the Imperial Army!" A cry like a shriek stabs her throat. "They aren't a command-by-direction army! Fucking hell, this—they've changed to mission oriented!"

Command by direction is a rigid system where the procedure, route, and even tactics are given in strict orders and you merely do exactly what Command tells you to. Frankly speaking, even amateurs can be a decent fighting force if they follow the instructions, so in that sense, it's useful for armies created through mass conscription.

On the other hand, mission-oriented tactics are how extremely high-level pros do things. Command sets a "mission," and all the details are left up to the discretion of the subordinates… To put it another way, you can't possibly use this style unless you recognize your subordinates' initiative and trust their judgment and resourcefulness.

Is such a thing even possible in an organizational culture like the Federation Army's or the Federation's Communist Party's, where everyone is devoted to carrying out what the top decrees?

"…So it's possible?"

Tanya murmurs and cradles her head in her hands.

It can't be, she wants to yell.

It must be some mistake, she wants to groan.

It's absurd, her heart is screaming.

But all you can do in the world is look at reality as it is. Averting your eyes from what's real in search of what you want to see makes you a fool who can't even understand what's in front of your nose.

Guys like that deserve contempt. They're not the type you want to have as friends.

THE SAME DAY, IMPERIAL CAPITAL BERUN, IMPERIAL ARMY GENERAL STAFF OFFICE

To the staffers belting out triumphant melodies at the successive good reports from Operation Iron Hammer, the announcement came like a face full of frigid water from the coast of Norden.

The encirclement's been broken? Everyone's expression stiffened in horror at the news.

The report that they'd been breached sent the General Staff, who had been convinced that victory in the east was theirs, literally reeling. This was Operation Iron Hammer, the major maneuver using the river as an anvil. If the critical river was crossed, and the enemy field army escaped, it was an utter failure.

The tension finally broke, and even the officers who had been dozing jumped up. Hanging on every word of the detailed reports that followed to explain what happened, they went through all manner of emotion and, at the next report, heaved a sigh of relief.

That is, the pocket including the headquarters was escaping, but a follow-up attack from an aerial mage battalion and armored unit got results. The rest of the pocket remained trapped.

"So for now…for now we're fine…"

It was enough for a few people to feel better. Operation Iron Hammer may not have gone off perfectly, but it wasn't a complete failure, either.

Still, anyone with some foresight furrowed their brow and groaned. Lieutenant General von Zettour of the Service Corps was no exception.

When he received the news from Lieutenant Colonel Uger, whom he'd been working hard as his assistant, he fell deep into thought; then, having agonized for a time, he spat in a pained tone, "…They got away?"

In a nutshell, he was stunned.

"I never imagined they would be able to operate in an organized way under these circumstances. The Salamander Kampfgruppe raided the headquarters, didn't they…? This is a huge problem."

"A h-huge problem?"

"If it's true, yes."

"We have records of their achievements as well as photographs. They definitely hit the headquarters in that pocket. There is even photographic evidence that a full general and other high-ranking officers were blown away. I can't imagine the report was falsified."

"Yes, of course I trust the reports from our troops," Zettour replied with a smile.

If this was a mistake or a fabricated report, there would actually be less cause for headaches. The big issue was that the breach happened due to the enemy's increased capabilities rather than an error on the imperial side.

"They're not such idiots as that. We can assume the headquarters was actually attacked. So do they have an officer who could salvage the situation, then?" Zettour spat in irritation. How could the Federation Army perform an organized breakthrough while under siege? …And after multiple attacks on the top?

"Sheesh, so the Federation soldiers have some talent, too."

"…But we did win."

Uger's point was true. It felt like crossing thin ice, but the Imperial Army on the eastern front had pushed the lines up dramatically, and the enemy field army was annihilated.

They were occupying enemy territory and had demolished the enemy's main forces. Now, even Moskva and other Federation cities were within reach of their attacks.

If the offensive had been even a little later...the enemy would have been able to regroup, and the Imperial Army might have been powerless. On top of that, the ground was turning from mud to dry dirt. The timing was perfect.

"Apparently, they really were able to rebuild a chain of command. It's good we were able to hit them now. It will take time for their strength to recover. If we can figure out a diplomatic solution during that time..."

It was the *rough-and-ready trumps polished-but-slow* thing.

Yeah. At that point, Zettour shook his head. *That Rudersdorf and I have different temperaments is simply human nature. Rather than being jealous of my old friend's talents, I should focus on my own strengths.*

"Colonel Uger, I want you to get some information from Intelligence for me. I'd like you to ask about Federation Army commanders, especially."

"Understood. I'll have them dig up everything they have."

"Please do. Just because we're getting close to negotiating a cease-fire doesn't mean we can let our guard down."

"I know."

"Okay," Zettour finally said, nodding.

"I'm counting on you."

[chapter]

V

Turning Point

"History isn't certain until it's written in the history books. And it's rare to find history that can't be rewritten."

Commissariat for Internal Affairs Loria

»»» MAY 11, UNIFIED YEAR 1927, FEDERATION ARMY PARTING MESSAGE «««

From: Western Army, Political Commissar Representative Hobrov and Commander Representative Lieutenant General Markov
To: Federation Army General Staff

Headquarters has given all remaining troops strict orders to withdraw. Command wishes to act as rear guard for their comrades' retreat. If even a single soldier can be saved, we're satisfied.

We are currently taking suppressive fire. At this moment of parting, Command would like to thank our comrades who fought with all their might. But we are unable to repay the sacrifice of our comrades fallen in the mud. Having lost air superiority, all we can do is pile up losses in vain.

Though it's well-known how vulnerable ground troops are when control of the airspace is lost, we take this opportunity to reemphasize that threat. The unique maneuvers the Imperial Army employed in Dacia have now been proven many times over in several other battles.

- *Even if achieving air supremacy isn't possible, stop enemy aerial attacks with an ambush if a chance present itself.*
- *Strive to improve weather forecasts.*
- *Aerial mage units put up a serious fight, so defend with your lives. Though the war situation has worsened, hold your ground.*

In response to some doubts related to rank issues, we believe that our troops proved their innocence with their flesh and blood. We hope you will recognize their contributions.

Additionally, we're at a disadvantage against an enemy with a less-rigid organization, so we require greater flexibility and agility on the operational level. We hope you'll consider these systemic issues.

- *We've noticed that repetitive phrasing in political commissars' messages and reports weakens the effectiveness of the ciphers encoding them.*
- *Our operations often seem to be found out when messages are sent. This seems to have led to the leaking of our HQ location. There's a good chance that was the cause of this aerial-mage-unit attack. Please use officer messengers and work to shorten messages as well as avoid repetition.*
- *Frequent use of ideological terms is an extreme weak point in terms of encoding.*

Please know that necessary intelligence being restricted during operations can invite extreme difficulties. But aside from Command, everyone did their best.

Letting our comrades die like dogs was entirely Command's failure, so please refrain from blaming the units beneath us. I wish luck to all our comrades in arms.

Long live the motherland, the party, and the people.

THE SAME DAY, MOSKVA, COMMISSARIAT FOR INTERNAL AFFAIRS OFFICE

The moment he finished reading it, the feeling he had was of a great nothingness. In response to the outcome of the clash with the Imperial Army, the commissar for internal affairs, Loria, emitted a deep sigh.

"...How awful. I never thought it would get this bad."

The official report, the copies of telegrams, and the insider he'd sent to inform him...

"Numerical superiority, plenty of equipment—we even improved the supply lines, and this is what we end up with?"

Their current status was more miserable than he could have imagined.

An enemy airborne unit caught them from the rear, and after throwing them into confusion, the Imperial Army, with armored troops as the main thrust, punched through their front to encircle and annihilate them. This army should have been doubly prepared for this day but collapsed so fast, the fight was like a scene from a poorly made propaganda film.

The only difference between that and one of those videos the party made was the gap between the heroes and the villains.

With the exception of the Federation Army, which was supposed to win, getting mopped up and being driven off by the Imperial Army, which was supposed to lose, everything was just like in the films. The fellows at the studio were apparently more talented in their pursuit of reality than one might think.

Shall I send them all to Sildberia? The resemblance was so uncanny that he half felt like actually taking out his anger on the filmmakers in that way.

"So this was a serious blow to the army, then?"

A little effort apparently wouldn't be enough to turn the war around. One read through was enough to see that. To put it plainly, this situation couldn't be solved with the all-purpose *lack of revolutionary spirit* line.

"Tell me something, comrade. Were there any issues with how the Western Army was operating?"

"I hear it was basically according to doctrine, sir."

This staffer had a lot of nerve for a mere colonel—implying that ultimately, it wasn't the army's fault.

Of course, that's why Loria had chosen him to serve under him.

"Just to confirm, when you say *basically*, do you mean there was some exception?"

"Apparently, there was some planning with the political commissars in the field to reinterpret orders how they saw fit."

"Comrade Colonel, I'm not blaming anyone. This inquiry isn't about making accusations. Could you perhaps tell me what sort of changes were made to the doctrine?" Loria continued, "If I felt like purging somebody, I could make up any number of reasons. I just want to know what the situation is on the ground. My question is clear, Comrade Colonel. What sort of changes did the commanders in the field require?"

"...I don't think it's the sort of thing that bears reporting to the Commissariat for Internal Affairs..."

"Comrade, I thought you understood me."

After all, the General Staff kept sending him liaison officer assistants like human sacrifices. Even this colonel had only recently been able to speak without flinching.

"To put it simply, they were slight tactical improvements made on the ground taking into account the skill level of the troops and the partial tactical withdrawal."

"Ohhh? *Slight?*"

"...Comrade, couldn't you please accept *slight...?*"

Although the purging of the military was a great success when it came to bending it to the army's will, when it came to acknowledging the officers' self-respect as specialists and making good use of them, it seemed his predecessor had gone a bit too far.

In the end, perhaps the omnipotent medicine of revolutionary ideology was pseudo opium. So the path to establishing socialism would require some adjustments. As long as they were trying to bypass a bourgeoisie revolution, necessary fixes should be made along the way.

"So I'd like to ask a question. Does our army need to make major changes on the ground?"

The colonel was silent, but at the point that he didn't blurt any denials, his true feelings were out. And to go a step further, those feelings were surely the feelings of the Federation Army's General Staff.

"Hmm." Loria nodded before giving his conclusion. "So there's an issue with the doctrine?"

"Comrade Loria, may I say something?"

"Our beloved comrade forerunners said that knowing the problem was halfway to solving it. Shouldn't we be happy to know where the problem lies? Smile," he said with a grin at the colonel, who was growing nervous. Then he continued, "Let's be frank. I didn't think we would lose this badly. Wasn't the army's estimation that even if we took a counterattack, we'd be able to end things in a stalemate if we made it a firefight?"

"I beg your pardon, but you probably want to talk to someone higher ranking..."

Grinning warmly, Loria peered into the colonel's eyes. Checking his reflection there, he seemed to be smiling fairly nicely. Nevertheless, every liaison officer selected by the General Staff ended up, unconsciously or not, backing away from him.

"May I hear what the General Staff thinks?"

Across the desk, the colonel stood at attention, and Loria felt it wrong that he was sitting, so he stood as well and reached out to put a hand on the man's shoulder.

The colonel had a fine physique with plenty of muscle... If Loria sent him to the *lageri*, he would be a decent source of labor. But specialists like him had to be made to contribute their specialized knowledge. Loria knew that was more profitable for the party and the motherland.

"Hey, comrade."

"Y-yes?"

"I'm merely interested in hearing what a specialist such as yourself thinks. I'm not going to tell you to turn in your superior or inform on anyone. You understand that, right?" Loria, for his part, had already stationed whistleblowers and informers in the General Staff by the gross. There was absolutely no need to have this colonel take that role. What he needed wasn't a report from an agent but the mainstream view of a specialist on the inside. "What are things like at the General Staff Office?"

"Honestly, the shock has everyone frightened."

"They're shocked? Hmm, kindly continue."

It was very easy for Loria to tell when someone was overly nervous.

The expression on the colonel's face as he agreed was one of someone trying his best not to have any expression at all. If Loria had wriggled his nose, surely the man's face would have tensed up even further.

That said, scaring him would achieve nothing. Loria urged him on in the tone he felt sounded like a loving father.

"I don't understand soldiers' thought processes perfectly, but I understand how you feel. I didn't expect the kind of losses we suffered this time, either. So?"

At Loria's comment, the colonel, nodding, opened his mouth to speak. "Our superiors sent in their pet security division and a division of artillery. We were fully expecting excellent results. No one thought it would end like this."

"Hrm." Loria growled and fell silent.

It wasn't as if it was a horrible habit, but higher-ranking officers of the General Staff were exceptionally talented at making safe remarks.

He was capable of discarding the linguistic flourishes, but he couldn't for the life of him fathom why the colonel felt it necessary to give a report that simply rephrased the word *shocking.*

...Is he that hesitant? In that case, I definitely have to know what's going on.

"Let's stop beating around the bush. What happened? I want to believe we put forth our best efforts, but..."

"...May I speak frankly with you, Comrade Commissar?"

"Of course, Comrade Colonel. Isn't that a given? If there is anything at all I can do for the people, I want to hear about it."

There, Loria realized he didn't phrase that well. The colonel before him, who had gone pale as a sheet, was like a little bird right before being sentenced to exile in Sildberia.

That wasn't Loria's intention this time, but...since he had used the same line to clean up a great many reactionary elements, including his predecessor, perhaps it would be better if he changed his phrasing.

"It seems like I should rephrase that, comrade."

"N-n-not at all—"

"Yes, I should." Loria shut him up with a wave of his hand. "Even if the army gets any punishment for the defeat, it will be left up to the court-martial. I personally guarantee that the staff of the Commissariat for Internal Affairs will not intervene. Relax," he said grandly. And the reaction was extreme. The colonel, who until moments ago had been one step removed from a corpse, came back to life like Lazarus.

"...Could you make that promise to the General Staff?"

"I'll support you at the party meeting. And I'll talk to Comrade General Secretary personally. Is that enough of a guarantee?"

"Thank you!"

"As long as you're happy. So?"

"Huh?"

Apparently, the colonel was so delighted, he had forgotten something important. Loria would endure the political commissars' unpleasantness only in exchange for *him talking.*

"I want to identify the problem. Then we'll report it to our comrades along with Comrade General Secretary and fix what needs fixing… Comrade, don't you think it would be difficult to defend the army if there wasn't a problem?"

To put it another way, if he didn't talk, there was no guarantee.

"…Well, the problem…"

"Yes, what is it?"

"A lack of air superiority. We failed to eradicate the enemy from the sky."

"The fleet was supposed to have received a good amount of reinforcements. Didn't it?"

"……Comrade. It…"

"Comrade Colonel, I can tell from your attitude thus far." Loria patted the colonel's shoulder with a sigh and sat back down. If he was being this generous and a man with guts still couldn't speak his mind…

It wasn't hard to imagine the existence of a taboo.

And what sort it was.

"Is this about aerial mages?"

"……Yes, comrade."

Though he replied timidly, it was probably praiseworthy that he'd honestly admitted it. Loria needed men like this.

"I'd like you to explain. Isn't the effect mages have on air superiority negligible? I've heard they can only be a minimal threat to planes."

"The issue is everything about them. This is an extreme example, but aerial mages mainly fight at lower altitudes. We have reports of Named who are flying higher, but they're in the minority."

"I'm aware of that. What about it?"

That's how that fairy came to visit Moskva.

If he had known, he would have personally done much, much, much—multiple times—more to keep her from getting away.

…He had given the point people who had made light of mages bodily reeducation, but this was such a huge defeat that he was compelled to feel that wasn't enough.

"Air combat at its essence is getting into position. This is the root of a large misunderstanding."

"I don't know much about it, but the idea is to get behind the enemy to fire, right?"

"Yes." The colonel nodded, and he began to explain the basics of aerial combat in a familiar way. It made sense that the General Staff had dispatched him as the liaison officer.

"According to ace pilots, practically everything depends on finding the enemy as well as a superior spot to fire from."

"I see. So it's not like the old days where you used to just point guns at each other and shoot."

"No, it's as you say. That's why it turns into a dogfight and getting into a good firing position becomes so critical. So," the colonel continued, "on this point, our mainstay fighter planes' specs are such that they're much faster than mages, which meant...that on paper, with those specs, they *were argued* to be superior."

With the repetition of the word *specs*, even a man who wasn't a military specialist could imagine what he was trying to say. Surmising that it must have been mere theory, Loria shook his head. "So what's the actual situation?"

"We can't even engage."

Loria gasped in spite of himself. It was easy enough to regain superficial composure, but inside he was troubled. *News to me...*

Of course, publicly, they had stressed that it was possible to resist mages with planes.

"Why not?"

"Planes need to land on runways, while mages can land anywhere their mission demands."

That was enough to explain that they had a choice. Once the colonel was satisfied the commissar understood, he said something rather quickly that Loria had never heard before.

"To be perfectly honest, rather than fighting it out with the planes, they can hole up at ground level and transform immediately into an anti-air firing nest."

"What about taking them out with the infantry?"

"It would be extremely difficult to defeat them with infantry firepower. Anti-tank rifles just barely work, but it's too hard to aim at them with bolt-action models."

In other words, from an operation standpoint, it was impossible to use infantry for this job.

"I thought we were able to boast that they were 'reactionary relics' slower than planes, weaker than tanks, and fewer than foot soldiers."

From the dumbfounded look on the man's face, Loria realized his childish comment was being misunderstood, so he hurried to take back his joke.

"I was kidding, Comrade Colonel."

It wasn't that he didn't understand. On the contrary, he knew what a little filly his precious fairy was. How satisfying it would be to break her.

"They can be deployed more freely than planes, their defense is solid enough to be comparable to a tank's, and they're also as multipurpose as soldiers, right? ...Sheesh, I thought I had it figured out in my head, but this really is a handful of a service, huh?"

The reason a military power like the Empire, or a highly militaristic organization like the Imperial Army, would make such extensive use of aerial mage units was that they were so convenient. It was impossible to laugh them off as anachronistic reactionaries clinging to magic.

He had to acknowledge their advanced maneuvers that had taken off the tops of not one but two, three forces. The Empire's magic army wasn't about ideological reaction—it was progressive.

"So only aerial mages can fight aerial mages? Hmm, but this is indeed a problem."

"Huh?"

Blank looks. *Right, these guys are soldiers, after all.*

"And it's awkward that the Western Army was emphasizing the contributions of the aerial mages, Comrade Colonel."

These guys are so dense, thought Loria, feeling slightly irritated. Soldiers paid too much attention to practical matters. He couldn't have them looking down on theory and politics.

"You must think we threw too many of them into the *lageri*, but this is a bit of a delicate matter."

"Why is that, comrade?"

"Doesn't it sound like *an excuse*?"

Though the colonel said nothing, his shocked expression showed that he acknowledged his mistake. Their view must have been clouded as they marveled that he had actually out and said it.

"...But they were trying so hard to tell you what was actually going on."

"And you're right, of course. The problem is that I and many other *nomenklatura*[9] weren't informed of any of this to begin with."

The magic officers during the czarist period had been a firm force of resistance against the revolutionary administration. Federation *nomenklaturas'* allergy to magic was severe. *Magic? We'll drive it off with science.* That's what they boasted, and in reality, they were close to eradicating the mages within the Federation, so it was difficult to change their mind so abruptly.

"...It can't be justified politically." A soldier groaned in a strained voice and Loria simply confirmed.

"I'm not sure it's necessary to be so extreme, but...if pressed, I'd say you're right. I mean, even Comrade General Secretary dislikes aerial mages." *So it's true?* they asked with their eyes, and Loria added with a wince, "If you faced resistance from them in the counterrevolutionary war, and more recently nearly got your house burned down by them, wouldn't it be logical to hate mages?"

"Yes, you're right, comrade."

"That said, we can't ignore the realities of the battlefield. We should be able to say *To hell with it* and reinforce our mage units in a big way."

"Reinforce...?"

Loria was used to being stared at in disbelief. But getting a look containing respect from sober soldiers undestroyed by ideology made even him blush.

"We have to use anything we can. That's war."

Digging up and learning the minute details about these creatures known as aerial mages while chasing the fairy, his precious one, was a major factor.

We can use aerial mages.

No wonder the previous establishment had made such good use of them. That was the conclusion this capable pervert of a political monster Loria arrived at. Though it was a sensitive matter, politically and

[9] ***nomenklatura*** Privileged individuals who exist in an equal society that has done away with classes. They're just on a list of those who work for the people and are not unlike anyone else in any other way. Of course, anyone who doesn't make that list will never get anywhere in life...

ideologically, to praise heroism and magic theory too much, he had to admit that aerial mage units had their uses.

"Haaah," he sighed quietly as he lamented, "at this rate, the state will regret not conducting proper magic aptitude tests."

Mages were the elites of the czarist era. In response to the revolution, mages had long been seen as enemies of their class.

In the context of the Federation, it was like being born in original sin.

For that reason, though the Federation's Communist Party recognized that mages required "reeducation," the idea of actually performing an extensive search for talent was missing. Well, that made sense. Nobody wanted to go anywhere near that taboo. To tell the truth, they had the technology to test for magic aptitude...but it was used to expose antiestablishment factions. If they wanted to throw someone in the *lageri*, they tested the person, and if they had the aptitude, they were locked up for being a mage in hiding. It wasn't called a "modern witch hunt" for no reason.

Sheesh. Loria shook his head.

His specialty was politics, not the military. Things outside one's area of expertise went better when left to an expert on a leash.

Shrugging, he winced. *I'm not cut out for this.* Then he reached for another document case and began to look over the neat bundle of papers.

"Now then, I have to read these results..."

They had suffered a major loss on the lines against the Empire. The politburo was even unofficially debating a temporary compromise with reactionary influences. *Wouldn't a cease-fire and peace happen if the Empire was reasonable?* It was easy to imagine many party members thinking that.

But...as far as Loria could see, it was unclear whether they would get a cease-fire, much less peace.

The Federation Army had suffered a major defeat. The Imperial Army was winning fight after fight. If no one could beat the Imperial Army, then peace was a kind of theoretical. And only a theoretical.

And a cease-fire would be difficult to accomplish. Loria remembered with a wince how many times they had gotten into battles over terms in order to reach a cease-fire agreement during the civil war.

All the numbskulls obsessed with how things "should" be clung to the word *probably*.

This was the definition of ludicrous. It took only one glance at human history to see how poorly this species understood anything. Putting together an encyclopedia of stupidity would be an undertaking on a national scale.

But he was looking forward to seeing the other side of the possibilities that *probably* presented. He was taking a close look at the documents that had been collected into a report so he could prepare for any potentialities when his brow relaxed slightly.

"...Oh?"

In his hand was a survey of living conditions inside the Empire. It wasn't a highly classified document, but public opinion in one's enemy countries could be surprisingly key.

Sometimes the nebulous spirit of the age transformed into something else.

"I figured the Empire was pleased with their victory, but...are they drunk on it?"

It's a possibility, but as far as I can tell from this editorial... Do they not even realize they're oozing this greed?

He flipped to another translated article and a smile crept across his lips.

"Oh, oh, oh?"

The fervent public opinion in the Empire was that fruits "worthy" of their "victory" should be demanded. Loria could appreciate that to an extent, but as far as he could tell, this was much more than he would have expected.

"A huge sum of reparations, outrageous demands... You want this much in exchange for peace?"

An EIC drunk on victory spouting grand nonsense about the Empire leading a new world order was one thing. And it was plausible that the people of the Empire wanted reparations.

But... That was as far as Loria could understand. If the environment in the Empire was such that they could dribble their ambitions all over the papers like this without any restraint, that meant something definitively different.

"This…this is… O-ohhh… It looks like we have horrible luck!"

He was sure that all imperial publications went through the inspections. That meant that for this article to pass, a censor had to feel that it had no issues. In that case, it represented "their" latent consciousness as a whole society.

"I thought there were people over there who understood politics, but…I guess they aren't the ones in power. This is just so…" *…fascinating.* He grinned inwardly. "More than enough is too much. Apparently, we don't have a monopoly on repeating your mistakes."

The Empire guarded its military secrets heavily, but in terms of politics, it was completely naive. They had far too little experience with this type of thing.

It made their awareness of espionage, which was not low by any means, a miserable thing. Even Loria, who considered himself immune from pity, wanted to express his condolences.

They were cautious against "spies."

It was both correct and idiotic. They protected only the things they wanted to hide and left everything else out in the open—despite the fact that the whole premise of information warfare was putting together innocuous little things like a puzzle to paint a bigger picture.

Loria's exhalation trembled with desire.

"So people really do support you when you're on the path to love…"

He thought he would have to give up on his sweet little fairy, but he was no longer anxious.

The war will continue long enough for me to pluck her.

"…This is what's so fun about ochlocracy."

The Imperial Army probably thought they were censoring the press… but censorship wasn't enough. What the newspapers needed was guidance, but the Empire must not have understood that.

The Empire was an old country, after all. They operated by tradition, so their imaginations were stuck in the old world.

They were right to call themselves, their Reich, a military power. Their state was built by the army. They knew nothing of political influence—they had only ever flashed their swords.

"How utterly fascinating and ironic…"

Meanwhile, in the Federation, the party was supreme. It was only natural that the Empire and the Federation had different strengths. And there was no reason one had to attempt to compete in the other's field.

"...So we really should fight with politics."

AROUND THE SAME TIME, FORMER ENTENTE ALLIANCE TERRITORY, THE NORTHERN LIBERATED ZONE (WHAT THE PARTISANS AND FEDERATION ARMY CALLED IT) / THE REGION CRAWLING WITH PARTISANS (WHAT THE EMPIRE CALLED IT)

Perhaps it happened because the Federation's change of direction was being discussed on a grand-strategy level. Someone rolled a die for fun, and the whole world began to change as a result.

The clash on what the Empire referred to as the eastern front became a huge turning point. The aftermath came like a flood and necessarily impacted the operations of the multinational unit in former Entente Alliance territory, which was considered a secondary front compared to the eastern front.

Like all things, it was the result of the guidance of an invisible hand trying to accomplish something that no one intended.

Yes, somebody called it an invisible hand.

Either way, it was inevitable that orders for redeployment of aerial mages under Commander Colonel Mikel would arrive from Federation Army authorities. If they were desperate for mages on the main lines, it made sense that they would scrape together seasoned troops from wherever they could get them.

...But theory was only theory in the end. Asked if it resonated, Lieutenant Colonel Drake was actually discouraged.

"I didn't expect to be withdrawing... I understand the necessity, but wow, it's a drag."

"I guess consideration for the partisans' interests won out in the end. We're only guests here. Even if we leave, it won't affect them that much."

"It's because they've been cautious that we can leave without being crushed under guilt."

"...I guess we should be grateful for their wisdom."

"No doubt about that." Drake nodded emotionally to Mikel's comment.

What started as information sharing and propaganda had grown into building a network. In addition to standard Entente Alliance language, they had been putting in an effort to learn some dialect to grab the hearts of the people, but now they were being told to withdraw.

"Barring other orders from the home country, we'll probably withdraw with you. The problem is how to get away. Should we just accept that it'll give off a huge mana signal and do a long-distance flight?"

"That's a bit too much ingratitude."

"Right."

The chance of mages lurking in partisan territory being high or low would surely be a large factor in how the Imperial Army would deal with them. Naturally, the partisans, who had the short end of the power imbalance, would hope the imperials would be cautious.

So the tactical intel of the departure of Mikel, Drake, and their troops was something they would want to hide for as long as possible.

"Still, it's only a matter of time before it comes out."

"...We gave some of our equipment to what few former Entente Alliance Army mages were left."

"Sorry, former mages? I never heard anything about that."

"I only learned of them officially just now."

"...Reserves?" Drake asked, but Mikel shook his head.

"Worse. They're the age of my dead grandmother."

"Oh man. War really does a number on respect for the aged, huh? Are they just decoys carrying orbs around? That's something else..."

"Well, if the orb reacts... And what's more, apparently, they all volunteered."

"Volunteered? They allowed that?" He refrained from saying, *Under these circumstances?*

"That's what it would mean."

"...I'll pretend I didn't hear that. Some of my subordinates are too sensitive to news like that. I don't want any more discipline issues."

"Makes sense."

"Politics is just such a pain. But war is even more of a monster. You never know what will happen tomorrow."

"You mean this world is just one big *lageri*? Ha-ha-ha, that's pretty funny." Mikel was trying to laugh it up, but his mouth was tense.

Drake was considerate enough to pretend he didn't notice, but he had the feeling he had caught a glimpse of something that left him no room to say anything.

"The world outside is still better, Colonel. Out here, I can fight as a human and die as a man of my homeland."

"That's what you want, huh, sir?"

"It really is. All right, let's explain to our guys that we're packing up... Well, the main lines will be a harder fight than we've had here—there's the potential to deal a real blow to the enemy. Let's think of it like that."

"Understood."

Reviewing their conversation, Lieutenant Colonel Drake stared silently into his mug of now lukewarm tea, feeling bitter.

Why is it that whether it's tea or your mood, they both have to cool down?

If he had to give a reason, the conclusion he reached wasn't very gentlemanly. Maybe it was inspired by the problematic individual sitting across from him, who made him a bit weary. *She's such a handful...*

"We're withdrawing? Now? At this critical moment?!"

"That's right, Lieutenant Sue."

"But the partisans are only just finally—finally—starting to accept us! If we would just hold our ground! We could free my homeland!"

Even Drake could understand what the look in her determined eyes was trying to tell him.

"I agree that they're accepting us. Even I agree with you there. We're withdrawing right as we're able to build a cooperative relationship. I'd be hard-pressed to say it's not unfortunate."

"Then!"

Most of the highly mobile imperial troops had been sent to the eastern front for the major head-on clash with the Federation Army there. The Devil of the Rhine who had so tormented him previously and the other enemy aerial mages hadn't been operating in their area of the former Entente Alliance territory, which meant things were going well. But that was also what gave Sue hope.

...So... Drake sighed before he spoke. "The situation has changed."

Things had changed so much, he probably should have added *fundamentally.*

"I'll give you a short explanation. The recent Federation offensive led to a decrease in imperial troops in and north of Norden, which gave us a major advantage."

"So then shouldn't we stay…?"

This girl arguing about whys was a first lieutenant in rank only; Drake realized, as an officer, that he had to give a straightforward explanation.

"I'm going to get to the point, Lieutenant Sue."

He knew telling her to shut up with his hands, mouth, and eyes would be rough. Nevertheless, he held up a hand, told her to shut up, and glared at her. Perhaps his final act of kindness was to withhold the *Just listen*.

"Unfortunately, our allies in the east lost. It was a major, full-frontal defeat."

"…What do you mean, they lost?"

It was never fun to be the bearer of bad news. And once they had learned that the Federation Army wasn't 100 percent pure Commie, it hit closer to home.

Colonel Mikel and other good people like him… And so many of them. Far too many must have sunk into the mud.

"The Federation's military, mainly the Western Army, carried out their counteroffensive as planned, but the operation failed. Problems piled up, and the counterattacks conducted by Imperial Army units have brought their lines close to collapsing."

Close to *is a kind way of putting it.*

Drake inwardly mocked himself. The intel and map made it obvious. The imperial units didn't let the awful muddy roads stop them in their resolute advance to the east. The Federation Army lines should have been stopping them, but they fiercely shoved them back.

The worst news of all was that decapitation tactics had been used. The Federation Western Army Headquarters, which should have been handling the situation, was almost completely destroyed.

"The details haven't been confirmed, but it's been reported that the regional headquarters has been annihilated. And the report mentioned a familiar enemy…the Devil of the Rhine."

Those words—*the Devil of the Rhine*—had a dramatic effect. Up until that moment, Mary had been keeping a discontented silence, but at the mention of that name, her mouth twitched nervously.

Her expression changed, and she stared at Drake for more information. He worked to keep from wincing and continued, "Apparently, they used classic decapitation tactics."

"Headquarters wasn't prepared for that?"

"That's a good question."

For a moment, he actually felt like he was having a conversation with a fellow officer. As a magic officer of the Commonwealth Army, it was only natural to learn from the battlefield. Drake had a curious fondness for talks and lessons like these.

"My personal guess is that…it would be weirder if they didn't have a defense plan. It seems reasonable to think that they got punched through despite that."

"You mean even after taking preventative measures?"

"I'm sure of it." Drake nodded without hesitation. "Those measures are just trial and error, you know."

"…So that means this enemy didn't leave room for a single error?"

"Right." Drake nodded as if he had been thinking the same thing himself. "And that mage battalion must have been those guys. If they were the ones who attacked the headquarters, then it makes sense that even the unexpected would turn to expected."

"And that's why headquarters fell?"

"Yes. That's how I personally see it."

Even a fully outfitted marine mage unit wouldn't have been able to prevent it with some half-baked preventative measures if they met some real, salty pros. If Drake himself was ordered to protect HQ from those guys, he was anxious that he would have a hard time unless he could come up with something awfully clever.

"When we get back, we'll be able to read a proper report. Are we on the same page, Lieutenant?"

"…Yes, Colonel. Your view makes sense to me."

How nice it is to just nod and say thank you. Sensing this was a good chance to have a talk with her, he continued, "What our allies have found out so far is that the chain of command was destroyed so suddenly that things fell apart. Then it was an encirclement-and-annihilation battle."

Decapitation tactics. They came around so often, they might as well have been the Imperial Army mage units' traditional performing art.

Apparently, even if you resisted by strengthening direct support and using every anti-air gun you had, imperial aerial mages would somehow find a way through.

After Mary heard that explanation, she asked a single question. "Were there any other reports about the Devil of the Rhine?"

"There are signs she's operating on the eastern front. Unfortunately, it's hard to get any information besides that. Sorry." As he apologized, he finally got to the point. "So that's why we need to move. All our fighting forces must head to the eastern front. That's what joint HQ decided."

She glanced at him. The look in her eyes, like that of a child who didn't want to go home, got on his nerves. If this was a marine magic officer of the Commonwealth, he would have told her not to be so servile, to have the self-respect of an officer, but…she was a volunteer and part of a group who had been through a short, accelerated training program.

It was an awkward situation, but Drake felt he had no choice but to argue her over to his side, so he spared no effort and said all he could. "Experienced mage units like ours are needed on the front lines. We may be receiving guidance from the Federation units, but our presence on the forward-most line will demonstrate an international united front."

"S-so you're telling me to just abandon the Entente Alliance?"

"Don't misunderstand, Lieutenant. That's definitely not what I'm saying."

It was clear as ever that to check the Empire, it was necessary to compel them to carry out operations on multiple fronts. Or, rather, it was even more important now. The strategic value had risen since the Federation's major defeat on the eastern front.

There isn't a single soldier who feels nothing for their home. Soldier or not, who doesn't have feelings for their home? It's natural to have a bond with the land you were born on.

So for once, Drake could sympathize with this Entente Alliance girl Mary Sue. No matter how crazy she was, how embarrassing, or if her emotional grasp of the ideas could use some work, in his head, he respected her feelings.

"I understand how you feel. So I promise you as an officer and on my honor as an individual: As far as I know, the higher-ups don't have any intention of abandoning it, either. At least," he continued, "according to Colonel Mikel, the Federation intends to continue their support. They're in a tough spot themselves, which is probably why they're hoping the guerrillas will dominate the northern part of the Empire."

Weapons aid, intel support, and training if necessary—the Federation Army was working hard to provide the orthodox basics of partisan support.

"But wouldn't real support mean staying?"

"...Honestly, I'm not so sure."

There was a simple reason the option of remaining didn't come in his conversations with Mikel. It was just that clear how badly mages were needed on the main lines.

"I think we're pretty effective at supporting the partisans..."

"...It's not as if we have no effect, that's true. But it's also the case that the type of support we can provide is disjointed and limited."

"What do you mean by *limited*?"

"The Republican Army tried things like long-range mage-unit advances and militia support on the Rhine front, and everyone knows how that turned out. What happened at Arene was undesirable, to put it mildly."

The plan for a mass uprising of militia supported by aerial mages had seemed perfect on paper, but it was powerless in the face of the overwhelming force of a regular army.

The besieged troops may have been holed up in the city, but if they couldn't disable the enemy guns, they ended up as mere targets. Whether the world wished it so or not, it had to be acknowledged as reality.

"But here we—"

"You're trying to say that since the enemy is dispersed, they're somewhat subdued?"

Sue nodded, and in part, her impressions were correct. *Unexpectedly*, perhaps it should be said...the Imperial Army had become distractingly restrained and polite in response to the threat of mages mixed in among the partisans.

"I guess we should take it that they're using what they learned cleaning up on the eastern front to deter partisans."

"They…learned?"

"That's right." Drake nodded. "They've realized how foolish it is to overreact to sporadic attacks. But there's a limit to these things…"

Once a threshold was crossed, they would necessarily turn into beasts driven by raison d'état. If partisans and mages holed up at the root of the communication lines or a foothold put up organized resistance, a heavily armed unit would show up.

"Ultimately, the harassment we're carrying out is within what the enemy can accept. So don't you think it would be better to do something more than harassment on the front lines instead?"

"But if you can't leave the unit, I could…"

He had expected her to say that, so he wasn't surprised one bit. And even Drake could understand. The love for her homeland that made her want to stay, want to continue resisting, was commendable. But his position was such that he had to reply with a sober expression. "If we're going to fight a clean war according to the rules, I'm not sure a solo mage staying behind for a combat mission will fly. Regardless of the interpretations for a unit's fighting, the interpretations for a single combatant are split."

"That's ridiculous. I—"

"It's not that I don't agree with you, but it's thanks to those ridiculous rules that we're just barely maintaining human society. That's just how it goes."

"How can you—?"

"Please appreciate our situation, Lieutenant. It's undeniable that our being dispatched here was based more on political factors than military strategy. Listen." He broke things down to persuade her, hoping she would understand. "Sending a large aerial mage unit was an unprecedented measure to begin with. Considering how the war situation is worsening, the only right move is to withdraw before things get more complicated."

If they were stuck trying to withdraw after the Empire sent a cleanup unit farther north than Norden, partisan trust in the Federation and Commonwealth would be compromised.

Should I just spell it out? Drake braced himself to speak. "If we act now, we can use the worsening war situation as justification to move." *You get it, right?* He looked at her.

Withdrawing wasn't a choice that felt good for anyone.

But now and only now could they pull out with the least friction. At this point, it was still possible for everyone involved to find common ground.

"I'll be frank, Lieutenant. If we have to beat a fighting retreat, and your homeland gets caught up in it, you'll see a jump in losses."

He was trying to be logical and meet her in the middle, not just drown out her voice. *This would be so easy if she would just understand.* With that hope in mind, Drake said a prayer as he gave her his final conclusion.

"We're moving out. Have the troops get their stuff together."

"...Yes, sir."

"You get it?"

If she would understand, even if reluctantly... If she would just understand as an officer, as a soldier, with some part of her mind...

"...Will we...or I...be able to come back again?"

"Let's hope so."

"Hope? ...Understood."

"You do? Thanks."

That was a little nod she just did! At that moment, a weight was lifted off Drake's shoulders—he could have cheered.

Even naval artillery shells are lighter than this! he thought; his face muscles were threatening to grin, but he pulled them into a sober expression.

"If we can, it would be great to see everyone again."

"Yes, it would be great if we could all safely meet up in the future."

"Well, I guess I'll get packing."

"Please do."

Sue looked the same as ever as she saluted, but to the extent that he could see her endeavoring to imitate the officer manual, he could at least term her a novice soldier.

Has she ameliorated some of the nonsense in her behavior?

...No, what is it? Something standoffish? Wait. He abruptly called out to stop Sue as she was about to leave the room. "Could you wait a moment?"

Something was bothering him.

That was all.

But Drake's hunches were what had allowed him to survive so long.

"Lieutenant Sue, tell me something honestly."

"Sir?"

"Having discussed it this much, I think you understand that we can't leave you behind, but..."

"...Ngh. Yes, sir."

"You want to stay so badly that you would go absent without leave?"

"Colonel Drake, please..."

"I can't let you do that."

"...There's no way?"

Contrary to how easy her expressions were to read, she sure lacked understanding as usual. *What can we do with her?* Drake was realizing that he was out of ways to persuade her.

He could shout her down or throw every bit of logic he had at her, but this one's determination wouldn't be rocked by anything so simple.

With no other choice, he reached out a hand and called up the Federation-side HQ.

He was used to the procedure of the interpreter picking up on a single ring and challenging the caller. "It's Lieutenant Colonel Drake. I'd like to leave a message for Colonel Mikel. Can you tell him that I have someone here who needs convincing from one of his political officers?"

"Yes, Colonel... But *convincing*, sir?"

From the slight gasp and puzzled question coming over the receiver, it was clear that the man didn't understand what was going on.

Well, of course he didn't.

Why would an interpreter have any idea why a Commonwealth soldier would be requesting *convincing* from a political officer?

"He should understand if you tell him I'd like First Lieutenant Liliya Ivanova Tanechka to speak with her friend First Lieutenant Mary Sue. She seems to be awfully homesick. I feel like a friend would be able to get through to her better than someone like me."

"Understood," the interpreter responded, and after a brief exchange in Federation language, he relayed that they had agreed. "That can be arranged. Was there anything else, Colonel Drake?"

"Thanks. That's it. I appreciate it."

When he clunked the receiver back into place, he gazed up at the ceiling in spite of himself. *Things should be fine for now, at least.*

...Or maybe I should hope they will? But no, political officers follow orders well enough to make themselves useful.

"What a mess this is."

I never thought the day would come that I'd rather have an obedient Communist as a subordinate. That's just terrific. I've never even daydreamed of it since my first day in the service.

"...Shit. I get it, but... Why does there have to be such a huge discrepancy?"

Ever since the Great War broke out, so many aerial mages had fallen, yet the imperial units remained their army's sharpened spear tip?

The enemy mages burned army headquarters while my subordinates are off living in their own worlds. O God, whatever is this trial for?

AROUND THE SAME TIME, EASTERN FRONT, IMPERIAL ARMY FORWARD POSITION (AT THE CROSSING)

Even flawed, what is a victory if not a victory? Especially if it's a definitive victory that will probably go down in history.

The eastern front is broader than those where we wiped out the Republican Army, but when the enemy carried out an all-or-nothing offensive, we surrounded them in a reversal. That's virtually a golden formula for crushing the enemy field army.

Having come this far, the Imperial Army has realized its long-cherished desire.

In the strategic realm, this was our second encircle-and-annihilate operation. And what's more, the victory comes with a huge leap forward compared to the time we did it when our own territory was under attack.

All's well that ends well. No one is thinking about trivial errors during the last step. In the end, it was such a brilliant breakthrough in the east, which was deadlocked not so long ago.

This is what it's like to get a supremely sweet sip when you're dying of thirst in the desert. Or maybe it's even better than that. A complete victory is a seductive wine that can steep you in feelings of omnipotence.

We won, our enemies lost, and the name of the Reich, crown of the world, has been proclaimed far and wide. At this point, the Federation will have to start thinking about a compromise.

Even Lieutenant Colonel Tanya von Degurechaff is overjoyed, hopeful that the Treaty of Brest-Litovsk[10] is just around the corner.

That's what a magnificent victory it was.

On the operational level, it must have been definitive.

"Ha-ha-ha! Wonderful! This is wonderful!"

With a smile like she's gotten exactly what she wanted, Tanya strokes her relaxed cheeks in spite of herself.

When was the last time I smiled from my heart?

After getting thrown into this stupid world by Being X, I've been struggling in the Reich with its mess of crazy neighbors, and finally, finally, there's some light at the end of the tunnel.

I'm ready to raise a hearty cheer.

Though we may have let some of the defeated remnants get away, all that faces us is the Federation, having lost its field army. If the Council for Self-Government is encouraged by our military victory and becomes even more pro-Empire, peace and security should be possible after the war.

...It'll be at least twenty years of peace. Given that much time, they'll secure a splendid position in society, defect, make a name for themselves, or carry on with a peaceful, secluded life—they'll have the freedom to choose how to live.

Freedom. Yes, golden freedom.

And so, with the camera First Lieutenant Serebryakov procured from somewhere slung around her neck, Tanya and the other officers of the Salamander Kampfgruppe even have enough time to take a commemorative photo.

"Colonel, would you like to take a photo?!"

"Please do!" Tanya replies to her camera-wielding adjutant, practically

[10] **Treaty of Brest-Litovsk** The peace treaty between Germany and Russia (the Soviet Union) in World War I. Of course, Germany's victory in the east is often ignored, since they failed to win in the west...

shouting, *It's worth commemorating!* in her buoyant mood, standing on the bridge they captured and posing.

"What a great job the airborne guys did securing this position unscathed! And I never thought we'd have so much film!"

"It reminds me of Moskva."

"Moskva, Lieutenant?"

"Yes." Serebryakov nods with an unaffected smile. "Because we used film we borrowed from the Federation."

"...Oh, that's what you mean, right."

Photographs and video may be different media, but the two occurrences shared the fact that they had played around with equipment acquired on the ground. Just like Sun Tzu said, being able to procure supplies in enemy territory is such an advantage. It's efficient, cost-effective, and, best of all, doesn't take a thing out of your own pocket. Tanya is in such a good mood, she asks Serebryakov for something she never would normally.

"Once the photos are developed, bring me a few. I'd like to hang them up."

It may be quite different from selfies on social media, but it's always a good idea to have some material to show off. Photographic evidence for discussing one's career with a worldly air is incredibly important—*I was there that day.* It's a practical application of signaling theory, or perhaps an extension of it.

"Of course! Please expect the highest-quality finish!"

"I will, naturally!"

Then she smiles and strikes some poses. Maybe she goes a little overboard, and just as it hits her that other people are watching, too...

"You're in a really good mood, huh, Colonel?"

"Ha-ha-ha! You bet, Major Weiss. I'll say this, since it's you I'm talking to...but *I'd be an awful party pooper if I wasn't happy right now.*" When she asks, "Don't you think?" with a sidelong glance, everyone laughs, proud looks on their faces.

Great coordination, she thinks, though she can't overlook the stern face on a mid-ranking officer she sees out of the corner of her eye.

...Apparently, he heard me making fun of him loud and clear.

"Hey, Colonel von Degurechaff. Congrats on the victory."

"Oh, if it isn't Colonel Calandro!" She salutes ostentatiously as if she only just noticed him.

He salutes so sincerely—he must be good at putting on the right persona for the occasion. "I congratulate you on behalf of your ally Ildoa."

"Thank you. The airborne guys really pulled it off. No, it must have been the organic coordination among all the troops and our allies."

"Perhaps," murmurs Calandro. The esteemed Ildoan guest worked so hard, but…Tanya and the others have pulled off such an outstanding victory that they're a bit excited. "Please allow me to commend you on the splendid job you did. Only hearing really is…nothing compared to seeing. Whoever said a picture is worth a thousand words had the right idea."

"Oh?"

"Personnel, teamwork, support—I feel like I've gained a peek at a high-level way of combining these elementary factors."

"I'm honored," Tanya replies adroitly with a smile. "Thank you so much for your kind words."

"…You don't have to stand on ceremony. Those are just my genuine feelings."

"Well then."

"Congratulations, Colonel von Degurechaff. Your state has really done it. I'm sure a cease-fire is only a matter of time now… You could say there's a diplomatic out in sight now, right?"

"If we don't get tripped up. With all due respect, it's not within our grasp just yet."

"But practically, it is, no?"

"The difference between *almost grasped* and *actually in hand* is subtle but very real."

Once upon a time, the Empire let a rat called De Lugo escape. When we realized he was less like a rat and more like a tiger, troops were sent to the southern continent. And now it has become evident that a few divisions down there won't be enough.

Given that failure, she wants to make sure that this time, their victory is complete. Wishes come true if you don't give up. The army has the overwhelming advantage necessary to get the Federation to agree to a cease-fire. After achieving that difficult victory, the rest is up to the diplomats.

"Until the cease-fire is agreed upon and peace realized, we're still at war. And if it's war, then soldiers must continue fighting to win."

"Not one to let your guard down, huh? That's a fine thing."

Tanya looks back at Calandro. *Why would I?*

Tanya isn't such an imbecile that she would neglect learning from her mistakes and let victory slip away twice. Tuition for the teacher called experience is too high. Paying twice for the same lesson isn't cost-effective at all. Or really, it's just a waste.

"Security is the greatest enemy, they always say. And isn't the truth everywhere you look?"

"I see." Calandro cracks a tired smile. "You have a point. Generally speaking, you're right. But—may I say something?"

"Of course."

"You're young. No, I don't want you to take that the wrong way. What I really mean is, look at all that you've accomplished at your age. It's praiseworthy. But there are some things you will only realize as you grow older." He laughs it off as the babbling of an older man.

Tanya considers how best to argue back but realizes none of the options benefits her, so she responds with a polite, vague smile.

Silence is golden. Gold is justice.

"Ultimately, what wins is common sense. Colonel von Degurechaff, no one wants to continue this ridiculous war at this ridiculous scale. If I may say so, the current situation is abnormal."

"...I have next to no experience in society outside of the army, so all I can say is that we shouldn't rely on wishful thinking."

"But with these results, it must be a sure thing. Having suffered a defeat this massive, even the Federation... Ah, but any more than this is just trying to see the future, and it's not the sort of thing we mid-ranking officers should be discussing anyhow." Calandro chuckles, as if to say that he's making too many predictions. "Don't you believe in the victory of reason, Colonel?"

"I believe in my own reason. But I can't be sure about other people I hardly know. I expect them to be reasonable, but trusting them is difficult."

"But raison d'état is different from the personal sort, isn't it? Besides." He gets a far-off look in his eyes as he continues, "The members of the Imperial Army General Staff, at least, seem reasonable... Ahhh, errr, I really am saying too much now."

"Hmm, that's trouble for me. If a colonel is going to clam up, then won't a mere lieutenant colonel like me have to be even more silent?"

"You got me there. I'm not usually so talkative. It'd be a lie to say I don't have an opinion, though. I know I should just be celebrating your achievements... Congratulations—that's really all I can say."

To the opportunists, even if the Imperial Army's definitive win isn't awful news, it's hard to call it good. This is probably an embarrassing position to be in for a soldier from Ildoa.

It's a stupid farce, but Ildoa—even like that—and the Empire are allied nations.

"To be frank, I just didn't think this would happen."

"Didn't think it would happen?" *Interesting.* Tanya engages. She's incredibly interested in hearing on what basis Ildoa ended up trying to take advantage of the situation. "Is this a chance for me to discreetly inquire as to how the Ildoan General Staff thinks the war will go?"

"*Nein*, if you'll allow me to brush off the question like they do in your country. I don't doubt our ally's victory for a minute."

"Sure," says Tanya, about to thank him. Calandro is being awfully generous today. In the end, these guys are sensible.

So they weren't sure if the Empire could pull it off?

Well, that's a reasonable level of wariness, thinks Tanya. The Imperial Army may be on a rampage against the entire world, but that in no way guarantees a victory on this scale. And it was close, so you can't even say they made assumptions without thinking and ended up being proven wrong.

"At least officially?"

"Of course officially."

"Do excuse me. Everything you say is correct, Colonel."

Sharing an unspoken understanding is a strange bond. Shrugging our shoulders and making liberal use of the space between the lines is actually quite intellectual and not unpleasant.

"What a rude lieutenant colonel you are."

"Well, I was raised in the field."

"...I'm not sure what to say to that. Is this the sort of animal a Silver Wings recipient is?"

"Maybe."

Perhaps it's the anticipation of being able to participate in civilized activities like this more often once the war is over that's getting me excited.

Cease-fire, pacification, and then peace. At least I hope that's what happens.

"Well, I can't compete with that. I suppose I'll be going now."

"As long as you're here, why not tour the battlefield? I would hate for you to write in your official report that the Lergen Kampfgruppe didn't show you much of anything."

Tanya makes the offer out of pure goodwill. Calandro is nominally here to observe, and he's doing us the favor of going along with the "Lergen Kampfgruppe" fiction.

"As luck would have it, the principal officers of the Salamander Kampfgruppe, beneath the Lergen Kampfgruppe, happen to be free. I could have someone take you around."

"I appreciate the offer, but that's all right."

"Are you sure?"

That much entertaining we can do pretty painlessly..., Tanya was thinking, so she's caught off guard by this unexpected reply.

This is curious Colonel Calandro we're talking about. I thought he would be interested.

"Let's just say I spent the day having a good long chat with Colonel von Lergen. I can write that up with no trouble."

"So, then?"

"I won't interrupt your celebration. Have a wonderful time."

She is about to say, *You won't join us?* But she knows you're not supposed to do things you know someone won't like to anyone but your enemies. After all, Lieutenant Colonel Tanya von Degurechaff is an individual of common sense.

"Thank you. We will."

"Please do."

"Yes, sir."

Thus, with the mood still buoyant, the Salamander Kampfgruppe with Tanya in the lead raises a triumphant cheer in the direction of the far reaches of Federation territory.

We've annihilated multiple corps.

We've acquired a path to invade. And more than anything, the military supplies we were able to seize are like a blessed rain upon the Imperial Army logistics org.

"Colonel! One more shot!"

"Sure! I'll take some of you, too!"

Everyone mingles, beaming.

Struggling to focus and take a picture with a looted camera—errr, a trophy of war—isn't something you get to do every day. Though she knows how to work one due to having used them on reconnaissance, she never thought she would have the leisure to take landscapes and portraits; the scent of civilization nearly moves her to tears.

It's just such a beautiful fragrance.

"Hmm? Wait a minute."

Sniff, sniff. When she wiggles her nose, she detects a good smell. If it's real…it's something we haven't seen on the front lines in quite some time…

"Huh? Where'd that come from?"

"It's a special ration from the beloved party, Colonel! We stole it from enemy HQ when we attacked."

The camera, the alcohol, mostly provided by the Federation. *Ahhh.* Tanya shivers at the delectable horror of barbarian economics even as she enjoys them.

"Lieutenant Serebryakov! Use all our funding! Buy out the alcohol in the area and serve it to the Kampfgruppe!"

"Are you sure, ma'am?"

"Of course! Oh, and one thing before I forget. The airborne guys did a great job, too. I want you to pay our respects."

"Certainly. I'll distribute some to them in the spirit of sharing!"

Commies are horrible precisely because you can start to think, even as a joke, that Communism might not be so bad. If the unproductive practice of taking from havers went on forever, the efficiency of distribution in such a looting economy would be fantastic!

"Lieutenant Serebryakov, feel free use some of the classified funds from the Kampfgruppe treasury, too! Find something we can nibble on! I'm sure our fellow troops have plundered more than they can get through even with their numbers."

Encircling multiple Federation supply bases means we've seized a ton of supplies. It's just a bonus, but it's one of the reasons the food situation is better on the front lines than the home front.

In any case, wonderful victory, wonderful feast, and the smell of civilization.

Victory is just that great.

[chapter]

VI

Excessive Triumph

"Why? Why, though?!"

Lieutenant General Hans von Zettour

MAY 13, UNIFIED YEAR 1927, IMPERIAL CAPITAL BERUN, IMPERIAL ARMY GENERAL STAFF OFFICE

From: Imperial Army, Eastern Army Group Headquarters
To: Imperial Army General Staff Office

The attacking Federation Army has been repelled.

We are currently making provisional estimations of achievements on the eastern front.

Several divisions, including the main enemy forces, have been annihilated.

We are continuing to pursue the enemy and capitalize on our gains.

P.S. Arrange for transport of prisoners as soon as possible.

"We won, huh?"

"...We sure did."

The achievements of the Imperial Army were so massive that both the boulder and the willow could project calm. And if you questioned the outcome of the major maneuver battle on the eastern front, all you had to do was glance at the wall map.

Certainly at one point, the pressure was on in the east and they were forced to retreat quite a ways. There was disarray in the frontline units, wandering supply lines, and finally confusion at Eastern Army Group Headquarters—they had to admit that there was plenty to improve on.

Still, the results were there on the map.

"...We can probably even count Moskva and the southern cities among the options of where to invade."

"In *theory*, Rudersdorf."

"So it'd be tricky?"

That's not even the half of it. Lieutenant General von Zettour winced and made himself clear to his esteemed friend. "Rebuilding the rail network is impossible. Even right now, we're pushing the limits by sourcing supplies on the ground!"

A maneuver battle, which involves invasion on a large scale, is constantly faced with the limits of logistics.

If they were using interior lines strategy at home, procuring supplies would be easier. In their own, familiar country, they could've gotten backing from the self-governing provincial bodies and moved at full speed—that wasn't just armchair theorizing.

But in foreign lands, even the kindest group is made of strangers, like the Council for Self-Government. Just creating a strategic base in their hinterlands and invading openly hostile enemy territory was a logistics nightmare.

Establishing a supply base that could sustain a major invasion was beyond the Empire's national strength.

"We're really lucky we were able to capture entire enemy supply depots at their HQ. We're just barely able to make it with what the Council for Self-Government provided plus what we've seized—it's a miracle."

The secret to making ends meet all the time was simple—if you had the tactics from the old *Art of War* book that said to source your food in enemy territory.

"What if that stopped?"

"Then we'd really have to procure everything in enemy territory."

And Zettour didn't even want to imagine that scenario. Seizing enemy matériel could still be called a military operation, but there was a subtle but critical difference between seizing enemy supplies in the field and coercing people to give them to you.

"Specifically?"

Since he was asked, he had to answer.

"Organized looting."

"Looting? This isn't the age of mercenaries. Are you serious, Zettour?"

"I'm serious." He nodded at Rudersdorf. "That's where we're at. At the very least, hmm, to keep up appearances… Formally, it would be requisitions in line with military law. But I wonder how far military scrip will get us in enemy territory."

"Right," his old friend answered with a wince. Even he knew. Military scrip was about as reliable as a candle in the wind. Regardless of how it worked at home, in enemy territory, the only people who would trust it were those in the position of being forced to pretend to.

"What's the difference, even...between requisitioning with military scrip and looting?"

"...So we're demanding things that don't exist, and that's why we have to bend over backward. But we can't very well give up on our operation because of supply issues."

"I'd sure like you to."

"That doesn't sound like you, General von Zettour... We're soldiers, remember."

Zettour emitted a sigh, and Rudersdorf tossed a question at him point-blank.

"If, hypothetically, we were to carry out another advance under the current circumstances, what logistics measures would you take?"

"...Negotiating the cease-fire is higher priority, isn't it? With this outcome, even the Federation will have a hard time refusing to talk."

"Negotiation is only possible if the other party is on board. Have you forgotten?"

Zettour was about to reply that he hadn't forgotten, but then he realized what Rudersdorf was trying to say. "...I see. You think we need to plan for the possibility that they turn down negotiations?"

"Exactly."

"Honestly, I'm not sure how likely that is. Colonel von Lergen's report only just arrived, but...according to him, while there might be a battle over terms, a cease-fire agreement is only a matter of time."

"I read it. He reported that the Federation side was groping for the possibility of a cease-fire, right?"

"Yes," said Zettour, continuing.

The terms they had come up with via Ildoa were simple. All armies would cease firing along the current demarcation line. Occupied territories would be considered under provisional control and possession would not change hands.

But all demands for possession of regions the Empire effectively controlled before the war would be rejected. That would be a final solution. And then the Imperial Army would establish a demilitarized zone of a few kilometers around the border as a precaution. If necessary, there was leeway for occupation to guarantee security.

They had also included the stipulation that residents of occupied territories would vote on where they felt they belonged. Though they would have to keep track of multiple nationalities, if this came through, securing the Empire would basically be a success. Counting the nominal reparations, you could say they got almost everything they wanted.

"It's true that we argued a lot about the residents voting. To put it another way…we beat them so soundly that they had to set aside their complaints for a moment and get the cease-fire in place…"

"You don't think it's just something on the Federation side?" Rudersdorf couldn't deny it but felt it could be for other reasons.

Zettour rejoined, "Isn't it more like the will of all the belligerent states? Even the Ildoans, seeing such a victory, will try to get on our side by wrapping up the negotiations."

"It's all in the realm of possibility in the end."

"So we should prepare for the worst case?"

"You have another idea, General von Zettour?"

I see. Zettour nodded at Rudersdorf's comment and pondered in silence for a time. He did the math in his head, looked over all the available supplies they had, consolidated the reports from the field, and groped for a possibility.

But it was true that even amid all those inquiries, he couldn't keep the thought from bubbling up in the back of his mind: *After such a thorough victory, there's no way negotiations won't work out.*

The remnants of the Republic could expect support from the Commonwealth.

The Commonwealth could expect support from the Federation and the Unified States.

But public opinion in the Unified States wasn't up for joining the war. All the Unified States had contributed so far was lend-lease and voluntary soldiers. Of course, both of those things were extremely problematic, but they didn't add up to the presence of the Federation, which had actually joined the war.

Ultimately, the Federation Army's overwhelming matériel superiority must have been the pillar supporting the other states' will to fight.

And the Empire had just crushed it in the east. Not only that, but it must have shocked and awed everyone nearby.

With that, diplomatic resolution should be possible.

Zettour was steeped in those thoughts when the phone rang, bringing him back to himself. *A call on the direct line? The timing means...*

"This is Lieutenant General von Zettour... Understood."

"Good news?"

Zettour's old friend asked, clearly invested, and he nodded. "An emergency meeting of Supreme Command."

"Oh? And what does Supreme Command say?"

"They're considering the terms. Now the details will get decided... We'll finally have a path to ending this." *It's just a little further.* Filled with that emotion, he murmured, "The joy of harvesting the seeds you've sown. Such are the blessings of Heimat."

They had fought for their fatherland. With their honor, with pride in their breasts, they left the bones of their fellow soldiers behind and still leveled their guns. Their predecessors and ancestors must have protected their homeland in the same way, as would their descendants.

And that's why the present existed, an inheritance of the past.

"Well done, General von Rudersdorf. It's only a matter of time before you're made marshal."

And it seemed permissible to bask in the strange feeling of having fulfilled one's duty. Which is why Zettour found himself offering his colleague more extravagant praise than ever before.

"I'm happy to hear you say that, but I'm merely a deputy."

"It's obvious who was running things, though. Your achievements brought about these results. I don't think the Empire is so corrupt that it would pretend not to notice such astounding achievements."

"I'm grateful for your glowing evaluation. I think it's your specialty, but...I'm pretty sure there's such a thing in this world as appearances..."

"You mean it'll go in order of length of service? Still, though. Still." *Come on, now.* Zettour smiled gently. "Friend, you've done it. Be proud."

"I suppose I owe some thanks."

"To me? To the troops?"

"That should be obvious." He laughed, which was a relief. "To the troops."

"Yeah… They really pulled it off."

Which is why… Zettour shut his eyes for a moment and made a mental vow. *I have to end it this time, no matter what it takes.*

It was a happy daydream. It was extravagant, but he could believe in it. He felt that things really would be brighter going forward.

Let's admit it, though.

No, let's admit he was forced to admit it.

It isn't only wishful thinking but negligence.

THE SAME DAY, IN THE AFTERNOON, IMPERIAL CAPITAL BERUN, LIAISON CONFERENCE ROOM, SUPREME COMMAND MEETING

Lieutenant General von Zettour, who was participating in the Supreme Command meeting, stiffened at the unexpected response to his summarization of the negotiations that had happened via Ildoa at the post-victory course-of-action meeting and his presentation of the terms.

Though most of their eyes were exhausted, the civil servants wore well-tailored suits. Just like military officers, they were intelligent, knowledgeable cogs of the state… That is, they should have "understood."

Should have…

But what swirled in the meeting room was a violent emotion.

"Don't give us that drivel!"

The bureaucrats stood and pounded on the table, expressing their feelings openly.

"Are you serious, sir?!"

"These are *good* terms?! Is that what you're telling us?!"

Though rattled, Zettour confirmed. "With all due respect, indeed they are. I understand that these are the best terms available under the circumstances, and I support them."

"General von Zettour! You still call yourself a man of the Empire?!"

"Of course."

The room filled with furious voices wondering why. For the one getting the looks of murderous hatred, it wasn't a terribly comfortable atmosphere.

"How are we supposed to make peace with terms like these?!"

"...You say *terms like these* as if it's a bad thing." As if he was a teacher dealing with dense students, Zettour spat back and corrected them. These were the results after they made every effort. "But these are the best terms we're able to secure. If from here we go to a cease-fire agreement and peace talks, the terms will be realistic and likely to go through. Listen." He stared around the room and snapped at the disgruntled civil servants. "Our troops fought with all their might to get us these conditions! At least that's how I see it."

"Excuse me, General von Zettour, but these—*these* terms—are the best you could get?!"

He scoffed, as if to say, *Yes, they are.*

The possibility of a cease-fire and the debate over terms that would lead to peace were both secured only by bending over backward to make the best use of imperial military power—really getting the impossible done. They had won them by forcing the other side to see reason through victory in combat, but it wasn't enough? The light thud on the table was him nearly pounding his fist.

It had been an unconscious motion. But the others must have taken it as a provocation. They confronted him irately.

"I'd like to know what you think! We can't understand if you remain silent!"

But conversely, Zettour found himself beginning to regain composure in the face of their anger.

It was just like war. There was no reason he had to get all riled up and play by their rules.

Being able to choose meant having the initiative. Defense didn't necessarily equate to losing it.

Having considered various tactics, his brain suggested the approach of waiting for his opponents to wear themselves out. They may have been feisty, but being feisty only meant consuming energy.

"I'm fairly certain I've answered all these questions."

"...But those are *your* thoughts, General von Zettour. We want to know what the *army* thinks!"

Ironically, the more agitated the others got, the calmer he grew. Though he knew it was a bad habit of his, Zettour had too much pride to talk with fools.

He snapped at them that they must know.

"So?"

"Well, this is strange. Does the opinion of the deputy chief of the Service Corps really not count as the general opinion of the army?"

He must have used a tone for talking with idiots. The men didn't even hide their displeasure as they averted their eyes, and Zettour sighed.

"...General von Rudersdorf! You're the same rank. What do you think about this?"

"Honestly, I agree with what General von Zettour has pointed out."

"...Of all the—! But that victory was so massive!"

And it was indeed a great victory they had won in the east. It was the kind of victory that all soldiers dream of being involved in.

But perhaps the barking civil servants didn't understand that the General Staff knew quite well what that win was worth. Figuring that they wouldn't get it if he stayed silent, Zettour spoke up. "Yes. And it's precisely because we achieved such a victory that we were able to nail down these terms."

The remark got him doused in looks from around the room that said, *Surely you must be joking.* If looks applied physical pressure, he would have been skewered. *Well! What cold, sharp glares.*

I anticipated some degree of resistance, but this is beyond what I imagined. Zettour couldn't help but wince.

"Don't you understand the position the Empire is in?!"

He was reminded of the Oriental saying about teaching Buddhist sutras. When it came to the numbers, given that he had access to military secrets and everything else, there had to be only a handful of people who understood the situation better than he did.

"I'm fairly certain I have a detailed grasp on the Empire's position." His comment came mixed with a puff of purple smoke and a faint, bitter grin. That was the expert Lieutenant General von Zettour's true intention, his true feeling, and his regret.

If I didn't know, I'd be able to say something more optimistic...

"I believe I have a solid understanding of the current wartime strength of the state as presented by Supreme Command, including matériel distribution and human resources."

He was in charge of logistics, the Service Corps member responsible for the matériel mobilization plan, and he had a background in Operations.

The confidence that of all those in the room, he was the one with the best understanding of the situation ended up making him say, "Is there some sort of secret I don't know? If not, then my answer to your question doesn't change. There are no better terms in our current situation than these."

"If you're aware of our situation, that makes this simple. I beg your pardon, but revise your opinion. General von Zettour, with all due respect, the military is too focused on the present."

"And?"

"The losses the Empire has sustained, including those of national wealth, are too great."

"I don't see what you're getting at."

"You don't? That's strange…"

The civil servants heaved fed-up sighs and began arguing all together.

"We have to regain those losses somewhere. That thought doesn't occur to you? Unless we get reparations, the Empire is—"

"I know what happens then," Zettour interrupted.

They had wasted a fortune on this war and gotten almost nothing in return. And their young male workforce had gone extinct. Each shell that Zettour, as one involved in matériel mobilization, sent to the front lines was made by women and the elderly. Schoolchildren were producing daily necessities in the factories while prisoners worked the fields.

"I suppose the state goes bankrupt. In the worst case, the apparatus is also in danger and—though I say this with the understanding that it's a dreadful scenario—the imperial family might even be at risk."

"If you know all that, then—!"

They could tell him to do something all they wanted, but it wasn't a soldier's job.

"With all due respect, I'm a military man."

"What's that supposed to mean?"

"I swore loyalty to the emperor and the state to defend our fatherland from external threat. So it's self-evident, then, that the army shouldn't interfere in domestic affairs."

In short, the army shouldn't overstep its designated authority. That was a central principle that, as a career soldier, Zettour believed absolutely.

War, at its foundation, is an extension of politics. Military matters could never be superior to politics. If that was the case, it would usher in a nightmare of the state being driven not by grand strategy but solely by military strategy. The Imperial Army was the state's violence machine; it wasn't supposed to be the state itself.

"General von Zettour, I object! You have no qualms about letting the state's finances collapse? This is a serious matter!"

"Finances? Whatever about them? Are you so frightened of a gentle decline that you'd rush us straight into poverty?"

"Money, money, money! Money is everything! Do you not realize what it's like in a state that could go bankrupt?! Listen!" the officer of the Ministry of the Treasury argued. It was clear from the tense looks on their faces that they were not fooling around. "We have a mountain of credit in bonds! You can't trust scraps of paper that aren't backed by anything! How would we pay back the government bonds?!"

Are you serious? he thought. If they truly feared the state going bankrupt over waging war...that was absurd.

"I realize it's an extreme opinion, but if we need more scraps of paper, we can just print more."

Lieutenant General von Zettour was a military man. The tools of his trade were guns and its losses, soldiers. In other words, humans. The youths of the country would die.

...He wouldn't allow anything to take priority over them.

"Sure, sure, I'm sure the mint will just print more! So? What denomination of marks would you like?"

"States may have fallen into decline due to inflation, but that's better than the people losing fundamental belief in the Reich. We should just take pride in ourselves and deal with it."

"Neither of those should be hanging in the balance!"

Everyone's eyes were on him, pleading.

...Is it possible that they...understand what they're saying?

No, it wouldn't make sense for them not to. They must understand. Zettour revised his thought. Even members of the imperial family had died. That was the nature of this war, which wore on despite the mountains of dead. It was rarer for a subject of the Empire to not have lost someone close.

Which was precisely why Zettour couldn't comprehend these people. *They're saying not to let those sacrifices be in vain but then also to keep fighting, knowing that that would entail further sacrifices?*

"If one more win will earn us better terms, we should win just once more! We need to secure the critical payment that will allow the state to survive!"

"What exactly do you take the military for?! I won't have you mistaking this national struggle as an opportunity to gamble!" Zettour snorted, saying it was out of the question.

In response, the officer of the treasury shouted back with a crumpled face, not even trying to hide his tears. "It's a reasonable request based on carrying out our national policy! Do you mean to tarnish our reputation?!"

"Have you ever heard of 'cutting your losses'?!"

"And for that, you'd leave your family destitute?! We can still win! We should be able to negotiate more advantageous terms!"

They were getting nowhere.

That is, they were going in circles.

"You're saying we should cling to wishful thinking and continue the war? As the one in charge of the Service Corps, I absolutely cannot have you assuming our forces have energy to burn."

"After all the resources it's eaten up, you're saying our army is a paper tiger?!"

Even showered in criticisms of the giant, unsustainable consumption machine the Imperial Army had become, all Zettour could do was crack a wry smile.

"If our opponent cries uncle, we should be able to expect better terms, right?! In order to rebuild, we must get them, no matter what it takes!"

As Zettour icily watched the murmuring group, he reached the end of his rope. Upon a casual scan of the room, he suddenly hit upon a terrifying truth that nearly made his eyes swim. Whenever the red-faced civil servants shouted, most of the silent attendees were bobbing their heads in agreement!

Agreement? Agreement?!

They identify with that nonsense, of all things?!

"...Apparently, generals know war, but not how to finance it. Take the occupied territories, for example. The Federation's resources are within hailing distance."

Having been asked, *What do you think about that?* he had no choice but to answer. Suddenly, though, he found himself as terrified as an infantryman who had fallen behind and gotten separated from his unit in enemy territory.

"Beg your pardon, but are you saying that if we conquer them, we'll be self-sufficient?"

"Exactly. If we go forward with that system—"

The civil servant seemed to say they had a good chance, but Zettour saw where he was going with it and interrupted. "Sorry," he barked, "but I will not have us waging war according to wishful thinking."

Let's admit it. There was some huge disagreement here. Which was why he had to drive his point home.

"It's pie in the sky. Even if we went back to negotiate further, if the situation was different, what we'd have to do to get terms like these would—"

"If we pile up victories, the enemy's attitude is sure to change!"

...Victory, victory, victory!

These addicts and their omnipotent cure-all, victory!

Unable to hold back the true feelings he wanted to spew, Zettour nearly groaned in spite of himself. He was keenly aware now of why his predecessors had warned that the only thing more dangerous than a major defeat was a major victory, and it utterly horrified him.

Are they just arbitrarily convinced that we can still win? The atmosphere made him want to scream, *Are you serious?!*

"Excuse me, may I say something?"

"Go ahead, General von Rudersdorf."

It was his esteemed friend, who had been silent beside him, who chimed in. Having muscled his way into the conversation, he gave a straightforward summary of the situation.

"It's fine for you all to criticize General von Zettour. But this setting requires a composed debate. Why don't we review where we're at?"

"Very well, General von Rudersdorf. How do you see things? Since you're the one in charge of Operations, I'd very much like to hear your thoughts."

"Well, I'll tell you. But it would help if you'd specify exactly what you want to know. I can give you a clear answer rather than an outline."

"All right, then." The civil servant nodded. "Do you believe that the Empire cannot hope to win any further?"

"Hmm." Zettour and the others watched as Rudersdorf put a cigar in his mouth. As everyone in the meeting room stared, he boldly puffed away.

Finally, the gazes urging him to continue were enough that he slowly opened his mouth, exhaling a cloud of smoke.

"Frankly, it would probably be difficult. Look," he said, repositioning his cigar, and the civil servants were quick to shoot questions back at him.

"Difficult?"

"Indeed. Extremely difficult."

"But you're not calling it impossible."

A slight disturbance. An almost imperceptible aberration. The only one who noticed him furrow his brow as if to say, *That's not a very nice thing to ask* was Zettour.

To a soldier, there was no question more loathed than the one that had just been slung at him.

"...Would the army declare right here that it couldn't win? How could we do that to the imperial family and their subjects?"

He refused to answer in a roundabout way. Having said just that, he busied himself with his cigar once more.

But to anyone who knew the ways of these creatures, military men, the answer was too clear. Zettour's old friend was as good as admitting the limits of the army. He was probably using his cigar to disguise his sighs. A cigar was the optimal tool for holding one's tongue.

...Thus Zettour, who had become a much heavier smoker than he was before the war, understood Rudersdorf so well, it made him sick.

It was good of you to go that far. He could spare no mental praise for Rudersdorf's bravery and resolve. The ones who had sacrificed so much for this victory were the troops. The General Staff was thoroughly aware of how they had piled up dead in the east to wrench this victory from the

Federation. They didn't need the civil servants to tell them. The Imperial Army General Staff wasn't so far removed from reality that they could ignore the mountain of promising young people's corpses forming on the forward-most line.

The results of the war weren't yet decided. Why would a soldier irresponsibly announce that they couldn't win? After all the military expenses, human resources, and hardships forced on the home front, it wasn't acceptable for the army to flinch before the fog of war and say victory was impossible.

...If they realized at some point that there really was no way to win, maybe then they could say it. But there were possibilities remaining. Which was why Rudersdorf, in charge of Operations, couldn't spout nonsense like *We can't win*, even by mistake, yet he still hinted at their limits.

"...Do I make myself clear?"

Rudersdorf was asking, between the lines, for their understanding.

"General von Rudersdorf, General von Zettour. I'm asking you officially: Can that be said to be the consensus of the General Staff—and the army?"

It was a question they could answer immediately.

""Of course,"" they answered, nodding in perfect synchronization.

Now the debate must be settled. With that optimistic outlook, the tension started, just slightly, to leave his shoulders.

They needed a plan for reducing the burdens on the home front, and there was the whole process of getting from a cease-fire to peace. Even if there were heaps of things to do...

"...So you're saying that even if it would be a challenge, there's still a chance we could win?"

Wait. The gears of Zettour's mind stopped turning after hearing that incomprehensible absurdity. *Even if it would be a challenge, there's still a chance we could win?*

"We've heard what the army thinks about the situation. But further victories would be possible if the home front took the necessary measures, correct?"

"Please wait. What are you talking about?"

"General von Zettour, a question... Is it possible that if we agree to these terms in the negations via the Kingdom of Ildoa, we'll appear weak-kneed to our opponents?"

"...What did you say?"

The reply to Zettour's blank question was cutthroat. "I just wonder if we aren't making it look like we're rushing to negotiate. If our enemies think we aren't able to continue fighting the war, we won't be in a very strong bargaining position."

Someone else added a comment. *Someone from the Ministry of the Interior, perhaps?*

"I'll be frank. Do you have a solid grasp of trends in public opinion and sentiment? We can't accept a cease-fire and peace with these terms. And Ildoa's plan for the cease-fire is only temporary. It's not clear if it would even lead to peace or not!"

Zettour saw a man in a well-tailored suit stand up to follow the other speaker. *One of those Foreign Office poseurs?*

"While the military cease-fire negotiations may be within the army's purview, the official cease-fire and peace talks are the realm of diplomacy. Which means, as a matter of course, that jurisdiction should be handled by we of the Foreign Office. Isn't it overstepping your authority for the army to exercise power as it pleases in this matter?"

How come you can't even understand that much? is what most of the people in the room seemed to be thinking as they attacked him.

The stern looks he was getting!

He was nearly thinking it was the sort of glare you'd give your enemies but then stopped himself.

Maybe not *the sort of.*

"We hope for peace just as much as you. But it must come along with right and acceptable reparations. If justice isn't done...the hearts of the people won't be satisfied."

"You're prioritizing that over the restoration of peace?!" Zettour was about to yell, *You must be kidding!* but was interrupted by innumerable scowls.

"The time for prioritizing an unjust peace ended when the war began!"

"Sacrifices must be properly compensated!"

"We can't compromise so much! The Ildoan proposal is too easygoing!"

The refutations Zettour was about to deliver were forestalled as if they were treason, and he was censured. It was so absurd that he would have wanted to laugh the response off as an emotional argument were this not a meeting of Supreme Command with none other than the group of people who handled all the practical matters in the Empire.

...But not being able to laugh it off made it serious by necessity.

"Supreme Command does not interfere in military orders as a rule. But certainly it has the right to exercise its abilities to make a request regarding national strategy."

"...And that is?"

He couldn't very well scream, *Please don't!* Zettour had to face his fate, like a commander who realized the battle was lost.

"With all due respect, we'd like the army to win better terms."

"...Am I meant to interpret that as the administration's official opinion?"

"To be accurate, it's the will of the people and a valid request the imperial family agrees with. As such, we'd like the army to follow through on that goal."

From an institutional perspective, they were correct. As for the military perspective, for the longest time, Supreme Command was merely an organization that approved of the General Staff's decisions. But the actual authority to decide lay unmistakably with Supreme Command. Even Zettour had no way to object.

If he couldn't express his dismay, and arguing back wasn't allowed, then he would have to remain silent.

But what does one person's silence mean? Just as he was about to crack a self-deprecating sneer, someone ventured to speak.

"...Fine. You're telling us to win?"

Shut your mouth, Rudersdorf!! he wanted to scream.

Maybe he should have. But having been rendered speechless, Zettour couldn't even muster a wordless cry to stop him.

"We'll show you a victory... As long as you give us what we need, the army will win as many times as you want."

Zettour immediately shot a look at Rudersdorf, but it didn't reach him. As the civil servants, nodding in satisfaction, reported various details and the conversation went back and forth, Zettour alone was depressed.

How? Why?

THE SAME DAY, IMPERIAL EMBASSY IN ILDOA

News of a victory is always good. Especially when it comes with optimal timing. It permeates every corner of the body, naturally warming the limbs. In the sense of that familiar comfort, it is every bit as good as alcohol.

Like a good tequila or perhaps scotch.

As news of the victory spread throughout the Empire, all the imperial subjects at the embassy in Ildoa shared the same excitement.

The military attaché to Ildoa, Colonel von Lergen, shook his head. In the pursuit of accuracy, we should probably revise: These people, who were involved directly in diplomatic negotiations, were more ecstatic than most. The embassy was such a madhouse, they were downing fine wine like college kids.

It wasn't that they didn't have the will to moderate themselves. They understood the word *restraint*. They were adults with both age and standing. They were well aware of how bad it looked to lose control in front of others.

Yet here they were, sloshed.

The drinks were just too delicious.

Ildoa had mediated the negotiations between parties who refused to back down, not even hiding the fact that they were playing both sides. The representatives from the Empire, exhausted in both mind and body, had intended to simply enjoy a social drink, but before they knew it, they were mentally and physically overdoing it.

They were so sure the balance had tipped in their direction that they celebrated.

They really did it.

Lergen himself was one of those who cheered from the pit of his stomach.

News of a victory—it could only be divine assistance!

He was so moved, he nearly shed tears in spite of himself—they had done such a good job. Before he knew it, he was reaching for a bottle he'd been treasuring for years. Not only had he been keeping it since before the war started, but these days, you couldn't even get a reliable supply of this Commonwealth spirit in neutral countries.

When he undid the tight seal and pulled out the cork, he was greeted with a smell that was appropriately rich for the bottle's age.

Even just taking ice from the embassy's refrigerator and preparing to pour his drink into an Ildoan cut-glass tumbler was thrilling.

When, after carefully pouring, he was savoring the relatively mild—for 40 percent—experience, that warm font of energy permeated his heart.

"Delicious."

The quiet comment expressed his deepest feelings. Whether it was from an enemy country or not, a good drink was a good drink. He had long forgotten this flavor.

"I can really taste it. Words can't describe how indebted I am to the troops for this chance to drink something so nice."

Alcohol in his system made him chatty—especially when he was drinking mature spirits to celebrate a victory. It intoxicated him more than usual.

But decidedly not in a bad way.

It was a lightness that banished his anxiety about the future as well as his frustration. The feeling spreading through his body was accompanied even by a kindness like that of an old friend. The cool, melodious clink of the ice in his glass, too, was exquisite. It was like looking up at a clear blue sky.

Above all, this atmosphere!

Today I can even tip one down the hatch in the attaché office and no one will question it!

"Oh, Colonel von Lergen. You have good taste."

The one who spoke to him was the usually serious ambassador. But today there was a mood he couldn't hide written all over his face.

"If it isn't our ambassador! And you, sir? What's that bottle you have? If memory serves, that's the X-brand stuff the Foreign Office was keeping under lock and key for diplomatic use!"

Even under blockade, etiquette had to be maintained, or they would lose face. Lergen had been surprised to learn that part of the job of diplomats stationed abroad was to acquire wine.

"Ha-ha-ha! Right you are. It's a valuable bottle I smuggled back through a neutral country in my diplomat bag, but there's no being stingy today! I'm going all out!"

Apparently, the ambassador, who should be the one rebuking those getting out of line, had given instructions to hold a victory celebration and was in such high spirits, he was popping the corks on bottles of wine he had bought to send back to the home country for diplomatic use.

"Come, come, Colonel. Please have some. I hope you'll propose a toast to the Imperial Army's fierce fighting."

"Well, if you insist..."

Normally, every bottle was strictly accounted for. But just for today, there were no rules. He expressed his gratitude for the glass, filled to the brim, and admired the richness of the red liquid.

He had completely forgotten the scent of the real thing.

"To victory and the hard fight!"

"To our brothers-in-arms and their self-sacrifice!"

"Glory to the fatherland!"

What grand words to raise in cheers.

"God is with us!"

The moment the fixed wording left his lips, the possibility that it was actually *grace* came to Lergen's mind. The future of the fatherland would begin now. *So maybe*, he couldn't help but think. Perhaps pragmatists like him should be praising the Lord, too: *May it be so.*

So it was that among all the deeply moved men, he, too, engaged in congratulatory remarks.

"May the Empire reign always!"

""""Hooray!!!""""

Their arms around one another, the men in full dress boomed "*Prosit!*" and it must have thundered even outside the embassy.

Well, let them hear it.

It was a shout of the Empire's triumph. *A laurel from the heart bestowed on the heroes of the eastern front, the defenders of the fatherland, our Reich.* You could call it a joyful song.

Let us raise our voices out of love for the Empire!

Give in to the intoxication and belt it out—let it resound throughout this foreign land!

Perhaps it's not a respectable way for an officer to unwind. Even so, why should I hesitate?

Who could not *celebrate their nation's victory in words? Any human who has sworn loyalty to their country as a soldier is surely compelled to applaud its success.*

"C-Colonel von Lergen?"

"Hmm? Oh, from the on-duty group. You poor fellows. I had the kitchen make something for you. Was there not enough to go around?"

"No, it's…for your ears only, sir. May I ask you to come with me?"

The deferential mood implied that was no small matter. Though Lergen was riding rather high on their victory, it wasn't hard to detect the urgency once he composed himself.

"Let's go."

He apologized for causing extra work for the duty officer as he took him into the empty corridor. Even in one's own embassy, there could be ears that shouldn't be listening.

The duty officer scanned the area, seeming awfully nervous.

"What is it?"

"It's from the General Staff."

"…Hmm? You mean…the results of the Supreme Command meeting?"

"Yes, it appears to be. I thought I should inform you…"

The duty officer seemed concerned as to whether it had really been worth interrupting his superior's celebration, but Lergen reassured him with a sincere smile. "Thank you. That was the right decision."

It was a message from the home country.

And so soon—he was impressed. The timely classified message had his heart pounding with anticipation.

"I suppose I should read this in my office. Excuse me."

Moved that the home country would reach a conclusion about the negotiations so immediately, Lergen went back to his office.

It was hard to keep from grinning. *What a sap I am*, he thought, before realizing that there wasn't actually any rule keeping him from expressing his joy. Maybe if he was actually in the middle of negotiations, but in his current situation, it was only natural that the entire range of emotions be allowed.

"…Ha-ha-ha. It's been so long…" *…since I've smiled so freely.* He grinned wryly and hurried on. In one hand, he carried his glass of aged wine, and in the other, the encoded message that, based on when it came in, would probably illuminate how they planned to end the war.

If he didn't use the book in the safe in his room, he wouldn't be able to read it.

Though the signal itself was also encoded, if they were monitored long enough, there was a risk of the enemy deciphering it. In light of that, they exchanged messages written in a very specific way, which had to be compared to a cipher only Lergen and the General Staff possessed in order to make any sense.

I'm so excited to decode it, thought Lergen as he stepped lightly toward his room.

With the flush of the drinks still in his cheeks, his heart pounded in a way it never had before as he pulled the codebook out of his safe.

The pleasant buzz he felt wasn't only the alcohol.

What man would be able to contain himself? He'd had the honor of participating in the saving of his nation's destiny. Why wouldn't he be thrilled?

"Okay, okay. Here's the important part. I sure hope there's a coherent plan for how to end the war..."

Elated, he lined up the book and the telegram next to each other. Then he worked his quill pen for a time to decode it. When he reached a part that decoded as "victory on the eastern front," he flipped through the codebook, knowing what came next would be what he had been waiting for.

"...? Huh?"

Unexpectedly confused, he drained his glass like a pick-me-up and poured out a little more.

"Ohhh, how silly of me... I must have made a mistake somewhere."

His first thought was that he had gotten a bit too drunk. He smiled wryly at the glass in his hand and shook his head. It seemed he had made a terrible reading error.

"So this is... And this... Huh? No, but..."

His blood vessels, warmed with spirits, contracted as if he'd been showered in close-range cannon fire.

Without even realizing he had dropped his glass, Lergen stared at the telegram in horror.

"...What?"

After reviewing each word, each punctuation mark, closely, taking care not to miss any lines, he was still confused. *It's not a misreading?*

Couldn't it be? Please?

Or am I just not comprehending it correctly? Maybe...not?

He frantically reread it, but the content remained mercilessly unwavering.

An encoded telegram followed a template in official language that left no room for misunderstandings. There were no errors of reading, comprehension, or composition. The one who drafted it had to have been an outstanding officer. He had certainly done his job polishing this official document.

"Regarding the victory on the eastern front, we see fit to renegotiate and press for much greater concessions."

He wanted it to be a joke.

That's how he felt as he abruptly read the text aloud without thinking, but his brain still stubbornly refused to understand.

Well, he got it; he just didn't want to.

If he understood it, if he accepted it...

"'R-regarding the victory on the eastern front, we see fit to *renegotiate* and press for *much greater concessions*'?!"

This wasn't a message to confirm the adoption of the proposal that Lergen had struggled so hard to pull together. You could say it was bad news that the home country didn't accept, and it was.

Actually, he thought he had been prepared for potential bad news from the outset. But this? This wasn't one of the scenarios he'd had in mind. The worst case is always the horror you can't predict.

"...B-but I negotiated all...all of *this*..."

They didn't even consider all the friction and the struggling it had taken to reach this result.

"R...r-r-renegotiate? Go back to the drawing board?"

Is this really the home country's, Supreme Command's, the Empire's intention? When we worked so hard to reach a patch of common ground, and things were only just starting to take shape, at long last?

He groaned softly.

How?

Why?

The stupidity.

Lamenting in intricate layers that refused to form into proper speech, Lergen turned his bloodshot eyes back to the telegram.

He felt he had gotten everything he could get.

But it's not enough?!

You're saying it's still not enough?!

"...I never imagined the day would come that I'd understand how Colonel von Degurechaff feels."

It wasn't a surprise that he respected her.

She was an outstanding magic officer.

She was the complete package as an officer, a soldier, and a modern intellectual, so that much made sense. She may have been warped, but he couldn't deny his respect for her.

What shocked Lergen was his irritated remark that he sympathized with her complaints and confusion.

"...Why can't they just put up with it?!"

It was a scream.

It was a lament.

And it was a wail.

"Why can't they just accept things this way?!"

The Empire had invested too much iron and blood in this war. It was reaching the point that practically anyone with common sense could see that any more conflict was meaningless. These days had been nightmares—far too many precious lives, far too much capital, had melted away in an instant.

...And the light of a solution was gleaming only half a step in front of them.

"How am I supposed to get them to agree to these conditions?!"

It was right there. He had been transferred from the forward-most line in the east to the neutral country of Ildoa and waited anxiously for news of the victory for this chance!

It was because he had caught a whiff of the lingering scent of normalcy, which his home country had lost, in Ildoa, that he could claim it was worth swallowing the country's high price for mediation, some dissatisfaction withstanding.

He understood how abnormal the war situation the Empire faced was whether he wanted to or not. Muster everything the nation had to offer and scatter it across the barren swamp-like earth?

What good would that do?

He wasn't afraid to die for his fatherland, for his Heimat. But how many soldiers were they planning on sacrificing to fight over the Federation mud?

Lergen felt so ill that the ground seemed to sway. Dizzy, he leaned against the chair next to him.

The telegram's message was clear.

We, the Imperial Army, were victorious on the eastern front. During negotiations, we defeated the Federation so thoroughly that the world gasped; it was both a tactical and operational victory. From a purely military perspective, it could probably be celebrated as a strategic victory as well.

The Imperial Army is now in a position to carry out fine attacks on the Federation's major cities.

So now is the time to settle the discussion. That's what Lergen thought, and it should have been a vision that not only those in the embassy but anyone in the army who had a grasp of the situation could share.

After getting a good look at the general situation on the eastern front, even a child could tell that they couldn't continue winning for long. You didn't have to be a monster of a little girl to understand that.

It was simple arithmetic.

The Imperial Army had committed millions of people to the eastern front, and there still weren't enough. *Just try expanding the lines as things stand.* Even if they entrusted some of the military districts to local security organizations such as the Council for Self-Government, they could stretch only so far.

There were the vast occupied territories on the map—entirely too vast.

The Empire as a state didn't have the strength to maintain them, and the Imperial Army didn't have a plan.

"The General Staff knows that, but they still weren't able to stop them?"

Was it the civil servants? Or some nonsense spouted by noble-born officers who were elite in rank only? Either way was no good.

Lergen's mouth twisted into a frown, and he couldn't help but utter curses.

This message, already difficult to comprehend, and its clamoring insistence that they could keep going was the product of something growing too large.

This is what you're telling me? I'm supposed to just renegotiate at the drop of a hat?!

"Generals von Zettour and von Rudersdorf agreed to this?"

Well, they probably had no choice.

The Imperial Army had won.

No, they must have taken a chance. Under the circumstances, the usual methods wouldn't have been enough to move the lines eastward in a major way.

...Saying there was no gamble would be a lie.

"Ha-ha-ha...it makes me laugh. So did you win your bet? Or did you win the game but lose the match?"

He knew this was going a bit far, but he thought it anyhow: *It would be better if we had lost in the east.* That was absolutely not the sort of thing an active-duty officer could say.

Stunned, clenching that absurd telegram, he couldn't help but agonize. "We won on the eastern front. We won, so what's going on? What exactly are these seeds we've sown?"

MAY 14, UNIFIED YEAR 1927, EASTERN FRONT, IMPERIAL ARMY, SALAMANDER KAMPFGRUPPE GARRISON

Apparently, the flow of a river really can make people sentimental.

Victory in battle, upcoming prospects—for Tanya, who has hope for a bright future and is leisurely enjoying plundered coffee with a splendid view of the water, it's a fantastic morning.

Holding our current position until further orders come from the home country essentially means throwing ourselves into the usual building projects. Looking around, it's the familiar scene of infantry digging foxholes, field engineers running communications cables, and anyone not busy with anything else filling sandbags.

So why does it look so radiant?

"...The seed of a dream where the people can hope for self-government, a buffer zone between the Empire and the Federation, a friendly neutral space. It's probably safe to feel pretty good about the future." With that quiet remark, her predictions cause her cheeks to relax into a smile.

When Tanya first joined the army, she had a pessimistic attitude, since there was no choice but to join. But look at her now, a proud member of a victorious nation.

No, that's not it. Tanya shakes her head. *Not yet. It hasn't been decided yet.* How shameless it would be to count her chickens before they hatch.

But still...

"Diplomatic negotiations, cease-fire, peace. Each step will be difficult to pull off—that hasn't changed. But this victory was huge. If we can win in the west and in the east..." It would be a rare example of a successful two-front war. Tanya chuckles at the thought.

Dealing a severe blow to the nation's primary enemy and securing even better terms than expected when imposing peace would...not be bad.

That's a logical deduction. Rational analysis makes her confident that's how it will go.

And since she has no idea what is going on far to the west, she can innocently go on believing.

Because she is ignorant, she continues smiling hopefully. "The Empire has sown its seeds. Ahhh, I can't wait for the harvest. I'm not a fan of the source text, but as you sow, so shall you reap."

(The Saga of Tanya the Evil, Volume 7: Ut Sementum Feceris, ita Metes, fin)

Appendixes

Mapped Outline of History

Mapped Outline of History

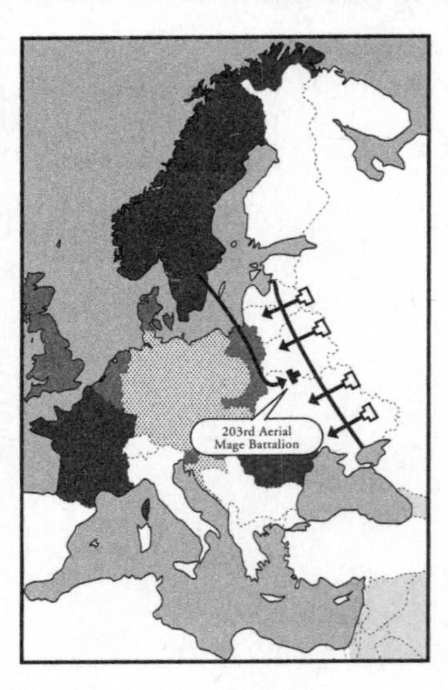

Federation Army Offensive

■ April 20, Unified Year 1927: The Federation Army launches an offensive all along the eastern front. The unexpected attack plunges the front-line Imperial Army units into severe disarray.

■ The Salamander Kampfgruppe's 203rd Aerial Mage Battalion is urgently deployed to the area along with other units.

■ April 22, Unified Year 1927: The Imperial Army gradually composes itself and organizes a retreat. Reinforcements begin work on rebuilding the lines.

■ Captain Ahrens's armored unit, a constituent of the Salamander Kampfgruppe, arrives at the front.

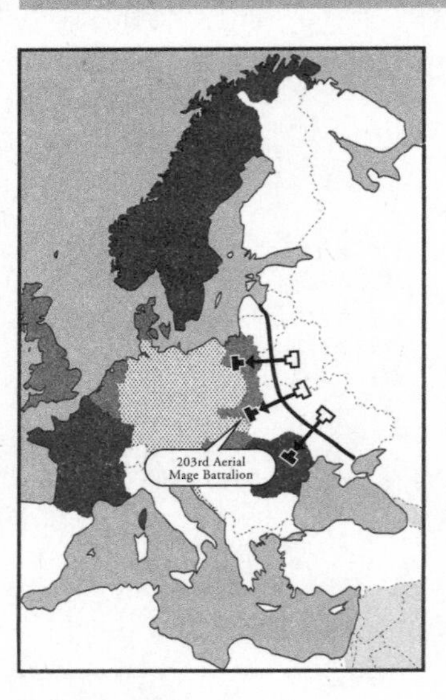

Federation Army Launches Second Offensive

■ April 26, Unified Year 1927: The Federation Army launches a second offensive. Having finished tightening up its lines, the Imperial Army holds and is able to counterattack in some places.

■ April 27, Unified Year 1927: The rest of the Salamander Kampfgruppe arrives in the east. Colonel von Lergen officially "takes up his new post."

■ April 28, Unified Year 1927: The Type T3476 Computation Orb becomes an issue on the eastern front. The Imperial Army is shaken by the enemy's new orb.

❸

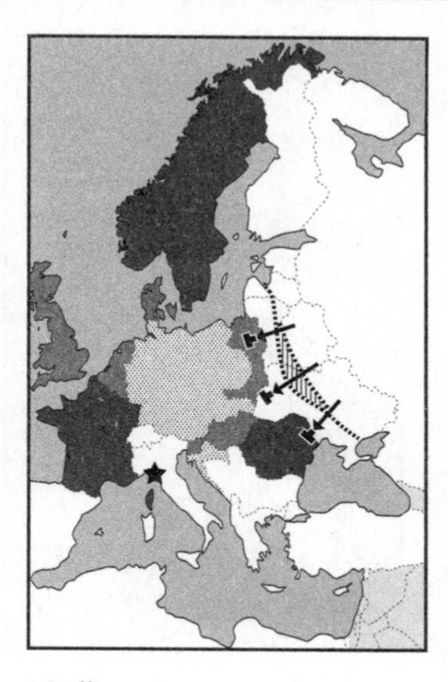

A Lull

1 May 1, Unified Year 1927: Preliminary negotiations begin in Ildoa.
2 The Imperial Army prepares for a counterattack on the eastern front by organizing and pulling back. Colonel Calandro arrives as a military observer.
3 May 2, Unified Year 1927: Several imperial units advance in search of the enemy. Small fights break out all along the eastern front.
4 May 3, Unified Year 1927: All imperial units on the eastern front are ordered to retreat. They reposition themselves on the newly designated line.

❹-1

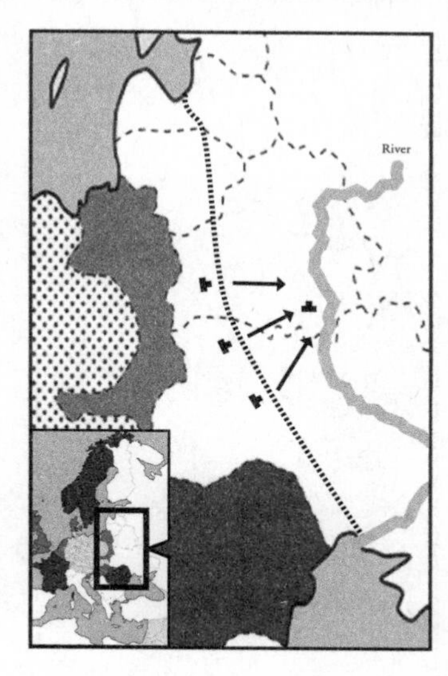

Imperial Army Initiates Operation Iron Hammer

1 May 5, Unified Year 1927: The Imperial Army General Staff initiates Operation Iron Hammer. Using their control of the sky gained in an aerial battle of annihilation, several moves, including an airborne assault, are made.
2 The Salamander Kampfgruppe participates in a major offensive. With the goal of joining up with the airborne troops, it begins advancing east.

Mapped Outline of History

❹-2

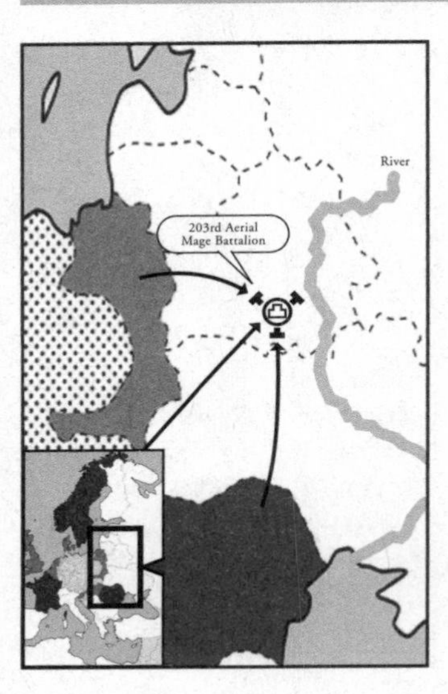

❸ May 7, Unified Year 1927: The Lergen Kampfgruppe makes contact with the Sixth Paratrooper Ranger Regiment and links up.

❹ May 8, Unified Year 1927: The Imperial Army General Staff learns what is happening on the eastern front. Orders to take out the encircled Federation Army Headquarters are issued.

❹-3

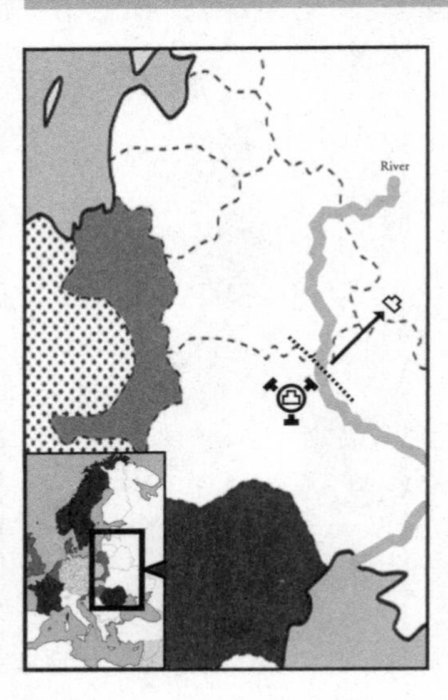

❺ May 11, Unified Year 1927: The Federation Army finds itself surrounded on the eastern front and launches an organized push to break through. Caught off guard, the Imperial Army reacts too late.

❻ May 11, Unified Year 1927: Federation Army Headquarters orders a massive retreat. (Those in the field act at their own discretion.) After that, there is a clash with the Imperial Army, and despite receiving assistance in the withdrawal, the Federation Army suffers devastating losses. (Some of the Federation forces did succeed in an organized withdrawal.)

❼ The highest authorities in the Federation Army decide to concentrate some units, including aerial mage units, on the eastern front, and despite receiving assistance in the withdrawal, the Federation Army suffers devastating losses. (Some of the Federation forces did succeed in an organized withdrawal.)

❽ Negotiations mediated by the Kingdom of Ildoa are well under way. At home in the Empire, a cry of victory erupts.

❺

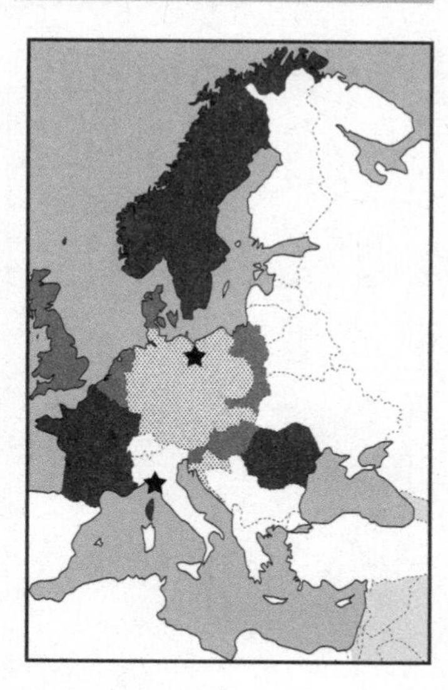

Declaration of Victory

1. May 13, Unified Year 1927: In the imperial capital, Berun, the Imperial Army General Staff officially declares victory.
2. Imperial Army Supreme Command holds a meeting to plan next steps. The proposal from the General Staff is rejected.
3. Diplomatic negotiations with Ildoa run aground.

Both the Empire and Federation grope for a resolution to the situation on the eastern front using their military might.

Though the Imperial Army achieves their military strategy goals with a major maneuver battle, a mismatch with the Empire's grand strategy is revealed.

The Federation continues to adjust the relationship between its government and military, with greater unity in mind.

Afterword

Hello, good evening, or to you valiant heroes who've been up and at 'em since sunrise, good morning. This is Carlo Zen with a greeting on the occasion of Volume 7's release.

Viva caffeine! And ramen!

Frankly, my greetings have been too formal. I have to make sure I don't forget my personality and uniqueness, my own color. I've engaged in some self-criticism and concluded that I have to stay true to my roots and goof around with confidence.

Now that I've reflected a little bit, on to the meat of this afterword. Some people might read this section first, so I'll refrain from spoilers. I value peaceful harmony.

The Saga of Tanya the Evil is about the misery of people stuck in the system and the absurdity of war. It's a tribute to labor wherein a young girl bites back her tears and works hard, facing the stress all working folks deal with daily at their jobs (huge lie). I hope that, with a cup of coffee in one hand, you'll enjoy Degu's struggles as if they have nothing to do with you. Or if, with a cup of coffee in each hand, you sympathize with moments that make you go "I totally get it. The higher-ups are always making us bend over backward with their plans!"—that's fine, too. Ah, for some reason, I keep finding tears in my eyes.

So, completely ignoring the demons lurking within the word *plan*, I'll assume that this has gone on sale at the end of December. Before this new novel arrives, Volumes 1 and 2 of Chika Tojo's manga adaptation will have already been released at a furious pace. And the anime should be starting in January.

Regarding the anime production... I've been able to

observe the recording, and all I could think the whole time is that pro voice actors are amazing. I can't say anything other than that, so...please look forward to the anime!

Last but not least, I'd like to thank everyone who lends me their strength. Readers, it's thanks to you that I've come this far!

And also, to the people who help out with the books. To illustrator Shinotsuki, the designers at Tsubakiya Design, the proofreaders at Tokyo Publishing Service Center, and my editor Fujita, thank you as always.

December 2016 Carlo Zen

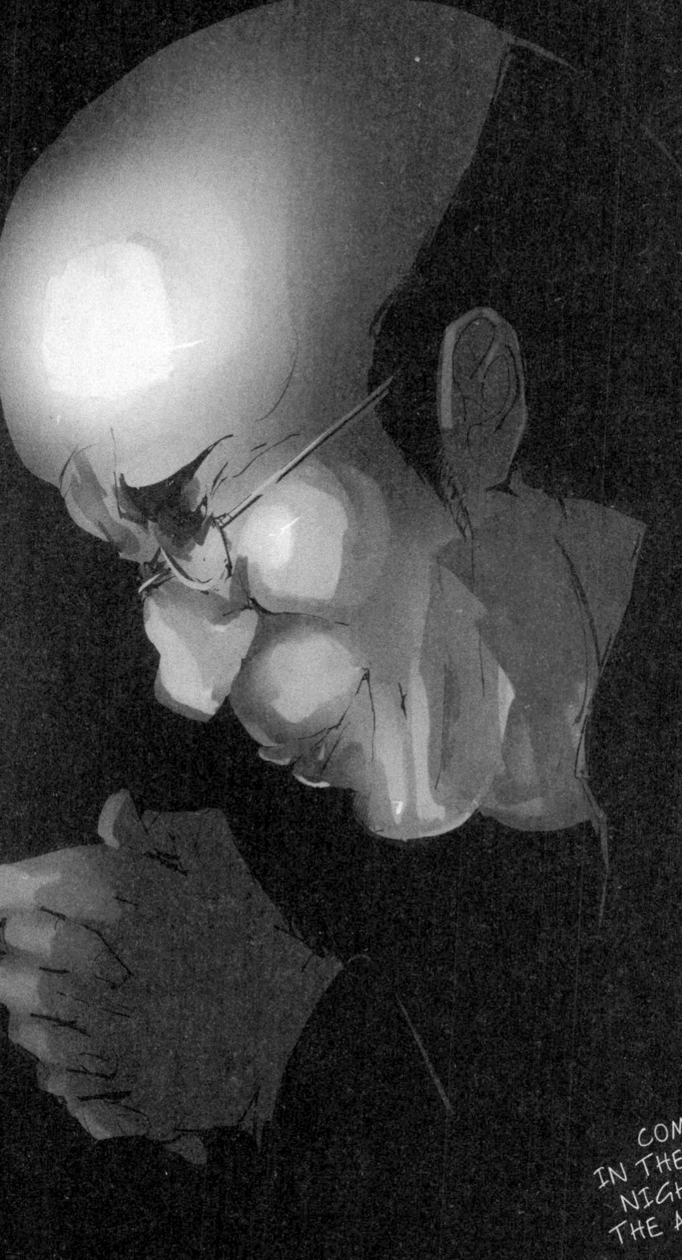
1:04
COMRADE LORIA
IN THE MIDDLE OF THE
NIGHT, THRILLED BY
THE ANIME BROADCAST

Her only choice
is to steel her resolve.
The little monster
girl is always headed
toward the front lines.

THE SAGA OF TANYA THE EVIL

In Omnia Paratus

[STORY BY] Carlo Zen [ILLUSTRATION BY] Shinobu Shinotsuki